THE BISHOP BURNED THE LADY

BILL PERCY

Black Rose Writing | Texas

First printing

ISBN: 978-1-68433-014-0
PUBLISHED BY BLACK ROSE WRITING
www.blackrosewriting.com

Printed in the United States of America
Suggested Retail Price (SRP) $20.95

The Bishop Burned the Lady is printed in Palatino Linotype

DEDICATION

This one's for the grandkids: Aspen, Cecilia, Charlotte, Ella, Jonah, Lydia, and Will. Grandchildren deserve a better world to grow up in than parts of this story describe. I trust that, having had such loving parents, when they start reading novels like this they will have a foundation of family and friends that will help them know that despite evil in the world, most people, like the folks in Monastery Valley, are good.

ACKNOWLEDGEMENTS

I must acknowledge Lorna Lynch, my editor and proofreader. She helped me to de-sensationalize a story that could all too easily have been overdramatized. My writing is always stronger for her careful tending. Oh, yes, Lorna also encouraged me not to spoil the ending by foreshadowing it on almost every page!

And then, there is the spectacular cover design by David Levine, graphic designer *par excellance.* He's designed the covers for all three Monastery Valley books: His designs can't help but grab readers' attention. Thanks, David.

Finally, to my trusted early readers—my wife, Michele, of course, an inveterate English teacher with her trusted red pen; my sister Sue, new on the team; Ken Stewart, Sara Wright, and Mark Cherniack, my "Minneapolis connection." Their insights and feedback took the book to the next level, and I am deeply indebted. And special thanks to Ken for sharing the stage with me at a conversation on the neuroscience of stories in Minneapolis in April 2017. He was superb.

Finally, my thanks to the clients I was honored to work with who suffered at the hands of abusers and traffickers. In *Bishop,* I could only hint at the faintest shadow of their experiences, but I am forever in their debt.

THE BISHOP BURNED THE LADY

PART ONE

MONDAY, LABOR DAY

1

As Ed yanked the cooler and folding chairs out of his pickup, he didn't bother to hide his irritation. "For a girlfriend, you're awful damn distant." A rotten opening to the question he wanted to ask her.

Andi was quiet for a moment. "Just thinking what a brutal five months we've gone through." She looked at him. "You haven't been much of a boyfriend lately, either."

"What's that mean?"

"When was the last time you were home in the evening?"

"Hey. Seeing patients all day, helping with the wildfires almost every evening in August, volunteering at the fire camps on weekends. Doesn't leave a lot of free time. And you were working overtime as much as I was."

Andi turned away.

Ed looked up at the ugly scar of the Hunter's Peak fire, 3500 acres halfway up the mountain, still smoldering. Thank God the wind had changed over the weekend, blowing the smoke out of the valley instead of blanketing it on their heads, as it had for weeks. There'd been talk of cancelling the fireworks tonight, but Magnus, whose field they were parked on, had decided to irrigate the field heavily and station the valley's four fire vehicles at the corners of the field in case of any stray sparks.

He pulled three lawn chairs from the truck. He heard Andi sigh.

"I'm sorry, Ed. You're right, we've both been crazy busy. No reason to argue with you."

He decided it was an offer of truce. "And tonight's for fun, not for arguing about not having any fun."

She grabbed the chairs. "Grab the cooler, will you?"

"Let the guy do the heavy lifting, eh?" *Lighten it up,* he thought.

Andi shrugged and started walking toward the field where families were already setting up their picnics. Ed watched her for a moment, wondering what was wrong. What Andi had said was true. Too true. It had been a lost summer, all work, no play. They were both feeling stretched way too far. The flood in early April, then Jared Hansen's threat to shoot his schoolmates and the surgery on his brain tumor in June, and weekend trips to Missoula so Grace could visit him, then the back-to-back wildfires in August. *We're just tired and grumpy like everybody these days,* he decided.

Behind him, a horn beeped. He turned. It was Grace's pink Volvo creeping along in a line of traffic finding parking spots along the dusty road beside the wide green pasture. He waved as she pulled abreast of him, rolling down her window.

"Hey, Northrup, could you please put a lawn chair in the back seat? I'm watching the fireworks with Zach's family."

"Andi carried them over already." He pointed toward the open field. "Find her and you can take one."

"Thanks, Northrup. Over and out."

As she drove on, Ed smiled. He liked how she always used his last name—unless she was annoyed with him. Times like that, she called him Dad. He set down the cooler at the edge of the pasture and looked around the green field for Andi. She stood fifty yards away. His last tinge of irritation with her vaporized; to him, she was the loveliest woman on this field...and he had his question to ask. Staying annoyed with her would be a lousy intro for that.

He lifted the cooler, grunted, and walked her way. When he reached her, he put down the cooler and touched her arm. "Sorry, pal. No call for me crabbing out the last night of summer."

Andi nodded, then pulled a bottle of Pinot Noir from the cooler. Silently.

"You upset about something?" He took the bottle from her.

She shook her head. "Yes. No. Don't take me personally. I'm one big menopausal nerve."

He moved closer. "Need a hug?"

She shook her head. "It'll just make me sweat."

Ed stepped back. "Well..." He didn't know what to say. Over Andi's shoulder, he spotted Grace strolling in their direction, eyes glued to her iPhone. It was beyond him how she managed to not trip over the chairs and blankets scattered across the field.

Andi sighed. "I'm sorry, Ed. God, let's reboot this and I'll try to resemble a human being."

He relaxed. "Don't worry about it, kid. Let's enjoy a fine summer evening." It *was* a fine evening, and if his question worked the magic he hoped it would, it'd soon get even finer.

The afternoon sun was passing behind the towering cottonwoods at the edge of the field along the river. Deliciously cool air moved gently through the early evening. He opened the cooler and grabbed two plastic glasses. "You ready for a glass of that Pinot?"

"Oh my God, yes!" She took the glass he held out. "Pour, before I turn into the Hulk."

Grace arrived. "Hey, step-girlfriend."

"Hey, kiddo. What's up?"

Grace held up her phone. "I'm looking for Zach and his family. Hi, Northrup."

"Hi, honey. Here's your chair." He held out the third lawn chair to her. "How's your day been?"

"Until just about now, it's been like sliding down a razor blade into a pool of iodine."

Ed laughed. "Why? What's wrong?"

"Last day of summer vacation and nobody could do anything. Zach was haying with his dad, and my girls were all doing, uh, *family activities*."

Andi laughed. "You meeting Zach here?"

"Soon as I find him." Grace resumed tapping her phone.

After watching her for a moment, Andi turned to Ed. "Think Magnus will make an appearance?"

It surprised him. "Why wouldn't he? It's his fireworks show."

Grace, beside them, still tapped her phone. Andi lowered her voice and leaned toward Ed. "After his trouble last spring?"

Ed quieted his voice too. "He'll be here, don't worry."

Without lifting her head and still tapping, Grace said, "Magnus almost killed the priest that abused him."

Ed's eyes widened. "How do you know that?"

"Magnus Junior told some of us."

"I'm always amazed at what you kids know."

"I'm always amazed at what you adults don't."

2

The lead vehicle, a dark sedan, edged slowly into the clearing that brooded under towering pines. The bishop ordered, "Stop here." Behind the lead car, a big van waited on the narrow forest road.

The driver nodded. "Yes, sir."

"Is the site ready?"

"Yes, sir." The driver cut the engine. "Virgil and Clinton say the shack—"

The bishop waved him silent and gazed quietly at the ancient weathered hulk, at its moss-covered shingles, its gray walls of gapped and mismatched boards, its warped door. "There is a window?"

"Yes, sir. Around the corner from the door. Clinton broke out the glass and nailed a couple two-by-fours across it."

"Good." The bishop pointed toward two two-by-fours resting against the wall beside the door. "Tell me."

"When we're ready, Virgil will nail them across the door. There will be no chance of escape."

The bishop nodded again. "Well done. And the witnesses?"

"Here." He pointed to where a large rectangle had been cleared of its weeds, down to the dirt. It was about ten feet long, maybe six wide.

The bishop considered it for a long moment.

"Unsatisfactory, sir?"

But the bishop shook his head. "Acceptable." He pointed at the edge of the forest, behind the rectangle. "What is that pile?"

A mound of junk rested against the trunk of one of the towering ponderosas hemming the clearing.

"It's the cabin's contents, sir. We wanted nothing left inside that could be used."

"To escape?"

"Yes, or for suicide."

"Excellent."

"Sir, I have a question."

"What?"

"Are you worried someone will see the smoke?"

The bishop took a long breath. "Perhaps. But it will not last long, and I cannot afford to wait. The lesson must be taught and then we move the product on." He pointed beside the bare ground of the rectangle. "Direct Guy to park the van there, and station Virgil and Clinton in their places. Then we will begin."

3

Grace stood facing Andi and Ed, fingers still flying on her phone. The third chair, folded, leaned against her hip. She looked up. "I could use a little of that Pinot Noir you guys are drinking."

Ed laughed. "You could use a twenty-first birthday, too."

"Northrup, please. You let me drink wine at home."

"At home." He looked out over the field, quickly filling with families. "This doesn't look much like home."

"Think of it as a temporary homestead." She grinned. When Ed simply smiled back, she added, "Okay, I'm with the program."

"Program?"

"Teetotalers Anonymous."

Andi laughed. Ed liked that sound. Grace went back to tapping her phone.

Ed watched a moment. "He's not answering?"

She glanced up. "He'll answer. I'm texting Jen and Dana, see if they're here yet."

Here was a fifty-acre field along the Monastery River, a tiny part of Magnus Anderssen's vast Double-A Ranch. Townspeople were gathering for his Labor Day fireworks show, his annual gift to the valley before the opening of the school year. Ed looked out at the other groups scattered across the grass, irrigated for a month and mowed by Magnus's crew over the weekend. By the time the fireworks went off, three-quarters of the valley's families would gather here.

Grace's phone beeped. "Finally!" she blurted. After checking the phone, she stuffed it in her pocket. "Zach and his boys are under the trees. Catch you later, guys." She grabbed the lawn chair and swung it over her shoulder, then went zigzagging through scattered blankets and lawn chairs toward the tall cottonwoods along the river.

Andi and Ed settled into their chairs, watching her go. After a moment, Ed shook his head. "Can you believe it? She's a senior already."

"Time flies when you have kids."

Three years ago, Mara Ellenson, Grace's mother and Ed's ex-wife, had abandoned the girl and disappeared. It turned out, Mara was dying and Grace had no other living relatives, except her birth father, who was serving a life sentence. When Mara died, Ed had adopted Grace. They buried Mara in the Jefferson Community Cemetery.

He took a sip of wine. "What do you think senior year'll bring?"

Andi chuckled. "She told me, 'I'm going to do everything seniors do.'"

"Hmm. Not encouraged by that word *everything*. I probably should make a mental Post-it to have another FDPB chat."

"FDPB?"

"Father-Daughter Preventative Biology. What do you think she meant by *everything*?"

Andi shrugged. "Drugs, sex, and rock 'n' roll, if her senior year is anything like mine was."

He looked at her. "What I was afraid of."

She touched his arm. "Just kidding. My mom died the summer before I became a senior. I pretty much hibernated the whole year. I was a wreck."

"I hope to hell nothing bad happens to her this year."

Andi sighed. "She's got a good head, Ed. Trust her."

"Her, I trust. It's not what she does, it's what happens to her I worry about."

Andi stretched. "Let's change the subject, not spoil the evening. We need a good time."

He nodded. "You're on. Perfect sky, silky air..." He wondered when the right moment would come for his question; it sure wasn't now. He'd almost driven their mood into the ditch. Again.

She looked up to the mountains. "Still dry up there."

He looked up toward the bare blue sky. "You know, just smelling fresh air again feels like a miracle. Thank God for the wind change." The second wildfire had been contained just last week, but both burns still smoldered behind them, high in the Monasteries. Ed took a long breath. The fragrance of mown grass and water anointed the air.

Andi looked at him. "You realize it's the first evening since Jared's surgery in June that we've spent together?"

Ed heard a tone that sounded like regret in her voice. "Yeah, I do. I've missed you, kid."

She patted his arm. "Even with all my whining about overtime and hot flashes?"

Ed stood and took her hand. "We're here now. What say we wander around and say hi?"

For a moment, Andi said nothing. Then she smiled. "You go." She stretched. "I'm going to sit here, sip my wine, and relax."

"Then I'm relaxing right here beside you."

He sat down and glanced over. She smiled again.

He almost asked his question, but decided to pour himself another glass of wine first. Wine warms the heart. He'd read that somewhere.

4

The big van pulled slowly into the clearing, and parked where the Bishop had indicated. The driver got out. At first, the woman beside him did not. He wore a sleeveless shirt and a milky orange ball cap. The bishop ordered him, "Guy, move them onto the witness area." He pronounced the French name, "Gee."

Guy opened the side door of the van, and the other men, Clinton and Virgil, roughly ushered out six terrified women and pushed them toward the weed-cleared rectangle, lining them up on the scalped dirt facing the shack.

The women—more like girls—were filthy, their eyes wild with terror; one girl pressed hers tightly shut. Old tears had streaked the filth on their faces. As they stumbled past him, the bishop's driver wrinkled his nose at their smell—sweat, urine, dried menstrual blood. The girls' brown foreheads shone with sweat, despite the cooling air. Their ink-black hair lay matted and wet against their skulls. Virgil and Clinton positioned themselves behind the girls, arms folded, waiting. Guy joined them, silently.

While the girls were being lined up, the woman who'd waited in the van, Beatrice, had climbed out and walked to the front of the bare earth rectangle. For such a large woman, her movements were fluid as a gymnast's, as graceful as her eyes were cruel. Now, facing them, she glared at the girls. "*¡Levántese y observen!*" she barked. *Stand and watch!*

The bishop moved to the edge of the witness area. One of the girls turned to look at him, and Beatrice swiftly slapped her. "*¡Ojos al frente!*" *Eyes to the front*. After the slap, though, Beatrice's own eyes briefly saddened and she fingered an amulet, a rusty triangle, on a string around her throat. Then she hardened again and threatened the girl with another slap. The girl cowered.

The bishop beckoned to Virgil and Clinton, then nodded toward the van. Guy remained behind the line of girls, his muscular arms folded.

Virgil led the way, and opened the rear cargo doors. He reached in and brought out the end of a rope, tugged it, softly first, then roughly. A woman, small like the others, so disheveled and foul that she might have been feral, was dragged out by the neck and fell to the ground. Virgil and Clinton seized her under the arms and stood her upright, facing the bishop, who walked slowly to her. The rope trailed behind her. Dried blood splotched her bare feet. Sagging against the men's hands, the woman whispered, *"Piedad, Señor." Pity, sir.*

The bishop slapped her face; her head banged sideways against Virgil's shoulder. One of the other girls cried out, and the bishop turned.

"Silencio," he said, very softly. Turning back, he directed his driver, "Remove the rope."

The driver opened his knife and cut the collar from around her neck, leaving a raw red scrape of blood. She started to drop again, but Clinton and Virgil yanked her up. The bishop approached her. Putting one finger below her chin, he slowly lifted her head and, like a priest bowing reverently over the holy bread, he leaned down and gently kissed her on the forehead. Her eyes drifted shut.

"Remove her," he ordered.

5

Andi took the wine bottle from Ed and topped off her glass. As she was putting the bottle back in the cooler, Pete Peterson, senior deputy in the Adams County Sheriff's Department, strolled up. Pete, like the other deputies, was quietly wandering, watching the crowd, absorbing the quiet murmuring conversations. It passed for crowd control in a community that mostly controlled itself.

"Ed, Andi." Pete grinned, saluting. "Look at you, lady, enjoying off-duty wine." Every Labor Day, Sheriff Ben Stewart chose one of his deputies to enjoy the fireworks off-duty, and this year, Andi had been the lucky one. "Me, I gotta make sure there's no mass murderers lurking." Pete chuckled.

Andi stiffened. An aftershock, she knew, from last April's high-anxiety Jared Hansen case, when the boy had amassed rifles and a pressure cooker and threatened to kill the senior class. It turned out the poor kid had a brain tumor, but words like *mass murder* still jarred.

Ed would call me post-traumatic. Probably am.

She shook it off and said to Pete, "Go protect-and-serve, partner. Me, I'm all about wine-and-fireworks."

Pete grinned. "Enjoy, you two. I'm on my appointed rounds."

Ed saluted. "Take care, Pete."

Ed's salute struck Andi as funny. For a moment, she enjoyed watching Pete chatting with families as he made his rounds. She took another sip of the good wine.

Without warning, her body caught fire. Heat swept over her chest and shoulders, up her throat. She made her mother's gesture, fanning herself. *As if this does any good.* She took a long breath, then another, then leaned down to the cooler beside her chair and retrieved the cold wine bottle, pressed it briefly against her wrist. "Refill?" She passed the bottle over to Ed.

He shook his head, so she pressed the bottle against her wrist again before placing it back into the icy cooler.

"Does that really work?" he asked, nodding at her wrist.

"Naw. But it's something to do." She wanted to tell Ed about the anxiety that sometimes came with the hot flashes, but didn't want to get into it, not tonight.

He chuckled. After a sip and a long gaze over the field, his voice sounded thoughtful. "I've been thinking. You realize I'm going on fifty-nine?"

Andi felt her eyebrow jump. "No you're not. Fifty-nine was last year, old man. Sixty's the next stop on that train."

"Huh. You're right. Think I'm in denial?"

"Like Moses in the bulrushes."

Ed laughed. "In de Nile." He looked out over the crowd. "Do I seem old to you?"

She stood up, took his hands, and pulled him up. "Try this." She wanted to push her complaining mood far away. "Dance with me, big guy."

Standing, he smiled. "No music?"

"Pretend. It's a two-step." They made small dance steps on the patch of grass in front of their chairs, humming. After a moment, she pulled Ed's body against hers.

He said, "Hey, you're leading."

"Damn right. It's been too long."

"Been missing in action for a while, haven't I?"

Andi nestled into him. "Shh. Not now."

They stopped moving, held their embrace a moment longer, then let go. A couple of wives sitting on nearby blankets gave a soft applause. Andi curtsied, and she and Ed sat and sipped their wine.

Long shadows from the riverside cottonwoods draped darkening streamers over the gathered families and their picnics spread on blankets or card tables or blue coolers with white tops. Quiet laughter floated across the field, punctuating the soft rustle of conversations. The westering sun hung nearly on the mountain ridges, and the cooling sweetness of the air spoke of evening. Graying dusk already brushed the Washington Mountains to the east.

She heard Ed clear his throat, usually a prelude to an announcement. She looked over at him. He patted her arm. "Like I started to say before Pete came, there's something I want to ask—"

Andi touched his arm, pointed toward the cottonwoods. Magnus Anderssen and her boss, Sheriff Ben Stewart, were walking their way. "Mack and Ben at two o'clock."

6

Ed saw Magnus smile as they approached. "Andi, Ed. Couldn't ask for a more perfect evening for the show, could we?"

Andi stood and gave him a hug. "Yeah, it is. How've you been, Mack?"

Everyone knew that Magnus had gone through a rough patch last spring. But few knew how he'd collapsed under the haunting memory of being raped by a monk he'd taken as a father-substitute as a young man.

Magnus looked over their heads toward the mountains. "I've been well, Andi. Luisa and I had a quiet summer—until the fires, at least." He nodded, his thick gray hair curling out under his Stetson. His face, always ruddy from the sun, was more creased than Ed remembered, but his eyes seemed filled with a soft contentment. Magnus nodded as if to himself, and repeated, "Yes, I've been good." He turned to Ed. "My friend, I've missed you. We haven't wet a line all summer." His big arms spread wide and they embraced.

"I'm glad to hear you're well, Mack." Magnus had turned to Ed for his professional help last spring. It had turned out well in the end, but only after long, tense weeks, and a flirtation with suicide. "How'd we get through a whole damn summer without fishing?"

Magnus smiled. "Hell, your plate was full."

"Too full. I've been working too much for an old guy."

Ben Stewart, the sheriff, grunted. "You ain't old. You're what, fifty-six, seven?"

"Sixty next month."

Magnus laughed, a deep rumble in his chest. "I'm sixty-two, and I feel thirty-eight. Except for the days I feel eighty."

Ben coughed. "Christ on a crutch, I'm fifty-six, but lately I been feelin' about seventy." Like an old bear gorging on autumn berries, Ben had gained a lot of weight over the past six months. He wheezed, and Ed realized that for most of the summer, Ben had often seemed out of breath. Ed had chalked it up to the smoke from the fires.

Magnus chuckled again. "Ben, when are you going to start jogging with Ed here?" He tapped Ben's paunch. "You could lose a few."

Ben looked sour. "Only runnin' I'm doin' is runnin' for sheriff." He coughed again. "Gotta say, I'm damn tired, though. Glad the election's a year off."

Surprised to hear his tone, Ed studied him. Ben had always been gruff, strong, and forceful; but tonight he seemed, well, diminished, pale. "I'm worried about you, man," Ed said.

"Ain't nothing to worry yourself about. We're here for fun." Ben looked annoyed. Then he gave a small cough, rubbed his midsection.

"Ben?"

The sheriff took a moment to catch his breath. "Gas. Jesus in a sidecar, you'd think a guy could belch without his friends' makin' a federal case of it."

Ed smiled. "Well, you can jog with me anytime, Ben."

"When cows write books." Ed laughed and clapped Ben on the shoulder. "Gotta go see my *workin'* deputies," he growled and walked off.

Magnus laughed. "I better go oversee the crew. Mostly they're ready, but it never hurts to do a final check. Enjoy the show."

7

Virgil and Clinton dragged the young woman into the shack. They came out and closed the door. Virgil padlocked the door, and held his hand up against it. Everyone heard the girl begin screaming, pounding on the decayed door and wall. The other girls glanced wildly at one another as Clinton nailed the two-by-fours across the doorway. One of the girls moaned in Spanish, and the large woman, Beatrice, stepped forward and slapped her twice. Again, her eyes saddened and she touched the amulet.

The bishop turned to Guy Flandreau. "Do it."

Guy opened a stoppered wine bottle and stuffed a dirty rag into its mouth. Clinton struck a match, held the flame to the rag, which caught. Guy carried it to the boarded window, holding it upright until the flame nearly reached the neck of the bottle. Clinton stepped behind the six girls. Another of the girls screamed and turned to run, but Clinton seized her and roughly threw her onto the ground, where Beatrice grabbed her hair and made her look at the shack.

The flame licked at Guy's hand. He swore loudly and tossed the bottle between the two-by-four slats of the gaping window. One of the girls fainted. The girl inside kept screaming. There was a massive *whump,* then silence; and then she screamed again, high and long-drawn, then higher-pitched, terrified, and then a blaze of sparks burst out the window and danced on the dirt below. Crackling flames, louder and louder, overwhelmed the girl's weakening screams. After a moment, she fell silent. The girls whimpered, but glares from Beatrice silenced them. Flames burst through the gaps between the wall boards, and then penetrated the dried brittle boards themselves, pushing out waves of heat and thick black smoke pulsing into the darkening evening sky. All the girls sank to the ground, moaning; the men forced them to watch as the shack convulsed in flames, heaving, then collapsing in with a crash, sparks soaring up. The smell of charring hair and flesh flooded the clearing.

One of the girls, eyes glazed, whispered in a lost voice, "*¿Porqué? ¿Porqué?*"

The bishop, his eyes dark, said, "*Ella eligió para escaparme. Elegí para castigarla.*" *She elected to escape me. I elected to punish her.*

8

As Magnus walked away to check his fireworks crew, Ed took a deep breath and said, "So, I'm trying to squeeze a question into the conversation, but it seems—"

"What the hell?" Andi sat up, pointing toward the crest of the Washington Mountains. A pillar of inky smoke boiled out of the forest into the sky. "Do you see that?"

Ed spotted it immediately, felt his breath catch. "Damn." He grimaced. "We can't take another fire."

Just then, Ben Stewart lumbered up and rested his hand on Andi's shoulder, breathing heavily.

Andi stood up. "What's your thinking, boss?"

Ben squinted. "Ain't never seen black smoke from a forest fire. Black usually means a building, but ain't no houses up that way. Fact is, there ain't nothin' up there. And 'less I missed it, we ain't had no lightnin' lately." He looked at Andi, then Ed.

Ed shook his head. "Nope. It might be a smolder flaring up."

Ben scratched his chin, still breathing heavily. "Hate to think it." He watched the smoke a while. "That looks pretty close to the Carlton County side. Let me call Harley Vogel. Maybe he knows somethin'." Vogel was the sheriff in Carlton County, Ben's counterpart on the other side of the Washingtons. He wandered off with his cell phone to his ear.

Ed studied the coal-black column. Around them, he could hear alarmed voices. Andi nodded at one family that had stood, pointing at the smoke. "People are still tense about fire. This could get ugly."

Ben came back. "Well, Harley can't see nothin' from his back yard, which is where he's hostin' his Labor Day steak fry for the deputies. Says he'll send their on-duty guy up to see what he can from the highway, but his helicopter guy can't go till morning."

"Why not?" Ed asked.

"Harley says the pilot's already toasted at the steak fry."

They all studied the thick boil of black smoke. Finally, wiping his forehead, Ben grunted, "Ain't sure I got it in me to go through another fire."

Andi said, "Maybe we ought to call Missoula County, have them send a chopper."

Ben gave a small hiccup. "Pardon. Indigestion." Absently, he rubbed his belly. "Naw. That black smoke just don't make me think wildfire." He paused. "Harley'll send up his chopper tomorrow morning. We'll take 'er from there."

Ed considered that. The Missoula helicopter could GPS the location, maybe even tell if the fire was growing; by morning they could have a team ready to mount the initial attack. It wasn't like Ben to delay like this.

The smoke pulsed up against the soft blue sky of the darkening evening. More people were pointing, talking to their neighbors. Ben said, "Crap on toast. Lemme start the word around that Carlton County's got it covered. No use startin' a general freak-out." He walked off.

As they sat down, Ed said, "Ben's never off duty, is he?"

Sipping her wine, Andi nodded. "Why I'm glad I'm just a deputy."

"I'm worried about him. He's put on a lot of weight, and he hasn't been himself since Marlene left." Ben's wife, Marlene, had divorced him suddenly and left the valley after decades of marriage. Ben had been in love with her till the moment her moving van drove off. Probably still was. "I'm surprised he put the chopper off till morning."

"Can't speak ill of the boss, but I get the feeling his heart's not in the job these days."

Ed caught sight of Brad Ordrew approaching. Andi must have seen him coming too. She muttered, "Look out, Leroy."

No love was lost between them and Deputy Ordrew. Last spring, during the investigation of Jared's threats to kill his friends, Ed had sheltered—no, hidden—the boy for two days in an attempt to figure out what caused his paranoia. Andi knew what Ed had done. When Ordrew, Andi's partner on the case, discovered this, he'd been livid. He'd tried to get Ed charged with obstruction of justice. The charge never came to pass, Andi hadn't been disciplined, and Ordrew had stewed all summer. He was a by-the-book, spit-and-polish cop, and hated what he thought was sloppy police work.

Andi nodded toward Brad, who was closing in. "Watch out," she said quietly.

Ordrew stopped. "Stewart said Carlton County's on that fire." He gestured to the mountain behind him, his eyes on Ed.

Andi half-smiled. "Yeah, we just talked to him."

"You think Stewart ought to ignore it overnight? Procedure would be, send a deputy up now."

Ed thought, *spit-and-polish*. He glanced down. Even after prowling the dusty road and walking in the green mown grass, Ordrew's shoes gleamed.

Andi said, "Ben talked with Vogel. They're on it."

Ed knew Andi would never second-guess Ben in front of Ordrew.

Ordrew shook his head. "Damn. Stewart will take the easy road anytime he gets a reason to. Goddamn pussy."

A couple of women nearby, babies on their laps, looked at him, their faces dark as he stalked away.

Andi smiled at the mothers. "Sorry about that. He didn't learn to talk till reform school." They laughed.

Ed held out his glass to Andi. "Fill 'er up?"

When she handed it back to him, he asked, "So what's Brad's thing?"

She sighed. "He doesn't think females should be cops. I ignore him."

Ed snorted. "You're a better man than I."

Her eyes widened. She whispered, "You'd like me to be the man sometime?"

"Deputy, language!" Ed chuckled, gesturing toward the moms, who hadn't heard.

As they sipped their wine and chatted with the neighbors, the smoke pushed up into the dusky sky, where the breeze caught it and smeared it northward. As dusk thickened, the smoke was hardly visible against the darkening eastern sky. The father of the family on the next blanket leaned over toward Andi. "Ben Stewart's passing the word, Carlton County's on top of it."

Andi, amused, thanked him, and muttered to Ed, "Ben at work."

Ed nodded and passed along the message to the families around them.

The last of the sun had gone, and the semi-darkness gathered around them. People's features faded, but their conversations were a gentle murmur, like a distant lowing of cattle in the night.

Ed leaned closer to Andi, ready to ask his question. But the first explosion lit up the fields, a billow of colored light-flowers, cascades shining and falling in arcs against the blackening sky. Great chrysanthemums blossomed over their heads, booming bursts and sparkles, followed by *ohs* and *ahs* from the crowd. Their light reflected off the mysterious column of smoke, but by the end of the show, that plume had faded to nothing, and Ed had decided to ask his question later.

TUESDAY

9

The next morning, Andi yawned in front of her computer screen. After the fireworks, they'd stayed up late to watch the stars, and around one a.m., just after they'd climbed into bed, Andi's cell phone had rung. She'd answered, sleepily holding the phone against her ear, shaking her head. After she clicked off, she plopped back onto the pillow.

"What?" Ed had muttered, half-asleep.

"Xav Contrerez, the night deputy, has been taken to the hospital. Ruptured appendix. I've gotta cover his shift."

Ed's erection pressed lazily against her bare leg. She brushed it away. "Stop."

"Damn."

"Suffer. I gotta go to work."

Remembering that exchange at her desk now, she smiled. Her office phone rang. Ben's voice pulled her out of the reverie. "In my office."

"On the way." She locked her computer screen and went down the hall to Ben's office. "What's cooking, Sheriff?"

He gestured her to a chair. "Something I need to talk to you about." His broad face was flushed, and it was not happy. He was breathing hard, as if he'd just climbed stairs. The Sheriff's Department had no stairs. "You probably ain't unaware that I ain't been functionin' at one hundred percent in recent weeks."

She thought, *More like months,* but shrugged. "Ben, it's not my business—"

"Just listen. Make this easier." He paused again, catching his breath. "It's sugar diabetes, 'cause of the damn weight I put on after Marlene left. I can't hardly move around much anymore. I got me a blood sugar crisis two, three times a day. Totally outa control." He wiped his forehead. "One's comin' on as we speak, low sugar this time." He reached into his desk and took out a tester and pricked his finger, then touched the blood drop to the test strip. There was a tiny beep and he read the result. "'Scuse me." He dug deeper in the drawer, took out an orange, quickly peeled it, and wolfed down a handful of pieces. "Little too much insulin last time. Too much sugar, too much insulin—I ain't figured out the damn balance yet."

Andi, uncomfortable, said, "Doc Keeley'll get it under control?" She tried, but failed, to make it a statement.

"We'll see. But meantime..." He stopped, sagging back into his big chair. "Takes a minute."

"Ben, if you—"

He waved his hand weakly. Andi felt her alarm growing. Finally, he leaned forward again. "Look. I ain't never been sick before, so this takes some gettin' used to. But damned if I ain't gonna beat the hell outa this thing."

Andi smiled. *That's Ben*. She waited.

Ben forced a weak smile. He wiped his sweaty forehead again. "The good news is, I ain't up for reelection till next year. Doubt I could do it if I had me a race."

He was already looking better. He rustled some papers. "I ain't tellin' the whole damn world, but you and Pete gotta know."

"Why me? Pete's senior, not me."

His color was slowly returning. "Your pal Bradley Ordrew's been makin' noises about my health gettin' in the way of me doin' the job. I want you to be my ears about that. He floats some crap, shoot it out of the sky."

"Brad doesn't talk to me much."

"Which I know. But you hear the other guys talkin', let me know. Worryin' about morale's my job. If he's trashin' me, I ain't about to let that crap fester."

"Hell, Ben. I don't like the feel of that. All I need's another reason for Brad to get pissed at me."

"He ain't gonna know 'less you tell him, damn it." As quickly as he'd said it, he looked sheepish. "Sorry. The sugar diabetes makes me short."

His outburst surprised her. Ben's temper wasn't the hot kind; it brewed, then came out cold and hard. "No problem." What would it hurt, listening for rumblings about Ben's health? "Okay, Ben, I'll keep my ears open. I just don't want Brad getting another reason to be on my case."

"I hear you. This stays between you and me. I know Ordrew's been rough on you since that Hansen case last spring."

"I'm handling it." She paused. "There is something, though. I need to tell you about—"

"I know you ain't a complainer, but Pete tells me he's hard on you. Talk to me."

"Uh, I..." She paused, then forged on. "Ben, Ordrew's crap with me I can handle, that's not what I need to tell you. Last night at the fireworks, he used some bad language, and it offended a couple of nearby moms with little ones on their laps. I'm thinking you should have a heads-up before a citizen complains."

Ben's eyes blazed. "What'd he say?"

"He called someone a 'fucking pussy.'"

Ben went red. "Goddamn. Some moms heard him, you say?"

She nodded. "They looked upset."

"Crap on toast." His face was red, but he looked weary. "Heart and soul of this job is protectin' the public, and public relations is part of that. Damn..." He sagged further. "You know my style, Andi. Whatever you guys say in the house is your business, but with citizens, I ain't about upsetting the moms of my county." He leaned back in his chair. "Okay. I'll be on that boy like rain on a picnic."

She smiled and started to stand up. "Thanks, Ben."

He tapped the papers again. "Hang around the department for a while. I just talked with Harley Vogel over in Carlton. He didn't want to send up the chopper 'cause the smoke's stopped, but I talked him into it. I expect he'll be callin' me back any time now, so stay close. I may need to send you up there."

10

Twenty minutes later, Ben buzzed again.

"In my office."

"On the way." *Damn,* she thought. *He's sending me up.* She yawned, and went down to his office.

As she feared, Ben said, "Harley called. His chopper guy found a small open space with a black pile in the middle that looks like char and ash. A little smoke risin'. Helicopter couldn't land 'cause the clearing's too small. GPS puts the site in Adams County, not Carlton. When I said I'd send somebody up, Harley tried to argue me out of it. So I want you to drive up and find this place."

"Why'd he argue?"

"No idea, but Harley 'n' me go way back, and he can be cranky sometimes."

Andi smiled. *And you aren't?*

He handed her a slip of paper. "Here's the coordinates. See if there's anything we should worry about."

"Shouldn't we send up somebody from Search and Rescue or the fire department? I know squat about fires."

Ben shook his head. "Negative on that. They're all volunteers, and I can't call 'em out unless we have a real fire or rescue situation, which we don't. So I'm thinkin', minimum, you go up and sniff around and see if there's still fire or embers. I don't want to wait and let another wildfire get a head start. You find somethin' to worry about, I'll call 'em out."

She tried suppressing a yawn, and failed. "Sorry, boss. A little tired here."

"Me too, Andi. I know you worked all night. I'd send Pete or Brad if I could."

Pete was on a domestic up north. "What's Brad doing?" She wanted out of this trip.

Ben grimaced. His hand brushed his chest. "Yeah, well..." He looked uncomfortable. "I shouldn't say this, but Brad don't play well with others."

"Others?"

Ben held up his hand for her to wait. He took a moment to catch his breath. His face had gone pale. Andi saw a few beads of sweat along his hairline. "Harley said he'd send one of his deputies up to mark the turn-in for that clearin'. Brad'll just get into a pissin' contest with him. Call Carlton dispatch when you leave and the guy'll be up there waitin'. Name's Mike somethin'. He'll meet you on Highway 36, just past milepost 47."

Andi sighed. "Okay, I guess. Seems like a waste of manpower." She chuckled. "Woman power." She turned to go.

Ben called after her. "It's fifty miles one way up to milepost 47, not to mention how far into the forest that site is. You'll be gone all day. I'm givin' Brad your assignments." He coughed, then touched his chest again. His lips were tight. "Serves his ass right."

11

Andi filled a go-cup with hot coffee, and stopped to say goodbye to Callie Martin, the gravel-voiced receptionist, dispatcher, and housemother of the department. Callie, on the phone, held up a finger and mouthed, *One minute.*

Andi waited. Callie, usually the crusty one around the department, had tears in her eyes. Her voice into the phone was soft. "Meet me tonight at the Angler. You and me need some girl time." After listening a moment, Callie said, "Five on the dot," and ended the call. "One of my girlfriends just got the word—breast cancer." Her eyes filled again.

Andi felt, again, a stab of something like fear. And a tug—compassion maybe, or something else. Maybe the word *girlfriend* had triggered it. *I need a girlfriend*. "Anybody I know?"

Callie nodded. "Maggie Sobstak."

"Oh, God." Three years before, Maggie's husband, Victor, and

Andi had both been shot during an attempt to break up a tax conspiracy. After, she and Maggie had gotten to know each other, without quite making it over the ridge into friendship.

Callie grinned. "Hey. Join us after shift. Wine and girl talk at the Angler."

She nearly said no, but stopped herself. "Breast cancer's kind of personal; I don't know Maggie well enough—"

Callie shushed her. "Don't be like that. Maggie likes you; she asks about you."

That caught her by surprise. "She does?" Something felt full in her chest. "Yeah, okay. If I get back from Carlton County in time, I'll be there." She said goodbye to Callie and stepped across the hall to Ed's office. Recognizing her loneliness had shaken her.

He stood to kiss her when she came in, but paused, a look of concern crossing his face. "You look like your best friend just moved away."

She shivered. "Maggie Sobstak's got breast cancer. And except for you, bucko, I don't have a best friend."

"Maggie? Damn!" Then he cocked his head. "You don't have a best friend?"

She waved that off. "It's rotten. My mom died of cancer."

"I remember. What's this about best friends?"

"Forget it. Just more whining. Anyway, Ben's sending me up to that burn we saw last night. It'll likely take hours."

"It's still burning?"

She shrugged. "Can't see any smoke, but you never know. Ben doesn't want us to let it start up again."

"So you'll be up there the rest of the day?"

"Probably. And look," she said, "if I get back in time, I'm meeting Callie and Maggie for a glass of wine at the Angler. Callie says Maggie needs 'girl talk,' and I kinda think I do too." She offered a thin smile. "After that, I've got to pick up a fresh uniform, then I'll be out to your place. But it's early to bed tonight."

"I'll miss you then." He smiled. "I missed you when I woke up this morning."

"Little Eddie missed me last night when I had to come in to work."

"You swatted him away!"

She winked. "Law enforcement's my first love."

12

She stood a moment in the parking lot, soaking in the exquisite September morning. Despite the weariness in her face and shoulders, the air invigorated her. She looked up toward the sierra of the Monastery Range, jagged granite teeth pushing into the cobalt sky, washed in yellow light, not yet dusted with snow. To the east, her morning's destination, the friendlier, rounder Washington Mountains were greener, softer, shadowed. A flatland Chicago girl, she felt more at ease with the Washingtons.

Brad Ordrew pulled into the space beside her, rolling down his window. "Where you off to?" His voice sounded almost friendly.

Andi stiffened, wary. "Up to check out that fire."

His smile faded. He rolled up the window, fast, turned off the engine, and jumped out. "You know much about fires?"

"This summer's wildfires sure added to what I knew before."

"I'm thinking Stewart ought to send somebody who knows what he's doing."

Andi caught the *he*.

"Anyway, there might be bears up there." He grinned. "Girls are scared of bears, aren't they?"

Andi waited a beat. "They're a lot more afraid of pigs, Brad."

His face reddened. He started toward the building, then turned and walked back. "Andi, this is nothing personal, but you know how I feel about woman cops."

"I know—you don't like them. And the hell it isn't personal, Brad. I'm one of them."

He moved slightly closer, too close. He pitched his voice low. "If I ever get the chance to run this *pigsty*, you'll tighten up your work ethic or you're history."

Ignoring her pounding heart, Andi stepped slightly back. "You'll never run this place, Brad."

He stood still. A vein pulsed in his forehead. But he pulled back, turned sharply, and stalked into the building.

Andi leaned against her vehicle and let the sun warm her face a few minutes more, taking calming drafts of the sweet-tasting air. Although she tried not to let Ordrew get to her, she couldn't help wondering what his thing was. Was it her, or women in general? She watched the shadows on the mountains flattening in the mid-morning light. Her heart slowed, and she eased up.

Then she chuckled, realizing that Ben was about to give Brad her assignments for the rest of the day. At one o'clock, he would have to cover her luncheon talk at the Ladies' League: Women in law enforcement. She almost laughed as she climbed into the SUV. "Let's roll."

She drove out of the lot, turned onto Division Street. Eight miles north of town, she turned east onto Highway 36. She rolled down the window and put her uniform hat on the passenger seat. The wind ruffled her short curly hair, feeling like Ed's fingers late at night. She yawned, and the yawn ended in another sudden stab of loneliness. For some reason, she thought of her mother. Her heart started pounding.

Not loneliness this time. Fear. What she didn't know was, fear of what?

13

Montana Highway 36 climbed, curving first up the benches below the mountains, then into the mountains themselves. She kept to the speed limit, occasionally rubbing her eyes to stay alert. She replayed the encounter with Ordrew. He wasn't nearly as threatening as some of the Chicago cops she'd learned to handle in her former life. His dislike of women might have amused her, except for the fact that one day her life might depend on him. Before that day, she'd have to find a way to smooth things over with him.

Ten miles further, she radioed the department, asked Callie to call Carlton County and ask for the deputy to meet her.

Fifty minutes into the drive, she passed milepost 47. Perhaps a tenth of a mile farther, another sheriff's car, sky blue with the red stripe of Carlton County, waited on the shoulder, flashers on. The deputy was leaning on the hood, smoking. She rolled slowly into the space behind him.

"Andi Pelton," she said, extending her hand when she got out.

"Mike Payne." His grip was firm, and his blue eyes penetrating. Dark hair curling on his neck, around his ears. He didn't release her hand when she loosened her grip, but she didn't mind. He smiled, let go her hand. "You're the one who got shot breaking up some cult thing a couple years ago."

She nodded, pulling her hand free. "Not a cult, a tax-resistance conspiracy. Not my favorite topic."

"I imagine not," he chuckled. "Good police work, though."

"Getting shot? Hardly."

"Not that. Catching the bad guys."

"Well, thanks." She let the compliment warm her. "Look, I'm on the rear-end of a double shift, so I've got to get to work before I fade out."

"No worries. I wasn't so keen on coming up here either, but I'm glad I can help out." He gestured toward a dry, two-rut track leading into a narrow break in the trees. "Here's our turnoff." If Andi had been driving by at speed, she'd never have seen it. "Our chopper guy says it looks to be about three miles in. He said the track looked passable."

Andi groaned. Mike's blue eyes looked concerned. "Sorry," she said. "Like I said, I've been on duty since midnight last night, covering for one of our guys who got sick. Three miles on that track is going to take a while."

He nodded. "Yeah. Let's take your truck. We're in your county here, and our chopper guy says the site is too, so you've got jurisdiction. And your SUV has higher clearance than my squad."

"You're coming with me? I thought—"

"Absolutely. My boss wants me to help you out."

"Good enough. Let's do this."

As Mike walked around to the passenger side of her vehicle, she realized she was glad Mike had met her. Driving alone deep into the forest wasn't her idea of a picnic.

14

The road was indeed passable, but rough, with dense forest pressing in on both sides. Branches scraped the sides of the SUV. Potholes slowed them. Everything looked sere, thirsty. The track wasn't entirely plugged with grass: two ruts in the weeds, neither well-used nor neglected. No snow yet. She took it slowly, driving for thirty minutes or so.

Mike talked pleasantly, mostly about hunting in these woods, which apparently he did whenever he could. "I'm curious as hell about this fire," he said. "I'll bet I've walked within a few hundred yards of the fire site more than once, but I don't remember any clearing like our chopper guy described."

Andi grimaced. "You sure of the GPS coordinates they gave us? I'd hate to think we're driving into nothing."

"Dwayne's a careful pilot and a good cop. He wouldn't get that wrong."

"Good." She heard her stomach rumbling. *Damn. Forgot to bring lunch.*

It was pushing a half-hour past noon when Andi slowly nosed the SUV to the edge of the clearing—which was, to her relief, right where it was supposed to be. It was perhaps one hundred feet in diameter.

They sat for a few moments, studying the scene. She saw crushed weeds—three sets of parallel ruts in the tall vegetation. She shut off the engine. "Let's stay out here. Who knows what those ruts are all about."

"Good call," Mike nodded. "Let's check the GPS, make sure we're in your county."

Andi pulled up the tracker on the SUV's computer and tapped the keys. In a moment, she read the coordinates aloud. Mike nodded. "That's what Dwayne gave us. Looks like it's your jurisdiction."

"You can still help."

"Sure can. So let's take a look."

Facing them, almost exactly in the center of the clearing, lay a jagged square pile of gray ash, perhaps ten feet on a side, eight or ten inches deep. Fire-blackened boards lay in the ashes, and two larger beams lay in the center of the pile, deeply charred. They climbed out of the SUV. Right away, Andi walked over to the parallel ruts at the edge of the clearing, the weeds crushed down. Mike joined her. "Three vehicles drove in here sometime, not long ago."

"Looks like it." Andi frowned. "Related to the fire, you think?"

"Hard to say, but ask me to guess, I'd say probably."

Avoiding the marks in the weeds, they walked over to the ashes. Andi peered around the clearing.

"Christ, this was one hot fire," Mike grunted, scuffling the bare burned soil around the ash pile with his foot.

Andi nodded. In the ashes near the edge of the fire stood an old potbelly stove, blackened now, sagging where one leg had partially melted. One of the charred beams had fallen and was resting on it. In another corner, a twisted rectangle of metal stuck up. "Looks like a bed frame," she said. "This must've been a cabin."

"From the location, I'd say a hunter's shack."

"Sure as hell wasn't a summer home. No plumbing I can see." She studied the ashes. "What if somebody died in the fire?"

Mike looked around the clearing. "No outhouse, either. I can't imagine anybody'd be up here at this time of year. Too early for bow-hunting, and there's no fishing anywhere up here."

"Not living here doesn't rule out dying here."

He nodded. "That's a point."

She surveyed the clearing again. A pile of debris under a ponderosa caught her eye. She walked over. A broken table, a couple of chairs, tools. A box of magazines. She riffled through a few. "*Life* magazines." She looked around. "Why would this junk be out here?"

Mike came over, looked a long moment at the pile. "Here's my guess: somebody set them out here to get rid of later. Could be, some old guy decided to burn down his shack."

Andi thought about it for a moment. *Why burn the cabin? And why carry all this junk out first? And why three vehicle tracks?* She turned back toward the fire scene, but noticed something. "Look at this, Mike." She pointed to a rectangular patch of bare earth perhaps twenty feet from the edge of the fire, six feet wide and maybe ten feet long. The weeds and grasses elsewhere in the clearing were autumn-length—twenty, thirty inches tall or higher—except for the crushed tire ruts she'd noticed earlier and what looked like stretches where someone had walked. Those weeds were merely bent over, but this strange rectangle was cut to the ground, and the chaff of weed-cuttings and blown dirt were scattered at the edges of the rectangle, as if blown against the surrounding weeds. And the perimeter around the ashy square was also scraped bare. A mass of marks could be seen in the dirt. "Footprints?"

Mike looked, bent over, studied the dirt. "Looks like prints. Not sure. Could be anything. This cut-down area does look odd, doesn't it?" He straightened, smiled at Andi. She liked his smile, young, friendly. "Who knows? Maybe he wanted to start a garden next spring." He chuckled.

Andi frowned. "But why burn your cabin if you want a garden in the spring?"

Mike laughed gently. "A joke, Andi."

"Got it," she said, a little embarrassed. *Must be a Gen X vs. Millennial thing,* she thought. She bent down again, examining the dirt floor of the odd rectangle. "There," she pointed. "Looks like a bare footprint. Toes and a heel." She spotted a few others. "Wow. More than one."

Mike bent over, moving in close beside her. She didn't move away. He stood. "What the hell?"

"I've heard bear prints can look human."

He nodded. "Sure can. But these are..."

"Too small for bear. And too many."

Mike nodded. "Put the footprint together with the tire tracks, I'd say human."

"So," she said. "We've got weird tire tracks in the weeds, three vehicles, and prints of bare feet in the dirt here."

She turned back to the tracks in the weeds. "I noticed that there's a low spot that's still damp over there."

He looked where she pointed.

"Check it out for me? Maybe we can get a cast."

As he went over to the ruts, she went to the edge of the ash pile, and stepped gingerly into the ashes. She pulled on the gloves she'd stuffed in her rear pocket, and bent over to lift the nearest of the charcoaled beams. That was when she saw the charred bones.

15

"Mike, come see this!" She laid the beam off to the side, stepped out of the ashes, and bent over, stood staring at the bones.

The bones wouldn't make a full skeleton; too many had been incinerated. A few ribs, a collarbone, she thought. Some of the skull and jaw. Half the pelvis lay amid dark ash. All the flesh had been consumed.

Mike stood quietly beside her, taking it in. Andi, straightening, said, "These are human."

"They look it, yeah."

"You doubtful?"

"Not really. But..." He wiped his forehead. "Gotta get our forensic guys up here."

Andi stood taller. "No, man. This is Adams County, and I'm calling DCI to evaluate this scene," she said. "There's too damn many questions and our county's resources are too small. Obviously, somebody died in this fire—or was dead before and burned in it. And if he or she was dead before, then how'd the fire start?"

"Must've been somebody in the vehicles, right?" He scratched his forehead, brow furrowed.

Andi smiled. He looked intense. Thoughtful. Cute. She nodded. "So either somebody died in the fire, or died some other way and was burned here. Three vehicle tracks and the footprints in the dirt tell me there were more than a couple of other people here."

"Unless there was just one vehicle that came up three times."

"Huh. Yeah, gotta consider that. It'd mean there were at least two people—the one who was burned and another to drive the vehicle out."

"Gotcha."

"I don't know if the fire was a crime or an accident, but either way, I want to seal this clearing and see what the DCI guys have to say."

"Devil's advocate for a minute?"

"Sure."

"Okay, these mountains are full of old hermits and crazies, not to mention hunters who get drunk at night. Lightning could've struck this tinderbox, with some old guy sleeping it off inside. This place is just too remote for a crime. If somebody wanted to kill somebody, why come all this way to do it and then leave the evidence?"

"That's a point." She hesitated. "Maybe. Was there any lightning yesterday?" She knew there wasn't.

"Not that I know of." He smiled. "I know, it's a long shot; but like I said, devil's advocate."

Something new caught her eye. Shards of glass, edges melted, fused. She walked over, into the ashes, and squatted next to the bigger shards, careful to avoid touching them. "What do you think?"

He joined her, looked for a moment, then reached toward them. Andi stopped his hand. "Gloves, Mike."

He closed his eyes, and his face reddened. "Thanks, Andi. If this is a crime scene, you stopped me from fucking it up." He pulled on his gloves, still blushing.

Andi stood. His embarrassment, so unlike Ordrew's arrogance, appealed to her. "No harm done. I'll call DCI and see what they find."

"We're in your county, so we do it your way. But it'd save a lot of time if I just took the bones to Carlton and let our coroner examine them." His smile was warm.

She liked his smile, but not his idea. "Let's do it by the book." Inside, she chuckled: *I sound like Ordrew.* "I'll get my phone."

At the SUV, she grabbed her jacket from the back and pulled her cell phone out of the pocket and swiped it on. No signal. She got in, keyed the radio, raised Callie, and was patched through to Ben. She briefed him on what they'd found, and asked him to make the call to DCI.

Mike rested his elbows in the open passenger side window, listening. When she signed off, she said to him, "My boss'll call them in. What's your thinking about those tire tracks?"

He shook his head. "Beats me. Like we thought, either three vehicles came in together, or one or two came different times. But the questions are when and why." He bent down to look at one of the tracks. "Truth is, I doubt these are going to help us."

She grimaced. She didn't want him to go slack on her. *Is this how Ordrew feels about me?* "It's worth a try." Getting out of her SUV, she squatted beside the deeper spot in one of the tracks, the one she'd noticed some moisture in earlier. It was closest to the rectangle where they'd seen the footprints. "This one looks like it could yield a cast. I'm going to cover it with an insulated blanket."

Mike looked at the sky. "I doubt it's going to snow."

"Probably not. But it'll keep animals from tracking it up. I'll ask the DCI guys to make a cast and try to trace the treads." The blanket covered six feet of the track. "While I take the pictures, you tape this scene. Around the whole clearing."

"Really? Who's going to find their way out here to violate it?"

"You're right, crime tape out here won't stop anybody. But it's the right thing to do, don't you think?" Her deference to procedure surprised her. Ordrew rubbing off?

He smiled. "Pulling your chain, Andi. You're right, again."

She laughed quietly. "Let's do it, then."

After she'd taken a couple dozen photos from all angles, and Mike had run yellow crime tape from tree to tree around the clearing, she stood a moment, surveying everything a last time. As they opened the SUV's doors, she paused, said, "This place feels wrong."

Mike looked at her over the roof. "Wrong how? The bones?"

"Them, and that rectangle and the barefoot prints. That pile of trash or whatever it is. Whatever happened here was no accident."

"Sure hope you're wrong," Mike said, then slipped into the passenger seat.

She drove them out to Highway 36, taking it as fast as she could, bouncing over a few potholes more roughly than she would have allowed with her own vehicle. Mike grunted at those jarrings, but kept quiet. She told herself she wanted to get back to Jefferson, to a glass of wine with Callie and Maggie, and an early sack time; the double shift was catching up with her. But she couldn't shake the foreboding that had come over her in the clearing.

At the highway, Mike opened his door. "Quite a ride out, Andi."

"Sorry," she said.

"Let me know when we go in again. I'll wear my crash helmet," he laughed. "Oh, and when you hear from DCI, give me a ring." He fumbled in a pocket, handed her his card.

When their fingers touched, Andi felt a charge. She put the card in her pocket. "You'll be hearing from me."

16

Driving down the mountain, Andi replayed the fire scene. The bones bothered her most. Whether the death happened before the fire or because of it, whose were they? It seemed only logical that someone had started the fire—no recent lightning recently. But if the bones belonged to whoever lit the fire, why had he stayed when the place was burning up? Maybe Mike was right, an old drunk hunter, passed out, unaware that his stove fire had ignited the cabin. Or suicide? There were too many easier ways to kill yourself. Murder? Hell, there were lots of less complicated ways to kill somebody than burning down a shack around him. And Mike made a good point: why drag somebody all the way out here and then leave the evidence?

The dots wouldn't connect. She sighed and rolled down the window, let the cool breeze restore her focus. Okay. Start with Mike's devil's advocate idea: an old hunter, drunk, passed out. Maybe his cigarette caught a magazine page, like those *Life* magazines in the junk pile? She thought back to the ashes, what she had seen. After a moment it came to her: it was what she *hadn't* seen. Nothing, just charred wood and ashes, the bones, and the shards of glass. No small utensils, no cups, no furniture except the half-melted bed frame and the potbelly stove. Wouldn't Mike's old hunter, drinking himself into a stupor, have had things—hell, a rifle barrel!—around him? She replayed her first sight of the bones. In her mind, she bent over to examine the bones.

"Focus," she told herself. But focus eluded her. When she was younger, her mind at a crime scene had been a laser. Unexpectedly, she felt the start of a hot flash. *Damn.* This time, though, the heat sweeping up her back came with a sharp burst of fear. She slowed, then pulled over and got out. Fifty yards ahead was a small bridge, so she strode down on the shoulder toward it. The mountain breeze, the small sound of water trickling in the nearly dry creek crossing under the road, the green of the tall pines cooled and calmed her. She climbed down toward the water, only a dribble this late in the season. She wet her hand and wiped her face. The heat was fading. What remained was a puzzling feeling of anxiety.

The scene?

Her cell phone buzzed back in the vehicle. She ran back and reached in for it.

When she heard Ed's voice, she stammered a hello.

"You okay?" he asked. "You're out of breath."

"Yeah. Ran to get the phone. And no, I'm not okay. I found bones in the ashes. Somebody died in that fire. Or at least I think so."

"That's ugly. Where are you now?"

"About forty-five minutes out of Jefferson."

"How about meeting me at the Angler for a beer when you get back?"

For no good reason, she felt a twinge of irritation. *I told him I'm meeting Callie and Maggie.* She sighed. "No can do, Ed. I'm meeting Callie and Maggie Sobstak there, remember? I told you in your office."

"Oh, right. You did tell me that."

"You're getting old, big guy."

She heard his snort. "Don't remind me."

"Like I said, I'll join you at your place after the Angler. I need to crash early."

She heard him rustling papers. "Look, I've got plenty of paperwork to clear up. Give me a call when you're wrapping it up with the ladies, will you?"

"You're a damn workaholic, Ed," she snapped, regretting it immediately.

He didn't answer for a moment, and she tensed. She started to apologize when she heard him chuckle, and relaxed.

"You're right, pal. I think I'll head home and make myself a drink."

"A drink? Not beer or wine?"

"Turning over a new leaf. By the way, I've got a question I want us to talk about."

Her jumbled feelings collapsed into a fog of weariness. "Nothing serious, I hope. Double shift's got me dead on my feet."

"I'll bet. Well, I'll keep it short. It's serious, but good-serious."

17

An hour later, Andi found Callie and Maggie out at the back of the Angler, on the deck overlooking the Monastery River as it flowed north through town. After the parched summer, the water was low, only its deeper channels moving slowly; dry dusty rocks, shadow-dappled, warmed in the late afternoon sun. Maggie, sitting with her back to the river, looked gray, shell-shocked. Callie saw Andi coming, gave a small wave.

Andi waved back. "Sorry I'm late," she said, glancing at the half-empty martini glasses shining softly in the late sun.

Callie shook her head. "Not to worry. Maggie and me had plenty to keep us busy."

Maggie forced a small smile. "I'm a little loopy," she said. "Callie's determined to get me drunk."

Might as well jump right in, Andi thought. "I'm so sorry to hear about the cancer." The word struck her with a jolt of fear. She ignored it.

Maggie smiled. "Thanks. Not what I was hoping for, but..."

Callie said, "I was telling Maggie, my mother had breast cancer the year she turned fifty. Lived another forty-one years, died in a car wreck, driving herself to bingo on a snowy night."

Maggie mustered a smile that only reached half her mouth.

Andi, thinking of the anxiety she'd felt, said, "My mom died of breast cancer. On my sixteenth birthday." Her throat thickened.

Both women turned toward her. Maggie reached over and took her hand. "I can see it still hurts."

Andi's grief took her by surprise. She'd learned to steel herself against this sorrow, and had left it behind years ago. Or thought she had. "I'm so sorry, Maggie. I should be thinking of you, not myself."

Callie snorted. "Girl, we all got mothers and we all got breasts, and we never get over losing either one. Don't worry your head." She waved inside toward Ted Coldry, the Angler's owner and bartender, who came out on the deck. To Andi, she said, "Here comes just what you need."

"Andrea, a glass of your usual Pinot Noir?" He saw the moisture in Andi's eyes. "I'm sorry, Andi. You must have learned about Maggie's problem." He smiled at Maggie and rested his hand lightly on her shoulder. Maggie patted the back of his hand.

Andi wiped her eyes dry and composed herself. "Yeah, Ted. Pinot...No, what the hell. I'll have a martini."

Callie lifted her eyebrows. "Atta girl!"

Ted's eyebrows arched and he grinned. "Vodka or gin?"

"My last martini was with my dad just before he died. He drank gin. Make it gin."

Maggie's smile came out sad, but it was a smile that this time reached her eyes. "You know what, Andi? I believe I'll join you." She wrinkled her nose. "It's not like I need to worry about my health for a while. Ted, I'll have another." She drained her martini and handed him the glass.

They all laughed. Ted left, and they talked about breast cancer until Maggie waved her hand. "I believe that's enough cancer talk."

Ted came back with their drinks. For a moment, they sipped silently, and then they talked about nothing related to cancer, mostly Callie's comical stories about sexual misadventures with her husband, Bill. Maggie talked about her volunteer jobs in the valley, and about how she was getting along with the new priest. The previous pastor, Ed's friend Father Jim Hamilton, had left the church and gone off to marry his priesthood-long love. Maggie was the volunteer church organist at St. Bernie's, and Father Jim had always let her pick the Sunday hymns. "The new priest's nice enough, but he picks all those stupid hymns from the 1950s." She shook her head, took another sip, then giggled. "Looks like I'm getting hammered."

Callie lifted her glass. "Steady as she goes, girl. This'll be a good story at the Society."

"The Society'll get a good laugh," Maggie agreed. She smiled a fuller smile.

Andi asked, "What society?"

Callie looked at Maggie, who nodded. "The Ladies' Fishing Society."

"What do they do?"

"Well, in the summer, we meet first Wednesday of the month by the river. In the cold months, we meet in each others' homes."

Maggie giggled.

Andi imagined them fishing in the summer, tying flies together amid amiable girl talk during the winter meetings. She felt that tug of loneliness again. She forced herself to say, "How's a woman get into the Society?"

"You get invited by a member." She turned to Maggie. "Should we?"

Maggie nodded, giggling again.

Callie looked at Andi, smiled. "All right. Why don't you come to our meeting tomorrow night?"

Andi gulped. "I don't fish."

Maggie and Callie both burst out laughing. "Oh, honey," Callie said, "we don't either."

18

After his last patient left the office, Ed sat down to write his notes on the day's sessions. As he'd promised Andi, he ignored the pile of paperwork on his desk; but these daily notes he could do in a few minutes, and then he'd head home for that drink. He hadn't had whiskey in ten years, preferring wine, but today he felt frivolous, dissolute, and surprisingly excited at the prospect. He grinned as he opened the first file. He'd barely started the notes when his office phone rang.

"Hey, Northrup, me and Dana and Jen—I mean Dana and Jen and I—need to pick up some stuff for Homecoming. I told you we're the Dance Committee, didn't I?"

"Yes, you did. When's Homecoming again?"

Grace's grammatical self-correcting tickled him. When she'd started her college search last January, she announced she was going to be either a lawyer, a journalist, or an FBI profiler, and he'd suggested that she start sounding like one. Three years ago, when he'd first adopted her, such a comment would have ignited an uproar. In January, she'd merely rolled her eyes. But last May, when they were negotiating about her car, she'd offered a deal: she'd work on her grammar if he'd buy her a car *before* senior year started. He'd agreed.

"It's on the thirteenth." She paused. "Northrup, I'm a little worried about your memory. I've told you the date a few times."

He chuckled. "Thanks for the concern. The thirteenth's early for Homecoming, isn't it?"

"Sure is," she agreed. "We kids don't make the schedule. Anyway, me and my girls—sorry, my girls and I—need to bring all the sets and decorations from the mini-storage, so can I please use your pickup? You can drive the Pink Vulva home." The car he'd found for her was a pink Volvo, which Grace and her girls had promptly—very promptly—renamed. Ed knew she trotted out the full name, instead of his preferred "PV," to tease him. He smiled.

"Sounds like a plan. I'm at the office."

"Uh, that must have occurred to me."

He chuckled. "Because you called me here."

"There you go. That's the old Northrup, sharp as a tack."

He was laughing again when they ended the call. Grace was having that effect on him more and more lately.

In ten minutes, she and her girlfriends burst into the office giggling.

"Hey, guys, what's up?" Ed tossed Grace his truck key.

"Hi, Doctor N.," Dana Harley said, and Jen Fortin gave him a little wrist-wave, still giggling.

"What's funny?"

Grace blushed. "Nothing."

Dana giggled. "Zach told Grace the back seat of the PV was just the right size for, uh, for you-know-what."

Grace jabbed her. "Hey!" She turned to Ed. "We don't *do* it, Northrup, we just *talk* about it."

That set Jen to giggling again. Ed composed that mental post-it note again: schedule that father-daughter preventative biology refresher. Soon. *And better buy some condoms before Homecoming.*

"Have fun," he said. "Will you be home for dinner?"

"Probably not," she said. "This'll take a while, so we'll stop at Alice's for burgers."

"Okay. Home by nine. School night."

"Negotiation alert: it's Homecoming business, and I'm a senior now. Ten."

"Nine-thirty."

She just looked at him.

He laughed and lifted his hands in surrender. "Okay. Ten."

Just then, Andi opened the door and came in. "Saw the lights on. Hey, Grace, girls."

Grace looked at her girls, then said, "Andi, can I talk to you? Privately, please?" She took Andi's hand and led her out of the office.

Ed looked at Jen and Dana. "What's that about?"

They both lifted their hands. Dana said, "No idea, Doctor N." But she looked sharply at Jen: *Keep your mouth shut.*

Jen said, "Would you tell Grace we're out in the parking lot?"

"Sure will. Good luck with the decorations."

He tried to go back to writing his notes, but mentally constructing that preventive biology talk distracted him.

19

Andi allowed herself to be ushered by Grace out into the common hallway and walked with her toward the front door. When Jen and Dana came out of Ed's office, Grace waved to them and called out, "I'll be out in a minute."

When they'd left the building, she looked urgently at Andi and whispered, "Andi, Homecoming's in two weeks, and I..." She blushed; this was the first time she'd confided like this in Andi. "I need some condoms. Can you get them for me?"

"Whoa, girl. That's a parent's decision, and I'm not your mom. Why not talk it over with your dad?"

Grace shook her head fiercely. "God, no. He'll be mad. You're my step-girlfriend, and anyway, you're better to me than my mom ever was."

Andi smiled and touched Grace's face softly, surprising them both. *The martini at work,* she thought. "I'll sound Ed out and see how he reacts. I doubt he'll be mad."

Grace looked skeptical. "Maybe not, but dads never want their daughters to grow up." She turned and hurried down the hall and out the door to the parking lot.

Andi watched her. *So this is how senior year is shaping up.*

20

After Andi returned to his office, Ed asked, "What was that about?" He suspected he knew.

Andi's cheeks had a martini glow, warm and sweet. She grinned. "Condoms. She thinks you'll go batshit if she asks you to get some, so she asked me to buy them. I said I'd sound you out."

He smiled. "I figured it was something like that. And so it begins."

Then he remembered, and his mood dropped. "How's Maggie? I've been feeling terrible about her all day."

"She's shell-shocked. But she had a couple of martinis and they loosened her up." She almost giggled. "Me too, as a matter of fact."

"Loosened is good." He winked, thinking about what it would be like to marry this woman. *It'd be fine.* He corrected his thought. *The finest thing I've ever done.*

She said, "I got invited to join the Ladies' Fishing Society. First meeting's tomorrow night." She yawned, deep and luxurious.

"I'd ask what the Ladies' Fishing Society is, but you look too..." He stopped. How did she look? Her flushed cheeks, her curly blond hair cut short. "Beautiful," he finished.

She blushed. "Thanks, big guy. Except for the buzz, I feel like somebody who's just finished two shifts in a dirty uniform."

21

After Andi drove into Ed's yard, she sat for a moment, watching the last lingering light. Twilight dusted the trees and grasses sloping down toward town. Distant rooftops nestled among the cottonwoods and tall pines of Jefferson. Interrupting the pleasant view, a flash of heat swept her, and with it, a flood of anxiety. She rolled down the window and waited it out. *The tension's about the bones,* she thought. Once the feeling faded, she gazed over the valley toward the Monastery range. The sun had set, but the air above the mountains glowed a rich gold. After a few minutes, she roused herself and went inside, carrying a pizza box, a salad perched on top.

"I'm bushed," she said, slumping onto a stool at the island. "Mind warming this up in the oven for me?"

Ed leaned over the island to kiss her. "Sure. How about a drink or a glass of wine?"

She pointed out to Grace's PV in the yard. "Grace in her room? And no thanks. I had that martini at Ted's, remember?"

"Yep. Turning over a new leaf?"

"Like you. So, Grace?"

He turned on the oven and slipped the pizza in. "Grace and her girls borrowed my truck to pick up some decorations for the Homecoming dance, then they're stopping for burgers."

She pointed at the glass on the counter. "That your drink?"

He smiled. "A Manhattan. Whiskey and sweet vermouth."

"You haven't drunk whiskey since I met you. What the hell. Make me one, too. Might perk me up."

"Or knock you out. Go relax. I'll bring you the drink and some pizza when it's warm."

She fell onto the living room couch and let her eyes close. He came in a moment later with her drink, and sat down beside her. "Fire?"

She nodded. "God, Ed. It was so upsetting."

"I meant, do you want me to light a fire?"

"Oh. Sure." While Ed started a fire in the wood stove, she described the fire scene, the bones, and all the questions they raised for her.

Ed sat down again. "You said 'we' a few times. Pete go with you?"

"Nope. A Carlton deputy. Nice guy. I think we'll work well on the case." She took a sip of her drink. "Hey, tastes good."

"Meaning?"

"Well, it's sweet, but has a nice bite to it."

"No, I meant the deputy. Why would you be working with a Carlton deputy?"

She chuckled. "Brain's not firing on all cylinders. Ben set it up. The scene's pretty close to the border between counties. In fact, it could even be in Carlton; borders are fuzzy up there. Anyway, Ben said Harley Vogel wants one of his guys on the case with me."

The oven timer chimed, and Ed got up. "I take it the Carlton deputy is more to your liking than Brad Ordrew."

"God, yes. He's smart, and nice. Good sense of humor."

"Good-looking?"

It hadn't occurred to her to use those words, but she immediately remembered the jolt she'd felt when he handed her his card and their fingers touched. She nodded, wondering about the breathy feeling in her throat. "Yeah, good-looking's the word."

"Hmm." Ed went toward the kitchen area. "I'll get the pizza."

Andi hardly spoke while they ate. A pleasant drowsiness—the drink, the pizza, and the warmth of the fire in the woodstove—came over her.

Ed noticed. "Just relax. I'll do the dishes, then we can talk."

She sighed. "Really, Ed, I'm fading fast. How about tomorrow?"

He looked up sharply, though he smiled. "I've been waiting a long time for this, Andi. Three years now."

Andi frowned. After being shot, she'd asked Ed not to push her about their relationship. To give her time. He'd been patient—more than patient. Still, his ignoring her weariness was annoying. "After all this time, what's the big deal about one more day?"

His smile faded.

"I'm sorry," she said. "That sounded bitchy. I'm tired and starting to get cranky."

Ed's silence hung between them for a moment, then he shrugged. "Sure, it can wait."

"No, I'll be okay. Why don't you make me another drink—put ice in it this time, water it down a bit—and we'll talk."

"Sure you want another one? Two's the limit for ladies."

"I'm no lady, I'm a cop. And something tells me I'm going to need it." The fire in the stove had made the room too warm. "Let's sit on the porch."

He made the drinks, and they put on jackets and went outside. She willed herself to relax, letting the evening air and the lingering blue light above the Monastery Range settle her mood.

Above the Monasteries, in the soft blue-brown twilit sky, three red lines in the sky, side by side, went down and west into the night. "Contrails," Ed murmured.

"Signs of a bad day coming."

Ed rested his hand on her shoulder. "Except for the news about Maggie's cancer, I've had a really good day."

"Lucky you. Mine sucked." *So much for relaxing,* she thought.

"Want to talk about it?"

"God, no, Ed. I want to hear what you need to say and then get some damn sleep." She took in a long breath. "Man, I'm sorry. Again. This case's got me spooked." She leaned back in the porch swing. "Talk to me." For no reason she could fathom, the contrails had upset her.

"Okay. I'll be quick. There's two things. First, I'm going to hire somebody to join my practice and, in a few years, buy me out. I'm thinking of Lynn Monroe, the counselor at the high school."

Andi jerked upright. "You're thinking what? You're a workaholic, Ed."

"I'm really excited about this, Andi. As you so gracelessly reminded me, I'm going to be sixty. Time to think about the next chapter."

"Jesus." She paused, trying to sort the tangled skein of her thoughts. "That sounds so *old*." She felt the sudden clench in her stomach, the high-alert she always went into when approaching a vehicle she'd pulled over. She felt her heart beating faster than this conversation deserved.

He laughed softly. "Old? Hadn't thought of it as old, just ready for something new. Like a Manhattan with my pal."

She stayed silent. *What the hell's bothering me here?*

He waited a moment. "I take it you don't like the idea."

She leaned back again and looked out over the night. "I'm only forty-nine. I'm not ready to slow down."

"I didn't say you had to slow down. But I want to do new things—or old things that are more fun."

"But you love your work."

He nodded. "Sure I do. But I like other things too, and I'm not doing them. It's time." He cleared his throat.

She stiffened. Ed always cleared his throat before something important.

"Which brings me to the second thing: I want us to get married."

She almost jumped out of the porch swing, her heart suddenly pounding, her chest tight. She could barely breathe. She moved to the front of the porch and leaned against a log post, trying to loosen herself up. It felt like breathing the smoky air during the wildfire, as if the air itself wanted to suffocate her. Behind her, she wondered if Ed noticed.

He cleared his throat. "When you were shot, you asked me to give you time, and I have. But we love each other." He stopped for a moment. "I want you in my life more than three or four nights a week."

Facing out into the dark yard, her heart still racing, she said, "You've been patient, Ed. I appreciate that." Her throat felt tight, her voice fighting its way out.

"Appreciate it, *but*..." His voice sounded calm.

She nodded into the darkness. "But, wow. I *am* in your life. When you say *get married* on the heels of saying you're getting old and want something new..." She paused. "Just, wow. That's a lot to absorb." She shivered. Something she needed to know seemed just out of reach. Her chest was not loosening.

He was waiting quietly. When she glanced back at him in the half-dark, he didn't have the squared-off, hard jaw that would speak of his anger. He smiled at her. She turned back toward the valley. The evening's first bat swooped across the yard, and she watched for it to circle back, but it didn't. Below them, down by the river, town lights twinkled like stars. She got it now: After her mother's death, Andi had resolved always to stay in control. In the past, when moments like this happened, Andi either controlled them or left the scene. Suddenly, she realized she didn't want to leave, and didn't know how to stay. And she definitely didn't know how to control this. She stiffened her back.

She returned and sat beside him and took his hand. "Don't take this wrong, but this scares me. Not that I don't love you, but I've never thought about us getting old. And the idea of marrying you makes getting old more, well, serious. I'm still young." When Ed didn't say anything, she wondered if he was thinking that menopause didn't exactly mean she was "still young."

After a moment, he said, "There's only ten years between us."

"Ten years is a long time."

"Hasn't been so far...but maybe you're right." He smiled in the dim porch light. "I haven't got any experience loving a younger woman."

Andi studied him in the dim light. He didn't seem to be taking her reaction personally. "I feel weird," she said. "Like wanting and not wanting it at the same time. Excited, but freaked. I need some time..."

He started to interrupt, but stopped. She heard a soft brush of breath. She looked at him; his jaw clenched, just once. After a minute, he said, "You know, I've been patient for a long time. I gave you the time you wanted. Now—"

"Whoa, cowboy. We're not kids here. You can't just drop a marriage proposal in my lap and expect me to go all starry-eyed. Getting married to an older man, that changes the equation. I need some time, and I don't need lectures about your generosity."

He looked at her. "Guess I touched a nerve." She could see hurt in his eyes, which almost infuriated her. He stood up and walked to the porch railing, placed both palms flat on the wood. "You afraid of something?" He didn't turn, but his voice was soft.

His words landed on her like a blow. Suddenly, she wanted to tell him about the rush of fear that had started accompanying her hot flashes, the clutching feeling deep in her chest.

All she said was, "I need some space." Space sounded right. Space to breathe.

He turned. "Meaning?"

"Damn it, Ed. I don't know what it means. It's a freaking phrase, for God's sake."

"Maybe this guy you're working with at the fire scene—"

"Stop! Just stop! This has nothing to do with him. It's—" She had no idea what to say.

"It's *what*, then? We're in love—or we both say so—and all of a sudden when I mention marriage, you need space? Space? God *damn* it, Andi!" He ran his hand through his hair, and was silent for a moment. "I'm sorry. I'm shouting. But what the hell do you mean?"

"Jesus, I'm no damn philosopher. Space means space. Time to figure things out. You're asking me to jump from A to Z, and I need to think about it."

She watched him taking long breaths. *Calming himself,* she

thought. *Not a bad idea. I should try it.* She said, "I know I'm a control freak, but this isn't about that. Not this time."

"You sure about that?"

No, I'm not. "This fire case, it's going to get ugly. Ben's diabetes. Ordrew's attitude. All I can say, I need time to think."

"Time, time, time." She could see on his face, in the shadows, the effort he was making to lighten it up. He took her hand and kissed it. "Well, take some time," he said, smiling again. "But just a little." A new twinkle lit his eye. "I'm not getting any younger, you know."

She slapped his arm and grinned. She yawned, deeply, the fatigue and worry, and now three drinks, pulling her down.

"You climb in bed, Andi," Ed said. "We can talk later."

She shook her head. "I'll be sleeping at home tonight, Ed."

He looked stricken, but nodded. "Ah. Space." After a moment, he said, "But sleep here. I'll take the couch. You've had, what? Three drinks, right? You shouldn't be driving."

The fact that Ed was right didn't pull the sting of staying when she really wanted to be alone. Andi took some extra time in the bathroom, holding a cool washcloth to her face. *He's right. Too much booze.* She studied her eyes in the mirror. Tense, red. *So what am I afraid of?*

The word *age* came to mind. Ed was turning sixty. Surprising herself, she thought of Mike Payne, his youth, his warm smile. She recalled the charge she'd felt when their fingers touched. To herself in the mirror, she whispered, "I don't need that complication, damn it." Outside the bathroom door, the phone rang. She checked her watch: *9:30*. Grace calling to say she'll be late, no doubt.

Ed's voice answered. After a moment, she heard him say, "My God. What happened?"

22

Ed listened as Melissa Hansen at the hospital told him, "We've admitted Grace for observation, It's only a concussion, but Doc wants to be on the safe side."

His heart was beating so hard for a moment he couldn't catch his breath. When he could speak, he said, "Is Grace...ah...all right?"

"There's the concussion, and she's in and out of consciousness. Nothing looks broken, although she has a few bruises and she'll probably have a bad whiplash. You don't have to come in at this hour—we'll give you a call if anything changes."

"What happened?"

"A car crash. I don't know all the details. Pete Peterson took her statement, so maybe you could—"

"Check with Pete, yeah. I'm on my way, Mel. Tell Gracie I'm coming, please." Ed had never felt such a hollowing out around his heart.

Andi was already out of the bathroom, looking at him. "Grace?" she asked.

"She had an accident. They think she's got a concussion. I'm heading in." He was already shouldering into his jacket, pushing through a growing sense of fear. Concussion? He knew all too well how bad a concussion could turn out. He'd had patients suffering for years from brain injuries. He shook off the thought, opened the door.

Andi grabbed her uniform jacket and weapon belt. "I'm coming with you."

Running toward her vehicle, she tossed Ed the keys. "You drive, I've had too much to drink." They climbed in. "What happened?"

"No idea. Melissa suggested talking to Pete. I guess he took the report."

"I'll call Pete." She was already dialing Pete's cell phone number. Ed glanced at her; she shook her head. "No answer." She left a message.

Ed pulled onto the highway and floored it.

After a few moments, Andi reached across and caressed his neck, then nodded at the speedometer. "Speed limit, big guy."

He looked at the dial and slowed. "Right."

"Maybe he's at the station." Andi punched numbers into her cell phone. In a moment, she said, "Pete? Thanks for picking up." She was quiet. "Yeah, we just heard. We're on the way in. What happened?" She listened. "Uh-huh. Got it. I'll tell Ed. Thanks." She ended the call.

"So?" he asked. Glanced at the dashboard—he'd picked up speed again, backed it down to the limit.

"She was stopped at Division Street, waiting for a car to cross from her right. A drunk rear-ended her, which pushed her out into the oncoming's path. The oncoming T-boned her on the passenger side, thank God. And thank God she didn't have any passengers. The guy who hit her is in serious condition. Broken sternum, collapsed lung."

Ed felt a sudden fury and tears blurred his vision. He slowed and pulled onto the shoulder. "Who was the drunk?"

"Burke Renton, works on the C.W. ranch. He's been arrested, DUI." She looked at him. "You okay?"

He shook his head and roughly rubbed his eyes. "No, I'm not. You better drive. I feel like killing somebody."

Andi felt her martini and two Manhattans. "Can't, Ed. Too much alcohol."

"Got it." He rubbed his eyes clear again and shook himself. "Let's go."

WEDNESDAY

23

The hospital lobby had chairs to try to sleep in—the operative word being "try"—but Ed couldn't sleep. Andi, exhausted and still feeling the alcohol, did, snoring quietly. When he dozed, after a few minutes he jerked awake, remembering the horrible nights, three years past, he'd spent in a chair outside Andi's ICU door after she'd been shot. Now, his daughter lay unconscious—not from the concussion, thank God, but asleep. Ed had sat with her for a couple hours, then joined Andi in the waiting room.

Somewhere in the night, Grace's boyfriend had come into the waiting room. Ed stood to shake his hand. "Zach. How'd you—"

"My mom's a nurse's aide. One of the nurses remembered me and Grace are, uh, going together, and called her."

Ed nodded. "She's asleep. Has a concussion. We're hoping she'll be all right." He stifled a huge yawn. "Sorry. Not much sleep on these chairs."

They sat silently. In a few minutes, Zach's chain-saw snores were twice the volume of Andi's. Ed sighed. Eventually, around five, he drifted off, but at six, Andi shook him softly.

She whispered, "Gotta get ready for work." She kissed him on the forehead. "Take care of our girl." He tipped his face up, and kissed her lips.

Andi gestured toward Zach, then whispered, "Young love."

A half-hour later, Doc Keeley found him in the same chair, glassy-eyed. When he came in, Ed sat up, then stood, stiff. "How is she?"

"A mild concussion," Keeley said, "but she woke up easily every time we checked her, and everything looks good now." He glanced at

Zach, who was stirring, but not wakening. "I think she can go home. I don't see any evidence of brain damage, although she's got a headache she'll probably keep for a few days. Give her ibuprofen, let's say six-hundred milligrams four times a day, as long as the headache's bad. Technically, she doesn't have whiplash, but she'll have a sore neck for a few days. We'll send her home in a cervical collar anyway. She shouldn't wear it more than a week, and it's better if she stays as active as she can. The ibuprofen and regular icing the area should help."

Ed asked him, "How about TBI?"

Keeley shook his head. "Doubt it. The impact was on the side, so her head moved laterally. She didn't sustain a direct blow to the head, as far as I can tell. Symptoms of traumatic brain injury can take time to manifest, though, so we'll have to wait and see. You know what to look for, right?"

Ed nodded. "All too well." In the 1980s, he'd treated a number of traumatized vets, before traumatic brain injury was well-enough understood. Failing those men was a painful memory. "Can I see her?"

When Ed and Doc entered her room, Grace was dozing, but woke easily. "Doc, I don't mean to be bitchy, but why'd you guys have to wake me up so often?"

Doc smiled. "Not nice, were we? We had to check that you didn't slip into a coma. It looks okay, so I'm thinking you can go home and sleep all day."

Grace nodded, then winced. Doc said, "Headache?"

"Yeah."

"You'll probably have it a couple of days. Take the ibuprofen like your dad tells you. It'll help." Doc turned to Ed, "Call me if anything changes."

Just as he was leaving, the discharge nurse came in and gave them instructions about the cervical collar. After the nurse left, Ed handed Grace a bag of her clothes and stepped outside.

A few minutes later, Dana and Jen came into the waiting room. Ed said, "Let me see if Grace is ready."

He checked and she was, though she asked him to help with her shoes. "I'm sorry, Northrup, but I can't bend my neck enough to see my shoelaces." Her grimace spoke volumes.

He tied her laces. "Jen and Dana are here to see you. I'll get them."

There ensued a flurry of hugs. "Omigod-you-could-have-died!" Jen blurted, which triggered tears and more hugs, which Grace gamely endured. And then Zach, bleary and yawning, came in. Grace's girls stepped aside, solemn in the presence of a love that faces almost-death, and made room for him to take Grace in his big arms.

Zach held Grace for a long, lingering time. "You're all right?" he whispered.

He was a big boy—six-three, offensive right tackle and defensive center linebacker on the school's nine-man football squad—and Grace disappeared inside his hug. Her answer came out muffled. "I have, like, a killer headache and my neck feels like shit, but I guess I'm okay."

Zach released her. "I was really scared, baby."

Ed lifted his eyebrows. *Baby*? He'd have to tell Andi about that. He liked Zach. A strapping kid from a ranching family in the northern valley, he treated Grace with sweetness and respect. Grace had confided to Andi that she might choose Missoula for college because Zach had already decided to go there to play Griz football.

Ed said, "Thanks for staying with us last night, Zach."

Dana's hand went to her mouth. "You stayed *all night*?" Her eyebrows danced as she glanced at Jen. "That is sooooo romantic."

Zach blushed. "No worries, Doctor N. Can I ask you something?"

Ed nodded.

"I gotta drive over to Missoula and pick up a load of fencing for my dad. Can Gracie ride with me?"

Gracie? Baby? "What about school?"

Zach reddened. "My dad, he says school's fine, but ranch work comes first."

Ed had heard that often enough in the valley. "I don't think so, Zach. I think we'll stay close to home today and make sure Grace's all right."

"Northrup, come on. I'm fine!" But he saw her flinch.

"Sorry, *Gracie,* a head injury isn't something to ignore." He saw her eyes narrow when he called her Gracie, which her mother, Mara, had called her. And which Grace had protested, every time.

She said nothing.

After another bustle of hugs and *omigods* with Grace's girls, Grace prolonged her good-bye kiss with Zach. Ed pretended not to notice Grace's hand drifting down, then squeezing, Zach's rear end.

That's her answer for me calling her "Gracie," Ed thought, bumping that father-daughter preventative biology chat to the top of the to-do list.

24

After tucking Grace into bed at home, Ed went into work and saw a few patients, but drove home at noon to check on her. She was still asleep, but he woke her for ibuprofen.

She woke up grumpy. "Geez, Northrup. Let me sleep!"

He held out a glass of water and the pill. "Take this, Gracie."

"Don't call me Gracie." She swallowed the medication and handed the glass back to him. She lowered herself gingerly to the pillow, obviously in pain as she pulled her blanket tight around her neck. She was asleep by the time he closed the door.

It was a quarter to six, work done for the day. Andi had agreed to check on Grace at four and give her another pill. Ed was already late for his Wednesday meeting with Ben on the corner. So when his phone rang in the office, he muttered a little before picking up.

"Dr. Northrup? We need to see you."

It was a woman's voice—hard, demanding, but tinged with fear and pitched low, as if she was trying to prevent being overheard.

"Actually, I'm just leaving the office. Perhaps we can make an appointment for another time?"

"When?"

He thumbed through his appointment book. "Tomorrow morning? Ten o'clock?"

Silence. Suddenly, her voice pitched high, panicked. "Help us!" Just as suddenly, the tone changed again, back to a harried, graveled sound. "Ten, then."

"Okay. Your name."

Ed thought he heard "Protect her," but quickly she said, "The name is John. Beatrice John." Her voice was replaced by the three beeps of an ended call.

Beatrice John. Ed jotted it into his appointment book. *Who does she want me to protect?*

25

Andi had called Ed to offer to make dinner for Grace before driving to the Ladies' Fishing Society meeting, knowing that Wednesday was Ed's evening on the corner with Ben Stewart.

"Thanks, Andi. I'll be home by eight."

"I'll be gone. The meeting's at seven, and I'm sleeping at my place, remember."

"Uh, guess I missed that one." He thought, *This space thing is going to get old fast.* "Okay, I'll cut it short with Ben. Tell Grace I'll be home around seven."

As he crossed Division Street to the Angler to meet Ben, he tried to parse Andi's reaction to his proposal—more space, more time—but gave up. *Something's going on with her.* He blushed, embarrassed at his next thought. *I hope it's not this Carlton deputy...*He pushed through the Angler door into the bar.

Ben Stewart, overflowing his customary barstool at the corner, said nothing when Ed took the stool beside him, apologizing for being late. Ted Coldry, as always, was behind the bar. "And you'll have what, Edward?"

Ted knew exactly what Ed would order, but it was their ritual, performed every Wednesday when Ed and Ben sat on the corner, which was *their* ritual.

"I'm going to have one of your delicious ales, Ted. How about the seasonal?" Since Ted and his partner, Lane Martin, had opened their brewery three years ago, Ed always ordered the seasonal.

"Good choice, Edward," Ted said, as he always did, grabbing a pint glass and pulling a tap handle. "This is Chas's latest, a new Belgian ale. It's exquisite." Ed knew exactly what the brewmaster's latest was. And it *was* exquisite.

Ben still hadn't said a word or even turned to greet Ed.

Ed patted the sheriff's broad shoulder, a slab like a mountain outcrop. "How're you doing, big guy?"

"Don't ask. How I'm doin' and how big I am ain't happy subject matters."

Ed thought, *Depressed.* "Why don't you come see me, Ben?"

Ben looked at him as though Ed had a spider on his nose. "I see you just fine, and that's all I want to do with you." He roused himself, coughing roughly. "Anyway, I ain't depressed. I'm sick."

"Andi told me. Diabetes."

Ben shrugged. "Doc'll get it on the run. Damn tough at the moment, though." He stopped, pressed his hand against his ribs.

"You all right?"

"Fine. Just gas findin' its way up." When no belch was forthcoming, Ben said, "So. Andi tells me you're thinkin' retirement."

"Uh-uh." He shook his head. "Not retiring, just cutting back, slowing down. Do more fishing." Curious: Had she also told Ben he'd asked her to marry him? Or that she needed time—and space—from him? Probably not.

Ben was subdued. "Yeah?" He lifted his glass and drained it. Ed noted a second wet coaster lying on the bar beside the one Ben was using. The sheriff now lifted his empty mug. "Mr. Coldry, this old sheriff needs some liquid salvation."

Usually an artist of riposte, Ted only lifted an eyebrow, then poured another glass of ale. "You're a constant surprise, Benjamin, but—"

"But I've already had my two, you're about to tell the damn world. True, true, and related. I ain't doin' business here on the corner tonight." Ben sat on the same stool, at the same time, four evenings of every workweek, talking with ranchers and business owners, with cowboys or couples—with anyone who asked for his time or whom he'd asked to join him, always with the aim of learning the lean of their thinking. Wednesdays, though, he reserved for Ed, and they traded gossip, talked about the psychological aspects of cases Ben was worrying about, or planned fishing or hunting trips.

Sitting with the valley's people on the corner had been his nightly habit since he was first elected in 1984; and every four years, when election season rolled around, no other candidate had the pulse—or the ready trust—of the valley's men and women that Ben had. And during all those evenings sitting on the corner, five every week, Ben never drank more than two beers.

In former times, before this last crazy season, Ed and Ben often camped a weekend beside a trout stream, and even then, two beers was Ben's limit, all day. Not two in the afternoon and two in the evening watching the fire. Two, period.

Ed's worry about his friend broke the surface. "You're drinking three, with diabetes?"

"Hell, it pisses me off!" He slapped the counter. "You'll analyze me, tell me I'm feelin' sorry for myself." He shook his head. "You'd be right." He growled at Ted, "Cancel that beer, Ted." He straightened his back as if it pained him. "I'm furious about this diabetes crap and I'm mad as hell at one of my deputies. Came bargin' in my office yesterday after Andi went up to that fire, givin' me hell about sendin' a woman to do a man's work. Ranted on and on."

"Ordrew?"

"The same."

"What'd you do?"

He breathed heavily for a moment, then seemed to settle down. Finally, he chuckled. "I just listened, then when he was finished, I said, 'Well, Brad, you ain't doin' no work standin' here pourin' out the verbal diarrhea, so 'til I see some goddamn *police* work outa you, I'll turn to Deputy Pelton any day. We clear?'"

Ed grinned. "How'd he take that?"

"Muttered some crap about women not bein' policemen, and swung outa the office. I got a kick outa hollarin' after him, 'That'd be police *officers*.'"

Ted was listening. "Benjamin, on Monday, Deputy Ordrew was in here, having dinner with someone I didn't recognize. My wait-person told me later he was complaining rather loudly that the sheriff's department is too lax in its enforcement of immigration laws. My waiter said the family at the next table looked offended, or maybe frightened. They were Hispanic, the Ortiz family. Good folks.

Ed said, "Hell, they're citizens."

Ben's face reddened. "Christ on a crutch." He rummaged in a shirt pocket, pulled out a pen, scribbled a note. "All I need's one of my deputies talkin' outa school, and this's the second time in a couple days. He does that again, you give me a call, hear?" His words were firm, but his voice wavered.

"I already instructed my staff to inform me if it happens again. I can handle offensive customers, Benjamin."

"Sure you can. But I need goddamn reasons to put the son of a bitch on permanent midnights. Handle him however you like, but call me when you're done."

Ed looked at his friend, whose face was a sickly red. Ted glanced at Ed. Ted was holding the beer Ben had ordered and then cancelled. "Edward, you want this?"

Ed nodded.

Ben turned to Ed. "Ed, I tire so fast." His voice brimmed with grief. His eyes reddened.

"Ben, you're sick."

"'And the sun also rises.'"

Ted, with the fresh beer still poised over Ed's second coaster, said, "Benjamin, I agree with Edward. I worry about you."

Ted was the only person in the valley who used full first names, or who could get away with talking to Ben like this. Ben long ago had chalked it up to his being gay, but Ed had disagreed. "Ted's a gentleman of the old school," he'd insisted.

Ben had snorted. "Old school? We talkin' Oscar Wilde here, or

Liberace?" It had not been the first time Ed had noticed Ben's well-hidden erudition.

Ben looked up at Ted, a long look. Ed knew Ben cared deeply for the bartender—though the sheriff teased him about his sexuality, his mannerisms, and his skill as a host. After a moment, Ben said, softly, "You know, Ted, I worry about me too. Thank God I ain't got no campaign to run this year. I ain't got the juice to give a one-word speech to an empty room."

Ted nodded. His reply was equally gentle. "You know, Benjamin, that I am prepared to be of any help I can offer."

Ben snorted. "I do. Ought to be, I bring enough business in this place."

Ed smiled. That sounded like the normal Ben: enough affection for one afternoon.

Ted winked at Ed, and said to Ben, "Take up ballroom dancing, Benjamin. It's terrific exercise. Lane can be your partner. He's divine on his feet."

Ben guffawed. "Which when I step on 'em, the poor guy ain't never dancin' again."

26

As Andi drove into Maggie Sobstak's ranch yard, unpleasant memories of her first visit there welled up. She'd been investigating Maggie's husband, Vic, who at the time was involved in an anti-tax conspiracy, so Maggie had naturally seen her as an enemy. Tension had crackled during their encounters. But yesterday's martinis at Ted's melted any leftover ice. Still, Andi wondered if this Ladies' Fishing Society thing was a mistake. She took a long, deep breath.

The Ladies' Fishing Society was already convened in Maggie's living room. Three ladies and one man. Momentarily confused, Andi stopped. *Wrong meeting?* But no. Maggie stood up, circles below her sad eyes—probably didn't sleep last night either—and Callie was smiling on the couch. The third woman Andi only knew casually, Bernadette something. But the man looked familiar; it wasn't Vic

Sobstak anyway. Then she had it: Lane Martin. And she was confused all over again.

Callie's last name was Martin. Was Lane...? No, no. Lane was Ted Coldry's partner, in business and in life. She relaxed. Lane stood up, all six-and-a-half slender feet of him, and held out his hand. As they shook, he said, "I would imagine that you're surprised at finding a gentleman member of the Ladies' Fishing Society," he said, smiling.

"I was. I am." She blushed. "Sorry."

Callie stood up to give her a hug. "That Gracie girl okay?"

"They think so. Mild concussion. I saw her fifteen minutes ago. She's sleeping."

"Good to hear. You know Bernie O'Reilly?"

Andi extended her hand to the big woman. Bernie brushed it aside and enveloped her in a hug. "We're not formal here, honey. Hell, Lane here's the lady-est member of the club, am I right? His *hors d'oeuvre*s are to die for. Even if he is a left-wing pinko queer." She looked affectionately at him; then a bell rang in the kitchen, and Bernie broke the hug and went there.

Lane bowed. "Guilty on all counts. Bernadette herself is a Republican red-white-and-blue hetero, but of the old school. Don't tell her, but she's a liberal at heart. And seriously, Deputy, welcome to our group."

"Thanks, Lane. And please, call me Andi."

Bernie emerged from the kitchen with a tray of appetizers. "Here's Round One, ladies. Hot from the frying pan. Pork fritters in honor of our new member."

Callie shook her head. "Shoulda warned you, Andi. Bernie always calls cops pigs."

Bernie's laugh made Andi think of Santa Claus. "Honey, when you grow up in Chicago, 'pig' is a compliment." Another booming laugh.

Andi smiled. "Don't worry, I just called one of our deputies a pig yesterday." She glanced at Callie, who nodded.

"That wouldn't have been Ordrew, would it?"

Andi smiled. "It would."

Bernie squealed. "Our theme tonight, ladies! 'Is Brad Ordrew's prickhood because of his gender or his personality?'"

Unwilling to back-stab a colleague, whatever she felt toward him, Andi hesitated. "Well, I'm not sure..."

Perhaps Lane interpreted her hesitation correctly. Kindly, he said, "If I may, let me put a slightly different spin on it. What have our personal encounters with Mr. Ordrew left us feeling about his approach to law enforcement?"

Andi relaxed again.

Bernie barreled on. "His asshole's too tight. He gave me a totally bogus speeding ticket last month. I was only doing eighty on the highway."

Callie laughed. "Speed limit's sixty-five."

"That's what the little prick said too. But there was nobody five miles behind me or five miles in front of me. Empty highway like that, us Montanans have a moral right to speed, same's we do to hunt, fish, and screw in the woods."

Everybody laughed.

Maggie raised her hand. "I need to get Andi a glass of wine, so let's put it on hold. Andi, red or white?"

"Red, thanks, Maggie."

Maggie walked toward the kitchen; over her shoulder, she said, "Not so sure we Montanans have a moral right to screw in the woods."

Bernie wrinkled her nose. "Sweetheart, you're not claiming you and Victor never...?"

Maggie stopped at the kitchen door and looked at Andi. "One of the Society's rules is what we say here stays here."

Andi nodded. "Agreed."

Maggie turned back to Bernie, "So to answer your question, every chance we got." Then she went into the kitchen.

Bernie clapped her hands. "I rest my case. In nature, let nature take its course. And that proves Bradley Ordrew's a prick."

Andi couldn't help herself. "But you weren't alone on the highway. Brad was there too."

Bernie made an "Oh!" face, and Callie clapped. "Good one, girl.

Facts are the only way you shut Bernie O'Reilly up."

Andi smiled at Bernie, said, "Just having some fun." And she thought, *Damn. I am.* "I'm from Chicago too. Worked for the Cook County Sheriff."

"Bernie will adore you for life," Lane said.

Bernie beamed. "Never happier than the day I left that damn city," she said. "You?"

Andi nodded. "It took me a little while, but the valley's home now."

Lane had picked up a fritter. "Hot," he said, approvingly. He bit. "Mmm. Scrumptious." He touched his lips with a napkin. "*Bon appétit,* everyone."

Maggie returned with a glass of red wine for Andi. "Maybe you'd rather have a martini?" She smiled, but Andi saw the sadness edging her eyes.

"No thanks. One or two of those a lifetime are more than enough!" She accepted the glass.

Lane stood. "I've brought some *hors d'oeuvres,* too. When we're done, I'll appreciate your considered opinions as to their flavor and interest."

Bernie laughed. "Lane, dear, the police contingent of our membership just jumped from twenty-five to forty percent, and we all know pigs live on donuts and beer. Asking them to vote on your culinary achievements could dunk your reputation in the toilet."

Callie said, "Whoa, cowgirl. One thing, I'm not police, I'm Reception and Dispatch. Two, who brought that smoked trout in Viognier and butter sauce?"

Bernie tilted her head. "Point taken. Those were damn near as good as a hot pastrami at Murry's deli."

Lane returned with another tray covered with assorted finger foods, which he put on the low coffee table, and said, "Let's move on. Imagine yourselves, if you will, at a fine restaurant in London, Paris, or God forgive me, Billings. When we're done, tell me if they win your love."

Andi stifled a laugh. Love for *appetizers*? She plated one of each kind. For a few minutes, everyone took small bites, chewed thoughtfully, occasionally looking at the ceiling.

Bernie burst out, "My sweet Lord, Lane, how do you do it? These honeys are crack-cocaine good!"

Callie added, "Lane, you deliver a bunch of these to the jail, I guarantee you the bad guys will bang on the jailhouse door, yelling 'I'll confess, just let me have some of Lane Martin's famous whores-dovers!'" Everyone chuckled.

A half-hour later, the hors d'oeuvre consumed and two glasses of wine in, Andi stretched. "I haven't slept much the last couple nights so maybe I'm slow on the uptake, but what do we actually do in the Ladies' Fishing Society?"

The other four looked at one another.

Bernie took it. "Sweetness, mostly we do just what we're doing. But tonight we've got a special item on the agenda." She looked at Maggie. "Tonight, it's about hugging a friend who's had some bad news."

Everyone but Maggie stood; surprised, she got up too.

Lane seemed to hang back. He was last to embrace Maggie, and he spoke softly to her as he did, but Andi heard: "Maggie, I may not be as vulnerable to having breast cancer, but I am entirely vulnerable to a broken heart when my dear friend does."

A mist clouded Andi's eyes, and she felt a rush of affection for this group of four friends; maybe she'd found a place to ease some of that loneliness she'd been feeling. She thought of Ed, who'd also offered such a place.

Then she thought of Mike Payne.

THURSDAY

27

Last night, Ben had called Andi at home. "DCI's sayin' they'll be at the fire scene tomorrow morning, around ten they think. Call the Carlton guy and meet 'em there."

"At the scene itself, or out on the highway?"

"Crap on toast, I don't know. Be there early and wait on the highway for 'em."

"Okay, boss."

On the drive up into the Washington Mountains this morning, she fretted about Ed's proposal. Well, was it a proposal? A desire? For a few miles, she let herself be angry, or at least conjure some vestige of anger. She didn't need a conventional family. Hadn't had one most of her life. Father a cop, mom dying when Andi turned sixteen, but sick for years before. Her own marriage ended after four months, when she caught her husband in their bed with another woman. Why ask for that again?

Be fair, she told herself. Ed isn't like that. But damn, four nights a week with Grace and Ed, three on her own, suited her just fine. What would marriage add? Would graduating from girlfriend to wife threaten what she and Ed had? Would climbing from "step-girlfriend" up to "step-mom" change too much with Grace?

A few miles later, though, she'd gotten past all that. Her evening with the Ladies' Fishing Society had left her with a calm sense of, well, home. Maybe friendships were in the cards. And maybe Ed was right—time to settle down and join the normal world.

Still, the age thing between her and Ed—she couldn't sort out why that affected her. Frowning, she decided she'd figure it out, eventually. She watched for the next milepost, finally saw it: 45. Two miles to go.

With a flush of excitement, she turned her thoughts toward meeting the DCI guys and learning what they saw in the fire scene. She'd deal with Ed's proposal—and that's exactly what it was—another time.

Mike wasn't waiting at the forest road when she got there. She parked off the shoulder a few feet, clicked on her flashers, and waited. It was only a few minutes before the Montana DCI van pulled up behind hers. She climbed out of her SUV and they introduced themselves. She hoped Mike would get there before they drove into the forest. She'd just told the DCI agents to follow her into the forest when Mike's sky blue Carlton County vehicle crested the ridge and pulled up nose-to-nose with hers. She smiled.

She made the introductions. "Mike Payne, this is Charlie Begay and Phil Oxendine from DCI. Phil likes to be called 'Ox.'" To the agents, she said, "Mike works for the Carlton County Sheriff." The men shook hands. Andi noticed Mike's eyes narrow slightly as he shook with Charlie Begay.

"Begay?" he said. "I had a buddy in the Marines, name was Begay."

Charlie smiled and said, "Probably a cousin. I've got hundreds. I'm Dineh."

Mike grinned. "Navaho! So was my buddy. From Bitter Springs, Arizona."

Charlie looked curious. "Yeah? I grew up in Page, maybe twenty miles from there. What was his name?"

"It was hard to pronounce; we called him Johnny."

Ox smiled thinly. "Plenty of Indians get their names changed because Whites can't pronounce them. I am Cree, Mike. My name is Pannoowau, so at school they changed it to Phil. It is why I prefer Ox."

Andi saw Mike blush again, and again felt the appeal of his

embarrassment. *A good man.*

Mike said, "We white folks do a lot of shit, don't we?"

"Not our worry, Mike," said Charlie. "Let's go to work."

Andi said, "It's a three-mile drive to the scene."

She kept things light with Mike as they drove into the woods, although he rested his arm across the back of her seat, close enough that she felt his heat. She said nothing; it was a warmth she was enjoying.

When they arrived, the two vehicles parked outside the clearing, nosed up to the yellow tape strung between the trees. Charlie ducked under the tape and went directly to the fire scene. He stood with his hands on his hips, surveying. Ox examined the tire tracks that Andi had covered before leaving on Tuesday.

"We can take a cast of this," he said, straightening up. "Good thinking to cover it."

Mike flashed her a thumbs-up.

"Thanks." She walked over to Charlie. "I found the bones right there." She pointed.

Charlie nodded. "I saw them right away too." His voice was soft. "Human."

She nodded. "Look at the glass shards there." She pointed again.

"Saw them too."

"Mike thinks one possibility is some old hermit or hunter got drunk, smashed the bottle, passed out, and maybe the potbelly or a cigarette started the fire."

Charlie looked for a long time at the potbelly, then shook his head. "We will check that theory out, of course. But I would say this fire started roughly where the shards are, which is about ten feet from the bones. From the look of it, an accelerant was used. Let me get a couple evidence bags for the bones and glass."

"Here, look at this first." Andi led him over to the bare rectangle where the weeds had been cleared.

Charlie stood quietly intent, hands on his hips. "Ox?" he called. "Come see what you make of this."

Ox turned away from his preparations for the cast and walked over, looked at the rectangle for a moment, then gave a low whistle. Mike joined them quietly. Charlie glanced at Mike, then said to Ox, "Looks to me like somebody mowed or weed-whacked this space. I am thinking weed-whacker. See the scatter? Thoughts?"

Ox took his time, then nodded. "I would say the same. There are no mower tracks in or out, just the prints of feet. There are circular gouge marks in the dirt, which a mower would not leave. And a mower would leave stubble." He looked from the space to the ash pile. "First question is, is this space related to the fire? And question two is, what is it for?"

Charlie agreed. "Andi, tell me again when this happened."

"Labor Day, in the evening. We spotted the smoke around seven."

"Three days ago." He squatted beside the area that had been scoured and ran his hand through the dirt. "These weeds have zero re-growth. Time frame fits. This may be related to the fire."

Ox joined Charlie, squatting by the rectangle. "Looks like something happened here we want to know about."

"I am thinking we have three things to worry about." Charlie looked around the clearing. "This weed-whacked rectangle, the tire tracks over there, and the fire." His voice shifted into a thoughtful muse. "Tell me if you disagree, but the fire probably was accelerated, and the accelerant came from one of the vehicles."

Ox nodded. "Or from inside the building, whatever it was."

Charlie nodded and turned back to the rectangle. "This naked ground stumps me, though."

"As long as we are counting," Ox said, "I see five issues. Your three, plus the bones and the glass shards."

Mike said, "Well, don't forget that pile. That makes six." He pointed to the junk at the base of the Ponderosa.

Charlie said to Mike, "Have you cataloged that?"

As they walked toward the pile, pulling on gloves, Mike took his notebook from his hip pocket. "We did. Found...let's see, one broken rake and two shovels, a sledgehammer, a rusty crosscut saw, two broken chairs, a mattress covered with stains and rips, an old kitchen table with initials or something carved on it, and a box of *Life* magazines."

Ox bent over the table and peered at the carving. "To me these look like initials, but they tell me nothing."

Charlie asked, "Andi, who owns this land?"

"It's federal."

"So whoever built this cabin, or whatever, was probably a squatter."

Ox was still staring at the trash pile. "Do you think it came from inside the building?"

Mike said, "I'd say so. Nobody drives three miles through the woods to dump things they could leave in the yard for the trash man."

"Good thought." Charlie eyed the pile, then squinted at their van. "We can load all this stuff in, I think. Maybe something useful will show up at the lab. Let me photograph everything."

Andi said, "I got good pictures; I'll email them to you when I get back to town." She looked at her watch: 11:45. "What can I help you guys with?" she asked. "I've gotta be leaving at noon. Got work back in Jeff."

Charlie nodded. "Understood. Show me what you did when you identified the bones."

"I was standing there, in the fire scene." Andi pointed. Her footprints were visible in the ashes. "I was lifting charred stuff, looking underneath. I didn't touch the bones. Mike was working there." She gestured toward the tire track. "Then I walked over to the glass shards, but I didn't touch anything. We talked about them, and then we photographed and taped off the area." They all looked at the yellow tape around the clearing.

Ox had joined them. "Did you get good pictures of the bones and the glass?"

"Let me show you." She went back to the SUV, grabbed the camera, and pulled up the photos. "These work for you, Ox?"

He studied them carefully. "Yes, good work, Andi." He handed back the camera. "Send them all along, will you?"

Charlie squatted beside the bones, studying them, "Ox, are you calling the ME or should I?"

"I will when we get back. Probably no reason for her to come up here, but she will want to examine these bones."

Mike said, "Andi already nixed this idea, but we should at least consider some hunter using the dry old shack, got drunk, tried to start a fire in that potbelly there, and the whole place just went up, boom. Probably his bottle exploded in the heat."

Charlie walked back to the edge of the fire, studied it again. "That is plausible, Mike. Plausible provided his ATV or pickup or horse or hot-air balloon or whatever he came in here with got magically transported away."

"Maybe he walked in. These old guys are nuts." He looked sheepish. "Just saying, so we can check it off the list."

"Walking in. That is a point." Charlie continued gazing into the ashes, motionless, as if he were meditating. "Except for two things: First thing, no vehicle at the highway, and we are at least fifty miles from Jefferson and twenty from Carlton. That is a very long walk for an old guy. Second thing, those bones there." He gestured at the skeleton. "They are either a child or a small woman."

Mike's eyebrows lifted. "You can know that?"

Charlie turned. "Oh, I can *know* it, but I cannot *prove* it out here." He smiled at Mike. "But back in the lab, we can." He turned back to the bones and started methodically searching the ashes around them with a trowel he'd brought from the van.

As he worked, something caught his eye. Using a soft brush from his pocket, he delicately cleared ashes from around the bones. After a minute of working gingerly, he lifted a small item between two plastic-gloved fingers. "Look here," he said, standing. Twisted metal, perhaps a half-inch in size, blackened. He peered at it, front and back, then said, "Looks like a cross. It might have belonged to the victim."

Andi looked at the cross, her eyes moist. She hoped the victim hadn't hoped the little thing would save her.

28

At ten in the morning, Ed locked his computer and stepped into the waiting room, looking for his new patient, Beatrice John. The room was empty. "Valley time," he sighed. Most of the valley people worked on one of the ranches, and ranch time had little in common with clock time. You learn to flex.

At 10:20, the door opened hesitantly. Eyes peered in through the small gap.

"Ms. John?" Ed said, pleasantly. The woman nodded, moving fully in, her face blank. "Let me take your jacket," Ed said, but the woman shook her head.

"I wear it," she said in the same hard voice as on the phone.

"Sure, that's fine. Well, come in," he said, gesturing toward his office. The woman went in and quickly sat in the chair Ed normally reserved for himself. He adjusted. Her fluid movements, like an athlete's or maybe a dancer's, caught his attention. Yet something about Beatrice John's presence warned him: do not push her.

"Did you have any trouble finding the office?" he asked.

The woman shook her head. "Not hard. Down the mountain to Jeff, turn left, go in the Sheriff's—"

He had the sudden impression she had cut something off. Her voice rasped. From smoking? An infection? No doubt, he'd learn eventually. For a moment, they simply looked at one another. Ed guessed Beatrice might be in her early thirties. She was overweight, unkempt, wearing dirty clothing: her physical appearance at odds with her grace of motion. Deep lines in her face spoke of suffering, sun, smoke. Black clouded eyes recoiled, jaw muscles worked. Her complexion was mottled and unhealthy. She rubbed her tongue over her teeth, stretching her upper lip. Her hair was stringy, black. Her heavy round full face was deeply tanned, or perhaps colored that way.

Ed made mental notes. "Can you tell me what you prefer to be called? And, please, call me Ed."

The woman stared at him, immobile except for the rhythmic clenching of her jaw. Her black eyes narrowed further. In her harsh voice she rasped, "Protector."

Protect her? "I'm sorry. Protect whom?"

The woman shook her head. "Protector."

"Your name is Protector?"

"I said it, no?"

"I thought you told me it was Beatrice."

Her eyes flickered, and she seemed to pull within herself. Her eyelids slipped down. For a moment, he watched as she seemed to fade from him. Her large body sagged in the chair. The aura of athleticism seemed to vaporize. He felt a chill on the back of his neck, like hairs rising.

In a moment, she opened her eyes. "I am Beatrice John. That is the name." Her voice had lost its hard edge, now sounding weary, broken.

His neck shivered again. "Thank you. May I ask you some questions?"

The woman nodded. He was surprised when she gave her address as "Wallace's Corner," a town he'd never heard of. She shrugged when he asked for a specific address, but offered only, "This side of Lincoln Pass on 36." She lived with her boyfriend, Guy Flandreau. She spelled it for him. "He's a Frenchie, like. Says it 'Gee.'" The G was hard. Did she have a job? No, no job, but she added, "Guy, he works at the parlor."

"The parlor?" he asked, thinking there wasn't a gambling parlor anywhere near.

"Funeral parlor, down in Carlton." When he asked what he did there, her face darkened. "I came here, not him."

He felt the heat of her irritation. *Mood swings? Change of voice tone?* "That's right. So, what brings you to see me, Beatrice?"

At first, her shoulders twitched, and she closed her eyes then blinked rapidly. Her body shifted subtly, straightened slightly in the chair, the shoulders lost their sag. Her voice, again, was a growl. "I heard you help people."

Again, his neck hair stood up. "That's right, I do. And what would you like my help with?"

Protector—or Beatrice—stayed silent, appeared again to drift. Her eyes nearly closed and her breathing slowed noticeably. She sat still, utterly still; Ed thought of a filthy Buddha. Her jaw's flexing and her tongue's probing had stopped. Ed waited a moment, then gently asked, "Protector? Beatrice? Can you hear me?" The fading in and out of her conscious awareness concerned him.

Her eyes opened slowly and her head moved slightly, her eyes darting around as if she were unsure where she was. In a moment, she said, "I hear you," but the words were tentative, uncertain. Unlike Protector. More like Beatrice, weary, burdened.

"You seemed to drift off there for a moment. Do you feel all right?"

The head tilted. "Would I be here?"

He smiled. "You're right, you wouldn't be here if you felt all right. So what doesn't feel all right?"

Again she drifted away into some kind of inner distance. Ed waited, fascinated, a bit worried.

Her eyes snapped open. "What?" The harsh, rasping voice again.

He felt a jolt, like fear. "What would you like my help with?"

After a moment, she spoke. "Headaches." As she said the word, she moved in the chair. Even though it was a slight movement, Ed was struck by its grace. *Posture changes, voice changes, mood changes, fluctuating awareness. Not good.*

"Tell me about your headaches."

Her eyes narrowed again. "You don't know how to help headaches?"

"Sure, but there are different kinds, and they're treated differently. I need to have some details so I can figure out what kind of headaches *yours* are."

The woman looked at him queerly for a moment, then muttered, "I don't know how to tell you. Ask."

Given the lead, Ed cautiously guided her into the details of headaches, growing increasingly concerned about what looked like alterations in her consciousness. A brain tumor? He felt a moment's anxiety. Jared Hanson's brain tumor last spring had been an ugly mystery; he didn't want another case like that. About fifteen minutes along, Protector—Ed decided the harsh, hoarse voice was Protector's—began to squint and rub her forehead.

"Are you getting a headache, Protector?"

The big woman slowly shook her head. "Had one all along. Worse now." Her hand reached under her shirt and pulled out a small amulet or pendant, a rust-red triangle hanging on a worn string. She began twisting it absently, then more roughly, and after a moment it broke loose from its string. She laid the amulet on her knee, and began rubbing her temples with both hands.

"Can I get you some water?"

She shook her head. "Gotta get to bed." She stood up, smoothly, effortlessly, her bodily grace contrasting with the agitation and obvious pain in her eyes. She went to the door. Ed noticed she was blinking rapidly.

"Beatrice, can you come back tomorrow? I'd like to see if I can help with your headaches, but we need to talk again."

She turned and looked at him. "What?"

"Can you come back tomorrow so we can talk more?"

"No. Not tomorrow."

"Monday then? So I can help you?"

"Help?" She seemed to be puzzled by that. "Monday." She nodded.

"Ten o'clock. Here, I'll write it for you." He turned to his desk and scribbled the appointment time on his card and handed it to her.

She looked a long moment at it, then blinked, then closed her eyes and swayed. Ed reached for her arm to steady her. Should he drive her to the hospital? She seemed to flinch at his touch, so he moved his hand away. Behind their lids, her eyes fluttered briefly. Ed again felt the cold brush across his nape.

She opened her eyes, once more blinking rapidly, confused, as if the room was too bright. She said, in a voice pitched much higher than either one before, "Bishop burned the lady in the fire."

Ed held his breath: It was a child's voice, terrified, neither the hard demanding voice nor the weaker one.

Bishop burned the lady in the fire? What fire? Ed said nothing for a moment, then said, quietly, "Would you like to sit down?"

But the woman looked at him once, her eyes glistening with fear, and then turned and rushed out the door.

Ed followed her, but she slammed the outer door, and he returned to his office. The amulet lay on the floor beside her chair, fallen off her knee. Grabbing it, he hurried after her to the parking lot. She was climbing into a rusty pickup. The man at the wheel had a florid scowl on his face. Ed held up the amulet and gestured for her to roll down the window, which she did, locking the door with her elbow with a loud *click*.

"You dropped this, Beatrice."

She reached for it, looking bewildered. But the man stretched his arm across, slapped her hand down, and grabbed the trinket. "She'd lose her fucking head if it ain't tied on." He pocketed the red triangle. "Roll up the damn window," the man ordered.

As she started it up, Ed said, "Remember, Monday at ten?"

The man revved the engine and pulled away, so Ed didn't hear the answer, but he thought the woman's head nodded once.

29

After work, Andi's cell phone buzzed. *Ed.*

He said, "You sleeping alone again tonight?"

"Hi to you too. I am," she answered, wondering how he was taking that. "Gotta iron a shirt for tomorrow."

"Ironing a shirt takes all night?"

"A joke."

"How about burgers at my place, then?"

Her heart sped up. "No big talks, okay? I'm trying to figure things out and I don't need anything new."

"Sure," he said. But she heard disappointment in his voice.

That evening, after hamburgers and salad, they moved out to the porch. The cooling grill and its dying coals ticked on the gravel in front of the stairs. Carried on the warm September air, cottony clouds drifted across the valley, glowing in the last pink light over the western mountains.

"How'd it go with the DCI guys and your sidekick from Carlton?" Ed asked.

She sighed. "Well. They agree the bones look suspicious. It's probably a woman. Charlie Begay—he's one of the DCI guys—said he'd call me soon as they know anything."

"And your pal, what's his name again?"

"Mike." Saying Mike's name conjured his image. Those dark curls. She leaned a bit away from Ed, uncomfortable.

"I can't help notice I mention your friend Mike and you move away from me."

"Give it a rest, Ed. There's nothing going on there."

"Doesn't stop me from wondering."

"Well, you're wasting your time."

After a silence that lasted, Ed cleared his throat, which put her on the alert. *Serious incoming,* she thought.

"You're right, I was being a little jealous there. Anyway, I wrote to Lynn Monroe, asked her to come work with me."

She turned her whole body, looked at him. "That was fast. So your big plan is charging ahead?" She stayed alert. Changing the subject from the murder—if it *was* a murder—brought a moment's relief, but where the retirement plan flashed, the marriage plan was sure to follow. Lightning and thunder. She felt her chest tighten again. For a moment, she tried to picture Lynn Monroe. Had trouble. Felt a pang of something.

He took her hand, but she pulled it back. "I think I need another glass of wine," she said. As she opened the front door to go inside, she stopped. "Want one? Or one of those Manhattan things?"

Ed looked at her for a moment. Then said, "Sure. Wine"

Andi went inside, and within a minute elbowed open the door with two glasses and stepped onto the porch. As she did, Grace drove into the yard, too fast. Braking, the PV skidded on the gravel and banged into the grill. Ashy still-hot coals poured out and ignited the dry grass. Ed hurried down and stamped out the small flames. Grace jumped out and ran around to peer at the front of her car. The cervical collar made her movements awkward. "Omigod, Northrup! I'm so sorry! Is the PV okay?"

The flames safely out, Ed uprighted the grill and inspected the car. "Looks fine to me. Come on, Grace! Don't drive into the yard so damn fast."

From the porch, Andi heard the annoyance in his voice; annoyance actually meant for her?

Grace had already reached back into the car for her gear. "You're right. I'm sorry. I wasn't paying enough attention."

"Well, slow's the word from now on."

"So I can still drive the PV?"

"Let's just keep it reasonable, shall we?"

"That's called the editorial 'we,' Northrup. I'm the one who screwed up, so just tell me to keep it reasonable. You're already reasonable."

From the porch, Andi said, "Nice bit of contrition, Grace."

"Well, no worries." She climbed the steps to the porch. "And guess what?" She was excited.

"What?" Ed rejoined them on the porch and sat beside Andi.

She nudged him and whispered, "Look out, Leroy."

Grace didn't hear, and rushed ahead. "Me and Zach, I mean Zach and me, no, Zach and I, went down to the river, and we started—"

"Whoa, Nellie!" Ed said.

Andi chuckled. Ed wouldn't be talking about marriage for a while.

Grace ignored him. "—we started studying *Romeo and Juliet,* that's a play by—"

"William Shakespeare," Ed broke in, smiling. "We know, Grace."

She looked at Ed. "I'm sorry, did the middle of my sentence interrupt the front of yours?"

Ed laughed. "Sorry. What about *Romeo and Juliet*?"

"It's the test in English next week. While the sun was setting, Zach went back to his truck and brought, get this, a lantern, real shrimp, and a bottle of —" She stopped.

Andi watched Ed withhold comment; he seemed to be enjoying the delicious moment. *I'm enjoying it too,* she thought. Grace seemed to have forgotten she wasn't talking to her girls.

She gulped and went on. "Okay: a bottle of white wine. Zach said you drink white wine with seafood." She waited a second, watching their faces, and when neither of them reacted, she forged ahead. "Anyway, I'm, like, *so* ready for *Romeo and Juliet*. I love that play." She bounded into the house, intoning, "'O! She doth teach the torches to burn bright!'"

Andi chuckled. "Oh, to be young and in love."

Ed half-smiled. "I thought you were still young. And in love. It's me who's old, isn't it?"

The air stilled between them. She didn't answer.

"Andi, I want to loosen up the hold work has on me. I need to fish more, to spend time with Mack and my buddies. And with you. We both work too many hours."

Her chest tightened again. She sat unmoving, except for taking a small sip of wine.

"Let's get married."

She stood up, the tightness ratcheting up. "I'm not seeing how getting married gives us more time together, or gets you out fishing. You're a workaholic and I don't set my hours. The age difference..."

"Come on, Andi, what's this crap? The age difference hasn't been an issue before."

"I haven't thought much about it before. It's an issue for me. I've got to sort it out."

"All of a sudden." He paused.

Andi felt her heart speed up, guessing what he might say.

"Is it an issue because you met this guy up on the mountain?"

"I could take offense at that, Ed." She tried to make it sound friendly, but knew it sounded prickly. But beneath it, she realized she was pleased, and surprised, that he sounded jealous.

Ed took a long breath. "You could, or we could talk about it with the openness we've both earned from one another."

His voice was gentler. Andi relaxed a little. "Got me there." She sipped her wine. In the west, behind the dark serrations of the peaks, she watched the day's dying blue light. After a few moments, she said, "There's nothing here about Mike Payne. I like him, he's cute, and nobody passed a law against looking. And he's a good cop. But he's nothing you have to worry about." This time, it felt right. "So tell me why you're the one being so controlling this time?"

He seemed to be thinking about it. After a moment, he said, "You know how I'm not the kind of guy to fight very hard for what I want? I guess my training was always to put the patient's needs first. And as a kid, my parents expected the same thing, put other people's needs ahead of mine."

"You fought pretty hard to keep me in the valley after I got shot." She smiled.

"That was the first time I can remember doing that. It's been three years since then, and I guess I woke up to the fact that I really want this thing with you to take the next step. So, you're right, I'm being pushy and controlling, but I think of it as fighting for what I want. Fighting for change."

"I get that. But you blindsided me with this talk about changing your life. You change your life, my life changes. I *like* what we've got here, Ed."

He took a long breath. "So we're not talking about age, are we? It's about change."

At the word *age,* she felt a bubble of fear, and after it, a slow warming across her chest and back. The faint blue light in the sky had gone; full darkness wrapped the valley. Andi imagined them sitting on this same porch, Ed with a blanket across his lap, half-frozen from a stroke, while she sat staring out at the mountains, yearning to go dancing at the Dew Drop Inn or to linger over a romantic dinner at The Angler. She took a long breath, then told him this. All of this.

Ed sat quiet for a while. Andi wondered if he was hurt. But, finally, he said, "I get that. I have my own version of that almost every day."

"Nerves about getting old?"

He shook his head. Other than that, he was quiet.

"What, then?"

"It's my stuff. Craziness. Irrelevant."

"Jesus, Ed, you want me to tell you what I'm thinking, then when it's your turn, you pull back into your cave." She stood up. "I'm getting my gear and going home." But at the screen door, she stopped, turned back. "Oh, man, I'm doing it again."

He nodded. "Withdrawing if you can't control the situation."

She came back. "Yep." She sat beside him. "But I do need you to talk to me."

"You're right." He looked out into the Montana night. "What I worry about is some asshole shooting you on a highway stop because he hates cops...and you're gone. Or, you're alive and paralyzed. I don't have any idea what the odds of your worst fantasy or my worst fantasy are, but I understand your fears. I've got my own."

She held her breath. "I didn't realize that."

He sipped his wine. "I've learned to ignore it. You're a cop and I love you, so it comes with the package. I just ignore the fear until it fades."

Andi had nothing to say to that.

He repeated, "Just part of the deal."

"Ed, I'm where you are about my job. Any cop is. You just accept the possibilities. But about you and me..." For a moment, she wondered how to say it. "You've had three years to learn to ignore your fear about me. I need time to learn to live with mine." She paused. "Truth is, I doubt I would handle losing you very well. So if we were married, I don't see how I could handle you dying."

She glanced at him; the inside lights silhouetted his face so she couldn't make out his reaction. She got up, reached inside the door, flicked on the porch light. "I want to see you."

He said, "So, you wouldn't feel bad about me dying as we are now?"

Her breath caught. Losing him would crush her, married or not. "Of course I would. I love you. It's the age thing, not...not whether I love you."

"So it's not my age itself, but fear of losing me?"

She grew still, but her heart pounded. *Exactly*. But she said, "It's what I said. I'll work it out." She paused. "But give me some time."

"All right," he said. "I won't bring it up again, until you're ready to talk about it." He nodded to her darkened face.

She saw his nod. She also saw the hurt in his eyes.

30

Back home, Andi climbed in the shower. With hot water pouring down her shoulders and breasts, Andi felt a sudden desolation. Emptied, drained, lost. She washed her hair, always soothing when she felt stress. Except now. Her memory stirred.

Her father is leaving for work. His uniform ironed, his big black woven belt with its gun and Mace holsters and flashlight cinched at the waist. He kisses Andi's mom gently.

She puts her hands on his shoulders. She does this every time he leaves for work. "You watch out," she says softly. "I want you home after work."

After a kiss for Andi, he's gone, and she asks her mom, "Why do you always say you want him to come home?"

Mom looks at her a long time and finally sighs. "How old are you now?"

Mom knows exactly how old she is. The question signals: Don't ask what you're not ready to hear. "I'm almost twelve, Mom."

Mom nods. "Yes, you are. So you're old enough to hear this. Your father's a cop. Cops deal with trouble. One day, that trouble might take him away from us."

But Andi isn't ready to hear that. She holds back the tears that rush to her eyes, and soon she learns she cannot stop the dread that envelops her every time her dad goes off to work.

Under the hot water, Andi let the tears wash her face. Trouble had never taken her father, but hearing Ed express the same fear she'd felt every day for years tore open her heart. To think that she was causing him the same pain she'd known, the worst pain she'd ever felt—until her mother died. And knowing Ed still wanted her in his life, despite the daily fear: that was bigger than her thoughts could grasp. Or her heart. Probably, she should feel grateful, loved, secure.

All she could muster was sorrow.

In that sorrow, under the water and the tears, she remembered something else. Something that made all the difference.

FRIDAY

31

After a restless night pondering what she'd realized in the shower, Andi felt an urgency to tell Ed. At work, she was pouring herself a cup of coffee to carry over to his office before his nine o'clock patient, but Callie called from the reception desk. "Line four's for you, Andi."

Damn. But it was Charlie Begay at DCI, and her focus shifted fast.

Charlie got right to it. "It was definitely arson. An accelerant was used, probably gasoline. The shards were likely from a beer or wine bottle—I am thinking wine. Some ash on the shards was from cloth, not wood, so it was most likely a Molotov-cocktail type of thing. We will know more in a couple days, but I wanted to loop you in."

"Thanks, Charlie. What about the bones?"

"Human, a young female. Judging from what's left of the pelvis, they tell me late teens or early twenties, not much older than that. About five feet, maybe five-one. We are assuming the fire was the cause of death, but without more remains to go on, we might never know for sure. I have called in our forensic anthropologist, so maybe we'll get something better. We do not see any broken bones or signs of bullet entry, but because the fire consumed so much, we do not have enough bone mass to rule that in or out."

"How likely is it the fire killed her?"

"I would call it a reasonable assumption. Like I say, our forensic guy will maybe find something."

Andi heard the rustle of paper.

Charlie said, "We found prints on some of the junk stacked by the tree. Got one match to a Virgil Stark. Two convictions for procurement, one for rape, and two others for domestic assault. Served all five terms at Hardin, three of them concurrent."

Andi felt a charge. *Virgil Stark*. She jotted the information on her pad. "Charlie, that's great. I'll get on his trail right away."

"Okay. Now, the tire track. We are not quite as sure about it. It matches the original tires on Ford Econoline vans built between 1990 and 1996, but it is impossible to know for sure, unless we find the tire itself. But it was a van, we know that much."

"How?"

He chuckled. "Well, we *think* we know. After you left, Ox traced between six and eight sets of footsteps in the rectangle, and most of them went between the rectangle and where the vehicle was parked."

"Meaning what?"

She could almost hear his shrug. "Well, at DCI we *try* not to speculate, but from the number and direction of the tracks we could find, we figure seven or eight people walked from the vehicle and later back to it. So, speculating, we think the tire track and those footprints suggest a van, which fits Econoline tires."

Andi had been taking notes as he spoke, the phone cradled by her shoulder. Now she took it in her hand.

Charlie went on, "Also, Ox teased out a few footprints in the rectangle."

"Shoes? Can you trace them?"

"Good question. Both boots and barefoot prints. The barefoot prints were small, older kids or women, we think. Six people, looks like, all in a row."

"A row?"

"Yeah, like a lineup, although there was scuffing that obscured a clearer picture. Behind this line of twelve partial barefoot prints, there are four boot prints, big enough to suggest males. We're tracking the prints now. And in front of the twelve barefoot prints, another set of two boot prints, smaller by a bit. Also tracing them. No hits yet."

Andi thought about it. Bare feet? She opened her notebook, did quick scan of her own notes. She'd seen the one barefoot print in the rectangle. She had a thought. "Were there any signs of shoes or boots near the bones?"

"Only yours and mine. That ash pile is all wood and bone. And a trace amount of flesh, not enough to do anything with."

Andi thought about it. *Six barefoot small people, lined up.* "What way were the barefoot people facing?"

"Toward the fire."

Andi felt a chill. "An audience?"

"Interesting. Watching. That occurred to us too. The strange thing is, the two boot prints in front of the row of bare feet are facing *away* from the fire." He was silent a moment. "You know, the audience idea might fit with something else we found. In the ashes on the side closest to that rectangle, we found two piles of four ten-penny nails each, about four feet apart. On the west side, also right at the edge of the ash, we found two more piles, four nails in one, two in the other. Now, the interesting thing is, all these were blackened, but they're all new. Like I said, both piles were right at the edge of the ashes. There was also a small chunk of a charred two-by-four right near the nails on the west side. It was new wood, not weathered like the cabin. Get this: it had two nails driven through it."

"Connect the dots for me, Charlie. How do the nails fit with the people being an audience?"

"Well, I am speculating again, but suppose sixteen new nails got pounded into the outside of that shack before it burned to the ground. If you press me, I'd guess the locations of the nail piles and the piece of burned two-by-four would be consistent with something like bars across a door and a window, one facing the rectangle, one on the next side. Get the picture?"

"One question. You didn't find any other two-by-fours, just the nails?"

"Correct. That was an intense fire. We're lucky we got the one chunk."

She let that sink in. "You're thinking they nailed the door and window shut with a young woman inside." Andi rubbed her eyes. "And the people in the rectangle were watching for some reason." She felt nauseous. "Jesus Christ."

Charlie grunted. "Yeah." He waited a moment. "We have something very ugly here." Again, she heard the rustling of papers. "Oh, that metal trinket we found? We're thinking it is a *Milagro* cross, a little tin cross some Mexican women wear for protection."

"*Milagro* cross?"

"The word means 'miracle' in Spanish."

Andi drew a breath to quiet her stomach. "There was no miracle for that poor little girl."

32

Andi hung up the phone and took a sip of the coffee she'd poured to take to Ed's. It was cold, but not as cold as she felt. She tried to banish the image of the door nailed shut, the woman on fire. For a moment, her hands trembled. When she felt calmer, she went out to Callie's desk. "Can you run a name for me?"

"Can a butcher sharpen a knife?"

Andi mustered a weak smile. "The name's Virgil Stark. See if you can locate him. Thanks, Callie."

She went to Ben's office and knocked on the open door. "Got a minute?"

"Sure," he beckoned her in. His breathing was labored. "What's up?" His face was gray.

She told him what she'd heard from Charlie Begay. When she mentioned the possibility of two-by-fours nailing shut the door and window, he fell back in his chair. "My God, Andi. My God in heaven. Nailed her in and set fire to her?" His voice cracked. "I ain't seen, not in forty-four years—" A line of sweat beaded on his forehead. Now tears gathered in his eyes.

"Ben, are you feeling all right?"

He waved it off. "Ain't about me. Look, you get back up there and see what else you can dig up. When can you go?"

"Not till Monday, probably. I've got patrol this afternoon, and I'm off this weekend." She caught his strained look. "You give my patrol to somebody, I'll go up this afternoon. Or maybe you want me on overtime for this? I could go up tomorrow."

He shook his head. "Naw. Ain't nothin' happenin' up there now that can't wait for Monday. Oh, and call Carlton for that deputy to meet you. This one smells worse than anything I've seen in the valley, and I've seen it all. I don't want you alone up there. I'd go with you myself but I ain't—" He stopped himself.

"You're not feeling the greatest. I'm on it, Ben. Don't worry."

Again he waved away her concern. "I'm dandy. Go do some police work."

She nodded, noticing as she left how the line of sweat on his brow shone against his gray skin.

33

On patrol an hour later, Andi drove carefully along the ranch roads thirty miles north of Jefferson, crisscrossing the highway every ten or fifteen minutes, looking for sheriff's business on the dusty back roads of the county. She toyed with the idea of going up to the fire scene tomorrow, on her day off. Ben hadn't shown urgency, but she felt it. Coming up to a stop sign, she turned north.

Up ahead, she saw a rolling plume of dust barreling along the next road intersecting hers, east to west. *Way too fast.* She accelerated toward the dust. A pickup truck sped through the crossroad a tenth of a mile ahead of her squad. The driver was wearing a large cowboy hat. She turned in behind him, hit the siren and flashers, and closed the windows against the dust.

The driver didn't slow. Reaching the highway, he fishtailed north, gunning it, blue smoke rising from his tires. She swung onto the highway, jammed the pedal to the floor, and within a mile had him pulled off the shoulder. She was angry, but careful; and he turned out to be only nineteen, and scared. Foolish, not bad.

She went back to her vehicle to run his license and registration. She'd typed in the kid's information and was waiting for the report, when Callie's voice crackled on the radio: "EMTs to the sheriff's department. Subject unconscious. *Repeat. EMTs to sheriff's department.*

Subject unconscious."

Andi froze.

The EMT's reply came immediately. "On the way, Callie. Who's down?"

"It's Ben! Hightail it!"

Andi swore at the computer, tapping the screen to force it to work faster, realizing that was stupid. She grabbed the papers and ran up to the pickup, tossing them in on the frightened kid's lap. "Don't speed next time!" She dashed back to her vehicle, ripped a u-turn across the highway, switched on the siren and light bar, and raced south toward Jefferson.

PART TWO

SATURDAY

34

As she was leaving the hospital next morning, Andi ran into Ed as he came in. She'd spent the night at her place again. "How about a cup of coffee with me?" he asked.

She glanced at her watch. "I'm thinking of driving up to the fire scene, look it over again. I was just heading over to Alice's for breakfast before I do. Join me."

"Ben's doing okay this morning?"

"About the same as when we were here last night. Awake but groggy. No visitors still. Doc doesn't think he'll need to stay here more than a few days, to be on the safe side. He's more worried about the diabetes."

Ed nodded. "Still out of control."

"Yeah."

Ed had a half-smile on his face. "Sometimes, control can be good."

"Please don't start, Ed." She paused. Her realization in the shower came back. "Look, there's something I wanted to tell you, but I won't if you're going to start another argument."

"Speaking of control."

"Huh." She chuckled. "You're right. Sorry. Let's go eat."

Crossing Division Street toward Alice's, she said, "Doc says the heart attack might be a blessing in disguise. Keeping Ben in the hospital will let him get aggressive with the diabetes."

"Good. Who's running the department?"

"Pete. He's the senior deputy. The county commissioners named him Acting Sheriff last evening. Get this: Ordrew actually called the commissioners before Ben even got to the hospital, lobbying to be put in charge."

"What a prick."

"Calling him that demeans a perfectly good organ," she said, smiling.

He looked at her, eyebrows arched a bit, then grinned. "Now *that's* an opening I could park my, uh, truck in."

"Stop. I was defending the generic penis, not offering an *opening*." She held open the restaurant door, but Ed stepped back.

"Come out to the cabin, I'll cook us a real breakfast."

"Uh-uh, don't think so. Gotta drive up to the scene."

"On your day off?" He looked down, then up into her eyes. "Look, can I ask a favor? For Grace, not me?"

"Sure." She wondered if he thought she would pull away from Grace? "You can ask favors for yourself too, Ed. I'm not trying to get away from you or Grace. I'm her friend."

"You're a hell of a lot more than her friend."

"Yeah, I know." She smiled. "I'm her step-girlfriend. So what's the favor?"

"I'm helping the kids decorate the gym for Homecoming this afternoon. I could use your help afterwards."

"With what?"

"I'm taking her to the Angler for dinner, to talk about the rules for Homecoming."

Andi felt a catch in her breath. Homecoming rules meant family rules. "I don't know, Ed..."

"For your step-girlfriend?"

35

Andi hadn't driven up to the scene after all, but spent the day catching up on laundry and groceries. So before Ed and Grace arrived after their decorating, she sat alone in the blond-wood-and-red-brick dining room of the Angler, sipping a Pinot Noir and thinking about Ed's proposal. During the day, she'd been half-annoyed with his roping her into this dinner with Grace, but now she was glad to be part of it. Was she being unfair to him, backing away from his proposal? She had just about decided she was when her phone buzzed.

She read the screen: *Pete Peterson.* "Andi here, Pete."

"Hi, Andi. You know already that Callie ran that name, Virgil Stark, and got an address over in Carlton. I called Harley Vogel over there and asked him to send that deputy you've been working with—"

"Mike Payne."

"Yeah, him. To send him to check it out, and Mike just called me."

Her heart jumped. Maybe the break they needed. "Did they get him?"

"Sorry, no. Turns out nobody knows anybody named Virgil Stark, or Virgil anything. And a single woman lives in the apartment."

Disappointment rose from her gut. "Damn. I was hoping...Well, thanks for letting me know, Pete."

Ed and Grace joined her as she ended the call and rubbed her eyes vigorously, trying to erase the frustration.

Ed looked at her, concerned. "What's wrong?"

She shook her head. "Bad news about the case. Never mind."

They ordered drinks—another Pinot for Andi and one for Ed, Red Bull for Grace. When the server had gone, Ed cleared his throat.

Before he could say anything, Grace laughed. "I thought so."

"You thought what?" Ed asked.

"You're going to tell me the rules for the dance."

"How'd you guess?" Ed asked.

"Whenever you're going to tell me some rules, you clear your throat."

He looked at Andi. She nodded. "You do." She chuckled, amused and feeling older-sisterly toward Grace. *How do I know what an older sister feels*?

Ed blushed. He sipped his wine. "Well, okay then, I cleared my throat. Rules. What's your plan for Homecoming?"

Andi didn't expect Grace to cooperate, so her shrug and prompt answer was a surprise. "Me and Zach and my girls, sorry, Zach and I and Jen and Dana and their dates are having dinner here at the Angler. He's picking me up at five, dinner's at six, and the parade's at seven."

"Dinner's at six? It doesn't take an hour to get from our cabin to town."

Grace rolled her eyes. "Northrup! Think: Pictures. Corsage. You and Andi making a fuss about how beautiful I am." She smiled, and Andi looked at Ed, who chuckled.

Grace looked as if she just remembered something crucial, and turned to Andi. "You'll be home to help me with my dress and putting on the corsage, right? Zach'll chicken out at the last minute."

"You bet I'll be there." The idea of sharing Grace's preparations was the first pleasure she'd felt all day. "I wouldn't miss it. But I've gotta warn you, I'll be in uniform."

Grace relaxed. "No biggie. Everybody knows you in uniform. Wait." She frowned. "Why are you working on Homecoming Day?"

"All the deputies work Homecoming. It's a major league night for drunk drivers." She winked at Ed, knowing he'd seize the opportunity to talk about drinking.

He picked up the ball. "Hence the rules. How about after the dance?"

She sighed. "I'm seventeen—"

Ed and Andi sang to each other, "'I am sixteen, going on seventeen...'"

Grace gave them her *what species are you?* look. Ed laughed.

Andi said, "It's from *The Sound of Music*. Julie Andrews."

"The old lady who voiced Queen Lillian in *Shrek*?"

Andi thought, *Hell, I* am *getting old.*

Ed said, "I guess. We knew her a few years before that. Anyway, after the dance, what's going on?"

"The six of us are, uh, going over to Jen's for a party."

Ed wondered what the *uh* meant. Or if it meant anything. "And her parents will be there?"

"Don't you trust me? Next fall I'm going to college and I can stay out all night if I want to."

"When you're at college, what time you come home is your business. I still want to know whether Jen's folks will be home."

"I'm not lying to you, Daddy." Her smile softened the sarcasm.

Andi remembered similar debates with her father. "You're not lying because you haven't answered the question yet." She was amused. "When I went to my prom, my dad asked the same questions and I lied like a rug."

Ed frowned. "Thanks for the support, Ms. Openness." He turned to Grace. "Just a simple yes or no will be fine."

"It's not simple, Northrup. If I say no, you won't let me go. If I say yes, you won't believe me." Andi could tell she was using her reasonable voice, mature, adult. "So the answer is yes, they'll be home, not that it matters."

"Thank you, and it matters. I trust you. And when will you be home?"

"Geez, Northrup!" The reasonable tone slipped. "How should I know? Jen's parents will be there, so it's better if we just stay there, anyway."

"Because there'll be drinking?"

Andi laughed outright. "I'm sorry, Ed," she said to his affronted look. "Of course there'll be drinking. That's why the deputies are out in the dark all night."

He frowned. "Okay, then, can I ask this? Will you be home for breakfast?"

Grace gave up being reasonable altogether and barked, "Yes, yes, yes! Can we please have some finishment here?"

He couldn't help smiling at the word, and he reminded himself again of the need for that father-daughter chat before next weekend. "All right. Finishment it is." Then he lifted one finger. "Oh, one more thing."

Grace sagged. "*Please,* Northrup. I told Zach I'd come out and watch a movie tonight. You keep interrogating me, I won't get there till morning."

Andi smiled to herself.

Ed said, "This'll be quick. You'll be drinking, right?"

Andi sat back and folded her arms, watching, remembering so many similar conversations with her own father, missing him, sad and delighted at the same time. She'd never imagined being on the parental end of such a talk herself. She liked it.

Grace blushed, but looked squarely at him. "In moderation."

Andi laughed again.

"What?" Grace said, frowning at her.

"I believe I used exactly the same word with my dad." She unwrapped her arms and leaned forward, touching Grace's hand tenderly. "Promise me something. If you guys get drunk, please just stay at Jen's and don't go driving. I'd hate to be the one to take your license so soon after you got the PV."

"You mean, don't go out cruising around doing Car-yokey?"

Ed asked, "Car-what?"

She rolled her eyes. "Northrup, you're so old. It's singing to tunes on our phones in a car."

Andi glanced at Ed. His eyebrows were arched. To Grace, she said, "Skip cruising around doing anything. Just stay at Jen's. Please?"

Ed added, "And just don't get drunk in the first place. Moderation, remember?"

Andi chuckled. "In college, we defined moderation as an imaginary kingdom that exists wherever you drink."

Ed frowned, then laughed, but Grace looked puzzled, then irritated. After a moment, she turned to Andi. "Did you, ah, talk about..." She head-gestured toward Ed.

Andi sank, shook her head. *Condoms*. "I will."

When Grace went to the restroom, Ed asked, "What was that last about?"

"Have you had that preventative biology talk with her?"

"Not yet."

"Have it. And buy her some condoms."

36

Grace returned, grabbed her bag, waved kisses, and left for Zach's. As soon as the restaurant door closed behind her, Ed said, "You didn't take Grace's drinking very seriously."

"Kids drink after Homecoming, Ed. Don't you remember?"

"I never went. Hell, I never dated. I was going to become a priest, so I figured celibacy was something you had to practice ahead of time." He laughed. "The June before I entered seminary in September, I started taking cold showers. I complained one day and my dad said, 'Why the hell are you taking cold showers?' I told him I was practicing for when I got to the seminary. He laughed out loud. 'For Christ's sake, practice when you get there.'"

"He was right. That sounds, ah, masochistic."

"Sure was."

"You didn't sneak even once? Try to get a little T 'n' A?"

"Not in high school." He blushed. "Okay. I used binoculars to look into Rosa Escobar's bedroom across the street. When I actually got into the seminary, though, I started sneaking. Thank God."

"Didn't take enough cold showers, eh?"

He smiled and took a sip of wine. "Okay. So. Where are we?"

She leaned her elbows on the table and framed her face with her hands. "Right here, at Ted's."

"Seriously."

Annoyed, and not sure why, she ran her fingers through her hair. "You asked me here to help with Homecoming rules. Don't ambush me."

"Didn't mean to. I know you're working things out, but you don't have to figure this out alone. You've got me."

His voice was warm, and that counted. "I'm not even sure what *this* is," she admitted. "I realized something that maybe matters, though."

"Oh, yeah? What's that?"

"You know how I freaked out about your age? Or actually the age difference between us?"

He smiled. "Etched forever in my mind."

"Well, something happened when I was fourteen..." She closed her eyes a moment, looking into the past.

They're driving to the grocery store. Andi sees her mom, one hand on the wheel, the other hand waving in front of her face, like a fan. Mom says, "Jesus!"

"What's the matter?" Andi asks.

"These hot flashes are killing me, kiddo. Happens to every woman when she gets older."

Andi is scared. "What's killing you?"

Her mom looks at her, then back at the road. "It's complicated. Try this. Being able to have babies means a girl has lots of baby-making chemicals in her body. When you get older, you don't need babies any more, so your body knows it's time to stop making those baby-chemicals."

"We got that in sex class. But why do you have hot flares?"

"Flashes. I suppose it's the body's way of burning up the baby-chemicals."

"Oh." Andi looks out the window a long time. "So does this mean you're getting to be an old lady?"

Mom chuckles. "Well, it'll take a while, but yeah. I'm on the way to old-ladyhood."

Andi feels a sick place in her stomach.

She turned to him. "So it's not *your* age that bothers me, Ed."

"It's yours. Menopause equals getting old."

"Worse. Menopause means becoming an 'old lady.'" She'd thought telling Ed would have brought relief. Instead, she felt a twinge of dread. And with it, a wave of heat. She thought, *Screw it*, and fanned herself.

Ed looked surprised. "Hot flash as we speak?"

She nodded. She waited for the fear to worsen, but it never did. After a few moments, she cooled off. "Over. But no, I'm not done with this. Something still bothers me and I haven't figured it out. At least I've got this much: menopause equals aging. And I hate it."

"You're not *looking* old." He winked. "In fact, you're looking downright edible. Let's—"

She put up her hand. "I need to work this out, Ed. I want to be with you, but right now, whatever's wrong feels close and I have to work on it. I'm going to my place tonight."

The pleasure went out of his eyes. He grabbed his napkin and roughly rubbed his lips. She could see him thinking about what to say. "Okay," he said. "I can wait, if you'll agree to keep me in the loop."

She resisted. "And if I don't?"

"I'll keep asking, pushing. You won't like that." His eyes softened. "We love each other, Andi. Can't we share the figuring out?" He looked toward the ceiling a moment. "Look, I'll take back my proposal of marriage. You keep working out what it set off, we share what you come up with, and we'll see where we stand when you're done."

Andi tensed. She wasn't sure she wanted him to rescind his proposal. *Can't have it both ways, cowgirl.* She squared her shoulders. "Okay. Sounds fair." She stood. "It's a deal. You put your proposal out of play, I keep you informed. But that's enough for one evening. I'm going home." She softened. "It's not that I don't love you, Ed. I just need to...I don't know...face something."

Ed nodded, then stood and came around the table. "A hug?" He stopped, slapped his forehead. "Damn, Andi, I forgot to tell you a thing I heard on Thursday. About your fire case."

Her eyes locked with his. "What about it?"

He told her what Beatrice John had said: *"Bishop burned the lady in the fire."*

MONDAY

37

Andi listened impatiently to the ringing of Ed's cell phone at the other end of the line. She needed something, but even more, she wanted to hear the sound of his voice. After work yesterday afternoon, she'd driven south toward Mount Adams thinking she'd hike the Coliseum, which always cleared her thinking. Partway there, she'd stopped to help with an accident—a car had hit and killed a deer, and the woman, driving alone in the car, was having trouble dragging the animal to the shoulder. After they were done and Andi gave her a police report for her insurance, she decided to head home instead.

Finally, Ed answered. "Sorry. I thought the phone was in my dream." His voice sounded groggy. "Coming over for a quickie?"

She smiled. "If I didn't have to work, I'd be there in a minute. After morning report here, I'm going to see Ben, then drive up to the fire scene. Look, I need some information I should've asked you for after dinner Saturday. What's the name and address of the woman who said that thing about a bishop burning the lady?"

She knew what he would say, and she heard his sigh. "Andi, you know I can't do that. She's my patient."

For a moment she said nothing, half understanding, half exasperated. Then, "Ed, I'm sorry to ask, and I understand confidentiality. But we're calling this a murder now, and your patient knows something that might help us. I need to talk to her."

"She's a disturbed woman, and what she said could easily be some hallucination or delusion. I don't even know that what she said has a connection to reality."

Her frustration mounted. "Come on, Ed. Why'd you tell me what she said if you won't let me follow up on it?"

"Not up to me, Andi. I figured the word *bishop* might help you get started."

Andi stayed silent for a moment. *One more try.* "Ed, please. I won't upset her. I just need to ask her a few questions."

"I'm sorry, Andi. I just can't, unless you get a court order."

"Fine," she said, torn between understanding and aggravation. "Thanks for the help." But she pressed the *End* button harder than necessary.

38

Pondering some way short of a court order to get Ed's information, Andi drove to the hospital to visit Ben. As she pulled into the parking lot, heat flared across her shoulders and back and up her neck, her chest suddenly so constricted she could barely breathe. She rolled down the window, her breathing shallow. After a couple minutes, the hot flash faded, and with it the panic gripping her chest. *I understand menopause,* she thought. Hot flashes, mood swings, irritability, crazy periods. *But why anxiety?* She remembered Ed had said that anxiety meant different things, but often arose from some hidden pain that somehow threatened the person. Did something lurk below, something darker than menopause?

Above the hospital's roof, a spiral of smoke churned in the high canyon on the side of Hunters' Peak, above the scar of the summer's first fire. *Another one?* Her stomach clenched. Grabbing the binoculars from the console, she peered up at the mountain, searching for the source; but as she studied it, the smoke thinned and dissipated. *Clouds!* She let out the breath she'd been holding. Her chest relaxed. *Jesus, my nerves are raw.*

She climbed out of the SUV, and thought about her boss. A year or so after she'd come to the valley from Chicago to join the department, Ben Stewart had told Ed that Andi was the daughter he'd never had. Although Ben felt more like an uncle than a father, she'd always cherished that.

She went down the hall toward his room and pushed open his door cautiously.

He was sitting up in bed, frowning fiercely. "You goin' up to the murder scene today?"

"Yeah. Right after we visit. You feeling better?"

"Doc's keepin' me in. Wants to get the damn diabetes under control."

"You don't sound pleased."

"No piece of this is pleasin'. Damn good thing this ain't an election year. Couldn't win if it was. But that ain't *your* worry. Don't waste time here. Get yourself up to that site and see what you can scrape together about the damn murder. And call that deputy pal of yours and take him in with you. I got me a real bad feelin' about this one."

Mike Payne. Her mood took an immediate uptick as she pulled out her cell phone.

39

Driving up Highway 36, Andi pondered what they were going to look for at the scene. Very likely, DCI had removed anything that might qualify as a clue. But two facts—the door nailed shut and the audience—had jacked this case up to a new level of horror. Pete had put out an APB on Virgil Stark, and maybe that would pay off. Meantime, she had to hope they'd missed something in that clearing.

Ed, at least, had added a clue. Someone named Bishop? Or maybe someone who *was* a bishop? A real bishop? Or maybe some kind of nickname? She grabbed her cell phone and speed-dialed the department. The phone beeped. She looked at the screen. *No service.* She dropped the phone on the seat, punched the radio on, and grabbed the mic.

"Unit Three to Base."

"Got you, Three. What's up?"

"Callie, I need the addresses of anybody named Bishop in either

Adams County or Carlton County. Can you do that?"

Static, then, "Can LeBron shoot baskets?"

Andi laughed. "Okay, I'd appreciate the info as fast as you can get it. Over."

She replaced the mic, and made a decision: she'd explore the scene again, in case they'd missed something, and then she'd widen the perimeter into the forest as far as she could manage alone. Or, if Mike stayed, as far as the two of them could cover before dark.

As she approached the turn-off, Mike hadn't arrived. She slowed, then pulled into the dirt track toward the murder scene. She looked at her watch. As she did, the radio barked. "Base to Unit Three. Come in, Three."

That was fast! "Three here, Callie. What've you got?"

Static. "I've got Mike Payne from Carlton County Sheriff's office on the line. Wants to be patched to you. Want to take it?"

"Sure." There was a moment's static, then Mike's voice. "Hi, Andi, it's Mike."

"Hey, Mike. What's going on?" *He's not coming. Damn.*

"Look, I'm running late, caught an accident. Go on in and I'll join you as soon as I can get up there."

"Okay," she said, relieved. "Your ETA?"

"I've got maybe thirty-five, forty more minutes processing this crash, then the drive up, let's say an hour and a half."

He obviously planned to drive this forest road faster than Andi did. She liked that.

"Got it. See you then." She hooked the mic, looking down the tunnel of road into the forest. *"I got me a real bad feelin' about this one,"* Ben had said. Maybe she should wait? She shook her head. Waiting because the scene didn't feel safe didn't cut it. She put the SUV in gear and started in.

The narrow road looked wider than she recalled it, the tire-flattened grass ruts looking broader, better defined. Low-hanging branches were broken here and there, though many merely dangled and hadn't fallen. They brushed the SUV, but not as roughly as she remembered. She drove slowly, thinking about jolting Mike around the last time. After thirty-five minutes, she got to the clearing—and found things terribly wrong. As wrong as could be.

The clearing was empty. The yellow police tape was gone. The ash pile, the potbellied stove, the twisted bed frame, the debris, the rectangle, the tire tracks: all gone, the clearing bulldozed, scraped down to bare earth, not a weed left. Where the shack had burned, there was a shadow of black soot mixed with earth, but the entire area looked skinned.

Who did this? What had lain hidden in the debris that required this?

Breathing heavily, Andi took her cell from the seat, saw the blank screen, and grabbed the mic again. When Callie responded, Andi asked her to get Pete on the line. "It's urgent, Callie."

"You all right up there?" were Pete's first words. "What's urgent?"

"Somebody needed to hide something up here." She described the scene.

"Holy hell. Is the Carlton guy with you?"

"No. He'll be here in a while."

"I want you out of there, Andi. Don't wait, just get out. I'll send a team up."

Andi looked around, suddenly aware of her isolation, alone three miles down a lost dirt track. She unclipped her weapon. "Don't send a team, Pete. Mike's coming soon. I'm out of here. I'll wait on the highway."

40

But she stayed.

Her moment of fear had shifted rapidly to fury. Whoever had scraped away this crime scene, she took it as a personal affront. Telling herself that was silly did nothing to change her mind or reduce her anger. She let it focus her. She set about combing through the bare dirt floor of the clearing. She took a broken branch and drew six-foot squares across the whole area, then systematically examined each square in order. After an hour, nothing. All that showed were scrape marks from a large machine. Dozer, or maybe a Bobcat. She took a few photos of the marks in case there might be a way to identify the machine.

She moved into the surrounding forest, searching as systematically as she could for signs of anything left behind. Branches scraped her face, and thick foliage grabbed at her clothing, hindered her search. Undergrowth everywhere made seeing to the ground impossible. After another hour, she'd covered maybe a third of the area around the clearing, working her way about ten yards back into the woods. More than once she reached for her weapon when a branch cracked in the trees or a crow cawed. Despite her nerves, she kept searching, her earlier anger dampening more and more into frustration at the nothing she was finding.

After almost two hours, she was drenched, her brown uniform shirt stained black. She checked her watch. Where the hell was Mike?

A few minutes later, she heard tires crunch. Holding her breath, she drew her weapon, bent low, and crept quietly toward the clearing. She thought of Ed's fear that some crazy would take her out. She flipped off the safety.

A Carlton County sheriff's pickup pulled in beside hers and Mike stepped out. She let out a long breath and straightened, stepping out of the brush. She flipped the safety back on, holstered the weapon.

"Wow, you look..." He stopped, his eyes roving over her sweat-stained chest, but then over to the scalped clearing.

"Hot and pissed."

His face showed surprise. No, shock. He gestured at the bare earth. "What the hell?"

"I've been back in the trees searching, but so far, nothing."

"I'm damned." He looked around again. "This fucks our investigation big time. Whoever did this wanted to hide something."

"My thoughts exactly. That's why I've been in the woods." She filled him in about the victim, the accelerant, the nails. "They locked her in and burned her, for God's sake." Her anger blossomed anew.

"Christ, that sucks, Andi." He shook his head. "I'm just..." He waved his hand, almost angrily, at the empty clearing. "What the hell have we got now?"

Two desires clashed in her: One, for him to plunge with her into a full-out search of the surrounding forest. The other, unaccountably, for him to take her in his arms, let her cry out her frustration. She pushed that away. "I say we keep searching. I've only covered about two-thirds the area outside the clearing. I started there." She pointed to the place she'd first entered the trees. "And I finished there. I took it back maybe ten yards, at least where the underbrush let me." She pointed again. "Why don't you start there and I'll start at the other end and we'll work toward each other?"

His blue eyes danced. "That's the spirit. Let's take this fucking forest apart."

Exactly what she wanted him to say.

After a half-hour, on the ponderosa the debris had been piled under, she found a small piece of something red snagged on the rough bark. Bending low, she examined it carefully. Red flannel, a tiny triangle about half an inch on a side. Had the fragment been here when they investigated previously? She hadn't gone behind this tree, but Charlie or Ox would have seen it, wouldn't they? If not, it must've gotten caught when the clearing was violated. She straightened, thought to call Mike, but changed her mind. *Don't interrupt his search.*

From her truck, she retrieved the camera and an evidence bag, and returned to the tree. She pulled on her latex gloves. She photographed the fabric on the snag, then delicately lifted it free, placed it in the evidence bag, tagged the bag, and sealed it. Back at the truck, she filled out a Field Data Card. She locked the bag in the evidence box behind the driver's seat.

Mike stood behind her. "What'd you find?"

She jumped. "Startled me. A small piece of cloth was caught on that ponderosa." She pointed.

He glanced at the tree. "Show me."

She led him to the snag. He examined the spot. "Nothing else here now. Let me take a look at the cloth."

She shook her head. "It's in the evidence box, Mike. I've got chain of custody now."

"You're allowed to let me look at it as long as you still control it."

Correct. She unlocked the box, took out the bag, and handed it to him. He rotated the bag and squinted at the cloth inside.

"What are you looking for?"

"Nothing specific. Just want a good look in case I see anybody with a torn flannel shirt. Good catch, Deputy." He smiled and handed her the bag.

She dropped it into the evidence box, relocked the box, and turned back to Mike. "Did you find anything?"

He shook his head. "Nope. But I sure generated a powerful thirst. How about joining me for a beer down in town?" His eyes were smiling.

She actually thought a beer with him sounded perfect. Then she shook her head. "No, but thanks, Mike."

He looked down.

Andi felt awkward. "I'm, uh, with someone, Mike. It's not that I don't like you..." *Not at all.*

There was that warm smile again. "Well, happy for you, Andi. Does going with him make having a beer with me a sin?"

It is if I'd enjoy it too much. She smiled. "No, but I have to get back to Jeff. How about I take a rain check?"

41

Ten o'clock arrived, but Beatrice John didn't. While he waited for her, Ed thought about how she'd acted last Thursday. Dimming and fluctuating consciousness, her eyes fluttering behind closed eyelids like someone dreaming, or blinking rapidly when they were open, the odd changes in her voice. He'd had that chill-on-the-neck feeling before, on the few occasions he'd encountered a patient with multiple personalities...

Whoa. Too soon to go there.

But what about the names? Beatrice? Protector? The headaches fit with dissociative disorders like multiple personality, but they could be caused by many other things, and probably were. After he saw her this morning and learned more, he'd call Charlie Merwin, his best friend in grad school and a clinical psych professor at the University of Minnesota, before this went much further.

While he waited, Ed read a couple of journal articles he needed to catch up on, then checked the clock. 10:40. Might not need that call to Merwin; he doubted Beatrice John was coming back.

He went out into the hall to check the mail. On the floor outside his office door was an envelope, an unfamiliar rusty color. His name, in childish printing, was scrawled on the face. He opened it. A single sheet of the same odd-colored paper. The same scrawl: "She has been taken away."

Alarmed, he went back into his office and called Andi's cell phone.

42

Driving out from the denuded crime scene, Mike's vehicle tracked her the entire way. Though she tried to focus her thoughts on the destruction of the crime scene and the single flannel clue, she kept imagining Mike looking at the back of her head. No, not imagining it, *feeling* it, as if his eyes were touching her.

She had barely turned from the forest road onto Highway 36 when her cell phone buzzed. It was Ed. She pulled quickly onto the shoulder and pressed *Talk.*

"Andi, it's me. Look, I've reconsidered about the patient's name. I—" The line went dead, and she heard a long beep. The screen showed only one bar, flickering.

Damn. She grabbed the radio mic. "Unit Three to Base. Come in, Callie." She waited impatiently.

"Base to Three. I'll have your names in a few minutes, Andi."

"This is something else, Callie. Ed just tried to call me and we got cut off. Get him on his cell and then patch him to me, will you?"

"Sure. Give me a minute."

In a moment, she was back. "Got him. Here he comes."

When she heard Ed's voice, she said, "Sorry. Terrible service up here. What's going on?"

"That new patient, the one who said the bishop burned the lady? She didn't show up, but somebody left the strangest piece of mail. It's an odd color, kind of a rusty pink, and it says, 'She has been taken away.'"

What the hell? "What's that mean?"

"On its face, I'd say she's been taken away—either abducted, or simply taken someplace else. I don't know, but I've got a bad feeling about it."

"So, maybe abducted...? But why would anyone leave you a message about it?"

"No idea on that."

"Anything else written on the paper?"

"No, just 'She has been taken away.' So I decided I should give you her name and her address."

Mike's pickup pulled in behind her. He got out. Andi watched him walking toward her vehicle in her mirror, wondered what was up. He came up to her door. She lowered the window.

"You all right?" he said. "Saw you pull over, so I came back in case..." His voice trailed off.

He looked shy. Andi momentarily forgot Ed, her finger still on the *Send* button. "I'm good, Mike. Thanks."

Mike turned, started moving away, then came back to her window. "Reconsider? Join me for that beer?"

She released the *Send* button. Ed was saying, ". . .'s going on?"

She pushed the *Send* button again and said, "Sorry, Mike. Talking with Ed." Thought quickly, said, "My boyfriend. Thanks anyway."

Mike patted the door of her vehicle, said, "Got it," and went back to his truck and did a U-turn back toward Carlton. To Ed, she said, "Nothing's going on. Pete insisted I call Mike. He got concerned, I guess, when I pulled off the highway and came to make sure I'm okay. Then he asked me to join him for a beer. That's what you heard." She tried to smooth out her breath. "So, her name and address?"

"Is that guy with you now?" His voice had turned tense.

She checked her rear-view. "No. He's driving away. What's the woman's name?" She pulled a clipboard and pen from the rack.

He didn't answer immediately. Then, "Okay. Her name is Beatrice John, that's J-o-h-n, although she also gave the name 'Protector.'"

"Say that again."

"Protector. I don't know what it means. She lives at Wallace's Corner. Wait, my handwriting is hard to read..." She waited impatiently. Ed said, "It's near Lincoln Pass, which is on Highway 36." He paused. "Nothing more specific than that. No phone number."

"Lincoln Pass? That's close to where I am."

"One more thing. After her last session, she got into a pickup with a guy who I think is her boyfriend. He slapped her arm pretty hard for no reason I could see."

Andi frowned. "Did he write the note and take her away?"

"I don't know, but I doubt it." He paused. "I've got a suspicion Beatrice is a multiple. One of her personalities might even have written the note. It's far-fetched, but possible."

Andi mused. "Also speculative, right? How'd the note get outside your door, if he'd already taken her away?"

"No clue. Sorry."

"What's this guy look like?"

"He was sitting in his pickup, but I'd say pretty tall. Wore a strange-colored ball cap—orange, but not a hunter's blaze orange. He had big arms, looked strong. He was wearing a wife-beater shirt, you know, with the sleeves cut off at the shoulder? And I think he had a tattoo on his right bicep, but I'm not sure on that. Mid-thirties."

She was jotting notes. "You have the boyfriend's name?"

"Let me look." After a moment, he said, "Yeah. Guy Flandreau." He spelled it out. "It's pronounced Gee, not Guy. Lives with Beatrice John at Wallace's Corner."

"I've heard of Wallace's Corner, but I don't know where it is; there's no town around this area. I'll call Callie and find out." Her frustration over the destruction of the crime scene was shifting toward excitement. "Thanks, Ed. I appreciate the information. I'll check it out while I'm up here." As she started to end the call, she thought of the red fragment of cloth in the evidence box. A wild hunch. "What color was the guy's wife-beater?"

"Hmm. He was in shadow, but I'd say kind of reddish."

"Huh." She tried to think of another question. "Well, okay. Thanks for the information."

"Sure. I didn't get to know Beatrice, but I hate to think she might be in trouble."

Andi nodded, looking out across the valley toward the mountains on the far side. Their rough serrated ridges, their strength usually a comfort to her, loomed sinister above the valley. "I'm not thinking she is. I'm *knowing* it."

43

After they broke the connection, Andi radioed the department again.

"Callie, I got a couple new names for you to look up. First, though, I need you to Google Earth the town of Wallace's Corner for me. I need directions from where I am."

"Where are you?"

"Highway 36, just west of milepost 47."

"You want the addresses of the Bishops when I come back?"

Andi thought about it a moment. "Just any who live along Highway 36. I'll get the rest when I'm back at the station."

After a few minutes, Callie was back. "First thing, there's nobody named Bishop along Highway 36. Now, Wallace's Corner is between milepost 43 and 44 on Montana 36, on the north side. There's no streets, though. Doesn't hardly look like a town. Google just shows six buildings around a central area, like some kind of compound. Can't be farther'n a football field off the highway, behind the trees. On the screen, looks like you can't miss it; though, up there, God only knows. You want backup?"

"Don't think so. I'll just scout around."

Static crackled, then Callie's voice broke through. ". . . those names you've got?"

"Right." She spelled out Beatrice John and Guy Flandreau. "Got them?"

"On it already. You be careful, hear?"

"Thanks, Callie. Will do."

Andi reached milepost 43, but she'd seen no road or turnoff since milepost 44. Lincoln Pass had been at milepost 45, so maybe she'd gotten confused. She turned around and drove back slowly a mile over the pass, then turned again and repeated her first search. She kept her flashers and light bar on to warn vehicles coming up on her at speed, and drove slowly, peering into the dense forest crowding the north side of the road. She passed milepost 44 again, and slowed more. About halfway to milepost 43, she saw it: a narrow grassy driveway on the right. She turned in, feeling her heart start to beat faster.

She rolled slowly along the opening between looming dark trees, and sure enough: about ninety yards in, the driveway opened into a wide graveled yard, surrounded by buildings arranged around the perimeter. Her tires crunched on the gravel.

An old two-story house stood to her right, with a gray picket fence enclosing a parched yard. The paint had long ago peeled off both the house and its fence. The windows were dark, with no visible shades or curtains. Had the house been abandoned?

Dead ahead squatted a much smaller cabin of peeling gray wood, with a similar unpainted picket fence around its front yard. To her left, in the center of the area, a long garden grew inside a high wire-mesh fence. *Not abandoned, then.* Beyond the garden, a new-looking two-story pole barn filled the third side. The barn sat square and true, unlike the house and the cabin, which seemed to lean. Completing the compound were two large sheds and a garage along the fourth side. A rusty, battered pickup truck sat in the garage. Pines and fir edged up to the buildings on all four sides.

Andi shivered.

Movement. A squat man came out of the barn. Though his form was clear, Andi couldn't make out his features through the garden fence. He closed the barn door carefully, locking it, walked around the garden toward her, stiffly, limping heavily on his right side. As he drew closer, she was struck by his ugliness. Five and a half feet tall, with a head too large for his body and a face crevassed with scars and massed deep wrinkles. Large wing-like ears flanked eyes spaced too wide in his head, with a bulbous red nose beneath. The hair peeking out from under his stained cap was thin and dirty gray, and his eyebrows were bushes of ashy hair, the same color as the tufts growing in his ears. His lips were thick and red, and he kept licking them. His lips made an odd tic, as if he were talking to himself. They exposed broken, yellow teeth. *He must be ninety*, Andi thought.

He walked toward her, eyeing the sheriff's vehicle. She got out, after unsnapping her holster.

He extended his hand. "Cassius Delbo, Sheriff." His hand, like his head, was oversized, or perhaps the rest of his body had simply shrunk faster. The hand was thick with callus, but his grip was soft.

"Deputy Andrea Pelton, Mr. Delbo. Is this Wallace's Corner?"

"Died in '06. Built the shack." He pointed his thumb over his shoulder at the small house.

"Wallace died? In 2006?"

"1906. Bought the place from his grandson back in 1945, after the war."

"I see." She didn't. Wallace died in 1906, then bought the place from his own grandson forty years later? *Doubt it*. She surveyed the compound. "You have a well-kept place here," she said. The garden, in the center among the buildings, showed neat rows of vegetables alternating with autumn flowers, encircled by the six-foot deer fence. Very attractive.

"Proud of it," he said, his voice raspy. "Got me a little furniture business, you see." He jerked his thumb over his shoulder toward the newer, large barn. "Build custom furniture for rich bastards—pardon the French—all over the country. Assholes mostly, but pay real good. Brings you up this way?"

"I'm trying to find a woman named John, Beatrice John. I was told she lives at Wallace's Corner." She remembered the second name. "Or maybe she's named Protector."

"Well, no Protector, but Beatrice. Livin' in old Wallace's shack." His thumb indicated the smaller cabin. "But Thursday last week, up and lighted outa here. Never asked for their deposit back. Strange, that."

"*Their* deposit? She wasn't alone?"

"Boyfriend."

Guy Flandreau. "What's his name?" She pulled out her notebook and pencil.

Delbo looked at the notebook. "Trouble? Don't want it here."

She shook her head. "I don't know, sir. We're just looking into some things that have happened. The name?"

He hesitated, then shrugged. "Flandreau. Guy Flandreau. Spells it English, *Guy*, says it French, *Gee.*

She noted that. "Thank you. Did they say where they were going?"

"Didn't say nothin'."

"Did you see them leave?"

"Doin' somethin' in the house there." He waved vaguely toward the main house. "Next thing, seen his tail lights driving out the driveway. Didn't think nothin' of it till next morning, not home. Looked in the window, knocked. Cleared everything out except the furniture. Ain't shown skin since."

"You cleared everything out?" She was having trouble with his sentences. No subjects.

He shook his head. "No. Them."

"Could I take a look inside?"

Delbo frowned, scrunching up his round face. It looked like he hadn't shaved in days, although he didn't have much beard, just old man's stubble. In fact, Andi wondered how he could even shave, his face so scarred with pocks and wrinkles. He shook his head. "Don't take much to that idea, Sheriff, all due respect. Rent's paid good till month-end, and ain't keen on violatin' their privacy."

Andi didn't press it. "Do you think they might have just gone on a trip, maybe a vacation?"

"Doubt it. Took everything."

"Anyone else live here, Mr. Delbo?" Someone who speaks in full sentences, maybe?

"Guy and Beatrice. Me. So just me now."

"What can you tell me about Beatrice? Did you know her well?"

"Hell's bells, don't know her at all. Fierce, the boyfriend. Kept her on a tight leash. One time, in the garden and comes out for a smoke—wouldn't let them smoke in the house, mind you—and struck up a chat. Well, out the door, boyfriend is, so fast never get further'n 'How you be this fair mornin'?' Just grabs her arm and drug her back inside. Of course, hollered to put out the cigarette."

He seemed allergic to using subjects for his verbs, but Andi thought she had caught the train of thought. "Did you talk to her, other times?"

"No, not much. Laid out the rent and the property rules and such, but wasn't one to talk."

Andi reconsidered the cabin. "I'd really like to take a look around their place, Mr. Delbo. She might have left information about a murder that we're looking into."

He was visibly guarded, eyes narrowing. "Well, now, real uncomfortable, all due respect. Nothin' to do with murder."

"I can imagine, sir, but if you won't open the place for me, I'll be forced to go down to Jefferson for a search warrant."

His eyes shot wider. "Aggravation." Annoyed, he waved a hand. "Guess, let you take a peek."

But the little place was clean. That is, empty, except worn and tattered furniture and three soiled books on a window sill. A stained bed in the cramped bedroom, a round linoleum table and two chairs in the kitchen, the usual appliances. But nothing personal. The bathroom towels hung on the racks, but the medicine chest had been emptied. Andi looked in all the drawers and under the bed and the couch. Nothing. Nothing under cushions or behind a chair. Nothing in the kitchen cupboards or the refrigerator, nor in the toilet tank.

When she lifted the tank cover off, Delbo said, "Learned you must be in how to hide things. Never woulda thought to peek there."

A closet off the cramped living room held a small furnace and hot water heater. Andi searched behind both, and removed the front panel of the furnace. Nothing that shouldn't have been there. She retrieved the three books—moldy, crinkled—resting on the window sill and carefully fanned the pages of each one. Empty.

But, in the bedroom closet, there was a shoebox on the shelf. "Do you mind if I open this?" she asked.

Delbo shrugged. "Ain't mine, and you're in now."

Inside was a stack of blank almost-rose-colored paper. Andi thought about Ed's note, on a "rusty pink page." She fanned the stack in the dark bedroom. Saw nothing on them. "Mr. Delbo, I'd like to take these with me."

"Bringin' them back? In case Guy and Beatrice show up? Don't want trouble."

She nodded. "Here." She pulled her notebook out and wrote a receipt for the pages, dated and signed it, and handed it to him.

As they left the shack, she knelt down and peered under the building. The foundation rested on the soil, no crawl space. "Is there a basement in this cabin?"

Delbo shook his head. "Nope. Built right on the ground."

As they walked back toward her vehicle, movement in a window of the larger house caught Andi's eye: a woman's face, round and brown, with black hair, turning away. "Mr. Delbo, I thought you said you were alone here."

"All by my lonesome. Me, myself, and I. And my furniture."

He must not have noticed the face. *Or he thinks I didn't.* "Sir, with all due respect, I just saw a woman at that window." She pointed. "May I speak with her, please?"

"Aggravation!" His composure failed. "First comin' onto my property uninvited, then askin' a bunch of questions, then lookin' into the cabin, now this. Of a mind to ask you to leave, Sheriff." But again he backed off when Andi mentioned getting a warrant to search the property more thoroughly. "My wife," he said. "Don't cotton to people, very shy woman. Ain't a talker. Don't want you gettin' her all upset."

"May I speak with her, please? I'll do my best not to upset her."

Slumping, Delbo limped into the house. She heard his voice, speaking softly. Then he led out a very small woman, shorter than he, Hispanic-looking, and half his age.

"Ma'am, may I ask you a few questions?"

"No speak," she said, in a heavy foreign accent.

Andi asked Delbo to translate for her, but he said, "Don't speak hers, she don't speak mine." He looked coy. "Makes for peace and quiet. Can't argue."

Andi looked hard into his eyes; he did not look away, but held her gaze until she broke it. She suspected Delbo of hiding more than this unspeaking and much younger wife. *Much younger.* Charlie Begay had said the bones belonged to a very young woman—likely younger than this woman, who looked maybe forty.

The wife had glanced nervously toward the barn a couple of times.

Andi said, "May I look in your barn, sir?"

Immediately, "Drawin' a line there, Sheriff. No. Please. Go." He folded his arms firmly across his chest. The pose did not bespeak fear.

"Again, sir, I will get a search warrant and come back."

"Well, do it. For now, leave it there."

She thought about it. *He's hiding something in that barn and he thinks he can get rid of it before I get back with the warrant.* Under the circumstances, she might be within procedure to insist on entering the barn without a warrant. But she doubted she had probable cause. Would an unspeaking wife's glances justify a search? *Shaky.* She wouldn't draw her weapon on an old man and woman just to search a barn. And she'd refused backup. *Damn.*

"Okay, then, Mr. Delbo. I'll be back with the warrant."

She nodded politely at the strange couple, and climbed into her vehicle. She doubted everything Delbo had said. She backed the vehicle around and drove slowly out to the highway. In her rear-view, she watched Delbo lead his small wife into the gray house.

44

Andi hadn't yet returned from the mountain when Ed's afternoon opened up. The day's final patient had called to cancel. He decided to drive down to the river and cast a few flies. But on his way, he thought of Ben, cooped up like a restless bull, and turned into the hospital lot. When he knocked on Ben's doorframe, the sheriff growled, "I'm supposed to be resting."

"Hello to you too."

"Christ on a crutch, a guy ain't gonna get a nap with you dropping in all the time."

"They told me the meds would make you cranky. How're you feeling otherwise?"

"Ain't no otherwise. It's cranky all the way to the bottom. Go away. Cure some depression."

Ed smiled. "I think Andi's got a lead on the arson murder case."

This lit Ben's eyes, and he pulled himself up in the bed. "Tell."

Ed described Wallace's Corner and Beatrice John. "She had Callie leave me a voice message. Andi's up there talking to them as we speak." He glanced at his watch. "Probably on her way back, actually."

"Who is this woman, Beatrice Jones?" Ben was as interested and alert now as he'd been grouchy a moment ago. *That's a cop for you,* Ed thought.

"John, not Jones." Ed told him what little he knew, including his suspicion she might have multiple personalities.

"Crap on toast. A nutcase's our only lead." Ben rolled his eyes.

"Not a nutcase. DID is complicated, but it's actually a reasonable reaction to prolonged child abuse."

"Did? Did what?"

"No, D-I-D, the initials. Dissociative identity disorder."

"Stick to multiple personalities. It's English." Ben was slipping back toward cranky.

"Anyway, if something happens that's too painful or shocking for a kid's brain to understand, the brain seems to partition that memory off from normal everyday memory. If it happens frequently over time—"

Ben waved him silent. "Shrink-wrapped goobledy-gook. I didn't understand a damn word you're sayin'."

"Sorry." He smiled. "The main thing is if she's multiple, she's not crazy. Her memories, if they jibe with what happened to her, can be very accurate."

"Well, go pick her brain then. Or brains. We ain't got a lot of time to figure out what happened up there."

"Well, that's the problem. She didn't show up." He told Ben about the note.

"Sweet Baby James! 'Taken away,' as in kidnapped? What the hell's goin' on up there?" Ben's rough hand slapped on the sheets.

Ed shrugged. "Easy, Ben. Can't be good for your heart. Andi'll get on top of it."

Ben sank back into the bed. "Geez. Tell me somethin' good."

Ed considered it. Finally, he said, "For your ears only, Ben."

"Speak."

"I asked Andi to marry me, but—" As he started to add that the proposal was temporarily—he hoped—off the table, Ben clapped his hands.

"Jesus Christ, this whole damn valley's been wondering when you'd pop the question! If this ain't welcome news!"

Grace had just poked her head in the door. "What's welcome news, Sheriff Ben?" She turned to Ed and handed him a list. "Northrup, could you please pick this stuff up at Art's? I want to cook pasta and shrimp for us tonight, and I have a Homecoming meeting in a few minutes."

"Sure." He looked over the list.

"Hey there, Gracie." Ben grinned. "Tell her, Ed."

Busted. Ed frowned. He shouldn't tell Grace until Andi made up her mind, especially now that the proposal was off the table. But the expectant look on her face? *What the hell.* "I asked Andi to marry me."

Grace squealed. "Omigod! Omigod! That is so amazing!"

"Is 'amazing' the new 'awesome'?"

Grace blew right by that. "Now I can go to college with a real mom at home! Omigod!" She rushed at Ed and threw her arms around him. "Way to go, Northrup! When's the wedding?"

Ed looked over her head to Ben, making what he hoped was a help-me-out-here face. "Well, Andi's not quite ready yet." He decided he shouldn't blab Andi's business. But did. "She's worried I'm too old."

Grace stepped back. "She's wrong! I need a mom before I go to college."

Ben chuckled. "Too old? Ain't nobody's too old for love."

Grace folded her arms. "I'm going to talk to her."

Ed frowned, his stomach a knot. But before he could speak, Ben grunted. "Grace, best not. Grownups can't sort these things out as easy as you kids do. Things ain't as clear."

Grace sat on the bed. "What do you mean, Sheriff?"

Ed relaxed. Three years ago, Grace would never have asked that question, just gotten annoyed at being told not to do something.

"Well," the sheriff started, then paused, as if finding words. "You and your friends, you've got your whole life ahead of you. College, boyfriends—" With a hand, he silenced her objection. "Sure, you got Zach now, and maybe he'll be the one, but there's a whole world of Boy out there. And jobs, and careers, and professions." He paused, breathing for a moment. Grace waited, her mouth slightly open. "You know, it's like goin' swimmin'. You got this big river—hell, a whole *ocean*—smack in front of you. If you jump in the wrong place, what the shoot, just swim back to shore'n jump again someplace new. You ain't in no hurry, you got time galore. Next year, you'll jump in that big river called college, and you'll have your shore right handy. Ed here and Andi and all of us here in the valley, well, we're behind you. We're your shore."

Again she opened her mouth, but the sheriff put his rough round finger against his lips. "Lemme finish, girl. I've had a heart attack, so I might just die on you before I get this little speech delivered."

Grace's face went solemn. Ed turned his chuckle into a cough.

The sheriff smiled at Grace. "So, I was where, exactly?"

Grace whispered, "The shore here is behind me, and the river in front of me?"

Ben sank back against the pillows, and took a few long breaths. "Andi, now, she ain't got a whole life ahead of her like you. Your daddy here, he ain't either. So they're doin' the right thing. Thinkin' it out, not just goin', 'What the hey, if I jump wrong, I got time to swim to shore,' 'cause maybe they don't." He reached out his broad rough hand and grasped Grace's small one. Very softly, he said, "Like maybe I don't." He looked, his eyes all kindness, at Grace for a long moment. "You takin' my meanin' here, Gracía?"

She nodded, smiling. Ed knew she liked hearing her name in Spanish. "Yes, sir, I think I am." She slid off the bed. "Thanks, Sheriff."

Her face was as solemn and warm as Ed could ever remember.

45

On his way home, Ed detoured into Art's Fine Foods for Grace's groceries. Since Art's death last spring, going in the store always gave Ed a small brush of sadness. He took a moment to think about the old guy, letting his sadness melt into gratitude for their friendship.

As he prowled the aisles for fresh angel hair pasta, three dozen small shrimp, capers, and a bottle of white wine, Art's hard wisdom and Ben's tenderness with Grace warmed him. Studying wine labels, he wondered, would Art have counseled him to wait before telling Grace about the proposal? Art's favorite advice was: "Sit your horse, Ed. Wait and see. Things get clear after awhile." Andi didn't like being pressured, and nobody could pressure better than Grace. Which could be disastrous.

When he got home, Grace was deep into dinner prep, dicing a large onion—tears on her cheeks—a couple of diced red peppers in one dish, quartered mushrooms in a second, spice jars lined up near the two sauté pans warming on the stove. Without looking up, she called, "Northrup, you didn't forget the groceries, did you?"

"I did not," he answered, pulling things out of the grocery bag. He watched her chopping for a moment. "You're a darn good cook, you know that?"

Her chopping stopped. She looked at him. "Yeah, I do. But it's kind of natural. Mara left me alone for dinner...lots. I used to watch the cooking channel."

"Ah." Just then, they heard Andi pull into the driveway. Ed was surprised. "Did you know Andi was coming?"

"I invited her." Grace glanced at him. "I won't say anything, Northrup."

"I appreciate that. Andi's got to work it out her own way."

"Yeah. Like Sheriff Ben said."

When Andi came in, she kissed Ed—on the cheek—and checked on Grace's progress, patting her on the back. "Nice work. I'm starving." Then she took Ed's arm and led him into the living room. "Sit down," she said, "I need to talk about my case."

As she sagged onto the couch, Grace called from the kitchen, "Andi, could you help me do these shrimp? I've got too many pans going at once."

Andi sighed. "Okay, kiddo." She got up, then put her hand on Ed's shoulder. "After the shrimp, mushrooms, and onions—my case."

46

After dinner, Grace drove her PV into town to do homework with her girls. Ed had noticed Andi flushing a couple of times during dinner. *Hot flashes?* As they cleaned up after dinner, she was silent and looked tense. He wondered if something unsettling had happened at the crime scene. Or maybe that other deputy, Mike something. He'd heard him ask her out for a beer.

"Something wrong?" Ed asked, pitching it neutral.

Andi grunted. "This damn menopause, getting a little tired of it, is all."

"Hmm. I've heard it's not temporary," he joked. He hoped it *was* menopause.

"Thanks for the understanding. Grab a towel and dry these damn dishes."

But when the dishes were done, Andi put on her jacket and moved toward the door.

Ed said, "You leaving? I thought you needed to talk about your case."

She seemed to hesitate. "I do, but..."

"Talk to me about what happened up there." He almost added, "with the deputy," but shut up.

For a moment, she looked away, then took a long breath. "You heard Mike ask me out for a beer?"

"I did," he said, his chest suddenly tightening. *Jesus, I'm reacting like a teenager.* "I heard you say no." *So why's she bringing it up now?*

"I'm feeling a little guilty about it."

He didn't want to ask. "Why?"

"I thought about saying yes and just not saying anything about it. That's not fair to you. There's nothing you need to worry about with Mike. He's just a nice guy and a good cop. I like him, but that's all there is."

"Sounded like he's a little further along on the liking curve."

"Jesus, Ed! I told you nothing's—" She stopped, then smiled. "My dad used to laugh at me when I got defensive. He'd say, 'That horse you're riding's pretty high, kid.'"

Ed chuckled, despite the tightening in his chest. *She said nothing's going on, so trust her. Lighten it up, man.* "Don't mind me, Andi. This is the first I've felt jealous since I was twenty. Not quite handling it with my usual suaveness." He grinned.

"Actually, it's kind of nice, you being jealous." She sighed. "Can I tell you about the case?"

"God, yes. Change the subject. It's embarrassing being a teenager again."

She took a long breath and told him about the obliteration of the crime scene.

It hit him like a slap. "Completely wiped out?" He thought of Beatrice John being "taken away."

"Completely. Whoever did it even scraped off the weeds and grass and then swept the area. No tracks showed in the clearing."

"Something needed hiding. Could one person have done it?"

"I can't imagine." She thought it over. "Well, yeah, maybe one guy with a Bobcat and a big enough truck..."

"Could Beatrice John being 'taken away' have anything to do with your crime scene?"

She didn't answer right away. "I'll think about that. Anyway, no, I'm thinking more than one person cleaned out the crime scene."

"Why?"

"From the scene before. All those footprints in the rectangle lined up like an audience, at least three sets of boot prints, two or three vehicles."

"Huh." He closed his eyes. "Are there any cults operating in the area?"

"Cults? Why?" She looked surprised.

"When you first described the murder, I thought it sounded like a ritual thing. I've worked with a few escapees from cults, and they often talked about weird, cruel rituals. Just a guess, actually."

"Hadn't thought about that. We're not aware of any on this side of the mountains. I'll call Carlton and see if they've got any on their side."

He watched her face as she held the phone to her ear. He was uneasy and she looked it too. He shook his head, annoyed with himself, and Andi frowned, covered the phone with her hand, said "What?"

"Nothing. Annoying myself. Ignore me."

She nodded. After a moment, she said hello and explained her reason for calling. She waited, whispered, "On hold." In a minute, she said, "Hello?" and from the audible edge in her voice, Ed figured the call had been routed to Mike. She hurried her question about cults, listened a moment, said thanks, and hung up. She looked puzzled.

"What'd he say?" Ed asked.

"Well, you heard me ask him about cults in their jurisdiction. He said he doubted it, but he'll check around and call me back." She stopped for a moment. "Surprises me, I guess. In our shop, we all know pretty much everything the rest of us know about what's going on in the county, things like this—we keep each other informed." She was silent a moment. "Curious, though. He didn't ask why I was asking."

"Probably assumes it's about the case."

"Well, he's been a good partner so far, maybe he's just busy."

Ed started to say it, stopped, then thought, *What the hell*. "Or he's more interested in getting in your knickers."

Andi's eyebrows went up, and then her laugh surprised him. "My *knickers*?" She laughed again. "The only *gentleman* getting in my *knickers* is you, big guy." She sobered. "One other thing. Thanks for giving me Beatrice John. After I left the scene, I found Wallace's Corner. Very strange. Your Beatrice John left with her boyfriend on Thursday and hasn't come back. Between then and today, somebody bulldozed that clearing. So maybe you're right about there being some connection. And the old guy who owns Wallace's Corner is lying to me."

TUESDAY

47

At seven in the morning, Andi sat down at the conference table for morning report. The anxious feeling she'd had since waking up hadn't abated. For no reason she could finger, her mother was much in her thoughts; and Ben Stewart's empty chair at the head of the table made her uncomfortable. *As if he died*. She recoiled from that thought.

Pete Peterson cleared his throat and said, "Let's get this going. Henry, how was midnights?" Henry Pierce, just off the graveyard shift, said, "Quiet as a grave."

Andi flinched.

Henry went on, "No calls, no accidents, no drunks at the Dew Drop Inn, nothing. I got most of the latest *Longmire* read."

Xavier Contrerez grinned. "Oh, man, I love those books. That Victoria Moretti is so hot."

Chipper Coleman shook his head. "Naw, the big Indian's the best character by a hundred miles."

Pete smiled. "Okay, guys. Back to business." He looked at his notes. "Looks like swing shift yesterday evening was quiet too. Hope that holds up for a while. Okay, assignments: Brad, you've got morning patrol; Chipper, you're on it this afternoon. Bud's on the evening shift all week, but he's testifying this morning on the Clifford DUI case, so if he drops by, he'll be tired. Be gentle with him." The men chuckled. Andi hadn't been listening. He turned to her. "Fill us in about your murder case up on the mountain?"

Caught off guard, she hesitated a moment, hefting her mind onto the case, but her report about the destruction of the crime scene and the discovery of Cassius Delbo's nearby compound came out disjointed, and she saw a thin smile form on Brad Ordrew's lips.

When she finished, Ordrew lifted a hand. "Question?"

She nodded, on guard now.

"The crime scene was completely wiped out? You lost a whole crime scene?"

She recalled the snag of red cloth, and what Ed told her Beatrice John had said. "We have two new things: there was a small piece of cloth on a tree near the site, and we may have a witness, or at least somebody who knows something about what happened. If we can find her."

Ordrew grinned. "Lost her *too*?"

Andi felt her face flush. Ordrew stood up. "Well, I've got patrol this morning, so if there's nothing else, I'm outa here."

Pete, his voice low, his eyes flashing, said, "Brad?"

"Pete?"

"I think Andi deserves an apology."

Ordrew shrugged. "Then, Pete, why don't you give her one? I don't apologize for calling sloppy what it is." He turned and left the room.

When the door slammed behind him, Pete spoke to the deputies. "Andi and I are going up to Wallace's Corner. There may be someone there who knows what's going on." He shifted uncomfortably. "Can I assume nobody shares Brad's opinion?"

Heads shook. Xav said, "I'll partner with Andi over Bradley any day. Any day." Nods around the table followed his words.

Andi said, "Not your problem, guys. But thanks for the support."

"Don't pay him any attention, Andi," Chipper put in. "He'll ease up when he gets used to the valley. He's still working on LA time: all tense, all the time."

The others chuckled.

48

After morning report, Andi and Pete signed out one of the department's pickup trucks, visited Judge Flure for a search warrant, and Andi drove them up to Wallace's Corner. They'd barely left the parking lot when Pete said, "I'm sorry for what happened in there."

"I'm okay, Pete." She didn't add anything, and they drove five miles without a word.

Pete finally broke the silence. "You're not your usual self, Andi. Something bothering you?"

"I'm good. Just a little rough around the edges this morning."

As the road lifted onto the mountain, Andi looked out at the endless forest. At first, such wild growth had intimidated her: pressing too close, too dense to see what hid inside. One summer, back in Cook County, a shooter had hidden in the forests that lined some of the rural highways and taken shots at passing officers. Everyone had been on edge for weeks. Finally, Andi had been one of the targets. The bullet had crashed in through the right front windshield and had grazed her forehead before smashing the side window at her left. She'd almost driven into the ditch. Since then, stands of trees had spooked her.

But in recent months she'd noticed a change in the woods. No, in herself. Towering pines and firs now exuded an enfolding strength. Surrounded by the big trees, she felt competent, alive. Younger.

She was letting all that was happening confuse her. The murder, Ed's proposal, her attraction to Mike, the hot flashes—they were all pushing her around. She felt a growing anger, a need to push back. She glanced at Pete, then back at the road. He looked calm. A tall, strong, quiet man, balding, still handsome. Pete had been married to Lucy for nineteen years. He was six years older than Andi and he'd served the county well for almost thirty years. He looked across the bench seat to her, caught her glance.

"What?"

"You're right. I'm not myself."

"Lately you've seemed like a cop with post-traumatic stress. Irritable, frustrated pretty easily..."

"Huh." *Exposed*. She stared ahead at the road, drove carefully, feeling vulnerable. "It's complicated."

"Complicated? How so?"

Should she talk about Ed? She trusted Pete fully, and knew he trusted her. In the confrontation with the Reverend Loyd Crane three years ago—when she'd taken a bullet from Crane's henchman—Pete had been right behind her, and Andi knew that he felt it should have been him getting hit. He was a fine policeman. *You don't cure confusion by not talking,* she thought. "Ed and I are having some problems. Well, not problems." Why had she used that word? "He wants to get married, and I'm hanging back."

"Hanging back? You guys love each other. Or at least you act like it."

A deer jumped across the road in front of them. "Fuck!" she shouted, hitting the brakes a little too hard. Although there was no real risk, her heart raced. After she got her breathing under control and they'd covered a mile or so, she said, "Can I ask you something personal, Pete?"

He looked over at her, smiled. The sudden braking hadn't seemed to upset him. "Go ahead."

"Do you think my being ten years younger than Ed is a problem? For a marriage?"

He made a small, warm sound; it brought back the quiet sound her father made when something in the paper amused him, a sound associated in her memory with contented summer evenings on the porch, him reading the news, her absorbed in her Nancy Drew mysteries. He said, "Yeah, sure, an age difference matters. Someday it'll be a bigger thing than it is now." He glanced at her. "You know that Luce is twelve years younger than me?"

"Well, I knew you were older, but no, I didn't know by how much."

He nodded. "Yeah. My first wife died in 1992. Cancer. Luce's husband had died in the first Gulf war. We met at a grief group over in Missoula. For a while, she worried about the age thing too. Someday I'd be in the rocking chair and she'd still want to party." He chuckled. "Which we don't do much, anyway."

At the word *cancer,* Andi's anxiety had flared. She fought through it. "How did she work it out?"

He shrugged. "You'd have to ask her, Andi. All I know is, she did. And let me tell you, when I'm in that rocker and she's out dancing with some young buck, well, I'll have some pretty swell memories for company."

She glanced at him. His smile was tender. What a good man, she thought. What she said instead was, "Well, it bothers me."

Pete looked over at her. "Are you sure it's the age difference?"

She shook her head. "I don't know..." She thought about her realization in the shower.

"Could be you're worried about getting up there yourself."

Her throat tightened. *Right on target*. She managed a soft, "Nail on the head, Pete." And as she acknowledged it, she realized the second thing, and again, she could barely breathe.

49

While Pete knocked on the door, Andi stood back from Cassius Delbo's house, scanning the windows for any sign of the wife. Pete's knocking went unanswered. No sound came from the house; the windows remained blank, no movement behind them. When they turned toward the barn, however, Delbo stood framed in the big door. They walked around the fenced garden in his direction.

"Mr. Delbo, this is Acting Sheriff Peterson," Andi said. "We've brought a warrant to search your property, including the house, the barn, and all outbuildings."

Delbo reached out for the warrant and read it slowly. "Words from courts," he muttered, scorn in his voice, tossing it back to Andi. He stepped aside and pointed his thumb toward the interior. "Do what you came for. Won't find a thing."

After a half-hour spent opening doors and looking in drawers on the first floor, Pete took off his gloves. "It's what it looks like, a furniture shop."

Andi nodded. "On this floor, at least. I'm going up to the loft."

Delbo grunted, but said nothing.

As she emerged from the stairway, what she saw took her breath away.

She called down. "Pete, you better come see this."

Six narrow beds, three along each side, lined the walls. Neatly made, military corners, extra blankets folded at the end. Pete put his gloves back on, and together, he and Andi lifted the mattresses from their frames, saw bare floor under the slats. They opened and inspected each of the six cupboards standing beside the beds, and the footlockers at the foot of each bed. Empty, except each top shelf held toiletries, towels, and washcloths. Nothing hung on the closet rods.

Delbo had followed them up, waiting wordlessly at the door. She addressed him. "What is this dormitory used for, sir?"

He folded his arms, gave no answer.

They continued their search for hiding places, loose boards, indications of the room's purpose, but found nothing unusual. Nothing in the bathroom, except two sinks, two toilets in stalls, two showers. Andi noticed they were all very clean.

They filed down the stairs. Delbo remained silent. They asked him to let them into the house, which he did. As they went through the rooms, Andi noticed that the younger woman was not there. "Mr. Delbo, where is your wife?"

He did not answer.

An hour and a half later, they'd found nothing out of the ordinary. They moved out onto a back porch, which also revealed nothing. Pete stood at the door of the porch, looking out. "Andi, out here."

A thin track led into the forest that closed in on the tiny yard behind the house. About thirty yards into the trees, they found a large old trunk under a pile of branches.

Inside was a box of photographs, and three neatly folded stacks of clothes, encased in plastic. They opened the thin box of photographs: small groups of women gathered around Delbo, taken in the dormitory. Five photos, one picturing seven women, four picturing six. Thirty-one women.

"Six beds in the dormitory," Pete noted quietly.

Andi nodded. She fanned the five pictures out like a poker hand, studied them carefully. "Are these all different women, or are there repeats?"

"They look different to me."

She nodded. She flipped the photos over and studied the dates. "These are all about two or three years apart." She looked at the fronts again. "Passing through? In groups?" she mused. "Why no men?"

All the women had brown skin, dark eyes, black hair. Few stood taller than Delbo's shoulder, and those who did still did not reach his height. The bones in the fire—a small woman, young, five-feet or so. A Mexican cross.

Delbo, having followed them, was watching. "Who are these women, Mr. Delbo?"

Again he folded his arms.

Pete said, "Mr. Delbo, if you don't answer our questions, it may be necessary for us to invite you down to the sheriff's office. We'd like to avoid that if we can."

Delbo turned away, facing back toward the house.

Andi opened one of the plastic bags. "Pete."

The bag held folded shirts, t-shirts, and female underclothes. Pete opened a second: slacks and jackets. Andi emptied the first bag onto the top of the trunk and counted: eighteen of each item.

Pete said, "Three times six, eh?"

Andi nodded, examining the shirts closely. "All these clothes are small sizes." She looked at Delbo, feeling a shiver of excitement. "Mr. Delbo, we need answers here."

Delbo, his arms crossed on his chest, his craggy face dark, kept utterly silent.

"Mr. Delbo, you have a dormitory with six beds. It's obviously been used and recently cleaned. You have a trunk full of women's clothing, which you've hidden out here in the woods. You have photos of yourself with thirty-one women who look Hispanic to me." Andi noticed his eyes flicker. "I'm going to ask you one more time to explain who these women are and what that dormitory is for. If you remain silent, I am going to work under the assumption that human trafficking is going on here and that you are perhaps smuggling undocumenteds for the sex trade."

Delbo expelled a rush of breath. "Never! Never that! Despicable, rotten! Not me. Not here." He shut his mouth, but his face flared red.

Pete said, "Mr. Delbo, if you want us to accept some other explanation, give it to us. Otherwise, we'll have to take you in, pending a full investigation by the Immigration and Customs Enforcement."

Delbo looked about to spit. "Morons." He spread his hands in a gesture of surrender. "Ask, then."

Andi, playing bad-guy, shook her head. "I've asked, Mr. Delbo. We can see you're running some kind of operation with these women. What is it?"

"Prejudices trap you. See brown-skinned women, assume Mexicans."

"What should I assume, then?"

"Filipinas." He pointed to the photographs. "Wife's cousins."

50

Andi frowned to fend off a laugh at the absurdity. "Sir, I've about finished with my questions and I'm getting ready to read you your rights."

Pete said, "Mr. Delbo, you're asking us to believe that you have thirty-one Filipina in-law cousins?"

He nodded angrily, and turned and walked toward the house. "Come. Have coffee."

Pete and Andi replaced the clothes and photos and lugged the trunk into the kitchen, where Delbo, already sitting at the table, had poured three cups of black sludge. Leaning on his elbows and holding his cup in front of himself, the old man coughed. His face registered grief.

"World War Two. Captured on Bataan, the whole unit. Japs marched us forty-five days. Heard about it, you have. Day thirty-two, fell. Too sick to get up, gutted me with his bayonet, guard did. Left me there. Should've died in the heat. Didn't. In the dark, Japs gone, Filipina and her two brothers drag me into the jungle. Hide me, nurse me, keep me in her hut till MacArthur returns, drives the fuckin' Japs into hell."

It cost him, this story. He was breathing hard. His face had reddened at first, then the color bled out as he went on. Andi watched him carefully. Where was this story headed? How would it explain the thirty-one *cousins*?

Delbo gulped a mouthful of coffee, almost violently, then resumed. "After war, married the Filipina, name Lydia, and brought her to Montana, here. Built the furniture business, we. 1988, started hearing from her family in Maguindanao, gangs comin' in, called 'Muslim terrorists' now. Gangsters." He looked ready to spit again. "Few months after, her two brothers—helped save me, them—murdered, both. Raped their wives, gangsters did, then killed 'em. 'Lesson to the people.'" He grunted, half in grief, half in fury.

"Heard about Filipino in San Diego, smuggled relatives into the country. Wife wanted me to join. Went down there, lasted a couple years, brought over some cousins from Maguindanao. Turned bad, the Filipino, started bringing up Mexicans, slaves. Turned real bad, scared us. Came back here, kept hearing from Filipino cousins, and maybe some not-so cousins. Terrified, cousins were. Stayed to fight, men did, sent the women to me. Got routine, a few girls a year, wife's cousins or friends." He slurped his coffee. "Big families over there. Built the sleeping room over the workshop, I did, and teach 'em enough English to work, Lydia did. Found 'em work where I was deliverin' furniture to the white rich folks. Wanted servants, the assholes did. But better life than with the gangsters."

His voice caught, and he cleared his throat before continuing. He fanned out the pack of photos on the table, found one, tapped his finger gently on the face of one of the women. "Lydia, my wife. Died twenty years ago, heart wore out." His voice roughened again. "Asked me to keep it goin'."

He looked Andi in the eyes, challenging her. "So. You know." He looked weary, sad, but defiant. "Never stop, the gangsters. Ninety-three years old. Going to die soon, then who...?" His voice trailed off, almost a sob.

Andi listened, jotting in her notebook. The story was a black well of sorrow. *But I'm the bad cop.* "Well, we have to get ICE involved, Mr.

Delbo. What you're doing is against the law. Even if you're telling us the truth."

From behind them, a soft voice said, in clear English this time, "He tells the truth."

They turned. It was the wife. The new wife. Where had she hidden while they searched the house? Andi peered at her, thinking of the age difference. Probably not much over forty, forty-five tops.

She said, "Mr. Delbo's wife was my grandmother. I take her place here."

"You're not his wife?"

She shook her head. "Granddaughter."

Delbo stood, brushed between Andi and Pete, stood with the younger woman. "Leave her out. Suffered more than any of us." He said something softly to her, his voice infinitely kind, in a language Andi did not recognize. The woman left the room.

Pete said, "Has she got her documents, Mr. Delbo?"

Delbo said nothing.

"We'll have to take her in too, sir." Andi felt the cruelty of saying it.

Delbo's eyes filled with tears, which he brushed away roughly. "Information you may want. Let her alone."

Andi saw the opening; Pete probably did too, but he glanced at Andi. She said, "We can't make a deal like that, Mr. Delbo. The law's the law."

Pete looked directly at her: *Let's talk,* said his eyes.

Delbo barked. "Japs had *laws* too. Would have raped and killed Lydia, Japs would, for savin' me." He scoffed. "Laws." He shook his head, then nodded toward his granddaughter's room, and took a ragged breath. "Lost both parents, she, and three brothers to the gangsters. Disappeared, her husband. Gone from the islands, her son and daughter. Doesn't know where. Leave her be." His ancient eyes were again full of tears. He did not brush them away.

Andi, her own eyes damp, looked at Pete. "Let's talk," she said. He nodded.

Outside, she said, "I think he's telling the truth."

"Maybe he is, maybe he isn't. Not for us to determine out here."

In the house, Pete was the good cop, but here, in the yard, he was arguing the strict side. Andi thought about Ordrew's approach, strict law-and-order, procedure, protocols. He'd have arrested Delbo a half-hour ago, the story be damned.

"Look, we can't take them both in the pickup, so either we call for backup to take them in, or we come back tomorrow with a larger vehicle."

Pete frowned. "Which gives them time to run."

"He's ninety-three. This is their home, and we don't have a shred of evidence to contradict his story. It's plausible."

"But his being a trafficker is plausible, too. This *cousin* story could be a cover."

"Yeah, but if he's trafficking, there's no action here now, and we can't connect him to previous shipments. Hell, we didn't even know there *were* previous shipments till the fire, and we're not even sure that's what it represents."

"Not yet."

"And if he runs, he loses his infrastructure. Anyway, Pete, he's ninety-three years old. He's not going to last long."

Pete turned away. "I don't know, Andi. We're cops, not the judge and jury. It's not our call. If we leave them up here, we could have real serious egg on our faces tomorrow."

He was holding to his argument, but Andi sensed he wanted her to win. She thought about how, in the Longmire books the guys liked so much, Sheriff Longmire always waited, letting the other guy squirm until the words came out. She waited.

After a moment, he said, "You believe him?"

"I do."

Pete took a deep breath. "Jesus," he muttered. "You're damn near talking me into this." He turned away, leaned down, and picked up a small rock. He rested it in his palm, then suddenly threw it over Beatrice John's cabin into the deep woods behind. Throwing something away. Pete turned back to her. "If Delbo runs, Ben'll have no choice but to suspend us."

"Ben's in the hospital, and you're Acting Sheriff. You'll have to do it." She grinned.

Pete took a long breath, took off his cap, and rubbed his forehead. "Hell, Andi. I'm of two minds. I can see what you see—he doesn't smell like a trafficker to me. On the other hand, there's the illegal entry side."

"True. But here's the thing, Pete. I believe him, and I think he knows something about what goes on up here. If we hold the ICE over his head, maybe we can get more information. Sex trafficking and murder are a hell of a lot bigger than rescuing cousins from terrorists."

"Gangsters." He nodded. "You're saying we trade. We don't call ICE in return for good information on a bigger crime."

"I am. In Cook County, we did it all the time."

Pete took another long breath and held it a moment, as if he were counting. Then he let it out slowly, nodded, said, "Okay. Cross your fingers."

They went back inside.

Andi said, "You said you have information."

"Do. Said let her alone," he answered, nodding again toward his granddaughter's room.

"What's your information?"

"You'll let her alone?"

Andi noticed this verb had its subject. *He's moving our way.* "We'll delay taking your granddaughter in, provided you tell us what you know, now. And that what you tell us is true."

He waited a moment, then his body sagged. "So. Around here, sex trafficking, yes, but not by me."

"Who?"

His eyes closed. Andi shot a glance at Pete, who nodded. *Keep going.* When Delbo opened his eyes, he said, "On that dirt road back to that fire you folks've been scoutin'? Half-mile in, big brush pile on the right. Pull it. Side road. Follow it a mile, see where they meet. Call it a church. Covers for what they really do. Sellin' girls from Mexico."

Andi shuddered. A "*milagro* cross," Charlie had said. Mexican.

She made a mental note: *Church + Mexican girls + Bishop burned the lady???*

Pete said, "How do you know this, Mr. Delbo?"

"Mine to know, not yours."

Andi said, "No, sir. We need to know. If you found out in some way that endangers us when we go there, we need to be prepared."

Delbo looked disgusted. "No protecting from these. Evil." He gave a dry spit. "Live here, hunt here, know these woods. Came across their church years ago. How I know."

She said, "Why haven't you reported this earlier, Mr. Delbo?"

The old man's eyes dropped, the disgust on his face shifting to anguish. "Afraid of them. Wicked to their enemies."

"So you know them. Tell me who they are."

His eyes narrowed a moment, then he shook his head. "Don't know them. But worked with their kind in San Diego. Turned very bad, the Filipino did. Same as these people. Cruel. Anger them, you die."

Andi thought, *He knows something more. But he's bargaining with us too.* "If you are telling us the truth, Mr. Delbo, your granddaughter can stay. Tell me how you know about that 'church,' and not just a random walk in the woods. The truth."

He looked angry. "Found it hunting, didn't understand. Coming back from Carlton, groceries. Years ago. Saw line of trucks going in the track. Next day, followed the tracks, found it again. Knew."

Pete took over. "You know they call it a church. How?"

"Not them, I. Looks like a church. To me."

"And how do you know they run sex traffic through here?"

"Enough talk. Go, look. See for yourself."

"We'll look for that church. But if there's anything wrong with what you gave us, we'll be back here. Fast."

Delbo said nothing.

Andi and Pete started gathering the box of photos and the bags of clothing. Andi stopped. "Why would we take these if we're not charging him with anything?"

"To protect them in case we do?"

"Good point." They carried the pictures and clothes to the back of the pickup.

Delbo spoke a long while with his granddaughter, then joined them at the truck. "Not lying," he grunted. "Don't lie."

"Thank you for your cooperation. But we'll be back for more," Andi said.

He simply looked at the two officers. Then he nodded, his shoulders down. "Yes," he said. "Will be back."

Driving out of the yard, Pete glanced over at Andi. "By morning, they're in the wind."

She feared he was right. "If he is, I'll find him. And we'll know he's the bishop."

51

Back at Andi's desk, Pete poured two cups of thick coffee while Andi opened the evidence room and brought back the things she'd found in Beatrice John's cabin. They started deconstructing Delbo's story. The story of the cousins and the "gangsters" had gripped her; and the sex-trafficking information, if it was true, had shaken her. It wrapped a story around the small woman, nailed inside the shack and burned alive.

At first, the idea of an audience standing in the rectangle of cut weeds, watching the girl being burned alive, had been unthinkable. But now, what if it had been a group of young women, seduced by promises of income and the good life in *Norteamérica,* being taught a lesson?

"The question is, what kind of lesson?" Andi asked Pete.

"Perhaps the dead woman had resisted or tried to escape."

"So they bring a group of girls up here, one tries to escape, and they kill her to terrify the others, keep them docile."

"Been known to happen."

"So, we've got plenty of guesses, but not as many facts."

From an evidence bag, Pete pulled out the rusty-rose-colored papers that Andi had brought down from Beatrice John's cabin, thumbing through them. After a dozen pages, all blank, he found one displaying an odd diagram. "What the hell's this?"

Andi looked. "I missed this."

They studied it.

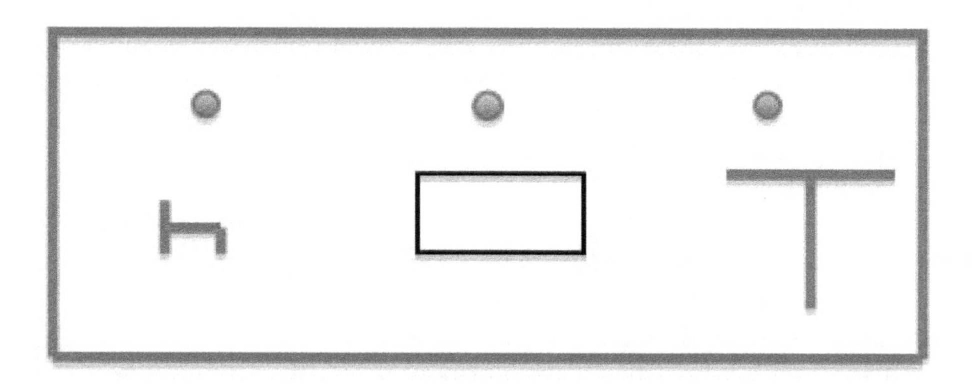

"I don't get it at all," Pete said, staring at the page. "To me, this sure as hell doesn't count as a fact."

Andi continued studying the diagram. "Well, it's a fact, but damned if I know what it means. I read it as 'ooo, hut,' which makes no sense at all." She took a sip of the sludge in her cup, almost gagged. "Wow, that's worse than usual." She held the page up. "Okay, we've got three new bits of information. One, Delbo's claim that there's sex trafficking up there. Two, the existence of this 'church'—if he isn't bluffing us. Three, this diagram, whatever the hell it is." She shook her head. "Maybe when we go up to this 'church' tomorrow, we'll learn more."

Pete grimaced. "Just remembered. I've got the monthly FEMA coordination meeting over in Missoula." He rubbed his eyes. "Man, I hope Ben's back soon. The pace's killing me, my own job and Ben's." He shrugged it off. "Okay, you have to work more information out of Delbo and you want to go to that new site. You need a partner."

"I'm thinking I'd like Ed to go up there with me."

"Ed? How come?"

"He told me that he's treated some cult survivors, back in

Minnesota. He says a lot of these so-called cults are actually part of drug or prostitution networks, traffickers, but they use religious symbolism to keep the group cohesive. We think this group has a bishop, which would fit with the religious angle. Ed might have insights when we find this 'church.'"

Pete nodded. "Good idea, but I want you to take another deputy with you. This thing looks dangerous to me; I don't want you going alone. Hell, I don't want *anyone* going alone."

"Won't be alone. Ed'll be there."

"Armed?"

Ed shot with cameras, not guns. "Got it." She immediately thought of Mike. "I'll call Mike Payne. He's on the case from Carlton."

Pete frowned. "Let's use him as a last resort. This is starting to be a real badass case, and I want our guys to be primary."

Andi held her breath. Disappointment that Mike wouldn't be with her wasn't a feeling she should be having. "Who've you got to send with us?"

"Let me check." He came back with the assignment book. "Looks like it'll have to be our friend Brad. I'll tell him. You tell Ed." He looked at her. "You okay with this?"

Damn. Trading Mike for Brad was trading down. But her desire to investigate the cult site trumped her disappointment. "Yeah, send Brad. I can handle working with him." If Delbo were in the wind tomorrow, Ordrew'd witness her mistake. *A risk I've got to take.*

After she and Pete locked the rose-colored paper and its strange diagram back in the evidence room, Andi checked off-duty and dropped by Ed's office and left a note. *"Dinner at the Angler? I need a glass of wine and a consultation with my personal shrink."* She wanted to process what they'd just learned from Delbo, and she didn't want Grace to be privy to the conversation. There were things in the world that a high school senior didn't need to know.

52

When Andi got to the Angler, Ed was already sitting at the bar chatting with Ted.

"Greetings, Andrea," Ted called out, and Ed turned toward her and smiled.

She waved to Ted, then touched Ed lightly on the shoulder. "Dinner?" she asked.

"How about a beer first?"

"Well, not at the bar. I need to talk."

Ed lifted his eyebrows, and followed her into the dining room. Ted called to Andi from behind the bar, "A martini, Andrea?"

She laughed. "How about a glass of Pinot Noir?"

"Your wish, *et cetera, et cetera.*"

Ed took a swallow of his ale, then said, "So. Your note was a little vague. In what sense am I your personal shrink?"

"The case. There's a bunch of dots I need to connect and maybe you can shed some light on them."

"Cool. Okay, dot-connecting and light-shedding coming up."

Andi told him what she and Pete were speculating.

"Your theory is maybe a woman was being trafficked, got out of hand somehow, and was burned to death as punishment?"

"And maybe the other women were forced to stand in the rectangle and watch. A lesson."

"Other women..." He looked up at the ceiling a moment. "You're assuming that's who left the bare footprints?"

"Uh-huh. Charlie Begay says there were as many as ten sets of footprints around the mowed area, and six of them were barefoot. And my informant says this group has a site where they meet, says it looks like a 'church,' which to me says 'cult.' It's near the murder scene."

Ed was nodding. "You're thinking the fire scene and this cult site are related?"

"Yup, exactly. Churches have bishops and a bishop burned the lady."

"So you want to find this place."

"I'm going up tomorrow morning. I want you to come with us." She watched his eyes narrow and hurried to add, "We'll pay a consultant fee." She hadn't cleared this with Pete, but she could always pay it herself. She expected Ed to say no, anyway. Too busy.

He surprised her again. "It's not the money. I'm wondering what you think I can add."

"You said you've worked with cult members. I haven't got any real experience there. You might pick up something I won't see."

He shook his head. "I've worked with victims, not active members. And it's been years."

She started to argue, but he cut her off. "Still, though, it's intriguing. I'll reschedule a few patients tonight when we get home."

Andi noticed his easy assumption that she'd spend the night at his place.

"You said 'we.' Is your Carlton buddy going with us?"

Andi looked at him, tense about how he'd react. "Brad Ordrew's the only deputy available."

He sipped his beer. "Hard to tell which of the three of us is going to have the worst time."

She chuckled. "You got that right, big guy."

He waited a minute, then shrugged. "All in the name of law enforcement. Okay, are we done with the case?"

As she was nodding, suddenly uncomfortable, her wine arrived.

She lifted the glass to her lips. *This'll give me a minute.* As she savored the wine, she tried to dredge up what she'd realized when talking with Pete, but Delbo's story and the information from Wallace's Corner must've buried it. "Did you know that Lucy is twelve years younger than Pete?"

"Actually, I did know that. How'd Lucy handle it?"

"Well, I don't really know. Apparently she did, though. And I will too."

His eyebrows lifted briefly, then he smiled.

She wondered if he'd taken that as a commitment of some kind. It did sound kind of promisey, didn't it? She felt her heart speed up.

But only for a moment, because Ed only smiled. "Take your time, pal," he said softly. And then, the bottom dropped out of her mind and she felt herself being sucked down a hole. The insight she'd lost roared back.

Ed, looking alarmed. "What's wrong?"

She looked at the ceiling fan, rotating slowly, trying different words for what she'd realized. "You know my mom died of breast cancer when I was sixteen, right?"

He nodded. "On your birthday, wasn't it?"

"Yeah." She felt something dark stirring inside. "A few months before she died, she'd had the chemotherapy and she was sick all the time. One day, she said she was hot all over. I asked what was the matter. She said, 'this damn menopause.'" Andi had to take a breath. Her heart was throbbing in her chest. "I must've put them together. If I go through menopause...I'll get cancer." Her eyes filled. She held her napkin against them, determined to let no tears fall. After a moment, she lowered the cloth, helpless against the moisture streaming down her face.

Ed laid his hand on the table beside hers, but did not touch her. She wanted to take it, feel his strength, but didn't. *This is mine.*

When she said nothing more and he spoke softly, she heard him from far away. "Oh, man, kid. You decided menopause causes cancer."

Terror flared at his words, as if she were about to die. "And cancer causes death. So menopause means I die."

Flooded, adrift, she took his hand.

WEDNESDAY

53

The next morning, before seven a.m. report, Andi had met Ed in the Department reception area. She'd spent the night at her place, alone, gnawing on what she'd remembered at the Angler. *Menopause means I'll die.* She could form the sentence without her eyes welling. That must be progress.

Ed kissed her. "How're you doing?"

"Didn't sleep. Thought a lot, though." She looked sheepish. "And cried a lot, mostly for my mom. You know what?"

"What?"

"Guess her age when she died."

"You're kidding."

"Nope. Forty-nine, same as me."

Pete pushed through the heavy glass Sheriff's Department door. He shook Ed's hand. "I see you're here. You're coming?"

Ed grinned. "Wouldn't miss it. Rescheduled the day's patients."

"Great. We got our very own cult expert."

"Wouldn't go that far. I'm no expert, but it's damn interesting."

"Interesting, eh? Not the adjective I'd use for these people."

Pete said to Andi, "I called Larry Wilkins at FEMA and told him I've got an emergent case, very hot. So I'm coming with you. I'm not happy it's just the two—well, three—of us. The place could be a trap. I'd like more firepower, but nobody's available."

"Brad's still available, isn't he?" Andi asked.

"Nope. Lannie called in sick, so I had to assign Brad to patrol this morning." Pete tossed her the keys. "We'll take the SUV. You drive."

Andi caught Ed's eye, and gave him a high-five look. Pete for Brad was trading *up*.

All the way up into the mountains, they talked over what they knew, picking at the edges of all they didn't know. Ed, in the second row, was quiet as Andi and Pete rehashed details. After a dozen miles, he said, "Boy, the more I hear about these people, the more serious I'm getting. These psychopaths are the real deal."

When they passed Wallace's Corner, Pete said, "Wonder if they're still home."

Andi looked sideways. "Well, if they haven't run yet, my bet's they're not going to."

"Who are you talking about?" Ed said.

Andi looked at Pete, who turned and faced Ed behind him. "Look, Ed, let's formalize this. I talk with Lucy about cases, and I know you guys do too; but legally, this is an ongoing investigation and giving you inside information could bite us in the ass if anything gets to a trial. You willing to sign on as our consultant, formally?"

"From what I know so far, this is way ugly. Sure. Sign me up. *Pro bono*."

Pete picked up the radio's mic. When he raised Callie, he explained and asked her to get the paperwork ready. "Dated this morning, nine a.m. I'll sign it when we get back."

Ed asked, "So what's going on with Wallace's Corner?"

Pete turned back toward Ed and explained their deal with Cassius Delbo.

Ed whistled. "Sounds risky."

"Damn risky," Andi said. "But I'm good with taking risks to save young Mexican women."

"Or men? They're victims sometimes too."

As Andi anwered, "Yeah, or men," the dirt road into the murder scene came up, and Andi turned in. Then, after a half-mile, they found the brush pile just where Delbo told them it would be. "Good sign," she said softly.

Pete grunted. "Unless he's this bishop character and the place has been bulldozed."

54

They pulled the brush pile aside, drove the SUV in, and a mile farther, they came to another, very different clearing. The surrounding forest was thicker, murkier than at the murder scene, and this clearing was larger, its dirt floor bare, no weeds or grasses. Used. Rather than soft soil, it was hard-packed, heavily trod. Strange furnishings rested in the space. Looking around, Ed shivered, and not for a chill. "This looks evil."

Andi grunted. "Delbo called it their 'church.'"

"This is no damn church."

The forest had been cleared in a carefully constructed circle perhaps sixty feet in diameter. The three studied the area without speaking. Ed felt his chest tighten.

In the center was a large square table, a two-inch thick slab of rough gray granite, dark-stained, resting on piled rocks. Between the table and the far edge of the clearing, three large posts rose out of the ground, each a foot in diameter and twelve feet tall. Ed thought, *Telephone poles, beheaded*. He shivered again, his anxiety growing. "I don't like this."

Andi nodded. "Bad scene."

The posts were fifteen feet apart, along a line parallel with the long side of the table, and were blotchy and stained. At the foot of the table was a T-shaped cross, maybe eight feet tall. Opposite the cross, as if at the head of the table, was a large wooden chair. Behind the chair, against the wall of trees, stood three small sheds, padlocked.

Pete whistled. "That diagram from Beatrice John's cabin. It's a layout just like this."

Ed asked, "What diagram?"

"One of the papers Andi found in Beatrice John and Guy Flandreau's cabin had a group of symbols." He squatted and drew the diagram in the dirt.

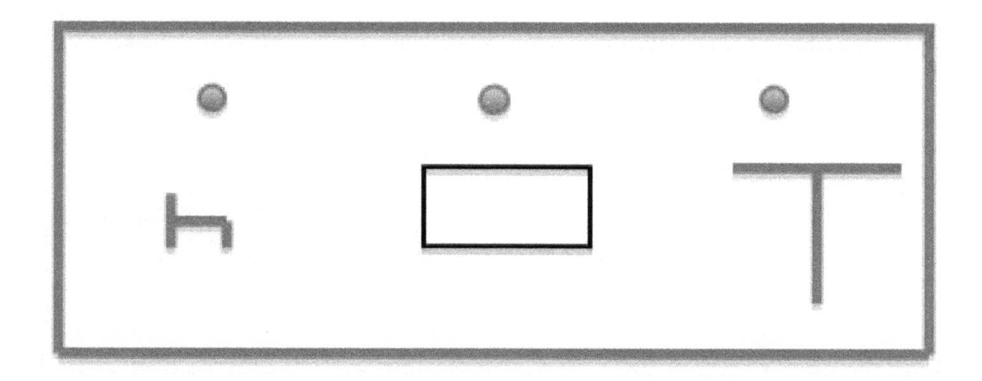

"So," Pete went on. "Picture this clearing from a bird's-eye view. The rectangle in the middle could be this thing." He pointed at the table. "The small circles above it could represent these, uh, those poles, and the T to the side, this thing." He nodded at the T-shaped cross.

Ed walked to the table and laid both hands on the granite, fingers spread, feeling the sticky texture, the cold rock. "This table's an altar."

Pete said, "Ed, don't touch anything. Your fingerprints'll be on it."

"Oh, man, sorry." He looked over at the T, made of heavy lumber, maybe ten feet tall. "The cross could be just a symbol, to give this place a church feeling." He shuddered. "Or they actually use it..."

Andi gasped. "What? To *crucify* people?"

"Don't know. Maybe just tie them onto it for a time. I've read that's not uncommon torture in some cults."

"Jesus."

The weak light seemed to dim further. Ed suddenly wanted to see sky. He looked up, but the forest canopy kept the clearing in gloom.

Pete pointed at the poles. "What are these for?"

Ed gathered himself. "I had a patient once who'd been raised in a bizarre Christian cult outside Minneapolis. She drew a picture with a setup something like this, except it was indoors. They tied members who strayed or broke the rules to the poles and punished them. She said they sometimes lashed them up overnight on a big cross. Other times, they would flog them."

Andi grimaced. "But the woman in the ashes wasn't flogged or tied up, she was burned."

Ed thought about it. "We don't know what they might've done to her *before* burning her, do we? I'd guess one thing, though: This place is for people who belong to this group, whatever it is. I'm thinking she wasn't a member—members are too valuable to kill." His stomach clenched. The murky light was menacing.

Pete went over and peered closely at one of the poles, the third one on the left of the clearing. He turned and called, "I'd say these are bloodstains. Let's get DCI back up to be sure." He pointed to a blackened eyebolt sunk in the pole about nine feet off the ground; there were two others, one at eight feet, the third at seven. "Eyebolts?" On the middle pole, the same arrangement. On the third pole on the right, there were two: one at six feet, a second maybe five feet above the ground. Pete looked at Ed. "For short, medium, and tall people, maybe?"

Ed nodded. "I'd bet on it. Tie their hands, then loop the rope through a higher eyebolt and either just let them hang there, or maybe flog them. That'd explain the bloodstains."

"Wait." Andi frowned. "I get tall and medium, but five feet off the ground?" Then she whispered, "Jesus."

"Yeah. Kids."

Andi and Pete looked at each other, their faces pale. His own heart was beating faster than he liked.

For a long moment, they said nothing. Then Pete turned and pointed. "Okay, what's the chair?"

Ed and Andi answered at the same moment. "The Bishop."

Pete said, "Explain."

Ed glanced at Andi, who nodded to him. "In cathedrals, there's always a throne for the bishop to sit on, presiding over the rituals. It's called a 'cathedra,' hence 'cathedral.'"

Pete said, "Ah."

Andi was gazing around the clearing, focusing on the row of padlocked sheds off to the side. "Man, I'd like to get inside these sheds."

Pete nodded. "Exigent circumstances."

Ed asked, "What's that mean?"

Andi said, "If circumstances call for a search but there's no time to get a warrant, and if those circumstances give us probable cause, we can search without a warrant."

Pete added, "People don't hide in the woods when they've got nothing to hide, and there could be a clean-up crew on its way up here any time now. Given the stripping of the murder scene, I'm thinking it's appropriate to break those locks rather than waiting for a warrant—which could give them time to destroy evidence." He turned to Andi. "Am I missing anything?"

She shook her head. "Not that I can see. But those locks are standard issue Master Locks. Let's see if any of our master keys work first. I hate advertising we've been here."

Andi went to the SUV and brought back a ring of keys, but after trying them all, no luck.

"Damn," Pete muttered. "Okay. I've got the real key."

He rummaged in the tool chest in the SUV and returned with a bolt cutter.

Ed grunted. "They'll know we've been here." He suddenly wanted to leave.

Pete hefted the bolt cutter. "You have a better idea?"

Andi studied the padlock and the hasp it closed. "How about a big slotted screwdriver? Maybe size eighteen or twenty."

Pete grinned. "Good thinking. Screwdrivers we've got."

Despite his unease, Ed looked at Andi. "You know screwdriver sizes?"

"My dad figured if I was going to grow up to be a cop, I ought to know what guys know."

"Huh."

Pete returned with a big screwdriver. Ed reached for it, but Pete shook his head. "As a consultant, you can advise us, examine what we determine to be evidence, and all that. But you can't actually participate in the search."

"Got it." He stepped away.

Pete pulled on his latex gloves. He struggled with the screws—very old, rusty—but finally extracted them and pulled the hasp from the wooden door. He repeated the work on the other two sheds.

When all three doors stood open, Andi turned to Ed, "We're going to do this search. When we're done, you can help us figure out what we've got. Mind taking a break in the SUV?"

"Not at all." His anxiety pushed in. "But let's not take too long."

As he walked to the SUV, he realized this was an Andi he'd never seen in action before: Brave. In charge. Competent. This sudden appreciation for her contrasted with his growing apprehensiveness. *No*, he thought. *Call it by its name: fear.*

55

Andi, gloved, worked through the first shed. There were iron implements of various shapes and sizes, some appearing to be old-fashioned shackles with dangling chains. Others looked like long pliers and pincers. After she'd photographed them and bagged two for evidence, she beckoned Ed to come. He walked over, and when he saw them, he grimaced.

"Your opinion?"

"My opinion wouldn't stand up in court since I'm not an expert. But they're for torture."

"Only good thing is," Pete whispered, after coming over to see, "they're rusty."

Pete's shed, in the middle, contained coiled bullwhips hanging on the back of the door, a stack of firewood, and on top of the wood, an orange bucket filled with green boxes of lye. "What do you guys think?" he asked.

Andi shook her head. "Keeping the wood dry. But the lye, no idea."

Ed looked in. "Cleaning would be my guess."

In the dark forest, a branch cracked. Andi and Pete both unholstered their weapons, and Ed's heart leapt. After a minute or so, when nothing emerged, Pete said, softly, "Back to work. Ed, you help

Andi—and keep it to yourself that you participated. I'm going to keep a lookout. Let's keep it quiet."

Andi went to the SUV and got Ed a pair of Latex gloves. "Here. Wear these." He pulled them on.

Beside the lye bucket on the woodpile was a nearly full five-gallon can of gasoline and a steel box of long matches. Ed went around behind the shed, where he found splits of pine and larch, stacked six feet high against the wall. To Andi he whispered, "This wood could get wet in the weather. Your idea that they're keeping some inside so it's dry when they need it makes sense." She came around and photographed the outside firewood.

Thinking about the likely use of the wood, he felt sick to his stomach. He went over to the altar and studied it. He kept his voice low. "Andi, can you take some scrapings from this stone? I'm thinking this is where they burn things."

Andi retrieved a tool from the SUV, and scraped it across the stone, brushing the scrapings into an evidence bag. "Looks like soot to me," she said.

Ed grimaced. "'Bishop burned the lady in the fire.'"

"You think they burned her here, then took her to the shack? Why would they do that?"

He shook his head. "Cover up the murder by burning the shack?" He thought a moment longer. "No, I don't think so. If she was being trafficked, they wouldn't bring her here. Didn't you say there were a number of people at the shack burning?"

As Andi started to answer, Pete returned. "Okay, I think we're alone." He went to the third shed. "Guys, over here."

He stepped back and pointed to a stack of seven old leather-covered books, wider than tall. Andi got a large plastic sheet from the SUV and laid it on the altar, then carried the books to the altar. She gingerly opened the first book. Yellowed pages were covered with columns and rows, with precise hand-printing in all the cells. "Accounting ledgers?"

One by one, she and Pete carefully opened the other books. All seven were the same: ancient, yellowed pages, columns and rows, neatly printed numbers and letters—but not whole words, just strings of what looked like random letters or numbers. They couldn't see any clear pattern, but, like the brooding forest around them and the grisly objects in the clearing, the ledgers felt evil.

Andi looked at the two men. "I want to take these back to the department and study them there, not here. We need to get the hell out of here."

"Sounds good to me," Ed murmured. "But if we take them, it's a dead giveaway that we've been here."

Andi took a long breath. "You're right. But we'll never figure these out up here, and I think they're too important to leave them." She blew on the top book. A gust of dust flew up. "These haven't been touched for a long time. Maybe they won't miss them."

"If you take the books, you might as well take the other evidence too."

Andi looked at Pete, who said, "It's your call, Andi." He scanned the surrounding forest. "I just want us out of here."

She nodded. "Let's get it logged in, put the doors back on, and get our butts out."

Pete looked in the third shed again. "Whoa. Look." Inside, where they'd been hidden behind the stack of books, was a stack of cardboard boxes. Printing on the sides read "Warriors of Yahweh," and beside the words was a small red banner with a white cross within it.

Andi opened the top box. Inside, flyers printed on rose-colored paper headed by the triangle logo. Under the same title, "Warriors of Yahweh," was a long paragraph. Andi lifted the paper. "This is English, but I'll be damned if I know what it means. We'll take these and study them later."

Over her shoulder, Ed whispered. "This paper's the same color as the note I got when Beatrice John didn't show up."

Andi studied the paper in the leaden forest light. She held it up toward the sky, dim light barely filtering through the dense canopy. "I think the color matches the papers I took out of Guy Flandreau's cabin at Wallace's Corner too. We're getting somewhere."

Another branch cracked. Ed jumped. "Let's get going."

Pete grunted. "With you, man. This place spooks me. Let's collect this stuff and get the hell out of here before we're sorry we didn't."

"I feel it too. Something's too close," Andi said. Then, angrily: "Let the bastards come." She grabbed the camera from the SUV. To Pete, she said, "While I photograph everything, bag what we're taking. We'll do the field cards when we get back." She turned to Ed. "While I'm taking the pictures and Pete's got what he needs from a shed, would you screw the hasps back on?"

"Sure. But let's hurry."

Ed waited anxiously near the sheds while Andi and Pete worked, feeling prickles on his neck, as if someone were watching. He looked around. Thick forest, dark trees, underbrush. His chest tightened. He started panting. "You guys about ready?" he said, very softly.

Andi's whisper carried. "Almost."

Pete waved Ed over. "Done with the first shed, Ed," he whispered. Ed began re-screwing the hasps. Done, he murmured, "I'm not feeling good about taking more time, guys."

Pete looked toward him. "Man, I'm with you. Fast as I can."

Screwing on the second and third locks, Ed's hands were sweat-slick. When he finished, Andi took final photos of everything looking undisturbed. "We're good," she whispered. "Until these assholes open the sheds."

Ed climbed into the second seat of the SUV, every nerve singing.

Turning on the engine, Andi muttered, "A damn mile out. Hope we don't meet anybody coming in."

Pete narrowed his eyes. "Just a precaution," he said softly, as he drew his weapon and held it in his lap. Andi looked at it, then did the same. Ed watched them, every muscle tight.

As they drove slowly out, Andi stopped at the brush pile. After they put it back in place concealing the road, Pete said, "Probably a waste of time. Once they find their stuff missing, they'll know we were here."

"Question is," Ed said, "what will they do about it?"

56

As they turned onto the highway, Pete asked Andi, "You planning to stop at Delbo's?"

She thought about it. "I'd rather come up tomorrow and talk to him. I'd like to dig into those books this afternoon."

"Your call," Pete said, then added, "I'd do the same."

Back at the station, Ed went to his office across the hall and Andi and Pete logged in the evidence. Andi piled the old books on her desk and opened the first one. As she'd thought up in the woods, they reminded her of accounting ledgers, but she couldn't make sense of them—some of the entries seemed like random strings of letters and numbers. She struggled with them for an hour, then groaned and gave up. Tomorrow. She'd tackle them again when she felt fresh. No use missing something because of fatigue.

As she stood to carry the books to the evidence room, Brad Ordrew walked in.

"Lucky break on the case, I hear," no congratulation in his voice.

She turned to face him. "We'll see." She took a breath. "Didn't appreciate the sarcasm this morning, Brad."

"Didn't think you would."

Andi just stared at him. Then, exasperated, she took the chance. "You've been pissed at me since I didn't tell you about Ed's hiding Jared Hansen."

"Think so?" He looked at the pile of books in her arms. "I wouldn't say I'm pissed. I just don't like cops breaking the rules."

"Just let it go, Brad."

He shook his head, then nodded toward the books. "The evidence you found?"

"Some of it."

"Don't lose it."

Fuck you, she thought. But she said nothing, and carted the books to the evidence room and signed them in.

THURSDAY

57

The next morning, a cup of coffee steamed on her desk beside the first of the seven books. Gloved, she opened it with care. She ran her finger down the first page, raising a fine feathery dust of weathered paper. Like a handwritten spreadsheet, each row had four columns. First, a column of consecutive numbers down the page—*numbered rows*? She thought—followed by a second column of eight-digit numbers. The numbers teased her, felt meaningful, but in a way she couldn't grasp. She mumbled to herself, "Yet."

She took a sip of coffee, and let her eyes wander over the strings of numbers, letting her mind empty out, sure that their meaning would emerge. It didn't. She muttered again, "Yet."

She turned her attention to the four column headings across the top of the page:

No.Da.Na.Prod.

She opened another page: The same. Then another, and another, all in the same format with the same headings and the same strings of letters and numbers. Opening the last book to its last page, she saw the same pattern, the numbers vastly larger now. She let the puzzle absorb her. She returned to the first book and its first column, and it sprang out immediately: ordinals! Row *1,* row *2,* row *3,* on down the pages. She went back to the last book's last page: The final row in that log was numbered 10,329. *10,329 rows across seven books.* She counted the blank rows at the back of the seventh ledger: 171. "So," she said aloud. "10,500 rows." She grabbed her calculator: *1500 rows per book. If they're consecutive.* She double-checked: The final row in each book was numbered one less than the first row in the next book. Okay, ordinals.

She took another sip of coffee, sitting back from the page for a moment.

So what were the long numbers in the second column? She turned back to page one and looked at the first row. The long number was 072307. Didn't make sense.

Yet.

Andi worked her way more or less at random through all seven books, checking the number strings. She began thinking that the books were logs of some kind. *But logs of what?* Each provided the same information in the same format, although the handwriting varied. First the sequential ordinal numbers, each followed by a string of eight new numbers. Andi went to the final row on the last page. The string in the second column was 101146; the one above it was 092246, and before that, 081646.

Dates! Excited, she grabbed a pen and rewrote the last number: *10/11/46*. "Damn," she muttered. She returned to the first row of the first ledger and rewrote that number as *07/23/07*. She checked a few dozen randomly selected rows through all seven books, and all the numbers could be rewritten as dates. They *had* to be dates, and given the age of the ledgers, they had to be from the last century. She added 19 to the string: the first was *07/23/1907*, the last was *10/11/1946*. *Thirty-nine years.*

1946. Something nagged her about that year.

She returned to the very first entries. Rows 1 through 4 had the same date, 072307. July 23, 1907. In column 3, the letters looked like names, although two were hard to make out, and in column 4 she found letters she couldn't interpret.

Yet. She focused, wrote out the letters in columns 3 and 4:

1. 7/23/1907 Joh_son, Mari_a cebf zrzo borq fbyq
2. 7/23/1907 Balkova, Belva cebf fbyq
3. 7/23/1907 Olafssen, Thr_nna cebf zrzo borq
4. 7/23/1907 Trask, Eugenia cebf fnpe

Old-fashioned names. Or maybe foreign names? She sat back again, reached for her coffee, and stared at the strings of letters beside each name. If they were names. She felt a growing sense they were. But the letter strings in column 4 made no sense. She played with possibilities. What if they formed one word? *Cebf zrzo borq fbyq?* Gibberish. Or four words? That meant nothing either.

Could they be codes? She wrote out the alphabet and, under each letter, she put its numerical equivalent, 1 through 26. But the results made even less sense than the letters. *I'm no code breaker,* she thought. She stood and stretched. Refocused on the dates.

The 1946 dates, the last ones entered in the last book, bothered her. Why did 1946 seem so familiar?

She opened her notebook and found her notes from the visit with Delbo. *Ah!* The old man claimed he'd bought the property from Wallace's grandson in 1946. Old man Wallace had built the little cabin in 1906. The first entry in the first ledger was July 1907. So Wallace or the Wallace family had owned the Delbo place during the same years, almost exactly, that the entries in the ledgers recorded. Was Wallace or his grandson—or both—connected with this group? Was Delbo?

What if Delbo hadn't been in the Philippines at all, had been in Carlton County, doing something recorded in these logs? What if he'd assumed some kind of control from Wallace in 1946? A sick heaviness filled her stomach. If she'd been wrong...

More questions: Did the fact that they'd found both the ledgers and the rose-colored flyers in the same shed mean the books had been created by the Warriors of Yahweh, who'd apparently created the flyers? Or did they have some kind of particular significance to them? If so, what kind of group were they, dating back to 1907, and maybe ending in 1946? And did her finding similar rose-colored papers in the small cabin rented by Beatrice John and Guy Flandreau mean she was involved? Or both of them?

Andi was suddenly unsure that the color of the flyers found in the shed matched the papers found in Beatrice John's cabin. She went to the evidence room and compared the two sets of papers: they were the same rusty rose color, the same velvety texture. Hadn't Ed described the paper announcing her "being taken" as rose-colored as well? She realized Ed hadn't given her the note he'd found. *Gotta get that.*

And don't forget Beatrice's words to Ed: *Bishop burned the lady in the fire.* If Beatrice John and her boyfriend were involved in the Warriors of Yahweh, and if they rented the small cabin from Delbo, was he involved too? She felt a queasy nausea.

Except...

Except the logs stopped seventy-plus years ago. Were there more ledgers that would fill in those missing decades? Was there anything to fill in? There had to be—the "church" in the forest was still active, she felt sure of it, and the arson and murder were current. She stared at the nonsense letters for a while, but nothing came. She decided to do a random riffle through the seven volumes. Looking for what?

Whatever she found.

After a few fruitless minutes, she opened the fourth ledger. Something dropped out, fluttered to the floor. She picked it up: a white business card.

Carlton Mortuary and Crematory

173 Main Street at Fulton
406-555-0174
Director: Richard E. Scopus, BMS, MFDA

A fixture in Carlton since 1946

"A fixture since 1946," she whispered. She double-checked the final entries in the last book: 101146. October 11, 1946. Which was the *fixture*? Richard E. Scopus or the Carlton Mortuary and Crematory?

Andi found an evidence bag and logged the card. She Googled the *Carlton Mortuary and Crematory*. Two pages of Carlton Mortuaries came up, starting with one in Carlton, Minnesota. Scrolling down, she found the Montana business near the bottom. On its website, the director's name was listed as Richard E. Scopus. *The card is current,* she thought. So either Richard E. Scopus has been director since 1946—which would put him close to a hundred years old—or the *business* had been a fixture since 1946. She typed some more, and it took only two minutes: Carlton Mortuary and Crematory was incorporated in 1946. Its first director was a Marvin P. Stark.

"Stark?" she wondered. Any relation to the vanished Virgil Stark?

She decided she needed to work through this carefully with somebody else. She dialed Callie's extension.

"Hey, Callie, Pete around?"

"Nope, out on an accident call. Want me to patch you through to his cell phone?"

"Uh-uh. I need some face-time. Thanks."

"Always proud to serve."

Andi chuckled, then dialed Ben's room at the hospital. When he answered, she didn't wait. "Are you feeling up to helping me analyze some evidence in this murder case?"

"Hell, yes! I'm so damn bored I been thinkin' of readin' a book. Bring it over."

She photocopied the business card and the first and last ten pages of each log, replaced the originals in the evidence room, signed them back in, and drove the six blocks to the hospital.

1907: one year after Wallace built Wallace's Corner. 1946: the end of the ledgers and the opening of the Carlton Mortuary and Crematory.

What the hell was going on?

58

Ben was propped up in bed when Andi came in. "Where's this evidence?"

The color in his face pleased her. "You're feeling better."

He waved it aside. "Ain't at death's door, anyway. Show me this evidence."

She handed him the copies, and told him about the full group of logs spanning the years 1907 through 1946. As she told him about the second column being dates, he grunted. "You sure of that?"

She shook her head. "But what other kinds of numbers would be organized like this?"

Ben stared at them for a moment. "Beats me. Okay, we'll call 'em dates." He looked at Andi. "So what're the letters?"

"Looks like a code to me."

Ben grunted. "Damn. Let's get Pete and your boyfriend over here."

"Ed? Ed's not a code-breaker."

Ben looked at her. "Ain't nobody's a code-breaker. But four heads're better'n three."

Andi called both men, but Pete was still handling a car crash. Ed answered, "I can get over in ten minutes, but I'm hungry. It's my lunch hour."

"Call Ted and have him send over some to-go food," she replied, then added, "On the department."

Ben lifted interested eyebrows. "Order lunch for us all. Get me a burger and fries. Doc's got me eatin' vegetables every damn meal, but I ain't no Buddhist monk."

Andi nodded. "Ed, get yourself lunch and get me the same as you order." She lowered her voice. "And a Caesar salad for Ben. With anchovies."

He heard. "Jesus in a sidecar, Andi. A *salad*?"

"Doctor's orders."

Ben sighed, a man caged. "Whatever. See if you can get a couple more chairs in here. I'll look over these pages." He held up the sheaf. "You sure all the other ledgers are the same as these?"

"All of them."

Ben peered at the pages, saying nothing. Andi went out to see the nurse about some chairs and a table.

After an aide delivered two folding chairs and a card table, Andi set up a work space. Ben was absorbed in the copies, and she took a bunch to study. A few minutes later, Ed arrived. Andi explained what they were doing, and handed him a pile of pages. The three silently pored over their sheaves. No one spoke.

After a few minutes, Ed held up a copy of the business card. "What's this?"

She explained.

Ben interrupted her. "Let's take 'er one point at a time. What the hell are these lists?"

"Wait, Ben." Ed was still looking at the business card. "The Carlton Mortuary is where Beatrice John's boyfriend works."

Andi felt a jolt of excitement. "Guy Flandreau? Jesus, that could be a break." Even as she spoke, a surge of heat flowed across her back and chest; along with it came the anxiety. She took a few breaths, waited a moment, and let heat and tension pass; the excitement remained.

Ben was asking, "Who's this Gee...what's-his-name?"

"Flandreau," Andi answered.

"Beatrice is that multiple personality I told you about," Ed added. "Flandreau's her boyfriend or something; they live together. And he works at the funeral home whose card Andi found in the books." He held it up.

Ben reached out and took the copy, studied it. "Think this place was started by Marv Stark. Him and my dad used to hunt together."

Andi frowned. "So he was a good guy?"

"Couldn't say. I never knew the man more'n to say hello when he'd pick up my dad. My old man wasn't one to put up with jerks, though." He handed the copy of the card back to Ed. "What say we talk about the lists now?"

Andi shook her head. "A minute. A couple dots just hooked up."

Ben looked interested. "Meanin'?"

"Guy Flandreau's girlfriend says 'Bishop burned the lady in the fire,' and the same Guy Flandreau works, or worked, for Carlton Mortuary, and Carlton Mortuary's business card is found in one of these ledgers—"

Ed held up his hand. "What Beatrice told me, to be precise, was that he worked in a 'funeral parlor' in Carlton, not a mortuary. Could there be more than one in Carlton?"

Ben shook his head. "Not so far's I know. Just the one. 'Course, I ain't been over there in a while."

Andi pulled out her phone. "I'll check." In a moment, she looked up. "Nope, just the one."

Ben grunted. "Soon's we get done here, go find this Gee character. Start at the mortuary and maybe you find something'll tie him to this damn mess."

"Yeah," Andi said. And thought, *And maybe not.*

"My turn, finally?" Ben growled. "What the hell are these lists?" He tapped the pages on his lap.

Andi nodded. "From what I saw, the names are all women's."

Ben frowned. "Women's names? How many?"

"Good question. Who's got the 1946 entries?"

They ruffled through their pages, and Ed spoke first. "Here they are."

"What's the final row number?"

"Ten-thousand-three-twenty-nine."

Ben snorted. "Ten-thousand-what? Hell, Doc's meds are turnin' my memory to bacon."

Ed laughed. "So, maybe ten-thousand-three-twenty-nine names?"

"If they're names, they're damn strange names."

"To me, they look like names," Ed said. "Maybe somebody at the department could start searching birth and death records?"

"Good idea, for a shrink." Ben pulled his cell phone out and dialed. While waiting, he said to Andi, "Where are those logs?"

"Locked in the evidence room."

"Right answer." On the phone, he gave Lannie McAlister, the deputy on duty, instructions to start searching the county's computerized records for the names. "Do a random ten pages from each log, Lannie, then call back with the results." Hanging up, Ben asked Ed, "What the hell does the mumbo-jumbo mean?"

"Maybe they're codes."

Andi said, "A big maybe."

Ed nodded. "Didn't you say the logs were meticulously entered?"

"I think so. Every one follows the same format, although the handwriting changes every few years."

"Same nonsense in the headings?" He squinted at the page. "*No. Da. Na. Prod.*?"

"The same, every page I looked at."

"Obviously, *No.* would be number."

"Yeah. And the second column is dates."

Ed nodded. "And *Na.* must be names. That, plus the same structure over, what, almost forty years, suggests they followed a template, which to me implies careful procedure." He looked at the other two.

Ben nodded. Andi said, "Yep. Makes sense."

"So. Following a procedure or template tells me that whoever kept the records wanted to convey information, not nonsense. These letters may look random, but they recur over almost forty years. They have to be codes."

"You're playin' catch up, Ed." Ben said, smiling for the first time. "I figured that out the minute I saw 'em."

Ed laughed, and fanned out his pages, running his finger down the column named *Prod.* "Andi, are these code letters the same in all the logs?"

"I only saw five clusters of letters—but remember, I only looked at random pages. Still, I saw the same five on every page I checked."

Ben squinted at his first few pages. "Ain't five anywhere on these. Just four's all I count." He leafed through the pile. "Ah, wait. This one's got five."

She grabbed her notebook. "Spell them out." She jotted the five codes on a notebook page, tore it out, and handed it to Ben. She made a second copy for Ed. "These are the ones I found too. Not saying there might be more on the pages I didn't look at, but..."

They all looked at her notes:

cebf, zrzo, borq, fbyq, fnpe

The three stared at the strings of letters, perplexed.

"Beats the hell outa me," Ben said. "Each one's four letters, but ain't no sense to 'em. They ain't words, just..."

"Strings of letters," Ed said. "But their regularity makes them codes, I'd say."

The door pushed open and Ted Coldry came in from the Angler, carrying three white plastic bags holding Styrofoam boxes. He set them down on the bed. "'Laborers are worthy of their hire,'" he quoted, looking pleased.

Ben snorted. "You slip a burger in mine?"

"Strictly Caesar, but extra anchovies, Benjamin."

"Extra tiny fish," Ben grumbled. "Can't even trust my own bartender."

Ted peered at the papers scattered on the makeshift table. "We're having a meeting in the sick bay?"

"'*We*' ain't havin' nothin', Theodore. Decoding some evidence, you gossip. Get your buns out of here—unless you get me a burger and fries."

"My deepest condolences, Benjamin." He twirled Andi's scribbled note around so he could see, and looked at the strings of letters.

Ben growled. "You never saw that, Ted. Official business."

Ted shrugged. "All are four letters long, which might be meaningful. Or not. Are there other strings?"

She handed him the copy of one of the pages, and he scanned the fourth column. "Look here," he pointed to a cluster in the middle of the page:

73. 071107	Gorka, Salva	cebf fbyq borq fnpe
74.071107	Jandro, Thomasa	cebf fbyq borq
75.080114	Darkins, Mena	cebf fbyq borq zrzo fnpe

"*Cebf, fbyq, borq* all appear in each entry. *Fnpe* in two, *zrzo* in just one."

Ben rustled his papers. "I got all them letters everywhere on my pages too. Real regular like."

Andi and Ed surveyed their pages and agreed. Ed said, "Looks like just the five words."

Ted scratched his head. "The pattern reminds me of something." They all waited while he closed his eyes. Then he opened them wide, smiling broadly. "I'm betting it's a reflected alphabet code."

"Ted." Andi burst out. "How do you know something like that?"

"And what in the good goddamn," Ben tossed in, "is a reflected alphabet code?"

Ted blushed. "I studied cryptology in college. Neal Stephenson's *Cryptonomicon* turned me on to decryption. Ever read it?"

Ed grinned. "Loved that book. What did you think about—"

Ben shot his hand up. "Hey! We ain't got us no book club meetin' here. Get back to the codes."

Ted saluted. "Yes, sir. So, a reflected alphabet code is a simple, primitive way of coding. You write the first half of the alphabet on one line, then—"

Ben interrupted. "Show, don't tell."

"Got it." Ted took a copied page, turned it over to the blank side, and wrote. "Top line, first half, like so:"

A B C D E F G H I J K L M
N O P Q R S T U V W X Y Z

"Then on the bottom line, the second half: The first half reflects the second half."

"That ain't helpin' us."

Ted ignored him. "What's the first word of those code words?"

Andi read "C-E-B-F."

"Perfect. P reflects C, R reflects E, O reflects B, and S reflects F. Now we have a new line of letters: *Pros*."

"Like I said," Ben grumped, "how the hell's that helpin'?"

Andi had been working out the other strings of letters. She held up her page. "The other words are *memb, obed, sold,* and *sacr.*"

Ben was looking downright cranky. "Still don't see—"

"Benjamin," Ted offered, "now we have actual words, or rather, abbreviations of actual words. Give me a moment, please." It didn't take that long. "All right. All of these are four letters long, which might be meaningful. I would guess that *memb* means *member* or *membrane*. The second one has to be *obedient* or *obedience*. Number three looks like *sold*, but there are other words that start with s-o-l-d, like *soldier*, or *solder*."

Andi said, "We're dealing with a cult, so *member* makes sense. *Obedient* does too. And *sold* would fit with sex trafficking."

Ed added, "So might *soldier.*"

Ted blanched. "A cult? You're kidding, right?" He looked around. No one answered. "You're not kidding."

Andi had never seen Ted so pale. "We can't tell you much, Ted. This is a murder investigation. We're letting you in more than we should."

Ted recovered, put a finger to his lips. "Very hush-hush. My lips are, proverbially, sealed."

Ben snorted. "And your ass will be proverbially grass if they ain't."

Ted lifted the back of his hand to his forehead. "Benjamin! As if I could even contemplate betraying confidential information. I am a *bartender*!"

Andi brought them back. "Okay, let's say we have *member* and *obedient* and *sold* or *soldier*. But *pros* and *sacr* are stumpers."

Ted looked back at the page, bent over, touching it lightly with his fingertips. After a moment, he straightened, his face stricken.

"What's wrong?"

"This is a sex trafficking cult?"

Andi nodded. "We're thinking so."

Ted whispered, "What if *sacr* means *sacrifice*?"

"Sweet Jesus," said Ben.

Ben's phone interrupted the tense silence. "Speak," he said. He jotted notes on the back of a page. "Okay. Write 'er up and lock up the evidence and note the chain of custody. Nice work." He closed his phone and looked up. "Lannie checked one hundred forty names, twenty from each book. Ain't a single one ever existed in our county, except two, Anna Alter and Paloma Martinez." He consulted his notes. "The names were numbers 2915 and 4770, dated 1928 and 1935, respectively. The names turn up in the valley, but now, not in 1928 and 1935. They're two kids, the Alter girl a five-year-old belonging to one of the cowboys on Mack Anderssen's ranch; and the other one, Martinez, is a town girl, a senior in the high school."

Andi asked, "So they weren't alive in 1928 and 1935."

"What Lannie said," Ben grumped.

"So none of the hundred forty names Lannie checked were born, died, or paid taxes here?"

"Looks to me."

Ed asked, "You don't suppose all ten thousand names are like this?"

Ben scowled. "Lannie's gonna hate *this* assignment."

Andi had been staring at the pages of codes. "Wait." The others looked at her. "We're assuming the names are accurate. What if they're not?"

Ed looked pained. "Pseudonyms?"

"Yes, or codes again."

"That's a hell of a lot of names to make up," Ben said.

Ed said, "Or a hell of a lot of codes to decipher."

"True," Andi said. "If you had to do it all at one time. But they didn't. They did a few one week, then a few more weeks or months later. If these are pseudonyms or codes, Lannie won't find a single one, except by coincidence."

Ted shook his head. "These aren't code names. If they coded rough abbreviations for the actual words, I doubt they'd use true codes that look like names. And even if they did, we'd see loads of repetition." He looked thoughtful for a moment. "And if they were content to use the reflected alphabet code, why use a different one for the names?"

Ed said, "There's no way to know for sure without going through every name to be sure none are repeated." He pointed at the stack of pages. "Andi, how many pages did you copy?"

"Twenty from each ledger. One hundred forty."

"And you have how many pages total? About three-fifty or so?"

"Didn't count, but that's probably close."

Ed closed his eyes a moment. "Okay, one-forty's about forty percent of three-fifty. That's a strong sample size. I think we can make a good judgment from these. Let's look for repetitions."

They divided the pile in four and started reading.

After ten minutes, Ed put his pile down. "No repetitions. And all mine are women's names."

A couple minutes later, all four agreed. No repetitions, all women.

Ben looked at Andi. "Your thoughts?"

"Let's have Lannie examine the missing persons records starting in 1946 and going back till they stopped being kept. He should only list the cases that aren't closed."

Ed said, "You guys have a scanner, don't you? What about having Callie scan the ledgers into the computer so Lannie can search them for any missing persons he digs up."

Ben nodded. "Good thinkin', people." He dialed Callie and dictated the instructions. When he hung up, he said, "I got me two very unhappy employees."

Ted spoke very softly. "I pray that *sacr* means something else."

Could *sacr* mean *sacrifice*? They talked about it, working their way around the ugliness of it. Not just trafficking: human sacrifice. Finally, Andi asked, "What else could *sacr* stand for?"

"Words having to do with the sacred, sacraments, that sort of word," Ed offered. "But we saw the torture instruments, the altar with something sticky on it that I'll wager is blood. It stands for *sacrifice.*"

What about the women's names *not* marked *sacr*? Why had they been recorded? And what did *pros* mean? Where did the women come from? Where did they go?

Suddenly, it exploded in Andi's mind. "These are production ledgers!"

The three men looked at her. "Meanin'?" asked Ben.

"Meaning, when our informant pointed us to the Warriors of Yahweh site—" She stopped. "Ted, you shouldn't be hearing this."

Ben looked at the bartender. "She's right, but stick around. We need every brain we can get."

Andi took a long breath. "Our informant told us that where we found these ledgers was the meeting place of a group that's involved in sex trafficking. These ledgers could be records of the women they brought through."

Ben growled. "They kept *records* of their crimes? Arrogant bastards!"

Ed shook his head. "Businessmen."

Ted asked, "Could *pros* mean *professionals*?"

Ed shook his head. "If they're traffickers, they're turning these women into prostitutes, not professionals."

No one spoke.

Finally, Andi said, "So maybe we have records of every woman who's been trafficked through that site between 1907 and 1946. Or been murdered."

Ed sighed. "People, I've got a patient to see in five minutes. This isn't going to be an easy afternoon." He left his Styrofoam box on the table, unopened.

Ben lay back against his pillows. "Maybe the records stopped in forty-six, but we got us a strange murder and a black church in the woods. So the good bet is, it's still goin' on, or at least somethin' like it is. And I ain't known a thing about what's happenin' in my own damn county." He sounded very old.

"These ledgers end in 1946," Andi said. "But our informant said they're still operating."

Ben straightened up. "Hold on. We're gettin' too hypothetical. We need a lot more than a stack of old books and some old fart who says he knows about a sex ring. 'Specially an old fart who ain't never came to us with it."

Andi nodded. "I'm going up to see our informant this afternoon." She didn't speak her thought: *If he's not in the wind.* "I'll push him hard to see if he'll point us toward the Carlton Mortuary and Crematory. After that, I want to meet the mortician, Richard E. Scopus. I *really* want to meet him."

Ben said, "Okay, people." He pointed at Ed's Styrofoam box as he sneaked his salad box under the covers. "Bring me my lunch on your way out?"

59

When Ed reached for his office door, he was surprised to find it unlocked. Usually he remembered to lock it. Even more surprising, Grace was in the waiting room, thumbing a magazine that must have been six years old.

"Hi, Northrup. Can we talk?"

"You've got a key to my office?"

"Uh-uh. It wasn't locked."

He grimaced. *Getting old, bud.* "What's on your mind?"

"My girls and me—I mean I—we're planning a college trip. We want to go October 22, 23, and 24. We're going to look at Missoula, at North Idaho College in Coeur d'Alene, and Gonzaga in Spokane. I'd like you to come with us." She lowered her head, still looking him in the eyes. "Please."

He smiled. "Taking it into your own hands. Good for you."

"Yeah, I figured if I waited for you, I'd go to college an old lady."

He chuckled. "Let me check my appointment book." He unlocked his inner office—at least *that* door was locked—and retrieved his calendar, thumbing to October. "Those dates are Wednesday, Thursday, and Friday."

"Yeah, but they're teacher meetings and stuff. We're off school."

"Well, I have some appointments to reschedule, but hell. You're on."

Grace jumped up, rubbing her hands. "Atta boy, Northrup. Makin' it happen!"

"Your girls are coming with us?"

"Yes. Their parents too. We'll be caravanning."

"You make motel reservations?"

"I thought I'd be nice and leave that for you, so you'd feel invested in the trip." She offered her sweetest smile.

"Ah. And I've got the credit card."

60

Andi couldn't shake the dread that had settled on her after they'd deciphered the abbreviations. Pete hadn't wanted her to drive alone to Wallace's Corner, and her own unsettled mood seconded his. But she talked him into it—no one else was free to go with her. As she drove up to Wallace's Corner, none of the forest's power nor the beauty of the day soothed her. She pulled off the highway where a small dry creek passed under the road. Dust on the rocks reminded her of ashes, of the fire scene. She scrambled down to the creek, sat on a larger rock, trying to feel a calm she couldn't quite reach. Overhead, the hard blue sky seemed blank. The words, *prostitute, member, obedient, sold* plagued her. And worst: *sacrificed.*

This isn't helping, she decided. She climbed back to the road and got in the SUV.

Wallace's Corner, as she and Pete had feared, was deserted. The house and barn were locked, but the garage stood open, and Delbo's ancient pickup was gone. She parked, went up to the door of the larger house, and pounded on it. After a couple of minutes, she went around to the back and repeated the pounding. She stood back and called out, "Mr. Delbo! Mr. Delbo!"

Answered by silence, she muttered, "Damn."

Same result in the shop/dormitory.

She leaned against her vehicle, thinking about how Ordrew would laugh. Another mistake, a big one this time. They should have taken Delbo in Tuesday, or stopped yesterday when they were up here. This was bad. Real bad.

She climbed back into the SUV. "On to the Carlton Mortuary and Mr. Richard Scopus," she said aloud. It didn't diminish her sense of futility.

She was halfway through dialing Ben's hospital room, when she hung up and called Pete instead. To Andi, Ben was still sheriff, but Pete was Acting. *Chain of command matters*. She gave a grim smile: Ordrew would like that.

When Pete picked up, she told him about Delbo vanishing and her plan to go on to Carlton to find Richard Scopus.

"No!" Pete nearly shouted into the phone. "We're talking killers here. You just wait till I get somebody up there."

"Don't worry, Pete. I can handle it."

"No. You wait."

"They may have already learned we were at their site. We could lose valuable time waiting around. Even an hour could make a difference." She didn't add her worry: that Cassius Delbo had betrayed them, had alerted the Warriors of Yahweh to close up shop. Or worse, that he was the bishop.

Pete paused a moment. "Well, go then. But I'm calling Harley Vogel to let him know you're coming down."

Mike immediately popped into her mind; having him with her would be good. "Ask him to have Mike Payne meet me, would you?"

"On it."

She smiled at the thought of seeing Mike again.

"Just be real careful up there, Andi."

"Will do." Andi knew Pete was worried about her getting shot again. She knew this because she was, too.

61

Richard Scopus greeted Andi in the homey waiting area of the Carlton Mortuary, his voice warm, even, and reassuringly calm, nicely tailored to the pastel colors of the walls and dark wood trim of the room. *Exactly the voice an undertaker needs,* she thought. At his invitation, she followed him into an office off the central hall. An entirely ordinary man: average height and size, maybe fifty, nothing about him unusual or memorable—except perhaps his clear, direct, gray eyes. Despite his calm and warmth, his eyes made her think of a wolf. He wore a conservative gray suit, white shirt, and restrained tie.

Scopus offered her a chair, holding it for her as she sat then seating himself behind his desk. "What can I do for you, Deputy?"

"I'm following up on a possible missing person case, sir. Doctor Ed Northrup, over in Jefferson, has a patient who seems to have disappeared—"

Scopus interrupted smoothly. "Please, call me Rick. And I know Doctor Northrup by reputation. A good man." His smile was kind.

Andi returned the smile. "Thanks, Rick. And please call me Andi. Anyway, we're worried about this woman. She's disappeared and we thought we should check in with her boyfriend, Guy Flandreau, but it turns out he's gone too and nobody knows his whereabouts. We are told he works for you, so I thought I'd drive over to see if he's here—

or if you can help me contact him."

There was knock at the office door. Mike stuck his head in. "Harley sent me over, Andi. Hi, Mister Scopus. Mind if I join you two?"

Rick smiled warmly, a look as well suited to his profession as his placid voice. "Not at all, Deputy." He stood. "I'm afraid I've forgotten your name." He extended his hand.

Mike shook it, said, "Mike, sir. Mike Payne. I've been helping Andi on a case."

"Ah. Is the case related to Guy's girlfriend?" he asked her.

She nodded, uncomfortable. She remembered the business card, and hoped Rick didn't know the real nature of the case Mike and she were working.

Rick was apologetic. "I'm afraid you came in vain, Andi. Guy left town a few days ago; something about his mother falling ill in Los Angeles. He said he'd let me know when he was going to return, but I doubt he will. I've already hired someone to take his place."

Damn. "What tells you he won't come back, Mr. Scop—, uh, Rick?"

He must have missed the question. "Is it standard procedure for a psychologist to notify the sheriff when a patient fails an appointment?"

Andi considered how to answer that. She'd said Beatrice John had disappeared, not failed an appointment. Other than that, though, Scopus hadn't given her any reason to distrust him. *The business card,* she thought, but that was thin. Anyone could have dropped the card into the ledger. She decided on candor. "Well, you're right, this is more than a failed appointment." She glanced at Mike, who smiled back. "We're investigating what might have been a murder, and we have reason to think that Guy's girlfriend might have information about it."

She watched him carefully, but detected nothing other than an understandable flicker at the word *murder*. His smile suggested concern. "You used an odd phrase, 'might have been a murder.' You're not certain?"

She shook her head. "Technically, we're not sure until we can learn more. That's why finding Ms. John is so important."

Scopus sighed, looking crestfallen. "I'm afraid I'm of no use to you then. I wouldn't know Guy's girlfriend if I tripped over her."

62

Scopus accompanied the two deputies out. He watched Mike cross the street and get in his squad, then walked beside the woman deputy to the Adams County SUV and opened the door for her. After she climbed inside, he patted the window as if it were her arm. When she drove off, he waved goodbye, kindly. He stood on the sidewalk watching the vehicle turn the corner. Then he went inside, locked the mortuary door, hung the "will return at" sign, and opened the door at the end of the hall. He went down the stairs to the lower level. There were two doors, one on either side of the lower hall. Outside the door on the right, on which the word "Crematory" had been stenciled, a man sat in a wooden chair, tilted back against the wall, reading.

"Bishop?" the man said, jumping to his feet as Scopus approached.

"Unlock it, Guy."

Guy Flandreau unlocked the door. Scopus said, "Leave us," and when Guy stepped out, Scopus locked the door from the inside and switched on the lights—sconces on each of the walls—that barely cut the dimness. A single lamp, unlit, hung above a metal table, its foot hinged to a large steel chamber with a glass door: the crematory. Beatrice John lay on the table, inert, naked. Her head was against the crematory door. Dead eyes, open, stared sightless into the unlit lamp above the table.

Scopus leaned over the body. "Protector, come forward."

For a moment, her body lay motionless, then her eyes slowly closed. Scopus repeated, "Protector," and started tapping her forehead lightly. "Protector, come forward now, as I count back from ten." He counted, pausing five seconds between each number. "Ten...nine...eight..." Her eyes began flickering behind their lids, slowly, then faster. He reached one. The eyes opened.

His face was professional, neutral. "Sit up, please."

Despite her large size, Protector rose to a seated position effortlessly, with a dancer's grace, as if lifted by strings. Her head turned to face him, but she made no eye contact.

He said, "Stand before me."

She slid off the table with the same fluid grace, as though lifted. Again, she made no eye contact. She was six inches taller than Scopus.

"Look at me."

Her gaze lowered to meet his eyes. "You called for me." Her throat sounded dry.

Scopus led her to a steel chair. "Sit, Protector. I have something to ask of you."

The woman lowered herself onto the chair. She seemed unaware of her nakedness. "Yes, sir?"

"Protector, I want you to summon the Child, but do not let her come forward. Please remain in control."

The woman looked at him for a moment, then closed her eyes. Her face slackened and her breathing slowed. After a few moments, she revived, though she did not open her eyes. She spoke softly. "We are here."

"Thank you, Protector. I will ask you a question for the Child, and I want to know her answer, in her exact words. Do not allow her to come forward, just relay her answer precisely as she gives it. Remind her what will happen if she disobeys me. Or if you do."

A brief spasm of alarm passed over her face, then she calmed.

He ignored her fear. "Here is my question: Did the Child tell the psychologist anything? If so, I want her exact words, please."

Protector stilled, her head tilted slightly, as though listening inwardly. Then she opened her eyes. "She told him, 'Bishop burned the lady in the fire.'" Protector looked calm, but her eyes flicked briefly to Scopus's face, then away.

Scopus frowned. "Another question, please. Did the psychologist tell the female deputy?"

This time, when her eyes closed, she appeared confused. Protector returned. "She doesn't know a female deputy, or the answer to your question. She asked you not to be angry."

"Is she telling the truth?"

Protector looked thoughtful. "I believe so, Bishop. Yes."

Scopus turned and paced across the room, then returned. For a moment, he stood silently above her. He slapped her face, once with each hand, two quick blows. Protector's eyes flared, but she remained still, alert, immobile.

His voice was sharp. "Protector, I am displeased with the Child and also with you."

Protector, alarmed, started, "Sir, I—"

"Silence!" he snarled. Protector's head snapped erect, her mouth tight. "The Child is a child, but your charge is to protect her. You should never have allowed her to speak to the psychologist in the first place." He went to the door, turned back to face her. "I cannot allow you to be free. You will remain here until I decide your punishment."

Protector closed her eyes.

"I will not punish you now, however. You will be comfortable." He pointed to the metal table. "Resume your place."

She moved to the table, again gracefully, as though floating in another atmosphere, and lay on it. Scopus ordered, "Focus on the lamp." Protector looked at the dark glass of the unlit lamp above her. Scopus began humming a quiet wordless tune: five notes, three rising then two descending. With the first ascending notes, Protector's eyes and the muscles of her face softened. With the first descent, her lids slid lower. The tune ascended again, the same three notes, and her eyes began to fade, the half-gaze locked on the lamp. On the second descent, her lids closed fully. On the third ascent, her breathing slowed. On the third descent, it almost stopped.

The humming stopped.

Scopus spoke, his voice clear, slow, monotonic. "Protector will lead the Child to the deep place...the deep place...the place of no light...no pain...no thought...no pain...no feeling...no pain." He continued like this for a couple of minutes, finishing with "Be in the deep place...no hearing...no sight...no smell, no touch, no warmth, no cold, no color...both, Protector, the Child, in the deep place." He paused for five beats, watching. The body lay absolutely still. She hardly breathed.

Scopus finished. To test his work, he took a stitching needle from its case and pierced one nipple. No response. He pulled an alcohol swab from a cabinet, cleaned the needle, and replaced it in its case. He unlocked the door and went out into the hall. Guy stood up. "I am finished. After you lock the door properly, see me in my office."

Guy bowed slightly. "Bishop."

PART THREE

SATURDAY

63

It was the earliest Homecoming game anyone could remember—only two weeks into the school year. August heat and forest fire smoke had cancelled pre-season practice, so nobody was particularly surprised that the Jefferson Grizzlies were trounced by the Sentinel Spartans. After the game, Ed drove Grace back to their cabin to get ready for the Homecoming parade and dance. His new pickup had been recruited as one of the royalty floats in the parade, so while Grace showered and started her prep, he washed the truck and waxed it to a shine. Then he draped the decorations the girls had made over the sides of the truck and lashed them down.

Andi arrived around 4:30, in uniform, and kissed him lightly.

"Love a girl in uniform," he said. "Grace'll be a half-hour. How about—"

"Whoa, cowboy," she said. "Let's keep it on the Homecoming thing." As they went inside, she turned. "Do you ever *not* think about sex?"

"Not around you. You're a testosterone pump."

"Must be a burden."

He started to sing, *"She ain't heavy, she's my lover."*

"My God, you're ill."

He laughed. "By the way, I had my Preventive Biology Talk with Grace. She reminded me it was the third time. Oh, and I gave her a condom."

"Just one?"

"Damn." He felt his face redden.

"Yeah. Even you can do it twice or three times, and you're sixty."

"Huh. Still fifty-nine for a month. Wait a minute." He went into the bathroom, returned, handed her a box. "Give these to her?"

"How'd she handle you giving her the condom?"

"Moral outrage," he chuckled. "'Northrup! How can you even *suspect* me and Zach of doing it?'"

"But she took it, right?"

Ed sighed and nodded. "Geez. I'm not ready for this."

Andi had patted his shoulder and shook the box. "Don't worry, Dad. She'll have as many condoms as she'll need."

She knocked on Grace's door. When Grace opened it, Andi went in and firmly closed the door to Ed. Over her shoulder, she said, "No boys allowed!"

Ed enjoyed hearing their giggling and their happy voices, though he couldn't make out the words. No doubt, they were talking about the dance and the after-party. And the condoms.

Zach showed up with the corsage at five on the dot, trussed into his tux—a 230-pound penguin. Andi came out of Grace's room, enjoying Zach's handsome awkwardness as he shook hands with Ed, as if they were meeting for the first time. While the guys talked, Andi poked her head into Grace's room. "Zach's here."

Grace gulped. "How do I look?"

Although there was no need for it—Grace was stunning, she thought—she said, "Turn around once, slow."

Grace did, and Andi smiled. "You look perfect, girl. You'll drive Zach nuts. Wait a minute or two after I leave, then make your entrance. Walk slow."

Grace nodded, looking embarrassed. Andi went out first and told Zach, "Grace'll be out in a minute." Zach was gulping too, and had a bead of sweat on his lip. Andi loved it.

Ed noticed Zach's discomfort. "Want a glass of water, Zach?"

"No thanks, sir. Just a little warm in here, and I—"

Grace's door opened. She stepped out, looking down, shy; she demurely lifted her eyes to her beau. Andi watched a look of pure adoration sweep over Zach's face. And like doting fathers throughout time, Ed grinned at her. She felt a flush, of pleasure this time, not heat.

Ed, camera ready, started shooting.

Zach, this year's Homecoming King, carried the Queen's tiara in a purple Crown Royal bag and Grace's corsage in a white box. After some awkwardness juggling the tiara bag and the flower box, Andi saved him by taking the bag so he could get at the corsage. When he approached Grace, the corsage in one extended hand and the pin pointing at her like a sword, Andi almost laughed aloud at his look of fierce concentration. He bit his lower lip as he struggled to pin the flower on Grace's dress without touching her breast. When the first line of sweat edged his brow, he gave up and handed the flower to Andi, his face blazing red.

Grace, grinning, said to him, "Chicken."

64

Ed moved his sparkling blue pickup into the line for the Homecoming parade, right ahead of Bud Groh's shiny red Ford F-250, which would carry the Royal Court—the princesses and princes. Queen Grace and King Zach would ride in Ed's spiffy new Dodge Ram. Soon, the royal party would be coming out of the Angler and mounting their "floats" (Ed had laughed when Dick Harper, the social studies teacher and parade manager, had called the pickups "floats"), which were parked and waiting on Division Street in front of the restaurant. The band—if one could call five drums, a trombone, a trumpet, a guitar, and six baton twirlers a band—was collected, giggling and horsing around, ahead of the floats. Ed got out of his truck and pulled a three-foot stepladder from behind the seat and set it up for the Royal Couple to climb aboard. *To mount their float,* he corrected himself.

Ed had fussed with pride when Grace announced she'd been elected Homecoming Queen. But she'd shaken her head. "Northrup, think about it. Our senior class has nine girls: Jen, Dana, me, Cara Olson, and five girls in the band. I only won by one vote."

"Well, I'm still proud of you."

Grace had grinned. "You're easily emprided, Northrup."

Ed looked at his watch. Six-forty-five. He paced around the truck, checking the tires, the handholds. Carrying the kids in his truck violated one of his oldest rules: nobody stands up in the bed of a moving pickup. Years ago, the woodshop class had built handholds for the bed of any pickup truck. Ed climbed up and put his weight against the structure, wrestling to dislodge it. When it failed to collapse, he sighed. *Guess it'll hold.*

Just then, the swarm of prom-attired royalty boiled out of the Angler and into the street, with billows of excited chatter, mostly girls' voices and squeals of laughter. The boys, having not yet loosened their ties (although some shirts were hanging partway out already), walked with studied dignity, their rented suits and ties requiring a certain coolness, a looking-away over the heads of the giggling girls. Zach, as king, limped—he'd had a tough game—in the lead, glancing adoringly now and then at Grace, whose smile made Ed's heart beat faster. *Easily emprided, be damned.*

The princesses—Jen, Dana, and Cara—and their princes approached Bud Groh's truck, parked behind Ed's. Bud's wife, Lorna, would drive, because Bud was out in the street interviewing people for the Monastery Valley Radio station he owned. Ed double-checked the stepladder placed behind his tailgate for Zach and Grace to use to get aboard. When they arrived, Ed offered his hand to Grace, but she smiled and turned to Zach, taking his hand, mounting the ladder queen-like. Ed offered his hand to Zach, but Zach gave a brisk, single head shake, and mounted proudly.

Once in their places, Grace kept turning around to wave to her princesses behind. The giggles and chatter among Jen, Dana, and Cara carried up to Ed, who was stowing the stepladder and putting up the tailgate. Zach stood very still, hand on the hand-hold, attempting nobility beside his queen. Grace turned often, smiling at him. Ed climbed into the cab and started the engine. Dick Harper stood on his ladder in the front and yelled instructions through his bullhorn, then dismounted, moved the ladder aside, and blew his air horn to signal the start.

Ed leaned out his window. "Grab your hand-holds, kids!"

"Northrup," Grace shouted back. "We have to wave. We're royalty!"

He grunted and leaned his head back in the cab. "Schmoyalty." Just then the last of the band's three lines began to march, and he stiffened, envisioning his foot slipping on the gas and the truck mowing down the band, spraying royalty all over the street. He gingerly shifted into *Drive*, softly pedaled the accelerator.

There was no mowing. No spraying.

Stationed five blocks down Division Street, Andi heard the air horn and watched the parade begin to move slowly toward her. The spunky little band was belting out the school song; she watched their legs moving in unison as they marched toward her. Ed had looked so happy earlier, watching Grace and Zach, taking pictures of the kids, and of her with the kids, and remote pictures of all four of them. A family moment. She'd found herself loving it, and she wondered if it were her future. It would be the closest she'd come to family since her father died. She sighed. Even if she didn't marry Ed, there wasn't anybody else she'd want to make a family with.

Without warning, she was engulfed in heat. She took off her hat, trying not to fan herself. She looked around; no one was looking at her, so she loosened the top button of her uniform shirt. She felt cornered, much more afraid than usual. She looked around again, suddenly alert: was she picking up some threat in the crowd? Everyone seemed excited, waving, smiling. No one looked suspicious.

No. It's what I thought before: Menopause means cancer, and cancer means I die. She tried to settle herself.

The band was reaching her. *Focus*. She shook herself, took in long deep breaths, put her hat back on. She focused on the one of the drummers, in the third row, a slight girl carrying a big bass drum, looking very red in the face. The sun was nearly down and the air was deliciously cool, but she looked heat-struck. Andi called out to her.

"You feeling all right?"

The girl looked over and grinned, a wide white look of delight. "Awesome! I get so excited when I drum!"

By mid-parade, four blocks along Division Street, Ed was thoroughly enjoying himself. Cheering people crowding the sidewalks waved, called his name, and Grace behind him was in a frenzy of waving and blowing kisses. He glanced back: she and Zach were leaning on the hand-holds, perfectly stable. He resumed his grin.

With about a block to go, he spotted Andi standing beside her department vehicle parked halfway onto the sidewalk, light bar flashing—because Ben liked the look of the flashing lights. Andi was saying something to one of the drummers. He gave a friendly toot of his horn, and was horrified to hear its enormous blast. His old truck had had a dismal squeaker of a horn; he'd never used this new one, which could've served a tug boat in a night hurricane. Alarmed, people stopped cheering and looked toward the blare. The girl with the big drum stumbled at the blast, but quickly regained her footing, still drumming away. When she'd staggered, Andi had frowned and moved toward the girl, then glanced his way and shook her head. Ed thought she looked shaken.

But as he rolled past her, she shouted through the window, "Nice horn!"

As Ed's truck passed slowly by, Andi watched Grace waving to the crowd. At the cabin helping Grace, she'd caught herself thinking more than once how young and vibrant Grace had looked, her whole future an open book, her skin so smooth and glowing. The girl's young breasts were taut and pert, and Andi wondered how Ed could find her own, still nice but losing to gravity, so enticing. Now, as Grace moved by on the truck, she looked even lovelier, happily waving to the crowd. "A beautiful young woman," Andi whispered to herself. Watching Grace beside her king, she realized she was experiencing a delicious new desire: She wanted to share Grace's growing into her womanhood.

Grace squealed. "Andi! Andi!" Andi waved back, smiling. Accepting Ed's proposal would bring the unexpected satisfaction of being in Grace's life as she grew up. But...She forced herself to stop daydreaming, to focus on her job: the parade, everyone's safety. Thank God, the hot flash had faded, and with it the anxiety. Her new insight—menopause equals death—seemed to have stopped them both.

She watched the various school clubs and their banners march slowly by. There were only a few members from each club—the rest had gone to the gym early to claim the good tables. Finally, in the rear—the second place of honor, after the floats of the Royal Court—came the football team, most looking worn but happy despite their loss, strolling with their dates. Those few boys who had somber faces were being especially attended to by devoted girlfriends, working vigorously to drag out a smile. Andi chuckled to herself. Unhappy boyfriends mean dull dances.

And then they arrived.

Ed edged the truck into the high school lot and up to the door of the gym. Quickly, two teachers dragged a set of steps behind the truck, then a cute arbor arching over it, and opened the tailgate. The couples and the parents who'd arrived early formed an Aisle of Honor for the Queen and her court to proceed solemnly into the gym, amid cheers and whistles. As the court climbed out, Ed stood beside the tailgate, holding out his hand, but neither the queen nor her king took it. As she stepped down, Grace had turned to him, her eyes gleaming, and said, "Northrup, that was the most fun thing that ever happened to me."

He leaned across and gave her a quick kiss.

"Northrup!" she objected, but her smile never dimmed.

When the parade had passed her by, Andi climbed in her squad car and inched along behind the last football couple, the light bar flashing celebratory blue on their backs. She parked at the edge of the parking lot and made her way toward Ed at the Aisle of Honor. Ed kissed her.

She said, "Your daughter's lovely."

He nodded, and reached his arm around her waist.

She briefly nestled against him, then gently removed his arm. "No on-duty fraternizing with the public."

Ed whispered, "So when are you off-duty?"

"Eleven."

"Can I interest you in fraternizing later? Perhaps over a glass of wine? At my abode?"

Andi said nothing for a moment. She felt his arm tense. "Sure. I'll change into civvies and be over about, say, ten-thirty."

"Perfect." More tentatively this time, Ed squeezed her waist. "Don't wear too many civvies."

65

When he saw Andi's headlights coming up the long curving driveway, Ed poured two glasses of Pinot Noir. When she came in the door, he eyed her civvies. Tight workout pants, a tunic to mid-thigh, Keens.

"Sexy," he said, as they embraced.

"Comfy," she said back.

On the porch, they chatted about the dance and the kids for a while. The night air was September soft, warm with a hint of October. In the woods behind the cabin, an owl made night sounds. Andi said, "So...about our deal."

"Our deal?"

"That I keep you in the loop about what I learn in this space-time program."

"Ah. That deal."

"I realized something at the parade."

"Yeah?"

"I found myself looking forward to being with Grace as she grows up. I think I love her."

"You think?" Ed chuckled. He was silent a moment. "So?"

"So, what?"

"So, what stands in the way of you being with Grace as long as you want?"

She looked at him a long time. "Nothing. Unless you—"

"Unless I pressure you to get married." He decided to say his annoyance. "Come on, Andi, I'm not doing that."

She looked out at the impenetrable night. Beyond the yard light, the lights of the town below them seemed infinitely far. She turned back to Ed. "I love you, Ed. I'm just not ready yet. Something's left to figure out."

"Menopause causes cancer, and cancer means you die, right? Something's left?"

She shook her head. "Something else, something bigger." She sipped the wine. "I'll get it."

He chuckled. "Sooner or later," he said.

"Yeah. Sooner or later. Anyway, like I've said, I like what we've got. You, me, Grace. Four, five nights together, a couple nights at my own place."

"You like the independence?" He remembered her first marriage had failed, only a few months old.

"No, not exactly."

Ed waited; she seemed to be struggling. He realized, with almost a shock, how hard this was for her.

"Well, independence is part of it. It's more...I can't find words for it." She took a moment. "Not just independence, it's like, ah, this thing we've got, this sort-of family—I *like* the way we are."

"Together and apart." He could see that.

"Yeah, a bit of each. Being with you guys is great, and so is having my own place. I don't know, it's like insurance."

"Insurance? In case something goes wrong?" *Guess I get that too,* he thought. He'd seen plenty of couples over the years. No relationship's immune to trouble.

"I guess. Yeah, it's a comfort knowing if I, uh, had to, I've got a place to go."

"Huh." He took a moment to choose his words. "Well, sounds like you know your mind."

Surprising him, Andi's eyes filled with tears. She wiped them quickly.

"What's wrong?" he asked.

"Nothing." She sounded shaky. "I guess I'm just glad to get that off my chest."

Ed smiled. He laid his hand tenderly on her breast. "Anything else you'd like to get off your chest?"

She looked mock-sternly at his hand. "Yeah, big guy."

SUNDAY

66

Ed awoke just before eight. Warm early-morning light flowed through the big window; across the valley, the crests of the western peaks gleamed rose and gold in the new sunlight. Andi for a moment rubbed herself against him, and he wondered if she was in the mood again—last night, after wine and their talk, their love-making had been very sweet—but her soft rhythmic breathing told him she was still asleep.

For a couple of minutes, Ed looked out at the sky, then he got up to start the coffee. While it brewed, he went out onto the porch and let the cool autumn air breathe around him. The pines stirred in the gentle breeze. He was a bit surprised at how quickly he'd accepted Andi's desire for keeping her own place, had let go his urge to be married. But he had.

The coffee was ready indoors. No sign of Grace and Zach, he thought. The PV sat in the yard beside his pickup. He doubted they'd be back much before ten.

Andi slept all morning. He knew she had a lot on her mind, and he was glad she could sleep. When they'd talked about why he was being so pushy, he gave the truest answer he could. He understood it better now. Sure, fighting for something he wanted—and he had hardly known how much he wanted to marry her—was new to him and being clumsy at it seemed natural. But putting others first was its own manner of control, wasn't it? Always working toward their goals, not his own, was good medicine and good psychology, but controlling as hell in a personal relationship. He was realizing, as he sipped his coffee and watched the dawn-lit mountaintops, how he'd kept himself safe by being kind and compassionate and affirming. Only real jerks attack a nice guy.

Ed sighed. *Busted. I'm as controlling as Andi, just in my own way. Instead of fighting, she withdraws and I offer support.* Well, maybe that's changing for both of us.

He took his coffee inside and quietly did the dishes and tidied the cabin.

At ten-thirty, he called Grace's cell. It rolled to voice mail. He said, "Hey, Grace, give me a call. It's ten-thirty." At ten-forty-five, when it again went to voice mail, he hung up and dialed Jen's parents' home phone. It too went to voice mail. "Hi. Sorry, you've reached the Fortins' phone, but we're out of town this weekend, so leave a message and we'll get back to you Monday."

He almost dropped the phone: Grace had lied.

Will her parents be home? He'd asked.

She'd answered, *So the answer is yes, they'll be home, not that it matters.*

But they weren't home. And it mattered. He cursed himself. *I should've called Sam Fortin myself.*

Doubtless, Jen's folks believed Jen was someplace else—or hadn't suspected there'd be a party at all. He felt a gust of anger: why would they leave on goddamn Homecoming weekend? They were begging for trouble. Grace and Zach may have—

Whatever they did, why wasn't she home? And whatever she'd done, why hadn't he been more skeptical?

He went and gently shook Andi awake. She looked bleary. "Oh, man, too much *vino-y-sexo* last night."

He said, "Grace isn't home. Jen's family is out of town for the weekend."

She groaned. "Did you call Dana's mom, Kristie? She usually knows what's up with that bunch."

"Right." He dialed while Andi dressed.

When she came out of the bedroom, she looked like another hour in bed wouldn't have hurt. "What's the word?"

He kept his voice level, though his anger, he knew, showed. "Dana's date dropped her off sometime around three in the morning. Kristie woke Dana up and she said that Grace, Zach, and Jen and her date went to a motel in Missoula."

"My God! Three drunken hours one-way. Give me the phone." Andi dialed the department and spoke to the weekend dispatcher. As she listened, her face registered relief. "There were no accidents or incidents in the valley last night or this morning," she told Ed. "Marla's calling Missoula County to see what they've got."

About ten minutes passed before the phone rang. Ed snatched it, then handed it to Andi. She listened, thanked Marla, and hung up. "Quite a few accidents up there, mostly drunks, but no teenagers, thank God."

Ed called Zach's parents. He wasn't home either. They thought he was staying the night with another boy in his class. Ed called that family. Zach had not stayed there.

67

Shortly before noon, Zach's pickup pulled into the yard and Grace climbed out, wearing the after-party clothes she'd taken when she left in her Homecoming dress, which hung crumbled over her arm. Glassy eyes, pale face, mussed hair.

Andi kept her smile to herself. *Doesn't look so young and fresh this morning.*

Ed beckoned to Zach. "Come in, man."

Zach rolled down the window and yelled, "I gotta get home, Doctor N. My folks thought I'd be home sooner than this. I'll see you later." He backed around and drove down the drive. Fast.

Ed let Grace in, then closed the door.

"I gotta sleep, Northrup. I'm sick."

"I imagine you are. We call it a hangover. You're late too."

"I just wanted to hang with my girls over at Jen's. We had a good time. I'm going to bed."

Andi watched silently. How was Ed was going to handle the lie?

Ed said, "You weren't at Jen's. You and Zach and Jen and her date went to a motel in Missoula. We talked to Dana's mom. Jen's parents are out of town for the weekend."

His voice was pitched low, sounding softer than Andi expected. She suspected he was forcing himself to stay calm.

Grace looked at Andi, her glance a message: *Help.* Turning back to Ed, she apologized. "I'm sorry, Northrup. I blew it, I know that. Can I sleep for a while?"

Ed took in a long, quivering breath. Andi knew he was torn. Then he nodded. "Go to bed, Grace." Another long breath. "Sleep it off. We'll talk when you get up."

Andi laid her hand gently on Ed's arm, felt his tension.

Grace closed her bedroom door. They heard her sobbing for a short time, and then they heard nothing.

68

Grace slept, or at least stayed quiet in her room, until dinner. Andi left about noon to do laundry and get ready for the week. After she drove away, Ed had pulled out his fly rod and practice-cast in the yard. Midafternoon, he drove into town for dinner groceries. On the way, despite his disappointment at Grace's lie, he realized that he felt a touch of pleasure that his teenage daughter was acting like, well, a teenage daughter. And that he was reacting like, well, the father of a teenage daughter.

When he got home, Andi had returned. He prepped the steaks for grilling; she tossed a salad. He slid *au gratin* potatoes into the oven, calculating the time. "I'll throw the steaks on in about an hour and a quarter. Want a glass of wine? Grace won't be coming out of her den till we call her."

On the porch, Andi asked, "How're you going to handle this?"

"With your help, I hope," he answered. "She's doing something most kids do sooner or later. Still, her lying bothers me."

Andi nodded. "She's seventeen. You know how that was: You've got the itch to try everything, but not the courage to ask your parents' advice about getting drunk and having sex."

"When you put it that way..." He chuckled.

When it was time to grill the steaks, Ed knocked on Grace's door and told her dinner would be in twenty minutes.

Grace emerged onto the porch in fifteen minutes, looking rumpled, puffy, trying to show both contrition and defiance. Ed concealed a smile at the remnants of her obvious hangover. She hardly spoke during the meal. When they had finished, she and Andi did the dishes. Ed laid and lit a fire; he heard them talking quietly, and figured Andi was softening her up for the reckoning.

When they came into the living room, Ed began, lightly, "Well, I guess we need a talk, now that you're risen from the dead."

Grace didn't smile. "I screwed up. I don't see what there is to talk about."

Andi said, "Try this: Drinking so much when you're underage."

Grace bristled. "I didn't drink that much! This is food poisoning or something."

Ed glanced at Andi, who nodded. *Now's the moment*. He said, "Forget that, Grace. I could smell the alcohol when you came in. So let's start over. We're not going to kill you, but the truth will go a long way toward settling the whole thing."

Grace started to protest, but stopped and waved her hand, surrendering. "Whatever. I already apologized. I should've told the truth—now you'll never believe me."

"Try us." Ed noticed he'd been speaking as if he and Andi were a team. He glanced at her, caught her small nod.

Grace looked at them both a long moment, and told it all. "After we left the dance, Zach drove us to Missoula—everybody was drinking in the car. Everybody except him."

Ed sat up straighter. "Truth?"

Grace nodded. "Truth." She told them the name of the motel.

Ed knew it. *Good taste in lodging, at least.* He said, "One room or two?"

"Two. What do you think? I wouldn't sleep in the same room with Jen's boyfriend."

Andi laughed, and Grace looked surprised.

"And what did you do in *your* room?" Ed didn't want to embarrass Grace, but he did want to impress on her that truth-telling would work.

This time Grace blushed. "Can I get a little respect here?"

"Sure. Truth from you, respect from us. If you want to act like an adult, take ownership of what you do."

When Grace wasn't looking, Andi gave him a quick wink.

Grace deflated. "Zach drank three beers real fast, to catch up. We drank some more, and then we did it. Twice. It wasn't as great as everybody says it is. Zach got way drunk, and kept stopping and going into the bathroom to puke." She fell back into the couch, her look saying, *There*.

Andi said, "Romantic."

"Not so much." She looked angrily at Ed. "You satisfied now?"

"One more question. Did you—"

"Use condoms?"

He laughed aloud.

"What's, like, so funny?"

He settled himself. "I've been so anxious about when you'd start having sex, now that it's come, I'm relieved."

Andi giggled. "Nice choice of words, chief."

Grace smiled too, before Ed got it. Then, the light dawned: The word: *come*. Ed flushed.

Grace's smile faded fast and she looked drained. "Can I go back to bed?"

He nodded. "Think we can talk honestly about things?"

For a moment, Grace looked sulky, then she nodded. "I guess so. It's not so bad."

She went into her room and closed the door. Ed noticed she didn't slam it.

Andi was smiling. "She never answered your question."

"Which question?"

"About condoms."

"Damn. She didn't."

Grace's door opened and she stuck her head out. "Andi, can I talk to you?"

Andi glanced at Ed, then answered, "Sure."

He watched her go into Grace's room and close the door, relieved the confrontation had gone well, and filled with curiosity about what they were talking about in there.

In her room, the door again shut, Grace grimaced. "I gotta ask you something."

"Go for it." Andi liked the feel of the moment.

After a long hesitation, she whispered, "Is sex supposed to hurt?"

Andi was startled: This she hadn't expected. "Did it hurt?"

"Uh-huh." Grace looked ready to crawl under the bed.

Andi took a deep breath. *Above my pay grade, but what the hell.* For a second, she felt a stab of sadness she'd never had a chance to ask her mother such a question. "Well, probably every woman's different, you know?" She enjoyed Grace's wide-eyed look at the word *woman*. "For me, the first time I did it, it hurt a lot, kind of like feeling torn open."

Grace's eyes went wider. "Does it always hurt?"

Andi thought, *Whew. If she were my daughter, would I be able to have this conversation?* "No. People wouldn't do it if it always hurt. It gets easier every time, if you go slow. Eventually you'll enjoy it."

Grace nodded shyly, her eyes filling with tears. "I'm so relieved. I hated it, and I thought there was something wrong with me."

Andi sat down on the bed beside her and wrapped her in a hug. "Oh, girl. We always think that, don't we?"

MONDAY

69

The next morning, Andi drove to the department early, before Ed and Grace got up. Still night, really, only a faint brush of gray in the east. Her restlessness all night had surprised her. After the talks with Grace, about the motel and later about her first time pain, she'd felt good, appreciating how Ed handled his situation with Grace, and quietly pleased with how she'd handled hers. Her father had handled things differently when she'd stayed out all night after prom. He'd walled her off, refused to talk about it. She knew she'd blown it with him, knew he didn't trust her anymore. Her mother had died six weeks before, and now it felt like her father had died to her, too. She'd cried herself to sleep every night for a week, her grief slowly hardening into the seed of the control she ultimately resorted to whenever she felt threatened. She'd avoided him as strenuously as he'd shut her out. But he'd eventually brought it up one evening, casually. They'd talked like adults. It had saved them both. Or at least, she knew it had saved her from a loss she doubted, looking back, she would have survived.

She felt a welling of tears. She parked behind the station, letting them flow, not even caring what they were about. Today was her day off, and she'd woken feeling urgent about the case, which had waited untouched all weekend. For a while, she let herself feel the flood of grief, and relief. For her dad. For Ed. When she was calm, she wiped her face and looked at the mountains.

The sky had begun to glow a luminescent blue-gray, though the sun wouldn't be up for an hour, and the early autumn air was sweet.

Late stars dappled the dusky sky to the west. She got out of her vehicle, stood in the lot, and listened to birds singing the morning awake. She let herself relive and savor Grace's question from last evening, smiling quietly to herself. *Maybe moving from step-girlfriend to step-mom wouldn't be the end of the world.*

The unexpected beating of her heart surprised her. She took a long breath, expecting anxiety and heat. But after a moment, nothing.

Time to get to work.

Inside, she went into the evidence room, thumbed the ledger books studying the abbreviations. Nothing new revealed itself. After a few minutes, she decided to visit the church site again; her sense of urgency arose from the threat that it might be cleared, as the murder scene had been.

She called Ed, looking at the clock on the wall. *6:30.* When he answered, his breathing was ragged. "Did I catch you at an awkward moment?" she asked.

"Meaning?"

"Perhaps a conjugal visit with your hand?"

He laughed. "No, just in from my run."

"Ah. Look, did you sign those consultant papers with Pete? Are you officially on the case?"

"I did, why?"

"Can you come with me up to the cult site again? This morning?"

"Wow." He was silent a moment. "I've only got a couple patients this morning. Let me see if I can reschedule. I'll call you back in a half hour. Hey, wait. Isn't it your day off?"

Andi knew Ed disliked rescheduling his patients, and appreciated him doing it for her. "It is, but this feels urgent and there's nobody in the department who's free to go with me."

"How about your friend Mike?"

It surprised her. "Guess I didn't think of him. I'll call Carlton and see if he can do it. Don't reschedule anybody till I call you back."

She called back quickly. "It's Mike's day off. So can you do it?"

"Okay, provided my folks can reschedule. I'll call you when I know." He was back to her within ten minutes. "We're good. I'll see you in, what? An hour?"

"Make it a half-hour."

They met in the parking lot and climbed into the department SUV. Andi drove north to Highway 36, and turned toward the mountains.

"You cancelled two appointments?" she said, incredulous. "I'm impressed."

"Well, not cancelled, just rescheduled for this afternoon. But yeah, I'm trying. I told you—time to start slowing down, having more fun."

"You *are* changing. Fancy big-city drinks, rescheduling patients. What's next?" Immediately, she regretted saying that. "No, scratch that." She glanced quickly at him, then back at the highway.

He was chuckling softly. "Okay. So, what are we looking for?"

"I don't know. Something we missed the first time. I need more information and I'm running out of places to look for it." She thought of old Delbo. She suddenly felt the heat. "Ed, mind if I lower my window?"

"Not at all," he replied.

The breeze, a rustling blend of warm and cool currents, was bracing. Gold and ocher clumps of dried roadside weeds added a dusty tang to the air. Letting the cool air wash over her, she realized she wasn't anxious. Coming to the end of this crazy chain of feelings, maybe. After a few minutes, she felt better.

She looked over at Ed. "Brainstorm with me?"

Ed nodded. "Sure, go for it."

"I'm thinking Guy Flandreau's the link." She let her thoughts take shape as she worded them. "He worked at the mortuary, the mortuary card is found at the cult site, Rick Scopus says Flandreau disappeared the same time Beatrice did, after she told you that the bishop burned the lady in the fire. Flandreau's got to be the link. Could be, he's the bishop."

"There's a logic to it."

"Then there's the rose paper and the penciled message about Beatrice being taken." She paused. "He had to write it. And the paper probably came from his cabin."

"Question: The note only said, '*She* has been taken away,' so it might not mean Beatrice, right? And why announce it?"

She nodded. "Good point." She pondered it a moment. "Beatrice is the only 'she' who's disappeared, though, and whoever wrote the note left it by your door at the time of her appointment. Let's assume it refers to her. You told me the note's on the same color paper I found in Beatrice and Flandreau's cabin, and up at the church. If the note refers to her, he's the obvious suspect. Which makes me really want to look at him."

"I have another question."

Andi looked over at him. "I'm getting to it: if Flandreau took her, why would he leave a note?"

"That's not it. Look, I'm speculating here. I suspect she might have multiple personality disorder, but I've got nowhere enough diagnostic information yet to make a good diagnosis."

"What does that add?"

"If she is a multiple, it's just possible that *she*—or some part of her—left the note herself."

"Ah. One part, writing about another part, not realizing that they're *all* being abducted. But it's still a mystery how she got the note there."

He nodded. "Maybe she didn't know it was an abduction—if it was. Or maybe one part took control of the body and took another part away. Like maybe to keep me from finding out something."

"Is that possible?"

Ed nodded, but said nothing for a while. Then, "Or it could be just a pile of coincidences."

Andi shook her head, but when she glanced at him, he was looking out the side window and she realized he hadn't seen her gesture. "Cops don't believe in coincidences when the same bad guy shows up in them all."

"Shrinks don't either."

She glanced over at him again. This time, facing her, he was smiling.

The road crossed a culvert shepherding a creek under the highway, the creek she'd stopped at last week on the way to Delbo's. As they sped by, Andi glimpsed the dry water-rounded rocks. All the stream beds in these mountains were parched, the usual shallow pools nothing but stones. *Wildfire's still a threat.* A single match, a random lightning strike. Whoever had burned that site and killed that woman—she had little doubt it was the Warriors of Yahweh and that Guy Flandreau was involved, probably their bishop—had taken a horrible chance.

"The bastards could've burned down the valley. I'm pissed."

Ed looked across at her. All he said was, "They're polluting our home."

"Which is why I'm pissed."

Shortly, she spotted the narrow track leading back into the woods and the Warriors of Yahweh's site. "Here we go," she said. "If anybody asks, you sat in the car while I did all the searching." She glanced at him.

"Right." He was staring straight ahead at the narrow track.

Using the big screwdriver, Andi unfastened the hasps again. They took everything out of the sheds and meticulously examined every sheet of paper, every tool. They tapped each altar stone, listening for a hollow one. Ed even took an awl and pierced the firewood, piece by piece. After a couple dozen pieces, he wondered if he was being absurd.

They took scrapings of what appeared to be recent blood and vomit off the center post, hoping DNA tests might reveal something. Andi had brought a fingerprint dusting kit.

"You can *do* that?"

"Sure. I don't want to ask DCI to come up here again; they didn't find anything that gives us information the first time." But the kit revealed no prints on the torture tools, none on the throne, none on the altar, none even on the padlocks.

"They wear gloves, or they wipe this crap down," she muttered.

"Maybe they use the lye."

"Good catch, Doctor," she smiled.

Ed pointed at the fingerprint powder on the chair. "The powder shows—they'll know we were here."

She tensed, narrowed her eyes a moment. "Let them. Maybe one of them will do something stupid." She took one of the bullwhips from the shed and put it in an evidence bag. She—or DCI—could test it later. The Warriors of Yahweh be damned.

Next, they gridded and paced off every square yard of the tramped-down soil. They divided the surrounding forest into sectors. Andi put on a backpack and gave Ed a second one, each filled with crime scene tools. They explored each sector systematically, fifty feet back into the trees. She took the east side, and Ed worked the west. From deep in the trees she heard him call, "Andi, here!"

She pulled the crime scene tape roll out of her pack, cut off a couple feet, and tied it on a branch to mark her place. She made her way through thick undergrowth to him, forty feet into the forest behind the three tall poles. He pointed to a slightly worn track leading further into the woods. "It's probably an animal trail, but it feels more used than that. I think we should follow it."

Andi nodded. They pushed through the heavy brush, never losing the trail. After a few hundred feet, they came to another open space. A broad, low mound filled the space, nearly hidden under long dry grasses and brush.

"What the hell?" Andi said.

"It reminds me of the Indian burial mounds in the Midwest, only smaller. You have a shovel in the SUV?"

"Yeah. Open the rear door."

When Ed returned five minutes later, Andi was on her knees at the edge of the mound, her gloves dirty, a trowel on the ground by her leg.

She turned around to look at him. She held up a bone. "You're right."

With the shovel, they uncovered a pile of bones under a foot or so of earth. Ed hesitated. "This could be sacred ground. Maybe we shouldn't—"

"We're maybe three hundred feet from a scene where torture may have taken place, even recently. We know of a nearby murder that might be related, and we've got evidence that may suggest human sacrifice." She looked at the bones. "If these turn out to be old Indian bones, we'll replace them with suitable honor. But I have to get DCI back up here to take a look."

"That trail doesn't seem big enough to have been used for burials."

"Maybe years ago, it was. The journals stop in 1946." She paused, struck by a thought. "Wait. If they stopped that long ago, this trail wouldn't still be here."

Ed shook his head. "Maybe animals use it."

Andi nodded. "Yeah. The human kind."

70

As they drove out to the highway on the bumpy dirt track, Andi's certainty about the bones grew. She glanced over to Ed. "I need to call DCI about the bones. You mind?"

He shook his head.

She pulled over, picked up the mic, and called Callie, asked her to patch her through to Charlie Begay or Phil Oxendine. Waiting, she watched the dashboard clock impatiently, until Callie's voice crackled through the radio. "I've got Charlie Begay. Here you go."

"Hey, Charlie." She explained what they had found. He said, "You're in luck, Andi. Phil and I are available on Thursday, so we can get up there, say, mid-day then. That work for you?"

"Perfect, Charlie." She added, "You can determine the age of the bones, right?"

"Do you mean the bone age at the time of death, or how long it's been since the death?"

She thought about it. "Both would be good."

"Age at death is fairly easy. We've got a couple of good forensic anthropologists here who can look at that. Time since death's trickier, but they can ballpark it. Might take a while, though."

"Do you need me up at the site?"

"Not if we can find it. It's at that place you call a church?"

"Yeah. The bones are about three hundred feet into the woods on the west side of the clearing. You'll see the tracks Ed and I left."

"No need for you to drive up, then. We'll take custody of the bones and get back to you. Could take a week, maybe two, once we get the bones."

"Thanks, Charlie."

"Are you still working the case with Mike?" Charlie asked.

At the name, Andi felt a sudden stirring, an unusual arousal. "Uh, yeah. He's on it." She signed off, embarrassed.

Ed asked, "Get what you need?"

"Uh-huh." She looked out the window a minute, confused at her rush of feeling. She collected herself. "They'll be on it Thursday."

71

A mile later, she reached over and rested her hand on Ed's neck. He glanced at her, smiled. "Excited about finding those bones?"

"I am. Thanks for helping me on this, big guy."

"My pleasure, pal."

She smiled. "Would you mind stopping at Wallace's Corner? I want to see if Delbo is back."

"Delbo? He's the guy with the Filipina girls?"

"The same."

Cassius Delbo was there, although he claimed his granddaughter was not. "Thank you, Sheriff. Appreciate it, giving us time." He glanced at Ed, sitting in the vehicle. "Him?"

"A friend. He knows something about cults."

Delbo said nothing.

"Deputy Peterson and I will keep quiet about what we learned about your, ah, work here, as long as you help us." She paused to frame her question, decided on the frontal approach. "Sir, do you know who the Warriors of Yahweh are?"

Delbo took a short step back, as though pushed. He shook his head. "Dangerous people. Don't know them."

"Mr. Delbo, if you don't know them, how do you know they're dangerous?"

"You saw the place?" the old man whispered.

Andi nodded.

"Then. Dangerous." He folded his scrawny arms across his chest.

"I need you to tell me everything you can, Mr. Delbo. These people could have committed a murder."

Delbo smiled grimly. "Not could have, Deputy. Have." He stopped for a moment. He did not relax his arms. "Learn what I can. Tell you when I do. But dangerous. Very dangerous."

Andi considered his answer. "I need to know what you know, Mr. Delbo. Other women might die."

His arms stayed folded. "When learn, will tell."

Andi's anger surged. "Damn it, Delbo. How do you know? Who do you know? And how will you learn what you can? I need you to stop the bullshit and help me." She wanted to arrest him, grill him. But he wasn't a man to wither under questioning. She walked a few steps away, breathing herself calm.

"Women might die, Mr. Delbo," she said, looking up into the forest.

There was no answer. She turned to him, but he stood still, arms folded. "Learn what I can, Sheriff. Then call."

"How, damn it? How will you learn? And when will you call?"

He said nothing. She knew he was closing down. Again, she considered arresting him, knew that would make the closing down permanent. "You call me. Or I will come back, Mr. Delbo."

"No. Stay away. Learn anything, will call you."

Andi looked at him. *What's he hiding now?* She glanced over his shoulder at the barn-dormitory. "If you're holding out on me, Mr. Delbo, I will find you and we'll end your operation."

Delbo laughed, a creaky, ancient sound. "Day comes want to be lost, no finding."

WEDNESDAY

72

In the forest clearing, Virgil Stark cut the duct tape binding the young man's hands, and seized one wrist. Another man grabbed the second wrist and they tied the young man to the tall center pole, his hands strung up above his head. They tugged on the rope, lifting the man onto his toes. The bishop nodded and Virgil cut off his shirt, exposing the flesh of his back. Overhead, clouds gathered, the already dim filtered light fading.

Scopus, frowning, clenched his jaw. Someone had broken into the sheds and taken things, valuables that he had insufficiently protected. It was an insufferable error, and if anyone else had made it, he'd have visited horrific consequences on them. He hadn't figured out who'd stolen the ledgers, though he had his thoughts. If it was some kid or a random hunter, probably nothing would come of it. Vandals. He doubted it was vandals, though. The padlocks were unbroken. They'd unscrewed the hasps. He felt a gnawing certainty: it was that woman deputy. She was too close.

He noticed Virgil looking at him, waiting. The young man tied to the post was trembling.

The bishop shook his head. Let the fuck-wit wait. He had been a good shipper so far, and letting that girl escape was bad enough. But lying to cover it up? This isn't some college frat house where people pretty up their stupidity with lies. This is business. You invest in your product, you take orders for it, you transport it, you deliver it, and you take payment. When somebody breaks that chain, you punish them.

He braced himself, looking at the man, who was trying to stand tall, pretending to be unafraid. When they hurt business, you beat them like the dumb animals they are. He noticed the intense silence of the forest. The crowd of disciples—the bishop was under no delusion that they were *believers*—stood quietly, eyes down to the ground. Men, twenty-five of them, seven others missing. He would deal with them later. Four women, hard-eyed, angry. *Sheep*, Scopus thought. *Time to instruct them.*

"You failed us, driver," he intoned sharply.

The young man jerked against the rope.

"You lost a shipment, then you lied to cover it up. Carelessness like that hurts our cause. You must be punished." The bishop glared at the crowd, cowing them, forcing them to reflect: *this could be me*.

The young man tried to speak, to defend himself, but his dry throat turned his sounds into croaks. The bishop barked, "Silence!" and nodded to Virgil, who stood off to the side of the group, ready with the bullwhip. He'd told the bishop, earlier, quietly, that the second whip was missing. It inflamed Scopus further.

Virgil cracked the leather sharply across the young man's shoulders. He screamed, and Scopus lifted his hand. Virgil coiled the whip, holding it at his side. To the people gathered on the far side of the altar facing the flogging pole, Scopus barked, "You are witnesses. This happens when one of you betrays our mission by impurity, by deceit. Yahweh tolerates no failure, and His sacred mission must be fulfilled, or there comes wrath. Worse is deserved, but Yahweh is merciful."

He dropped his hand, nodded curtly at Virgil, who planted his feet squarely and began to flog the young man methodically. The initial screams turned into grunts; bloody lines welled up and dripped down his back. His back turned into a mass of tangled flesh. His grunts faded into a long moan. The man vomited, then lost consciousness and hung from the rope. The bishop signaled a stop. "Clean him up," he ordered. To the women, who held their heads low and avoided his eyes, he snarled, "Clean the Temple."

Virgil and another man cut the boy down and laid him on the

ground, on his stomach, then threw a bucket of water on his back. The others, silent, poured lye into buckets and added water, and began cleaning the pole of blood and vomit.

The bishop turned to his driver beside him. "Follow me," he ordered quietly. They walked into the forest. When they were screened from the others, he spoke. "The police have been here. There is fingerprint dust on the altar, and our old logbooks and some tools are in the hands of the female deputy. I require them back. Get them for me."

The man tilted his head. "That's pretty tough. They'll be locked in—"

"Silence." He fixed the man's eyes with his own. "I require them."

The driver looked down. After a moment, he muttered, "Bishop."

73

Andi drew morning patrol, and had been driving the usual circuit of back roads for about an hour when her cell phone buzzed. The screen read *Mike Payne*. Pleased, she pulled onto the shoulder and hit *Talk*.

"Hey, Andi, what's cooking?"

She filled him in about the bones and Delbo's evasions.

"Wow, that's huge. And I've heard of that Delbo character. Actually..." He didn't finish.

"Actually?"

Mike cleared his throat. "Well, I shouldn't talk out of turn, but Delbo's a person of interest to us here."

"Really? What for?"

Another hesitation. "Look, it's sensitive. You'll keep this between us?"

She considered it. "I will, unless it affects us over here in Adams County."

"That's fair. We've been watching him for a couple years now. We're thinking he's running a sex trafficking ring through that compound of his."

She felt a flash of irritation. "Damn it, Mike, why the hell didn't you tell me?"

"We have to catch him with the girls, and we're keeping an eye on him. If he got wind of us sniffing around, he'd be gone."

"I'm not so sure, Mike. I've been talking with him, and he gives me a pretty convincing story of what he's doing. What you're saying doesn't jibe with my instincts. When he told me and Pete—"

"Who's Pete?"

"Peterson. Senior deputy. Acting Sheriff while Ben's out. Anyway, we both thought his story hung together."

"Hmm. And your instincts are pretty good, so..." He paused. Andi could almost hear the wheels turning in his head. "What'd he tell you?"

"He's been rescuing relatives of his wife in the Philippines. Saving them from the Islamist terrorists."

"Huh. Saving his wife's family or running girls for sex." After a moment, he sighed. "Facts fit either way, don't they? Look, I don't want to step on your toes—but we're going to keep watching him. Maybe you and I should go talk to him together?"

"Let's hold off. He's been cooperating with me, and if I bring you in now he might shut down."

"Okay. If you trust him...But we've gotta keep our eye on him over here. That fair?"

Do I trust the old man? He hadn't given her a strong enough reason not to, yet. "Sure. I guess neither of us wants to spook him, and sooner or later we'll figure out what he's really up to." She remembered that he'd called her. "So, what's this call for?"

"I've got a question. Can I get a look at that little piece of cloth you found? I think I can help you identify it."

"Really? What've you got?"

"We're working another case here, it's a big load of nothing. But it involves a red flannel shirt, and there's a little tear on the arm. I'd like to compare the fabrics."

"Ah, man, that'd be great if they match."

"You planning to come over to Carlton any time soon? You could bring the piece with you."

Andi considered it. "Wasn't planning to, but..."

"No problem, I'll drive over to Jeff, maybe Saturday, around lunchtime. I could use some of those fantastic ribs from that restaurant you've got. The Archer?"

"Angler. You sure it's not too much trouble—it's my case, I should really be the one driving."

"No trouble at all, and there's those ribs."

"I really appreciate this, Mike."

He laughed. "I want to bust this case as bad as you do. See you Saturday."

They ended the call. Driving back onto the highway, she let her excitement about the bones and Mike's information build. This might be the week.

Capped off by lunch with Mike. Hmm. How would Ed feel about that?

Hell, how did *she* feel about that?

74

After her shift ended at four, she drove the five miles to Ed's. Her excitement about the case had given way to discomfort. Was it guilt at the pleasure she took from anticipating lunch with Mike? She'd thought about it all day. Guilt? *Sure is,* she thought. She chewed on that as she drove up his curving drive, then decided to ignore it. *Lunch with a colleague's no sin.* By the time she rolled into the yard and got out, she felt better, but a little apprehensive about how Ed would react when she told him.

They sat on the porch watching the sun set over the mountains.

"You're quiet," he said.

She took a long breath, then said, "I've got something to tell you."

He looked at her. "You sound serious."

"I got a call from Mike a little while ago. He thinks he has information about the case, and he's coming over to Jefferson Saturday to look at our evidence and maybe help identify somebody. He wants to have lunch at the Angler. I don't want you to get any ideas, so I'm telling you up front."

After a moment, he shrugged. "Well, it's your call." Like the shrug, his voice seemed neutral. Painfully neutral.

"Don't, Ed. I'm trying to be honest here."

Their eyes met for a brief moment. He looked back out into the evening. "I'm just disappointed. Saturday's the day we were going to go to Missoula with Grace for her SATs."

Ouch. "Damn. I forgot. Look, I'll call him back. I can make a run over to Carlton tomorrow."

Ed ran his fingers through his hair. He shook his head. "Don't do that, Andi. I'm just being stupid. You've got to work your case, I get that."

She felt a flutter of heat, but more powerfully, gratitude. "Thanks, Ed. Understanding helps. And just to be clear, there's nothing going on between Mike and me. He's good looking, but I'm with you. Period." She thought of the weekend past, their candor, sharing Grace's lie and then her honesty, the moment alone with Grace in her room. She placed her hand on Ed's arm.

His smile seemed real. "Good looking, eh?" He grinned. "I don't care where you get your appetite, as long as you eat at home."

She laughed.

"So, what do you think Mike knows about the investigation?"

Just then, Grace's PV slid into the yard. Her regular parking place was a pile of scrunched up gravel from her many too-fast stops.

"Hey, guys," she called out, climbing onto the porch.

"What've you been up to?" Ed asked.

"After school, me and Dana—I mean, Dana and I—went over to Jen's for pizza and SAT prep. I'm nervous. We've spent so many hours with that damn SAT practice book we're getting testarded."

Andi chuckled. "Testarded?"

Grace assumed a lecturer's stance. "*Testarded*: The state of walking brain-death caused by too much SAT prep." She yawned. "Andi, you're coming with us to Missoula Saturday?"

"Uh-uh. I've got a...meeting." She glanced at Ed, whose eyebrows had a curious arched look.

"Bummer. Well, I'm tired. Beddy-bye."

"Goodnight," Andi said to her back.

Ed chimed in, "Sleep well, kiddo."

In answer, Grace let the screen door slam, and they heard, from inside, her faint "Sorry."

Andi said, "What were you asking, before Grace arrived?"

"What do you think Mike actually knows about your investigation?"

"He says it's about the little piece of red cloth we found. He might know whose it is."

"What little red piece of cloth?"

She explained. "If he's got somebody who left it there, maybe that'll give us a handle on the case."

"A name," he said.

"Yeah. God, that'd be good." Sudden heat flared across her chest and back. She pulled off her jacket and unbuttoned her shirt. "Jesus. I could strip naked and still be on fire."

"Do it." He grinned. "I'll personally hose you down."

FRIDAY

75

Two nights later, Andi sat on Ed's couch thinking about tomorrow's meeting with Mike. He'd called to say he was coming over the mountain around noon, and again mentioned the ribs at the Angler. To think the fabric might lead them to a suspect excited her. So she didn't feel guilty about the lunch: lunch with a colleague was just that. Really.

The TV was on, but Andi was hardly watching it. Grace paced, restless, in front of the set.

"You're a bundle of nerves," she said to Grace. "Come sit down." She patted the cushion beside her.

"Can't. I'm too nervous about my testathlon tomorrow. I need sleep, but I'll just lie there and worry and by tomorrow I'll have brain-crash. No way I'll score high enough to get into college." She paced some more.

Andi grimaced. "Look, you're making me nervous. Go pour yourself a half-glass of wine, and bring me one too. That'll settle you down."

After she got the wine, Grace fell onto the couch and they clinked glasses. "Here's to success tomorrow," Andi said. Which thing? Grace's test, or her meeting with Mike?

They heard a vehicle drive in. "It's Northrup," Grace said. "He won't like me drinking this wine. He thinks I should only drink on holidays."

"After Homecoming, I suspect your father's thinking has changed."

Grace grimaced. "I really screwed that up, didn't I?"

"Yeah, but you redeemed yourself."

Ed came in, looked at the wine glass in Grace's hand, started to say something, then shrugged. "Any more where that came from?" he asked.

Grace's eyebrows went up. Andi laughed.

A half-hour later, Ed said, "Better get some sleep, ladies. We leave for Missoula at five."

Andi grimaced. "I'm not going, remember?" She looked at Grace. "Sorry, kiddo. Wish I could be there."

Grace patted Andi's knee as she stood up. "I'm sure you'll redeem yourself."

Andi laughed.

Ed looked at her. "He's coming?"

"Noon."

"Ah."

Grace looked baffled. "Who's coming?"

"Mike Payne, the deputy from Carlton who's working with me on a case. He might have new evidence he wants me to see." She smiled at Ed; he didn't look jealous.

As if she hadn't heard a word, Grace said, "Man, these SATs make me soooo nervous!" She started pacing again.

Ed said to her, "You'll do fine, Grace."

Grace stopped pacing. "You know, maybe I need another glass of wine."

SATURDAY

76

Ed and Grace, groggy and grumpy, had left for Missoula at five in the morning. Andi went in to the department at nine, surprised at how warm the day was, and spent the morning combing through the evidence, once again, hoping to come up with something they'd missed. Nothing. As the morning passed, her anticipation about the fabric grew. And she was anxious to hear from DCI about the bones, although Charlie had said that might take a couple of weeks.

Right at noon, her phone buzzed. Marla, the weekend receptionist and dispatcher, said, "Visitor in Reception, Andi."

Mike wore shorts and a tight t-shirt. He carried a small backpack, one strap slung over his shoulder. "Hey, Andi. Great to see you."

"Hi, Mike," she said, relishing the rush of pleasure at seeing him. Marla, usually buried in a crossword puzzle, looked up curiously. Andi felt herself blush. "Can't wait to see whether we've got a match. Shall we do it?" She blushed again, wishing she'd said it differently.

But Mike appeared not to notice. "Absolutely. I brought the shirt." He patted the backpack.

"Okay, right this way." She led the way to her cubicle. Standing in front of her desk, she bent over and typed her ID into the computer and logged into the EVIDENCE folder. She typed the ID again, and her name and the date and time automatically filled in. She checked the box beside the line: "Small fabric piece. Item 17092314." Over her shoulder, she sensed Mike watching her. Again that throat-tightening rush of pleasure.

"What's your system?" he asked. "Over at Carlton, you have to log into a secure server and provide your ID or the evidence door won't unlock."

"Ours works much the same way, with an old-fashioned twist."

"Which is what?"

"You'll see." She locked her monitor and stood. "Follow me."

She led him down to the end of the hall, past Ben's office. She stopped at the door labeled "ACS 17."

"ACS 17?"

"Adams County Sheriff, room 17. Evidence room. We call it a locker, but it's much bigger than that."

He laughed. "Huh. We just use numbers."

The lock safe was built into the wall beside the door. Andi stood close to the keypad, shielded her hand, and punched in her ID. The safe door clicked, and she opened it, extracting a foot-long steel pipe, to which a large key ring was attached. She turned around and showed Mike the pipe-and-key. "The old-fashioned twist."

Mike looked at the pipe. "Clever. Won't fit in a pocket and get lost. I'll have to pass that along to Harley. Our key keeps going home in a deputy's pocket."

They both laughed. Andi unlocked the door and swung it open.

Inside the big room, almost a small warehouse, industrial shelves stood in rows. In the middle of the room, a large table held a stack of Latex glove boxes, and an organizer—an old silverware tray—filled with tools.

Andi found the shelf holding the cult-site evidence box and lifted out the plastic bag containing the tiny shred of red cloth. "Now for the good part." She pulled on Latex gloves from the box on the table, opened the bag, and, with tweezers from the organizer, picked out the small red piece of fabric. Carefully, she laid it on a clean tray.

Mike put his backpack on the table and unzipped it. He took two gloves from the box, then pulled out an evidence bag containing a flannel shirt. He opened the bag and removed the shirt. The shirt was bright red. Andi frowned. *Wrong color?*

"We found this on another case over in Carlton, and it's got a rip in the sleeve. I'm hoping they match." When he carefully straightened the sleeve, she saw the tear immediately. He reached for the tweezers. "May I?"

She nodded. Under the bright light, she could already see that the colors were close, but not a match. "It's the wrong color."

"Yeah, it's close," he said. He very carefully rested the small snag on the tear in the arm of the shirt. "Shoot," he whispered. "Wrong shape, too."

Andi, swallowing her disappointment, opened the evidence bag so Mike could drop the snag back in. She sealed it, then took off her gloves and tossed them in the wastebasket under the table. "Damn," she whispered. "I really hoped...Well."

Mike carefully folded the shirt and returned it to its own bag, which he slid into his pack. "I'm sorry, Andi. We were both hoping." He pulled off his gloves and threw them in the basket, then replaced the tweezers in the tray.

After they locked the room and returned the key ring to the safe, Mike asked, "Lunch? Or are you too bummed?"

She shook her head. "I'd feel like a jerk having you drive all the way over here and not buy you lunch."

"Good, I'm starving. Every time I'm in Jeff I get the ribs at the Angler."

As they crossed Division Street toward the Angler, Mike said, "Don't give up. I might have some new information that could help us. I'll tell you while we eat."

77

Andi ignored Ted's curious look when she and Mike passed by the bar and went into the restaurant. After they found a table, she excused herself to use the restroom. "I'll be right back."

When she came back and sat down, she cut directly to the point. "So, your information?"

"Let's order first. I'm starved."

After they ordered, Mike said, "Look, I wasn't entirely honest with you when we talked about Cassius Delbo."

"Oh?"

"Yeah. We've had our eyes on him for a long time, serious stuff. I thought maybe I shouldn't reveal it, but Harley gave me the go-ahead."

"You already told me, sex-trafficking."

"You said he gave you his story that they're Filipina family members escaping terrorists."

Andi felt her stomach tighten. "Yeah. Not true?"

Mike shook his head. "No way. They're Mexicans."

"Have you seen any?"

"No, that's why we're watching him. We put a GPS trace under his truck, and we're just waiting for him to go someplace other than the grocery store in Carlton."

"Damn." She thought about it. "He gave us this story about being in the Bataan Death March."

"We heard that too. One of our guys went undercover on the building crew helping him build that big workshop and sleeping room he's got. Got the old fart talking about why he needed it. We looked at the military records of the Death March—there's nobody named Delbo listed."

"Shit. We didn't follow up." She felt embarrassed. Sloppy police work. Ordrew would be merciless.

Mike looked sympathetic. "I'm sorry, Andi. But look, he's got to be our guy. You've seen his dormitory, right?"

She nodded. "Man, this bums me. I'd pegged Delbo as eccentric, but honest."

The server brought their lunches. She waited till they were alone again, then said, "So how do we nail him?"

"Basically, surveillance. Like I said, we watch the trace till he makes a move. But he's our guy."

"How long have you been tracing his movements?"

"Six months, maybe a little more."

"Did he go into the fire scene on Labor Day?"

Mike shook his head. "Why?"

"Look, if he's our guy, he must have been there, right? He's old.

Maybe somebody drives him and you bugged the wrong vehicle. You might never see him do anything. Do you think we should arrest him on suspicion?"

Mike looked alarmed. "Whoa. If you do, we'll never get the evidence we need to convict. We have to catch him with the product."

"Product?" She thought of the heading on one of the columns in the ledgers: *prod*. Product.

Mike grinned. "Sorry. Trafficker lingo. It refers to the women they're moving. Anyway, let us do the watching. I've got a couple of guys working it with me, and the GPS is wired into our dispatch office, so if he moves, we'll know it."

"Not if he doesn't use his vehicle for business."

Giggles burst in from the entrance to the restaurant. Jen and Grace were coming into the room, and Grace spotted Andi. Her eyes darted quickly to Mike. She came across the restaurant, smiling. "Hey, Andi." Once again, her eyes flicked to Mike. Her smile faded.

Andi was swept up in a hot flash, and her heart started to pound. She could feel the flush on her face. She knew Grace could see it—and that she could misinterpret it. She said, "Hi, Grace. How'd the test go?" The heat was like the sun in August.

Grace looked back to her. "Sucked. I finished early. Probably went too fast." She looked again at Mike, then back to Andi, her eyebrows lifting.

"Grace, this is Deputy Mike Payne. He works for Carlton County. We're talking about a case I'm working." She turned to Mike. "Grace is Ed's daughter."

"Pleased to meet you, Mike," Grace said, shaking his hand. "Jen and me, I mean I, are starved. She turned to Andi. "You coming over for dinner tonight?"

Andi nodded. "I'll be there."

Mike watched Grace walking away. "A nice kid."

Andi nodded. The hot flash was easing. "She is."

She wondered what Grace would tell Ed. And what Ed would think.

78

Finding out took less time than she'd expected. As she and Mike were leaving, he stretched his arm over her shoulder to shove open the Angler's front door for her, but at that very moment it was pulled open from the other side, revealing Ed, looking surprised. Mike stumbled, steadying himself by dropping his arm onto Andi's shoulder. Ed stepped back, and his look sharpened.

Andi shrugged Mike's arm off her shoulder and said, "Ed! Grace's inside."

Ed nodded. "I know, that's why I'm here. You're..." He stopped.

"Mike and I were having lunch, talking about the case."

Ed nodded.

Mike leaned around Andi and extended his hand. "Nice to meet you, Ed. Andi says good things about you."

Andi looked sharply at him; she didn't remember saying *anything* about Ed.

Ed nodded, returning the handshake. "We have this thing: She says good things about me and I say good things about her." Andi couldn't read his voice.

Mike laughed. "Well, I gotta get back to Carlton. Thanks for lunch, Andi. Ed, Good to see you."

He pushed out the door and walked across Division Street to his car.

Andi looked at Ed, whose eyes had narrowed. "Ed, it was only lunch."

"Sure." He pushed past her into the restaurant. "I'm eating with Grace."

"Damn it, Ed, don't be a shit."

He stopped, turned. "Ah," he said, turned away, and walked into the restaurant.

79

By the time he pulled into his yard, Ed regretted being out of line. He put his things in the cabin, then went outside to split wood, debating whether to call Andi to apologize. After a handful of splits, he saw the PV pulling into the yard. He made up his mind to call. *Ten more splits.*

Grace watched him work, saying nothing. After another split, he stopped and rested the ax against the block. She said, "You were pretty quiet during lunch. You met that guy?"

"I did."

"What are you going to do?"

"I'll call Andi, and we'll talk. I got jealous and I imagine she's hurt. Or angry."

Grace pursed her lips. "If Zach caught me with somebody else, he wouldn't talk."

"No? What would Zach do?"

"He'd spank me," she said, then blushed furiously. "In a manner of speaking," she added quickly as she turned and bounced up the porch steps and went inside.

Ed watched the door slam shut behind her and picked up his ax. *Six more splits.*

When he called her at home, Andi didn't answer, so he dialed her cell phone. It rolled over to voice mail immediately. He left a message and returned to his woodpile. A moment later, his cell rang. *Andi.* "I'd like to come out."

"You need to ask?" Testy hadn't been his intent, but that's how he sounded to himself.

"We need to clear this up, Ed."

"Nothing to clear up," he said, softening his voice. "I shouldn't have reacted like I did. I trust you."

"Good."

"So come on out."

"I, ah..." She stopped. "I'll be there in a minute."

"A *minute*? Where are you?"

"Parked at the foot of your driveway. Wanted to get the lay of the land before I drove up."

When he heard her car drive into the yard, he felt a new commotion in his chest, a quiet swelling around his heart. Not anger or jealousy this time. Gratitude.

Andi walked over to him and looked in his eyes for a moment, then glanced toward the cabin. "Grace home?"

He nodded. "Just got here. Look, I'm sorry about acting jealous. It's just..." He didn't quite know the right words.

She touched his arm. "It's a nice afternoon. Let's talk on the porch." She climbed the steps. He leaned the ax against his chopping block and followed her. Had she cut him off?

From the porch, they watched the clouds smeared above the western peaks, their edges tinted gold and rose by the late afternoon sun, their interiors gray. The sky between the streaks of cloud was baby blue, soft, a blanket of delicate color.

Ed waited.

Andi took a breath. "I thought about it all afternoon. You being jealous pissed me off at first, but after a while, I think I get it."

That surprised him. "What do you mean?"

"You ask me to marry you, and I don't give you an answer, yes or no. I put you off, and keep putting you off. Then I tell you I want to keep my independence. Then you see this guy from Carlton I've been spending time with, and his arm's over my shoulder. I'd be jealous too." She paused and took another long breath. She gauged his look. Not angry. "Well, it's more than that. Remember when you first told me you wanted to hire Lynn Monroe, your counselor friend?"

"Yeah. You jumped all over me about my age."

"I did. But looking back, I think I felt jealous and couldn't admit it to myself."

"Huh. You being jealous would never occur to me. Did you know Lynn's a lesbian?" He couldn't remember ever mentioning that. "Not that I'm interested anyway."

"Huh. Didn't know she was." She sighed. "Anyway, since Mike drove over to check the evidence, I'd agreed to buy lunch, which only seemed fair. *Quid pro quo*, you know."

He thought, *Don't want to ask, but admit it, I'm curious*. "So how'd his arm get around you? What was the *quid* for that *quo*?"

Andi tilted her head a little. "He reached over my shoulder to push the door open, and you pulled it open and he kind of fell against me."

Ed studied her for a moment, feeling again the gratitude, a warm energy in his chest. "I'm sorry, kid. Big overreaction."

"I'm not making this any easier for you, either." She leaned against him, and he put his arm around her shoulder. For a few minutes, they sat quietly, watching the afternoon edging toward evening.

Ed said, "This helps."

She nodded.

"I take it the fabric piece didn't work out?"

"Nope." She stood up and went to the railing and leaned back against it, watching him. "You know, it's the weekend. Let's not talk about the case. We're kind of stalled till we hear from DCI about the bones, so I'm going to let it percolate."

"In your unconscious."

"In my unconscious." She continued looking at him.

"What?"

"Maybe you and I need a little percolating."

The tight, throaty, grateful feeling Ed had had before came back. All the way back. "Grace," he whispered, glancing inside.

She touched his lips. "Get a blanket. We'll walk into the woods."

MONDAY

80

Early on Monday evening after work, Ed chopped kindling from the splits he'd made on Saturday. *Feels good,* he thought. As he worked, he thought about Saturday afternoon and evening. After they'd *percolated* and then come home and eaten dinner, Andi had been quiet, within herself, but hadn't closed him out. Later in the evening, she'd surprised him.

"Do you remember what came to me...that menopause means cancer and cancer means I die?"

"Sure. It's a big insight."

"Yeah. I thought realizing that would resolve it, right? Well, during the Homecoming parade, just before you drove by and honked your horn—God, that's a loud horn!"

Ed's curiosity sped past that. "Something else?"

"No, it just came back, scary as ever."

"Ouch."

"Thing is, as I say it now, it sounds nuts."

"Well, the unconscious plays strange tricks."

"Maybe, but I know I'm not dying of menopause."

He smiled. "Whew. That's good to hear."

"That I'm not going to die, or that I know I'm not?"

Now, remembering the exchange, he smiled. Then he shivered. The weekend's unusual warmth was fading. He tossed kindling and a few splits in his wood bag and went inside.

Grace was listening to someone on her phone, bundled in a blanket on the couch in pajamas and robe, her face creamed, her hair towel-wrapped. After a moment, she hit the *End* button and dropped the phone on the couch.

"Northrup, I forgot to tell you something."

Ed said, "Mind if I start a fire?"

"Yeah, it's cold. Listen: You remember Ms. Monroe, the school counselor?"

"Sure." He considered whether to tell her, decided not yet. He had a sinking feeling something was going wrong with his plan. "Why?"

"She called just before you came home from work. I forgot to tell you."

Ed turned away from the wood stove, into which he'd been bundling wads of newspaper and laying kindling on top of them. He felt his heart speed up, relieved, almost excited. "When did she call? What'd she say? Did she leave a number?"

Grace grinned at him. "You're pumped, Northrup."

"Yeah. This could mean something really good." He rubbed his hands, and immediately felt foolish. He didn't know what Lynn had to say. *Too early for excitement, pal.*

"Well, you don't need to get all poly-gasmic about it. Just call her."

He lifted an eyebrow at her, then looked at the clock. "You think it's too late to call?"

Grace grinned again. "Come on, Northrup, you're dying to. Live dangerously."

81

Ed dialed the number and waited, listening to the rings.

"Hello?" He recognized the voice of Lynn's partner.

"Hi, Rachel. It's Ed Northrup calling for—"

"Is something wrong with Jayne?"

Momentarily confused, Ed said, "Jayne?"

She laughed. "Jayne Mansfield, my Volvo. You bought her for your daughter."

"Right, right. No, the car's just fine. It—" Rachel had shown real affection for the very pink Volvo. "She's just great." He debated whether to tell her Grace had renamed the car the Pink Vulva. *Not a good idea.* "No, I'm calling to speak with Lynn."

"Sure. About the job, I'll bet."

"Well, I don't exactly know. I'm returning her call."

Rachel laughed. "Oh, it's about the job. She's right here."

He felt a rush of excitement. *Hold your horses, bud,* he told himself. After a moment, Lynn came on. "Hi, Ed. Thanks for calling back."

"You're welcome. I assume you got my email?"

"Yes, that's why I called."

"Great. What's your thinking?"

She was quiet for a moment. "Uh, Ed, I'm flattered, of course. I've wanted to make the jump to private practice for years. But...I don't see how I can make it work."

The excitement drained out of him. "Can I ask why not?"

"Well, sure. First off, Rachel and I don't make a lot of money, and I need all three jobs I'm working now just to make ends meet. Missoula's kind of a pricey town to live in. I can't imagine you could offer me what amounts to a full time position right away."

"True." He relaxed. He'd thought about this. "Look, let me propose something. You're already here at the school two half-days a week. What if we start out adding one half-day, then another as your patient load builds? When you need more time, we can add a half-day at a time. If you can reduce your current jobs the same amounts over time, you could keep a steady income for how ever long it takes to build up your clientele here. Would that work with your current boss? Or bosses?"

"Just one boss, two clinics. I suppose we could negotiate something." But her voice sounded hesitant.

"Is there something else?"

"Uh, yeah. Rachel's a wellness coach—you know, yoga, nutrition, complementary medicine stuff—and she's worried there's not a big enough population in your valley to make a living. It's taken her years to build her practice here, and she's afraid to risk it."

"I don't blame her." He'd thought about that too. "What about a trial run? Say she comes down with you one day a week and we set up a studio for her. We'll find out if the population is big enough for a move, while she keeps her present client load in Missoula till we find out. Worst case, you end up just doing the part-time thing here."

"I can talk it over with Rachel. Maybe..." She hesitated "Ed, I can't see how you'll make any money on me."

"I don't need to make money on you, Lynn. I need a path to working less, and part of that is bringing in someone whose work I trust. Hopefully, someone who can take over as I get older." He thought about Andi's reaction to his saying that.

"I'm flattered, Ed. But how sure are you about the quality of my work?"

He smiled. "You know Chris Walther?"

"Sure, he's our consulting psychologist."

"Chris and I went to grad school together. We're old friends."

She said nothing for a moment. "You talked to Chris about me?"

"I did. He's high on you. He said I'd have nothing to regret."

Again, she was quiet. "Well, that's nice to hear." She seemed to rouse herself. "Okay, thanks for the call. I'll talk with Rachel, see if she might be okay trying it in stages, like you suggest. And if she's on board, I'll negotiate with my other jobs some kind of off-ramp plan, if I can."

"Thanks, Lynn. Those are big ifs, but I hope this works. I'd really like you to join me." He hesitated, then said it. "Just hoping you feel the same."

She chuckled. "Ever have a dream come true, Ed? I've wanted to work in a private practice since I was in grad school, but I figured it'd never happen. I'm dying for the chance."

Ever had a dream come true? Ed smiled. "Yeah, I've got a dream my fingers are crossed about. Real hard."

82

Ten minutes after his call with Lynn, Ed's phone rang again. The sound startled him. *Calling back so soon?* But no, the screen read *Magnus Anderssen.*

"Ed? Mack here. How you doing, my friend?"

Ed thought about that. "I'm good. I'm negotiating with a therapist to join my practice so I can start cutting back. Need more fun in my life."

"Good for you. Actually, that's why I called. How about Saturday, you and I drive up into the Monasteries and scout elk habitat."

Ed's heart soared. "You're on, man. I haven't been up there since last year."

"Good. Very good. And you and your lady? Ben tells me you popped the question."

Ed sighed. "That old gossip! Damn, don't spread that word, Mack. I popped it, but we're, ah, negotiating. She's really deep into the murder case—the girl burned in that Labor Day fire."

"Negotiating? Negotiating what? A prenup?"

Ed laughed. "Nothing like that. Just how it feels to marry somebody ten years older than yourself."

"Ah. By the way, I hear lots of talk around the valley about Andi's case. It's a murder for certain?"

"Looks that way. A pretty ugly one, too."

"So, you two getting married?"

"Getting closer, I think."

"Closer?"

"Mack."

"Back off?"

"Yep. I'll keep you posted. Andi's working on a lot."

"Got it. Take care, my friend. And take care of her."

"Ah, man. That's a given."

83

It was turning into an evening of phone calls.

"Ed? Ben here."

"Ben? What's wrong?" Ed had visited Ben earlier in the day, and he'd seemed better.

"Ain't nothin' wrong, it's somethin' right for a change. I'm home.

Doc Keeley says I ain't supposed to work for a month and I gotta walk three miles a day." He sounded disgusted, or maybe disbelieving. "Can you see me walkin' around town every day, like those old ladies with their little dogs? Might as well take up skydivin'."

"That's great news, though, Ben. Think of it as walking a beat. Bet you're glad you're home."

"Yep, that hospital was gettin' on my nerves. And we finally got the diabetes under control. Your lady home?" Ben knew that Andi spent four or five nights a week with Ed. Everyone knew.

"No, she's staying at her place tonight."

"Thinkin' about gettin' married, I hope."

"Or something." Ed felt uncomfortable discussing Andi so much. But what are friends for?

"Okay. I'll call her there. See ya at the office."

"Ben! Doc said no work for a month, didn't he?"

Ben hung up with a snort.

FRIDAY

84

Four days later, Andi drove patrol along the back roads in the north end of the valley. She thought back on the long and fruitless week. Most frustrating was the silence from Carlton. She'd called Mike twice, but he'd said that Delbo wasn't going anywhere. Groceries once, hardware once. Nowhere else. She'd repeated her worry that they'd bugged the wrong vehicle. He'd assured her they had the old man covered.

An uneventful morning of patrol done—as boring as almost always—she returned to the department. Just as she was turning on her computer, Callie called in from reception. "Line 3, Andi."

It was Charlie Begay from the DCI. "Good morning, Andi. Have you any progress at your end?"

"Frustrating. Nothing going on here. Carlton County thinks Cassius Delbo's our guy, but I can't see it."

"Delbo? The old man?"

"Yeah. So, how about you? Got anything for me?"

"It is your lucky day. First of all, the mound of bones you found is definitely a burial site; and we found two more mounds nearby, about the same size. The bones we have are not Native American bones, though, so we do not have to worry about dishonoring the grave."

"Least of our worries, right?"

"You have that right. These bones are Caucasoid. My forensic anthropologist cannot date them exactly, but she is thinking—and she wants me to tell you this is a very rough estimate—that the bones go back to the early to middle nineteen hundreds. Nineteen-hundred to perhaps nineteen-fifty. She cannot get it closer than that. I know it is very broad."

Andi jotted a note, thinking, *1907 through 1946*. "No, that's the exact time period we've got hard evidence that this group was active."

"The ledgers?"

"Exactly. Find any complete skeletons?"

"No. They appeared to have been thrown in the mound in such a way that many skeletons mixed together. Why?"

"I'm wondering if some of the names in those ledgers might belong to the bones."

"To identify someone using bones, we would need things like the person's medical records, before-death X-rays, or DNA samples."

"Nothing like that in this case," she said. "How hard would it be for you guys to catalog all the bones? Get me an estimate of how many people?"

She heard a sigh. "Oh, man, Andi, we are stretched here. I doubt we could do that in less than six months, and you'd have to get us some funding for a couple of contractor techs. And it would mean we would be tearing up the forest behind that site. You want this group to know we are on to them?"

"I'm sure they already know. You dug up the bones, right? And I've removed a bunch of stuff from their sheds."

"True. Well, we do not have the budget for additional tech support, so unless you do..."

She laughed. "Nope, won't happen. Well, thanks, Charlie."

"There's another thing. We found fresh blood and vomit on one of those tall poles. Somebody had wiped it down with lye and water, but enough was left. I doubt it was more than a day or two old. Two at the most."

"Jesus. Caused by what, specifically?"

"Couldn't tell you...but it does say whoever those people are, they are still active. I believe you said you confiscated a bull whip?"

Andi felt a chill. "We did. We left another one in the shed."

"Perhaps that was it. Of course, we cannot know."

"Thanks, Charlie. You're right that it suggests the group is active.

That's helpful."

"All in a day's work." The call ended.

Brad Ordrew came in, crossing the room and stopping beside her desk. "What's helpful?"

"DCI has some useful findings in the murder case."

He smiled, as if he were pleased. "Well, good for them." The smile faded. "Helps to have real police investigating for you, eh?"

"That's out of line, Brad."

"You're the one who's been losing evidence. Not my idea of good police work."

She held her annoyance. "The evidence in that clearing was destroyed, Brad. I didn't *lose* it."

"You don't *have* it, so it's lost. So is your only witness—lost." His face reddened, looking genuinely angry. "Take some damn responsibility."

She bit back her reaction. Instead, she evened out her voice. "Difference of opinion. I'm done with this discussion."

He shook his head. "I'm going to run against Stewart in next year's election. I'll win it too, Pelton. And when I do, believe me, you *will* be done here."

85

Andi watched his back as he sauntered down the hall, her feelings mixed: quick anger, but an unexpected trepidation along with it. Ben would win that face-off, right? Shaking the whole thing off, she dialed Mike Payne's number. No answer. She left another message. "Mike, call me. I've got some new information. We've got to move on this case." She felt her irritation flare at Mike's not staying in touch, then realized the irritation was with Ordrew; she was taking it out on Mike.

Ben walked in.

"Hey, you're not supposed to be here," she said. He'd been in the station every morning this week, gleefully violating doctor's orders. Despite his distaste for walking, he'd put in his three dutiful miles each day, and already his face had a healthy color. "You had your walk today?"

"Did. What's new on the case?" he asked, steering right past her question.

She told him about the dating of the bones. "I'm trying to figure out the connection."

"And?"

"Well, tell me what you think. The bones come from the first half of the last century, so 1900 through 1950. The logs are from approximately that same period, 1907 through 1946."

"So you're thinkin' it ain't no coincidence—the bones belong to the names."

"Could be, at least some of the names, the ones marked *sacrificed*. If that's what *sacr* means. Not that we could ever make that link stand up in court."

"How many bones we talkin' about?"

"Don't know. DCI can't do that for a while, unless we pay for it."

Ben grunted. "Never happen. Budget's so red it looks like we butchered a steer over it." He started to turn away, then came back. "Thing bothers me is, why 1946? Why'd the books just stop there? Doesn't your guy, that Delbo character, think they're still at it?"

That stopped her. Charlie Begay had just corroborated what Delbo had told them. *And if he's the leader, why'd he give us the cult site?* She told Ben about Mike's suspicion and surveillance of Delbo.

"Don't fit."

"Yeah. Charlie said there is fresh blood and vomit on one of the tall poles, so they must be active...so Delbo's tip bears out."

"So the question is, why ain't we found no logs after 1946?"

"That's one question. The other one is whether Delbo's giving us something that won't matter very long."

"Like they're plannin' to trash the site?"

"Something like that. I'm sure they know we've been up there and taken evidence. Thank God I've got good photos."

"So where are the logs since 1946?"

"Someplace else. Or they didn't keep them. Or the Carlton

mortuary got involved and things changed. Like maybe cremating victims, and not keeping records. Or keeping them in the mortuary."

"Find 'em. And I'm thinkin' you're on to something with that cremation angle."

"No way we can find out, unless the Carlton Mortuary and Crematory kept records."

"Ain't that the truth. Or unless you catch you a witness who talks." He turned to go, then stopped. "I keep thinkin' of that poor little girl, nailed shut into that burning shack." He ran his hands roughly through his hair. "You ever feel like the job's breakin' your heart?"

86

After lunch, Andi was still pondering the dates. In addition to the question of where the ledgers after 1946 might be, the timeframe nagged her. Was it reasonable to assume the burials and the ledgers stopped then?

Could Delbo be stringing them along? He'd come to Montana in 1946. What if he'd taken over the leadership from someone else and changed the operation? Could he be the bishop? She couldn't shake her intuition that Delbo wasn't involved—but was 1946 *really* coincidental? She jotted a note: *1946-ledgers end, Delbo arrives in MT, Carlton Mortuary opens*. Three dots. Do any connect, or are they coincidence?

Ben's famous saying, "Coincidences ain't," argued against it; but if Delbo was innocent, the date *had* to be coincidental. Or if "coincidences ain't," then Delbo wasn't innocent.

The business card: *A Fixture in Carlton since 1946*. Funeral Home and Crematory. *Cremation.* Guy Flandreau worked there, and he was the most obvious link connecting all these dots: He'd left with Beatrice John, who told Ed the bishop burned the lady. And the note Ed got was on the same paper as that found in Flandreau's cabin and at the cult site. Flandreau rented the cabin from Delbo. If the funeral home were involved—if Flandreau were the bishop, and if there were sacrifices—the bodies could be cremated. And if the Warriors of Yahweh were sex traffickers, no one would even know the identities of the victims, so no one—at least no one locally—would miss them.

Plenty of *ifs*, but she could feel something clarifying. If those *ifs* were right, Delbo could be clean—the rental *could* be a coincidence. But the other two dots—the crematory opening and the ledgers ending in 1946—might connect.

Wait. Was Flandreau old enough to have been working at the funeral home in 1946? He'd be in his early eighties now. Ed had mentioned something about a muscle shirt, and a tattoo. Most eighty-year-olds don't wear wife-beaters. Or tattoos. At least none of the eighty-year-olds she knew did. She dialed Ed's work number. Amazingly, he answered.

"It's me. How old would you say Guy Flandreau is?"

"Geez, that's tough. I didn't get a real good look. Maybe thirty?"

She felt herself deflate. "So Flandreau couldn't have been around in 1946."

"God, no. Nowhere near that old."

"Still," she said, "Flandreau may be the leader now, so I'm thinking the funeral home's involved." Then it hit her: if Flandreau wasn't around in '46, whoever *founded* the funeral home might be relevant. She said, "Gotta run. Just thought of something."

She ended the call and pulled out her notes. *Marvin P. Stark.* He'd founded the mortuary in 1946. The sole fingerprint they'd come up with tied to a Virgil Stark. She turned to the computer and brought up the new genealogy software they'd installed last year. She'd never used it before, and it took a few minutes to satisfy herself she wasn't going to use it now.

She hit the Reception button. "Callie, can you use the genealogy program?"

"Can the Pope speak Latin?"

"Huh. Okay, would you see if you can find out if Virgil Stark is a descendent of Marvin P. Stark, who lived in Carlton after 1946."

"Give me a few minutes."

Excited now, Andi wanted to be doubly sure she had her facts right. She went back over her notes, literally making dots and connecting the two that, at this moment, she thought connected. Her phone rang.

"I don't know what you deputies would do without me," Callie chuckled. "Virgil Stark is the second son of Marvin Stark, who died in 1997. That enough for you?"

Damn right! "Perfect, Callie."

This strengthened her suspicion that the elder Stark might have either led the cult from 1946, or had somehow been recruited to help them dispose of bodies. *Wait. Am I remembering the date right? Is it 1946?* A mistake would be crushing—and Ordrew would never let it be forgotten.

She entered her ID, locked her computer, and headed to the evidence locker to double-check the ledger and the business card. Well, okay, quadruple-check. *Pretty anal,* she thought, but she didn't care.

The shelf that she and Pete had put everything on was bare. *Moved?* Frantic, she checked all the remaining stacks, every shelf. The evidence—all of it: ledgers, tools, rose-colored papers, bullwhip, fabric, business card—gone.

She leaned her forehead against the top shelf, barely able to breathe.

87

Her heart pounding, Andi grabbed the sign-out sheet to see who had checked out the evidence. The last signature was Pete's, Tuesday, and he'd checked out no individual items. *Why would Pete move everything? And to where?* Only two other signatures appeared for pieces of the evidence: hers two weeks ago for the logbooks and the business card and six days ago for the red snag of cloth; and Lannie McAllister's for the logbooks—two weeks ago, when he'd done the random search of identities and found none living in the valley. *Damn!*

Sick to her stomach, Andi relocked the room and hurried to her computer and pulled up the tracking log, which registered the computer-entered IDs. Just as on the sheet, the electronic log showed that she'd gone in last Saturday, and Pete on Tuesday. He'd been on his usual rounds Tuesday, which meant he'd have entered the evidence room to make sure everything was in its place. That should have been the last entry. Should have been.

But the most recent entry was *her* ID, at 12:59 a.m. Wednesday morning. *Two days ago!* She fought off panic, breathed deep, forcing herself into a state of icy concentration. Who'd used her ID? All the deputies had access to everyone's IDs, so it could've been any one of them. She hated to think that, but where else to start? Who would want to stop the investigation cold?

A better question: Who would be hurt by this? She would, of course. And who'd want to hurt her? Brad Ordrew.

She stiffened, riveted by a fierce focus. She went to Callie's desk. "Callie, who was on midnights Tuesday night?"

Callie looked startled. "You look dog-bit."

"Something big just came up."

"Okay. Midnights Tuesday. Deputy or dispatch?"

"Both."

Callie tapped some keys and peered at her screen. "Deputy was Lannie. Dispatch was Marla—Evie called in sick. Why?"

She hesitated. Word getting out about the missing evidence would be trouble for the department, so she said nothing. "I've got a question for them. I need to know if there were any periods of time early Wednesday morning when Lannie was on a call and Marla..." She wondered how to phrase it. "When Marla might've stepped out, maybe for a smoke."

"I can answer the first one." She typed a few commands, again peering at the screen. "Lannie was called out on a drunk and disorderly at 12:36 a.m., returned at 1:42." She looked up at Andi. "Marla doesn't smoke."

Calling Marla could wait a few minutes. "Ben still around?" she asked, her voice stiff.

Callie frowned. "What's going on?"

"Trouble in paradise. Can't say much till Pete and Ben okay it."

She paused. Ben, despite coming in every morning, was technically on medical leave for two more weeks, so Pete was still Acting Sheriff.

"Ben's home. Says it's too quiet around here."

"Won't be for long. But I'll call Pete."

She returned to the squad room and called Pete's cell phone. He didn't pick up. She went out to Callie's desk again. "Do you know where Pete is, Callie? I just tried to call his cell."

"No answer? He's up north meeting a couple ranchers about a fence break. Let me radio." Callie sent out a call for Pete to contact the station a.s.a.p. In a few minutes, he was on the line, and Callie patched him through to Andi.

"What's up?" he asked.

She told him.

"Crap." His voice shook. "It was all there on Tuesday. Nobody's signed it out?"

"Nobody signed the log...but there's more."

"What?"

She told him about her ID.

"This is bad, Andi." She was grateful that he didn't add the obvious: She had to be the prime suspect. But why would she have moved—or stolen—her own evidence? And why would she call Pete to tell him?

For the moment, she didn't want to mention her suspicion about Ordrew. "I think I should tell Ben. Technically, that's your call, though, being the Acting."

Pete was quiet for a long moment. "I'll call him. It's on my watch. Geez, Andi, this is terrible. If word gets out our evidence room isn't secure, all the convictions based on our evidence go up in smoke."

She didn't say anything for a moment, thinking, *It's Ordrew. To get at me*. She recalled how often lately he'd brought up her "losing" evidence. Or his smirk when he said, about the election next year, "I'll win it, too, Pelton. And when I do, you *will* be done." This would give him all the ammunition he needed.

The icy focus blurred into a wash of anger and dread, and she felt like she might throw up.

88

When Pete hung up, she waited until the nausea had retreated, leaving a dark dread. She dialed Marla's home number.

"Hey, Marla, it's Andi. Question: Tuesday night, say around 1:00 a.m., did anybody come into the department?"

"Like who?"

"Anybody. One of the guys, a citizen, anybody."

Marla was quiet. "Ah, Andi, this is hard. If I tell you something, can it stay between us?"

"Probably. It depends what you tell me."

Another silence stretched on. Finally, Marla said, "Uh, no. Nobody came in that night. It was real quiet."

"You sure?"

Marla sighed. "Damn. I knew I'd get caught. I wasn't at the desk for a little bit Tuesday night. The baby got sick and Johnnie asked me to come home and help him."

Andi narrowed her eyes. "Wow, Marla. You left the desk uncovered?"

"We got a procedure for that. We set the system to forward any calls to the hospital operator. We do that from time to time when one of us has something pressing to do or has to go to the bathroom. Thing is, I've never left the station before."

"So what time were you gone, exactly?"

"Oh, I don't know. No, wait. I left just after Lannie caught that D & D call, and got back, maybe forty-five minutes later." Her voice got shaky. "I suppose you've got to tell Ben. I mean Pete."

"Let me think it over. Thanks for telling me, though. Best not do it again." She ended the call. So the station was empty roughly between 12:45 and 1:30 in the morning. And the theft happened at 12:59. Coincidence? Or was the thief watching?

She heard Ben out in reception, and stood. He paused at the squad room door. "Andi! My office."

They'd just gotten there when Pete came in, back from his

business up north. Ben told him to close the door, then looked at Andi and, as he flopped into his chair, said, "Pete called me. I'm startin' with the hunch it ain't you who stole the evidence, but I need to hear it from you."

"It wasn't me, Ben. Trouble is, I look responsible for it." She told them about her suspicion of Ordrew, then felt she had to fill in a blank. "Last Saturday, I opened the evidence room with Mike Payne, the deputy I'm working the fire case with from Carlton. I don't know, he might've gotten my ID somehow."

"Doubt it, but let's do us a little experiment." He led them down the hall to the squad room, and pointed at Andi's chair. "Sit here," he said. "Exactly where was this guy standin'?"

"I wasn't sitting, I was bending over." She took that position, then indicated where Mike had been standing while she typed her ID.

Ben took his place there. "How tall's this joker?"

She looked at Ben. "An inch shorter than you."

"Good. So for me, your shoulder blocks the right side of your keyboard real good—if I can't see it, he couldn't either. Pete, you stand where you can see the whole keyboard." After Pete came around the desk to where he could see, Ben said, "Pete, you and me, memorize what she types. Andi, type your ID, usual speed." They watched her fingers. Her shoulders were hunched with tension.

When she was done, Ben said, "Hell, that's nine digits typed real fast. I got the first two: 43."

Pete said, "I got five, but I thought they were 54903."

Andi relaxed, a little. "The first five are 53992."

Ben snorted. "So we can rule the Carlton guy out. Him gettin' your ID's 'bout as likely as findin' condoms in a nun's pocket."

Despite her tension, Andi chuckled.

They returned to Ben's office. Ben sat heavily. "Like I said, it ain't the Carlton guy. We got us an insider." He rubbed his eyes. "Crap. Shoulda stayed in the damn hospital." He looked at Pete. "Hate to say this, Pete, but you gotta take the shift from whoever's on midnights tonight and check everybody's desk and any place somebody could stash something from the evidence. See what you can find."

Pete nodded. He looked sad. "My gut reaction is, who'd be stupid enough to leave it here in the department? I sure as hell wouldn't." He frowned. "I know I've gotta do it, but hell, distrusting my friends galls me."

Andi felt that too. "Want me to come in and help?"

Ben grunted. "Bad idea. At the moment, you're suspect number one. You let Pete do it. Now get your buns outa the station till we know more."

It was going to be a long, restless night.

SATURDAY

89

Andi heard the phone ringing, and drifted up from sleep that had been a long time coming. Ed was answering. She glanced at the alarm clock: *6:03*.

"It's Pete, for you." Ed's voice was husky with sleep.

She was wide awake, instantly, her heart racing.

"Andi, can you come in?"

"What did you find?"

"Not over the phone. How soon can you be here?"

"Twenty minutes. I'm on my way." She got out of bed.

Ed was awake. "You remember Mack and I are scouting elk today?"

"Have fun. I'll be spending the day in hell."

Pete closed Ben's door, gingerly, as if it were wired to a bomb. "I feel crappy about this, Andi, but you need to know what I found."

"Do I want to know?"

"You need to. I called Ben, he should be here any minute."

As he spoke, the door opened and Ben came in. "What we got?"

"It's lousy. Just lousy." Pete pulled an evidence bag filled with bits of paper and handed it to Ben. Andi moved closer and studied it as well. Filling it was rose-colored confetti, and what appeared to be shreds of the Carlton Mortuary business card.

She looked back to Pete. "Where'd you find this?"

"In your bottom drawer."

90

For a short while, they sat in silence as Andi fended off a strangling anger that had forced her to jump up and pace the office.

After a couple of minutes of her pacing, Ben said, "Cool your jets, Andi, we gotta do us some real hard thinkin'."

She nodded, and sat. Gripped the arms of the chair.

"So where are we?" Ben asked.

Pete cautioned, "Let's go slow. Maybe there's an explanation. Andi, did you shred any of the evidence for some reason?"

"Hell no!" she snapped. "I know this looks bad, but Jesus Christ!"

Ben said, "Calm yourself. You ain't the only one who ain't likin' this much. Either I think it's you did it, or I have to think one of my other deputies did it. Either way, it's a rotten choice on a Sunday mornin'." He ran his stubby fingers through his hair. "Well, ain't no use bitchin' about this. Andi, I got me a couple questions, and then you better go on home while Pete and me sort this one out."

Her insides felt hollowed out. For a moment, she could only look at him while she gathered the strength to ask it: "You're thinking it was me?"

"Hell, no. But all I know for sure is: one, it ain't me, two; I'm pretty sure it ain't Pete; and three, I ain't able to convince myself it was you. But the evidence says you."

Andi nodded, calmer. "You said you have questions."

Ben scribbled hard black circles on a piece of paper, not looking at her. "You able to give me any other suspects?"

She thought about Ordrew's threat, and his overall dislike of her—of female police in general. To her, it made him a suspect. But he could claim she was out to get him, couldn't he? *She said, he said.* It was her ID, not his, that opened the evidence room door.

She took a long breath, composing her words. "Without the evidence, the investigation is back to zero, and the only one who seems interested in me screwing up the investigation is Brad. He, uh...damn, I hate to sound whiney, but on Friday morning, he told me if he wins the election next year, I'm gone. He doesn't think women belong in police departments."

Ben continued scribbling black circles. "So you're thinkin' it's Ordrew."

Andi hesitated. "If it's inside, I'd lean toward him. But..."

"We ruled the Carlton deputy out." He shot a glance at Pete. "Agree?"

Pete narrowed his eyes. "Yeah, boss. But spell your reasons out anyway."

"First thing, he ain't got no motive."

Andi nodded. "Mike's a good cop. He wants to solve the case as much as I do."

"Second thing," Ben said, "our experiment. It ain't possible he could see numbers on the right side of the keyboard." He gazed at the ceiling. "I've known Harvey Vogel thirty-five years. He's lots of things, but he's a damn good sheriff, and he don't have no corrupt deputy in his shop."

Andi felt her heart sink. "But what if you have one in yours?"

Ben nodded sadly. "Ain't what I want to think, but it's what we're pointin' at, no?"

Pete scratched his head. "What about the Warriors of Yahweh? Could they have done it?"

Andi frowned. "We don't know enough about them. I suppose we should consider it."

Ben pressed more hard black circles into his notebook. "Find out what you can. Me, I ain't got the feelin' some outsider could get in the station and us never hear about it."

Andi sighed. "During about forty-five minutes around the time my ID was logged in, the station was empty."

Ben's face reddened. He crumpled his doodle sheet into a dense wad, squeezing hard. "What the hell's that mean?"

"Lannie was out on a call and Marla went home for forty-five minutes to take care of her sick baby. She said they have a procedure—they set any 911 calls to forward to the hospital operator—"

"That goddamn procedure's for emergencies. I don't give a good rat's ass what's her excuse!" Ben threw the wadded paper at the wastebasket, hard. "Marla was on *duty,* damn it. What kinda department am I runnin' here?" The ball of paper bounced off the rim onto the floor.

Pete said, "I'll handle Marla, Ben. Don't give yourself another heart attack."

Ben shook his head, disgusted. "So some asshole from that gang might've gotten in here, but how'd they get into the evidence room? Any chance one of them has your ID?"

While she opened her wallet and thumbed through her cards, Andi let her thoughts run quickly through all that had happened in the case. Not once had she set eyes on a member of the Warriors of Yahweh, that she knew of. Ed had glimpsed Guy Flandreau, but only for a few seconds. Beatrice John he'd known a few minutes longer, but Andi couldn't draw a line from that to the department's evidence room. Her department ID was there. "I don't see how they could," she said. "Hell, even if they did get in the station while Marla was gone, they would've had to break down the evidence room door."

"Whoever did it, *did* have your ID," Pete said.

"So we're back to Ordrew," she said.

"Ain't wanted to bother you with this," Ben said, "but Jack Kollier called me from Missoula couple days ago, said he was doin' a story and wanted a confirmation. He said, quote, 'a reliable source' told him you failed to protect the crime scene up on the mountain."

"He referring to the murder scene being scraped clear?"

"The same."

Her anger rekindled. "Shit. What'd you say?"

"Told Jack to go to hell. Didn't you think last spring that Brad was leaking information to Kollier about the Hansen case?"

"I did."

"Takin' your evidence fits what he's been sayin' to a T. He could call Kollier, tell him you stole it." Ben got up and walked over to the wastepaper basket, stooped, picked up the wad of paper, and threw it directly into the basket. "Crap on goddamn toast."

"Okay, it turns my stomach, but let's say Brad's our guy," Pete said. "But the evidence—the ID and the shredding in your drawer, points right at you."

She nodded. "So I should leave."

Ben held up his hand. "Hold your horses. Got me a couple more questions." He looked hard at her. "If you were sheriff, what's your next move here?"

She took a deep breath, grateful that Ben trusted her so deeply. "First thing I'd do is dust my keyboard, see if Brad's prints are on it."

Ben nodded. "Yep. Just what we'll be doin'. Pete, you handle that?"

Pete looked skeptical. "On it, boss, but if it's Ordrew—or any cop—they'd know not to leave prints."

Ben nodded. "Thought of that. But let's hope he slipped up." He paused, then added, "Take the keyboard and do it in the evidence room, Pete. Don't let nobody see you."

After Pete left, Ben said, "What else?"

"We need to find those logs. Maybe whoever stole them got sloppy and left some prints on them."

Ben frowned. "I'm bettin' those logs are ashes at the bottom of Ordrew's, or somebody's, fireplace. He'd be stupid to leave 'em anyplace we could find 'em. And if he's one of them Warriors, those bastards fix their problems with fire."

Andi shook her head. "I can see Ordrew wanting to discredit me, but I don't know about him being in the Warriors. If it was the gang, and somehow they got my ID, my hunch is they wouldn't destroy them. They've got a long tradition of careful record-keeping. I'm thinking they're re-hidden, probably with the logs for 1947 and on."

"You ain't found logs for any time after 1946, right?"

She grimaced. "Yeah. So it's possible they don't exist, and the Warriors of Yahweh aren't as interested in records as they were before 1946."

"Me, I ain't thinkin' it's possible. I'm thinkin' it's probable."

"Okay, but I can't see Brad as a Warrior of Yahweh."

"Because?"

"He's not criminal, he's anal. He's law-and-order, procedures, protocols. What he doesn't like about me is I'm not as obsessed with that as he is."

"Okay. But if Brad's thinkin' about derailin' your investigation, that's criminal."

"By derailing the investigation, he derails me. Like I said, he wants me gone."

Ben closed his eyes. "And if we ain't fixed this pronto and word leaks, I'll have to suspend you. Maybe fire you."

They looked at each other somberly for a long moment. Ben shook his head again, cleared his throat. Pete came back into the office. He shrugged helplessly. "The only prints on your keyboard are yours."

Ben cleared his throat. "We knew it was a long shot. Back to them logbooks. I got me one more question, Andi. If it's Ordrew, why would he keep the books?"

Andi was relieved to get past the talk of suspension. She thought about Ben's question. "He keeps them a year and during the election campaign, he drops the bomb, accuses you publicly of failing to protect evidence, and then, just before the election, he heroically 'finds' the logs, cameras rolling."

Ben nodded. "Fits. Kills two birds with one stone: you and me. If you're right, our boy Bradley might be law-and-order, but he's rotten wrapped in rules. So the solution is: find the damn books."

"They could be anywhere," Andi said, standing to go.

Ben nodded. "Like findin' a mouse turd on a mountain."

WEDNESDAY

91

For three days, the tension hadn't let up. After the meeting with Ben and Pete on Saturday, Andi had gone home. As she'd unlocked the door, the thought had stunned her: Whoever planted the evidence in her bottom drawer in the office might have broken into her house and left more evidence there. *My God, what if he burned the ledgers in my fireplace?* She found no ashes, though, and set about methodically searching every possible hiding place, glad of having something more useful to do than waiting and worrying.

Around five, Ed had called. "I'm back from the mountains with Mack. Want to meet me for dinner at the Angler?"

"Uh, I can't, Ed. Something's come up at the station. I'm, kind of, waiting to hear from Pete about it." She could wait at the Angler as well as at home, but she hadn't felt up to small talk. Or any talk.

"Serious?"

"Could turn out to be." She had decided not to mention the missing evidence until she heard from Ben and Pete. If they decided to suspend her, the story would come out soon enough.

"Well, if you hear from Pete, let me know. The invitation stands."

But Ben hadn't called until late on Saturday evening. "Me and Pete decided mum's the word," he said. "News gets out about this clusterfuck, every conviction based on our evidence goes up in smoke. We'll just give 'er a while to settle out. Face that nightmare later."

She took a breath. "So I'm not suspended?"

"Not yet. As long as just you, me, Pete, and whoever stole the goods are the only ones who know, we'll keep it under the radar. 'Course, once the story breaks, I ain't got no choice, I'll have to suspend you. Meantime, keep workin' your case like nothin' happened."

So over Monday and Tuesday, she'd struggled to appear normal. A half-dozen times, she'd called Mike about Delbo, the only direction she could take the case at this point. She wanted a line on Guy Flandreau, and the line to Flandreau went through Delbo. Or Scopus? No, Flandreau had left the mortuary. She figured if he came back, he'd first contact Delbo for a place to stay.

Mike returned her calls each time, but begged her not to interfere with Carlton's surveillance. Hanging up the last time, she ignored her annoyance with him and considered: Carlton was convinced Delbo was running a sex slavery ring. If they were wrong, waiting was wasting time. But if they were right and she interfered...not a good choice.

But she couldn't feel it. The old man had given them too much, and she recalled his vehemence, his outburst of anger and disgust, when she'd accused him of sex trafficking.

So, mid-Tuesday, tired of inaction, she decided: If she wanted Flandreau, she'd go after Flandreau. She'd worked the phones on a new APB for him, and called fifty or sixty—she lost count—sheriff's and police departments in southern California, and then in the mountain regions of Montana, Idaho, and Wyoming, to follow up on the APB. She rode her assigned patrols, answered routine DUIs and domestics when it was her turn, and behind it all, quietly tried to forge a link between the missing ledgers and Brad Ordrew.

This morning, she was no further along on any of it than she'd been on Sunday morning, except she was growing more certain Ordrew had stolen the evidence. He'd been far too civil for the last few days.

—

Around nine, Ben barged in to the deputies' squad room and clapped his hands briskly. "Great walk this mornin'," he said. "Nice nip in the air."

Andi smiled through her tension. "You the guy who hates walking?"

"One 'n' the same." He rubbed his hands briskly together. "Let's go talk about this damn murder case. Why don't you get your boyfriend and we'll have us a sit-down. Pete told me he's our consultant now. I'll find Pete."

Andi called Ed's office, invited him to join them in the conference room.

"I'm free for a half-hour. Be right over."

When Ed joined them in the conference room, Andi smiled at him. "I was just telling Ben that I talked yesterday with the Southern Poverty Law Center and they know these Warriors of Yahweh. Apparently they started as a prison gang, but now they're outside too, and their gig is running drugs and Mexican girls for the sex trade."

"That fits with something I've discovered." Ed laid a folder on the table.

Andi wondered if Ben hadn't heard him, because the sheriff asked, "We sure it's the same gang?"

She shrugged. "I'd bet on it. SPLC isn't wrong about people like this. I found a dozen groups on the Internet using Yahweh or Warrior in their name, but only this one named Warriors of Yahweh, in that exact form."

"Leadership?" Pete asked.

"Four main guys. Three are doing life in maximum security, one at Parchman Farm in Mississippi, and two at Corcoran in California. One is out, living in Crawford, Texas. Montana leadership's unknown; in fact, SPLC thinks there may not be any state leaders. Apparently, outside the prison system, the individual groups are more like sleeper cells, running their own operations independently. SPLC says their religious propaganda is a cover to keep their drug mules and peons in line."

Ben said, "Your guy up at Wallace's Corner? He a possible?"

Andi frowned, then looked at Pete. "I'm doubtful," she said. But she added what Mike Payne and the Carlton sheriff thought.

Ben grunted, and they all looked at him. "Me and Harley talk once, twice a week. He ain't never mentioned that."

"Mike says they've got him under surveillance. Says his story about the Bataan march is bogus. Says no one named Delbo is in the official record."

"Hmm," Pete said. He opened a folder and pulled out a sheet, sliding it across the table toward Andi. "When I get a few minutes, I've been doing some Internet searching too. A few days ago, I found a list of the missing and presumed dead from the Bataan Death March. Delbo's name doesn't appear, but there's a Corporal C. M. Delbourn, from Choteau."

Andi held her breath. Could this be the answer?

Ben, as if reading her mind, said, "'Delbo' ain't much of a stretch from that."

Pete nodded. "Agreed. Also, he apparently did some prison time in 1949-50."

"Maybe he hooked up with this gang then."

Andi shook her head. "SPLC says there's no evidence this gang existed until the late 1990s." But learning Delbo had done time shook her.

Ben growled, "Jesus in a sidecar. So how do those logs connect with a gang that ain't even around till eighty years later?"

Andi looked at her notes a moment. "SPLC says the Warriors, like a lot of trafficking cults, move in on existing small-time cult-type groups. They basically take over. The gang offers the local cults muscle and money, and the cults give the gang a local distribution channel for drugs and an underground railroad for the women. Also, a cut of the revenue. And the religious cover."

"Crap," Ben said. "So we maybe got us a local bunch of some kind taken over by the Yahweh guys. A local group none of us knew diddly about." He shook his head, then turned to Pete. "What was Delbo's charge in, when'd you say, 1949?"

"Kidnap and transfer of a minor over state lines."

Nobody spoke for a moment. Andi felt her already-thin confidence in Delbo stretched thinner. On top of the missing evidence and her responsibility for it, the possibility that she'd badly misjudged Delbo weighed on her.

Pete continued. "It seems a few months after his conviction, his lawyer presented new evidence that the victim was a relative by marriage from the Philippines and that she'd asked for his help getting into the U.S. That had been the defense in the trial, but there hadn't been any real evidence before. Seems the charges were changed to traveling with a minor without parental consent and his sentence reduced to time served. Very strange, but it fits his story."

Andi sat up straighter. "Say that again."

Pete did.

"So he was importing a Philippine woman...a relative of, I suppose, his wife's."

"Yep."

Andi felt a flood a relief. *Gotta call Mike about this, soon as the meeting's over.* Then she thought, *He must know about the conviction already. It's probably why he is so set that Delbo's trafficking.*

Ben walked over to the coffee machine and poured himself a cup. "So we got, what, Delbo's maybe the bad guy and maybe not?"

Andi said, "I still think his story hangs together, especially with what Pete just gave us. But Delbo knows *something*. Every time we mention ICE, he drops another lead."

"ICE?" Ben dropped into his chair, and they told him about Delbo's smuggling Philippine relatives over the years.

Ben took it in, then looked sadly at his coffee. "A goddamn pile of bad news on a mornin'. First we got us a prison gang runnin' sex workers, next we got us an informant's been doin' a little traffickin' on his own. You let him go?"

Pete said, "He came back, though. And he talks if we goose him."

"Well, then get the hell up there and goose him till he squeaks." He stared at his coffee, then muttered, "Oh, what the hell," and poured cream and sugar into it. After he'd stirred it, he said, "How good's his story about Philippine relatives? You say Carlton's got it down as bogus?"

Andi said, "I'm inclined to believe him, especially with that conviction reversed in '49."

"And you, Pete?"

Pete nodded. "Me too, boss."

Ben waved a hand. "I ain't the boss till Doc signs my ticket."

Ed cleared his throat. "I might have something of interest." He opened the folder. "First, here's that message about Beatrice John being taken to put with the evidence." He slid the rose-colored pencil-scrawled page toward Andi. There was an awkward silence. Andi hadn't confided in Ed about the missing evidence.

"What?" he asked, looking around.

Ben picked up his coffee cup; a little sloshed on his desk. "Nothin'. So what'ya got there?" He pointed at the folder.

"A buddy back at the University of Minnesota is a psycholinguist who has done work on cults' use of language. I sent him a copy of the Warriors' tract. I've got his analysis here." He pulled a single page from his folder. "I asked him two questions: What does he think the propaganda means, and why does he think they kept such meticulous records in their ledgers." He cleared his throat. "I need to mention this is all speculative. Until we actually talk to one of these Warriors, we can't know their real thinking and motives."

Andi reminded them, "You know, the people who kept the ledgers and the Warriors aren't one and the same. In fact, they're almost certainly different groups."

Ed nodded, then began reading:

"The document has multiple encoded references to sexual intercourse and discusses an alleged culture of sexual excess that is evil or demonic. A recurring theme: They supply the 'enemy' (the 'lustful public,' probably) with their 'objects of lust' in order to 'trap' them. Then by satisfying their lusts, the 'enemy' draws God's attention and punishment. A common, almost banal rationalization used by many kinds of prostitution rings taking cover behind pseudo-religious rhetoric—'we are pure, we supply impurity in order to purify the world.'"

Ben growled. "And how does this purification happen?"

Ed looked up. "By Yahweh's fire."

No one spoke.

Finally, Ben asked, "Ed, you have a copy of that tract on you?"

Ed extracted the rose-colored sheet from his folder. "Here you go." As Ben took the page, Andi glanced at Pete. *Evidence,* she mouthed. He nodded. They all listened as Ben read slowly.

"We are Yahweh's Warriors, which are not defiled with women nor deterred by the lusts of the heart. We are they which follow Yahweh faithfully, which attack His enemies and pierce them in their sin, in their sinful vessels. We are Warriors against those which are defiled, but are ourselves undefiled by the world's Jezebel adulteries.

"These Warriors of Yahweh destroy any man which hurts them or impedes their work by breathing Yahweh's fire on them, and thus our enemies will be destroyed.

"We who are Warriors of Yahweh deliver to our enemies the objects of their lusts, but we feel no lust. We procure for our enemies the fruits of their desires, but we do not eat those fruits. We are faithful and pure, procuring evil but untouched by it. Let our enemies satiate their lusts through us, and thus be destroyed by the harsh wind and hot fire of Yahweh. We are His Warriors!"

Ben looked around. "Thoughts?"

Pete nodded. "Read that second paragraph again, but substitute "woman" for "man." Ben did so. Pete looked around. "Seems to describe the fire scene, if you ask me. A young woman became an obstacle in some way and was punished by fire."

Andi looked at Ben. "I was struck by that word 'procuring.' Read that again."

Ben searched for the word. "'We procure for our enemies the fruits of their desires, but we do not eat those fruits. We are faithful and pure, procuring evil but untouched by it.'" He looked up. "That the part?"

"Yeah. Procuring's an old term for pimping, right?" Ben nodded. Andi continued, "So, they pimp sex slaves but they themselves are pure of heart." Anger thickened her throat. "Hypocritical bastards."

Ben leaned back in his chair, resting his big hands on his belly.

"Ed, you asked your guy two questions. What'd he say about the ledgers?"

"Again, it's speculation. He thought the original group kept them as business records. He doubted there was any religious motive for them. And if you guys are right about the Warriors not being around in 1946, the ledgers won't tell us anything about them."

"Jesus. *Business*. Did you ask him why there's no books after, what is it, 1946?"

"No, I didn't. I doubt he'd be able to answer that."

Andi said, "Let me connect some more dots. We know the mortuary was opened in 1946 by Marvin Stark, who was Virgil Stark's father. Virgil's fingerprint showed up at the murder scene. It's plausible that Virgil's father somehow got involved with the original cult in 1946. He might have been the leader, or maybe he was recruited to cremate victims. It's plausible too that maybe at that point they stopped keeping records at all. We just don't know."

Ben slapped the table. "So let's get our butts up to Wallace's Corner and put Delbo's precious ass against the wall."

Andi frowned. "He's ninety-three years old, Ben."

"Meanin' he might croak tomorrow. So go squeeze him dry before he dies."

92

Mike was off duty when Andi called the Carlton County Sheriff's office, but the receptionist offered Andi his cell phone number. He answered.

"Hey, Mike, just calling to say I'm changing direction on Delbo. My boss just ordered us to push him hard. We've got to find out if he's the leader of the trafficking ring; and if not, who is? I think he knows a lot more than he's giving us and I can't wait any longer."

"Andi, don't. I think he's about to move—he's been quiet as a mouse for too long."

"He's no mouse, and I'm going up, boss's order."

"Damn it, Andi, you push him, he'll know you're getting close.

It'll blow everything."

Andi heard anger in his voice. "I don't think so, Mike. Delbo believes we're looking at the Warriors of Yahweh, not at him. He thinks we trust him. If I push him, your investigation isn't compromised. You're still off to the side. He won't think we're on to him about sex trafficking unless he puts you and me together, and so far he hasn't got any reason to do that."

A long silence. Finally, Mike said, "He's our guy, Andi, I'm sure of it. If you push him about the Warriors, he'll figure you're getting close, and close means close to him."

Probably true, damn it. "Okay, tell you what: I'll wait an hour. Have your boss call Ben Stewart and if Ben agrees to wait, I will. If not, I'm leaving in an hour with a search warrant."

"Shit." Another long silence, then, "Okay. An hour."

For the first time since they'd met, Mike sounded angry. She understood his position: His case was going down the drain. Like hers.

93

An hour passed. Andi knocked on Ben's door. He and Pete were looking at the overtime budget, and neither was smiling. "Ben?"

He looked up. "Come."

"Have you and Harley Vogel made a decision?"

"Me and Harley? What decision we talkin' about here?"

"He was going to call you and argue against my pushing Delbo."

He looked at Pete. "You take any calls?"

Pete shook his head. Ben said to Andi, "Well, then, he ain't called. What's this about?"

She explained Mike's surveillance.

Ben grabbed his phone. "Lemme call Harley." He dialed and waited. "Harley, Ben Stewart here....Feelin' damn good, actually. Heart's pumpin' like God made it to and the sugar diabetes...Yeah, got that too, but it's gettin' under control." He listened, then covered the mouthpiece and whispered, "Thinks this is a social call." After a moment, he said, "Gotta rush this, Harley, just a quick question. You got any problem with my deputy questioning Cassius Delbo, that old hermit up at Wallace's Corner?"

He listened, then said, "About the fire, the murder case I told you about." Listened. Nodded. "Many thanks, Harley." Ben hung up the receiver. "'No problem,' he says."

"Huh." Andi was surprised, but glad the way was clear. "Okay. I'm on my way."

Pete looked at Ben. "I'm up for a little road trip. This budget crap gets on my nerves, and Andi needs backup."

"Go. Only thing more deadly than budgets is a pissed-off bad guy with a gun. I'll finish these up, leave 'em on the desk for you to sign."

Andi smiled. "Pete, we'll leave in—" She checked her watch. "A half-hour. I'll order some sandwiches from Ted."

Back at her desk, she considered dialing Delbo's number—to drive up only to find him missing would be worse than a waste of time. But she decided not to tip him off, and put down the phone.

Through the window, she saw new snow, the season's first, drifting softly down.

94

Andi got sandwiches and coffee to go and she and Pete were just climbing into the department SUV when Ben trotted into the parking lot. Andi rolled down her window. He grinned, "Let's roll. Ain't a good day for budgets, and I ain't supposed to be workin'." He opened the side door of the SUV and got into the back seat. "Beautiful afternoon for a ride. First little snow."

"Ben, you said it yourself, you're not supposed to be working."

"Not supposed to be doin' lots of things, but that's not my problem. Lovely day. Let's go see us this old trafficker."

Andi glanced at Pete, shrugged, and turned the ignition.

The snow that had started softly during the morning continued. It was dry and powdery, and the wind blew it off the highway. Still dry, the roads were fine, and they made time. From his back seat, Ben kept up a steady stream of chatter, some about the case, but mostly happy chit-chat.

"You're in a fine mood this afternoon, Ben," Andi said, glancing at him in the rear-view.

"A good walk'll do that for a guy," he said.

Pete turned to face him. "Okay, Ben, what's this about walks? You hate exercise!"

Ben chuckled. "Never knew my neighborhood's got a bunch of women joggin' or walkin' every mornin'." When Andi and Pete looked at each other, he continued, "Don't go gettin' any ideas, but they're kinda takin' me under their wing. My neighbor, especially. Bernie O'Reilly. She's a hoot, from Chicago like you, Andi. They really hustle, so I sorta hang back and," he chuckled again, "enjoy the view, you might say."

The two in the front seat burst out laughing, and Ben grinned.

Andi nodded. "I know Bernie. We're in a ladies' group together."

Ben chuckled. "Bernie told me about that. Ted's boyfriend's in it, no?"

Pete looked at her.

"He does the best *hors d'oeuvres*."

As Highway 36 mounted the western flank of the Washington Mountains, the snow grew heavier. The plow hadn't come through, so Andi slowed and switched into four-wheel drive. Ben munched cheerfully on his roast beef sandwich; Andi had no appetite and had given him hers.

"Sure pretty up here," Ben said. "I forget how nice 'n' white the mountains get."

By the time they reached Delbo's drive, there were probably four inches on the ground. The driveway into Delbo's yard was unplowed, but the SUV had good clearance and four-wheel drive. Andi stopped anyway at the turn-in and surveyed the snow.

"No firm pavement under that snow. Think maybe we should walk?"

"Drive in," Ben said. "Got nothin' but my tennies on." He leaned into the front seat, peering at the driveway. "Ain't no tracks comin' out."

"That's the good news," Pete said.

"Unless he left before it started snowin'."

"That'd be the bad news."

Andi drove the SUV into the yard.

A track opened by a snowblower connected the house and the barn, and Delbo's pickup stood in the open garage, snow drifted against its rear tires. They found him in the woodshop, pushing red boards through the table saw.

"Mr. Delbo?" Andi called.

When he didn't hear her over the scream of the saw, they waited, careful not to startle him. When he switched off the saw and it whirred to a stop, Andi said again, "Mr. Delbo?"

He jerked, then turned toward them, angry. "Kill a man, creeping up."

Pete apologized. "Sorry, sir. We came to talk about—"

"No more talking."

Andi looked at Pete. He nodded, and she took over. "That's beautiful wood, Mr. Delbo. It's cherry, isn't it? My dad did woodworking after he retired."

Delbo turned to look at her. "Hobby or work?"

"Hobby. He was a police officer."

The old man softened a bit. "Good wood, cherry. Hope he handled it right."

"We need to ask some questions, sir."

Delbo shook his head. "Answered questions already." His glance lingered on Ben. "Who're you?"

"Sheriff Ben Stewart, Delbo, and you can drop the *no-more-questions* crap."

Delbo sized Ben up, and after a moment, shrugged. "Ask your questions. No more answers, though." He grinned.

Ben frowned, but folded his arms and leaned against a counter, letting Andi take the lead.

"We need everything you know about these sex traffickers."

"Already told."

"Who are their leaders?"

"Bring in Mex girls and sell them in Chicago, St. Louis, and Minneapolis."

"Wasn't the question, Delbo." Ben's voice was hard.

Delbo looked pissed, so Andi added, "Please, sir, we need to know about the leaders."

The old man went to a pile of uncut cherry wood planks and lifted one, sighting down its length. "Too fresh," he muttered, and dropped it on the pile. The next was straight, and he held it by the end, trying to flex it up onto the saw table. It bowed and he was laboring, so Andi quickly picked up the other end and placed it where he was aiming.

"Thank you, young lady," he said, and made some measurements with a tape and pencil.

Andi said, "Mr. Delbo, we need your help."

Delbo continued measuring. "Knew a man in California worked for guys like these. Told the police something, a small thing, figured never know it was him, the gang wouldn't. Nailed his hands to the bedroom doorframe, his feet to the floor. Took turns raping his wife in front of him, in his own bed. Took him down, tied 'em together on the bed back to back, burned his house to the ground." He took a hard breath, made some pencil marks on the plank. His voice came out thick. "Stuff you don't want to know. Not now, not ever."

Pete caught Andi's nod, and said, "That's a horrible story, you're right about that. But we've got ICE banging down our doors trying to get at you, and I can't hold them off much longer unless you help us. I can protect you as one of our informants, but no other way."

"Ain't no informer." Delbo turned his back and switched on the saw. Ben moved quickly and switched it off. Delbo glared at him, but Ben was a foot taller, more than thirty years younger, and probably a hundred pounds heavier. Delbo narrowed his eyes.

"Whatever we call it," Pete said, "if you help us, I can protect you. If not, I can't. And you dying in prison isn't going to help your granddaughter."

Delbo smiled a real smile. "Your prisons are water to me. Already died once. Fear those guys who made those bones. Them I'm scared of. ICE comes for me, I'll manage. No managing if those boys come for me. So you people go." He sighted along the board again, resting his hand on the power switch. "I learn more about them bones, call."

Ben snorted. "Ain't our job to call *you*, Delbo."

Andi translated. "When Mr. Delbo learns something, he'll call us." She looked at Delbo. "That right, sir?"

The old man grinned as he nodded. "Sheriff, girl listens better than you." Then he glared at Ben, daring him to interfere, and switched on the saw.

Andi stepped in and switched it off. "How do you know about the bones, sir?"

"Know one thing: bones there before I came. Not my business. I learn more about them, call." Again, he switched on the saw, and began slowly pushing the long board through the blade.

Andi looked at Ben and Pete, and pointed to the door.

As they drove out onto the plowed highway, Ben growled from the back seat, "That ain't how it was supposed to go down. We got diddly."

Pete turned to him in the back. "I think he's softening up, Ben. He said he'd call."

Ben snorted. "And if wishes was fishes..."

Andi said, "Did you notice his sentences at the end?"

Ben, leaning into the front seat, said, "What about 'em?"

"He put subjects in front of his verbs. He didn't say, 'Learn about them, call,'" he said, "'I learn more about them bones, call.'"

"Meanin'?"

"I'm thinking he's identifying a bit with us. He's on our side."

Pete said, "Pretty strong statement based on a pronoun."

Andi laughed, then grew serious. "I thought he looked genuinely afraid of the Warriors of Yahweh. Did you see his eyes when he told that story?"

Pete nodded. "I thought that too. Maybe you're right."

They drove a few miles in silence. Andi broke it. "I don't think

Delbo's the leader. All the connections we've uncovered funnel through Guy Flandreau. We find Flandreau, we find the Warriors of Yahweh."

Ben grunted. "And what kinda crap have we found then?"

95

Andi came late to the Ladies' Fishing Society. When Callie opened the door, she picked up the sober mood right away. She whispered to Callie, "What's wrong?"

Callie whispered back, "Maggie's under the knife Friday."

Chagrined at forgetting, Andi felt a now-familiar chill. Cancer. Menopause means you die. She waited for the jolt of anxiety, but it didn't come. Instead, just a soft enveloping sense of care for Maggie. She breathed gently, hoping the dread would stay away.

As she was hanging up her jacket in the mud room, Andi listened to the conversational murmur from the living room. No boisterous laughter, but no thick gloom, either. She waited at the doorway, not wanting to interrupt.

Lane was saying to Bernie, ". . . and Vic's got to be back here as soon as he can. The calves aren't weaned yet, and the fall haying got set back by the snow today, so I'm going with them to St. Pat's. Once Maggie's out of surgery and settled, I'll stay there and Vic'll come back to work. When she's ready to come home, I'll bring her over."

Bernie said, "Honey, that's the goddamned sweetest thing I ever heard from a man." She chuckled. "You're not quite a man, though, are you?"

Lane smiled. "I know a gay woman that sounds like an owl."

Bernie said, "Who?" Then she looked surprised when everyone laughed. Lane went to join Callie in the kitchen, patting Bernie on the head as he passed. He stopped when he saw Andi, gave her a quick hug.

Bernie laughed. "Damn, I enjoy that man!" Then she looked guiltily at Maggie.

"I can use a good laugh, Bernie," Maggie said. "I'm not dying, you know."

Andi went into the living room to join them. Bernie said, "Oh, look who the cat dragged in."

"Sorry I'm late," Andi said. "Working a tough case."

She sat beside Maggie, touched her knee. "How're you doing?"

Maggie nodded. "Hanging in. And I found an upside to cancer: Vic's stepped right up. Doing dishes every night, checking on me during the day, rubbing my feet. He's like a teenager in love."

Everybody chuckled. Callie and Lane came in from the kitchen with the first tray of appetizers. Lane said, "Glad you made it, Andi. Just in time for sweet and saucy jalapeño poppers and cranberry chili meatballs."

Andi realized she was starving. "Wow," she said. "Looks delicious."

For a few moments, the conversation quieted as everyone tasted. Then Callie said, "Let's talk about Friday."

Maggie shook her head. "No talk about Friday. The surgeon says it'll be easy, just take the lump and check the nodes. Then the radiation starts in two weeks. I'm not worrying till I have something to worry about."

Lane looked surprised. "Breast cancer isn't something to worry about?"

She shook her head again. "All done worrying about that. Next thing's the lymph nodes, and my philosophy is, no use fretting over them till I find out they're trouble."

A hot flash swept over Andi, and she was fanning herself before she knew it. Everyone looked at her. Adding to the heat, she felt embarrassed.

"Ah, the lady-fan," came from Bernie. "Got the change going on, eh?"

"A while now. It's been a struggle."

"Girl," Bernie said, "the whole thing's a struggle, no? First the curse, then the change. Hell, I haven't finished it yet, and I'm almost sixty. Burns my tushie."

"Literally."

Callie laughed. "I haven't started yet, but Bill says sleeping next to me is like a night-long hot flash. Guess I run on the hot side."

Bernie shook her head. "Callie girl, you're the hottie in this group by a long shot! Except maybe for Lane."

They all chuckled. Lane spoke quietly. "Andi, your feelings about menopause?"

That's the question, isn't it? She wondered how to answer, then remembered why she'd accepted Callie's invitation to join the Society: she was lonely. *You don't make friends by holding back,* she thought, and sighed. "It's been strange." She told them about her first insight: menopause causes aging.

"Hon, that there's a thought won't win you any scholarships." Bernie laughed, then added, "Come to think of it, being born causes aging."

Andi chuckled. "Well insight number two was that menopause causes cancer." She stopped, looked at Maggie. "Sorry, broke the no-cancer-talk rule."

Maggie shook her head. "No, tell us."

She told about her mother going through menopause and receiving her diagnosis at the same time. "I was just fourteen and even though it's irrational, I believed menopause caused the cancer."

Lane nodded. "Fourteen's the age for, what shall I call it, poetic thinking. When I was fourteen, I had a crush on one of the boys on my block. I told the priest and he said I was going to hell if I didn't get over it. Trouble was, the crush already was hell. So I did my best to listen to the priest. Believed him till I was twenty-four."

"Unless I'm deaf, dumb, blind, and stupid, something changed your mind," Bernie tossed in.

Lane nodded. "Ted Coldry." Everyone smiled. "Sorry to interrupt your story, Andi. Please, go on."

"One last insight was the real source of my nervousness." She considered that word. "Hell, it wasn't nerves, it was anxiety. The thought was, *menopause kills you*. I must have connected my mom's dying of cancer with her menopause. Crazy." It surprised her how easily she'd told the story.

Bernie shook her head. "Hell's bells, that's not crazy at all. When the change started for me, I couldn't admit what was happening. Saw my doctor every couple weeks with some new theory or another. Depression. Parkinson's. Dementia. You name it, I had it. Finally, after six months, he took my hand, real sweet, more like my daddy than my doctor. 'Bernie,' he says, 'do you know what makes a woman eligible to join AARP?' 'Uh-uh,' I said. But I knew, and I got it. 'So there's nothing wrong with me?' He shook his head. 'You're fine as a day in spring.' 'Hell,' I told him, 'I'm like the dog days of August.'"

Andi laughed with the others. Somehow, in the past few minutes, something had fully shifted inside her. It wasn't age, and it wasn't cancer, and it wasn't death. It was just menopause. Then something else came to her, a grief soft as the day's first snow.

With menopause, it was official: She'd never be a mother. She felt her eyes fill.

Bernie had been watching her. She whispered, "You're not done, darling."

Andi nodded, but wasn't able to speak.

"We'll wait," Bernie said, reaching for another sweet and saucy jalapeño popper.

Everyone was quiet, watching Andi. She found it excruciating, yet comforting. For the first time since her mother's death, she knew she could speak of a thing she felt powerless about without needing to run, needing to control the situation. She just had to wait till her throat opened.

After a few minutes, she said, "I'm nobody's mother...and now I won't be."

Callie smiled. "Look around the Ladies' Fishing Society."

"What?"

"Nobody here's anybody's mother. Or father," she added, nodding to Lane. "And if you don't mind me saying it, you've got one blessing over the rest of us."

Andi felt her eyes moisten again. "What's that?" And she knew.

Lane said it. "The love of Gracie Northrup."

—

When the meeting broke up and everyone had given Maggie a farewell hug, the outside air was cold. Stars were sharp in the dark sky. The morning's snow still lay fresh and blue on the grass. Andi trembled with the first delicious shiver of earth's long shift toward winter.

She decided she'd go home to Ed tonight. And Grace.

FRIDAY

96

Word came from Vic Sobstak at St. Pat's hospital a little after noon. Callie came into the deputies' squad room to tell Andi: Maggie's surgery went well, and there'd been no cancer in the lymph nodes. She could come home Sunday, if all stayed good.

Andi's emotion surprised her. Tears came as she sat at her desk, thinking about her mom's surgery news—nowhere near as good. But Andi's tears weren't for her mother, or herself. They were relief that this new friend of hers would be coming back to the valley and the Ladies' Fishing Society.

Callie waited as Andi grabbed a tissue and wiped her eyes, then patted her on the shoulder. "You and me both, Andi," she whispered, dabbing her own eyes.

WEDNESDAY

97

Five days passed with no news from Delbo and no word back from the APB on Guy Flandreau. Andi fielded the usual routine of accidents, intoxications, small-scale domestic calls—and a more serious assault, by a logger on his eldest daughter for having gotten pregnant. Except for the last, nothing out of the ordinary. Unlike Andi, the deputies were bored. She, though, was exasperated. She wanted to see Delbo again, but Pete and she agreed that they should wait, at least a couple days, hoping he would call as he'd promised.

When Andi came in to work, Callie pulled her aside. "We got bad news."

Alarmed, Andi said, "What?"

"Maggie's back in the hospital."

Her heart staggered. "Why? I thought the surgery was successful. She came home on Sunday—"

"It was successful, and yeah, she's been home. Her incision got infected, though. Vic took her to see Doc Keeley yesterday, and Doc put her in the hospital last night. She called me this morning."

"Oh, man." She shook her head. "Hospital? Must be bad."

"No, don't say that. Infections aren't cancer. Doc'll get it under control. She'll be okay."

But Andi's sense of foreboding was back. It wasn't panic, though. *Thank God for small favors*. But cancer can kill.

98

After she got off duty, Andi drove to the hospital to visit Maggie. Although she was still on an IV, she was already feeling better. "Doc says tomorrow, maybe Friday, I can go home."

"That's great." A gust of heat hit Andi and she started fanning. "Is it hot in here, or just me?"

Maggie smiled. "Just you, honey. How *you* been doing?"

"Well, I'm not fighting it so hard. And the anxiety attacks seem to be over."

"Good. Real good."

"And you?"

Maggie sighed. "Guess the news is as good as it could be. Cancer didn't spread to the nodes. Soon's this infection goes away, they're starting radiation. Can't say I'm looking forward to that part."

Andi reached over and touched Maggie's hand, then gave her a quick kiss. "We'll be right beside you all the way."

When she stood back, she felt tears in her eyes. *Been happening a lot lately,* she thought.

That evening, after dinner, Grace drove into town for a "homework session" with Zach, and Ed and Andi sat on the couch watching the fire in the wood stove. Fatigue mixed with frustration about Delbo's silence and concern for Maggie. She was telling him about Maggie's infection and quick recovery.

When she'd finished and they'd sat a few silent moments, Ed put his hand on her arm. "I'm glad she's okay. Do you mind if I change the subject? There's something I keep forgetting to ask you."

"Go ahead. I'm done."

"Okay. Have you guys finished scanning those ledgers into the computer? I think I know a search trick to find any duplicate entries."

She closed her eyes. "No, they're not scanned."

"When do you think that'll happen? I think discovering duplicates is important, don't you?"

"Uh...yeah."

He looked at her. "You're not having them scanned? Why not?"

"I'm not able to talk about it, Ed. Like you and your patients. Pete and Ben put the lid on talking about the evidence." Truth, just not the whole truth.

"So something's happened."

She forced herself quiet, not even allowing a nod. She placed her index finger against her lips.

He smiled. "Got it."

She heard the PV drive into the yard. She watched the fire darting and crackling in the stove. Except for firelight, the room was dark.

Grace came in, stopped. "Are you two fooling around?"

Andi thought, *That would take energy.*

When Grace's bedroom door closed, Ed asked, "*Are* we fooling around?"

The phone rang before she could answer. Ed picked it up, listened, handed to Andi. "For you. It's the evening dispatcher."

"Hi, Diana. What's up?"

"Andi, I've got a call for you. Guy says it's serious. Want me to patch him through?"

I was tired. "Caller give a name?"

"No, he wouldn't. Talks kind of funny."

Delbo? Her heart jumped. "Yeah, put him through."

In a moment, she heard the rough voice. "Hello?"

"This is Deputy Pelton. Is this Mr. Delbo?"

"Delbo," he answered, his voice distorted and echoey. A cell phone? "Could be gettin' myself killed, but they're meetin' now. As we speak."

"The Warriors?"

"Nobody else up here, Deputy. Okay. Told you. If they kill me, it's on you."

99

Excited, she quickly called Pete at home. "Delbo called. They're meeting right now. We've got to get up there!"

"Whoa," he said. "Think, Andi. It's eight o'clock. By the time we get up there—"

"We're wasting time talking about it! This could be a break in the case. I've got to get up there!"

"Slow down, Andi. There's too much we don't know. How many people will be there? Are they armed? How do you think they'll react to a couple of cops busting in on their meeting? These people kill. Let's think this through."

"Damn it, Pete! I've done nothing but *think* about this damn case—I need to *do* something."

Ed looked alarmed. "What's—?"

She put her finger to his lips, focused on Pete's voice.

". . . you've got more courage than anybody I know, but you're not thinking straight. Going into that situation with no plan in the middle of the night could get you killed. Let me call in the troops and we'll have a meeting and lay it all out."

So frustrated she could spit, she said, "Look. You and I should drive up there and wait on the highway. We'll take license plate numbers when they come out."

"Uh-uh. Two cops, alone and isolated—these guys *eliminate* obstacles, remember?"

She suddenly knew how unreasonable she was being; still, it went against every instinct to pass up this chance. She took a long breath. *Think.* "You're right. Call in the guys and we'll talk it over. God, I hate wasting Delbo's tip. He might not give us anything else."

"I think that's why we're unprepared for this: We never really expected Delbo to tip us off, so we never planned for a last-minute tip. Sloppy."

She took another long breath. "I suppose that's true." She glanced at Ed, sighed.

He still looked concerned, but said nothing.

Her knuckles whitened around the phone. "Okay, Pete. But we gotta make that plan now."

"Well, if we try to do anything tonight, by the time everybody gets to the department and we hash it all out, those bastards will be long gone. Let's take the evening to think about what we're missing, and we'll put our heads together first thing in the morning. We need a plan for the next time."

"If there *is* a goddamn next time."

THURSDAY

100

Andi lay awake, knowing there'd be no more rest. The clock on her side of the bed said *5:33*. She lay quietly a few minutes, hands behind her head, looking out the window, listening to Ed's breathing, rhythmic, calm. The night and her sleep had been lost to exasperation about the case. She'd assembled the bones of a plan, but had no idea if it was worth anything.

Pete had been right, of course. Going up to the cult site last night could have turned disastrous. The Warriors of Yahweh were brutes. But she hated wasting Delbo's tip—not only because the Warriors had been vulnerable, but because the old man might clam up now. Or disappear.

She felt something toughen in her. She'd push Delbo today. Granted, he'd given them the tip—too late to use. She needed more, and she would get it, today. Although it was her day off, after she met with Pete, she'd drive up, catch Delbo off guard. Resolved, she climbed out of the warm bed. When the cold floor and the chilly air hit her skin, she almost crawled back in. But she didn't; she got ready and drove into town. She forgot to leave a note for Ed.

At the department, she announced her plan, but Pete—another early riser—shook his head. "No you're not. We need to have a meeting to make a plan, and I don't want you going up there alone."

She frowned. "I can handle Delbo," she said, instantly disliking the irritation in her voice. A good night's sleep would've helped.

"Nope. I'm not sending anybody up there alone. These people are bad."

"I need to do this, Pete." She hesitated, then said, "It's my day off. I can drive any place I want."

He looked at her, his eyes hard. "Give me a minute to look at the schedule." After looking at the computer, he said, "Okay, I'm your man." Now *his* tone contained irritation.

For thirty miles, they rode in silence. Halfway up the mountain, Andi had looked over at Pete. "I'm sorry, Pete. I don't mean to be so pushy, but I'm dying to break this case."

He grunted. "Lousy choice of words, Andi. Dying is precisely what I want you to avoid."

She held her eyes on the road. "I know. I appreciate you coming with me." She glanced at him again.

"Okay, I'm over being pissed." He chuckled. "Working on a murder beats figuring out how to stretch the budget ten ways to Sunday."

"And this Mexican girl's murder is worse than vicious." She felt a throb of emotion in her chest. "Charlie Begay at DCI thinks she might've been twenty. My bet, she's younger. Teen meat's all she was to these people." She gripped the wheel hard. "I can't let it rest, and it won't let me rest."

Pete said nothing. After a moment, he nodded. "I'm here, right?"

She looked back to him. "Right. You're here." She added, "Thanks."

Delbo was piling hay on his garden rows, on top of the early snow, which obviously had taken him by surprise. He stood up stiffly when they pulled to a stop, glared at them, then bent down again to his work.

As they approached, he worked the row. Not standing or stopping, he said, "Finished talking. Risked my neck to tip you off, nothing happened. No more."

Andi said, "We appreciated your tip, but there wasn't time to get the team together, Mr. Delbo."

"Wasn't time." Delbo continued spreading hay. "Lying on that Bataan road, gutted, had no time, me. But Lydia *made* time for me." His voice vibrated with contempt. "Didn't *wait*, Lydia."

Andi, containing her irritation, lowered her voice. "Look, sir. When you called, the meeting was already happening. You must have known about it ahead of time. You didn't call until it was too late for us to act safely. I don't call that a real tip. We've been giving you time. We've held off bringing in ICE because you told us you would tell something useful. Last night's tip wasn't useful—if it was even true."

He straightened. "Call ICE if you want. Granddaughter's hid. Can't find her."

Andi opened the garden gate and stepped inside the tall fence. She walked to Delbo's side. He glared at her.

"We're completely stumped, Mr. Delbo. We need your help."

He shook his head, looking directly at her.

She said, "Please. Who is the bishop?"

Fear flickered in his eyes, then he quickly looked down to the hay pile. He shook his head. Very softly, he said, "No more. No more."

Andi went very still. Something about the fear in his eyes stopped her. She waited, hoping what had caught her would clarify in her mind if she said nothing.

Pete stepped up. "Mr. Delbo, I think we're going to have to take you down to—"

Andi interrupted. "Wait, Pete. I say we give him a last chance."

She felt the emerging thought more than thought it, stilled herself again to let it find words. Might his fear do what she hadn't been able to: wear him down? He claimed to have already died, to not fear death. But she'd seen it flicker in his eyes. As long as he'd had his granddaughter to protect, he could be bold, for her. But she was out of the picture, safe. Delbo was old, ancient as the forest. Fear, like water over rock, could erode a much younger man.

What could it do to a man in his nineties, all alone, surrounded by evil, with no one else to protect?

101

"That was one royal waste of time," Pete groused. "I want to trust your hunches, Andi, but damn it, we should've arrested him." Andi turned onto the highway back to Jefferson. "You were going to push him. Why'd you back down?"

"Did you see the fear in his eyes, Pete? When I asked about the bishop? He's afraid, and he knows we can help him. He'll call." Although she felt sure of her decision, it surprised her too. Pete was right: She'd driven up primed to confront Delbo hard, to press him until he yielded the knowledge she knew he'd hidden somewhere inside himself.

"Huh. I think we should go back and haul him in."

"On what charge?"

"The ICE threat. We know he's imported undocumenteds."

"He's not afraid of ICE—or of us either." She softened. "I'll admit, though, it's harder and harder to see him as entirely innocent."

Pete, despite his frustrated tone, chuckled. "I doubt *innocent* is a word anybody's ever used about Cassius Delbo."

She thought for a moment. "Maybe I should go back to the funeral home. Maybe Rick Scopus has heard something from Flandreau. I'm sure he's our link to the Warriors of Yahweh."

"Call Scopus, ask him."

"No. I want to watch his eyes."

102

As she and Pete pulled into the department parking lot, her cell phone buzzed. *Callie*. "Got more bad news about Maggie," she said.

Andi felt a chill. "What's wrong?"

"The infection's worse. They sent her to Missoula. Bernie and I are driving over to see her Saturday. Come along with us."

"Sure. What time?" She shivered. Her mother's cancer had

recurred twice, finally killing her. *This isn't cancer,* she reminded herself. *It's an infection.*

"We'll take off around seven. I've gotta be back by three—I'm catching the p.m. shift this weekend. Shirl's got the flu, and Marla's baby's sick again."

"Oh." She thought quickly. Saturday she had the evening shift as well. "Sure, I'll go with you."

Andi hung up, unfocussed. Memories of her mother's death were blindsiding her. Pete, at the building door, looked then came back. "You okay?"

"Must show, eh? Maggie's back in the hospital in Missoula."

He grunted. "Shit."

Andi remembered Pete's wife had died of cancer. "Memories?"

He nodded, looking momentarily rough. He looked over the SUV, toward the mountains. "It's been a long time, but it's always close." He cleared his throat. "Ginny made my life worth living for a long time." He brushed at his eyes. "Thanks for telling me. I'll give her husband a call." He paused. "What's his name?"

"Victor. Vic."

"Ah." He nodded and turned toward the department.

Climbing out of her vehicle, she felt the now-familiar wash of heat through her body. *Hot flash. Menopause causes cancer. Cancer kills.*

She shook it off, suddenly angry.

SATURDAY

103

The trip to Missoula had sobered her, putting her anxiety about the case in perspective. The young woman burned in the fire was a human being. She deserved the department's hard work to learn what happened, to bring her killers to justice. And she'd get it. But would Maggie? Maggie was a friend. Andi thought about the Ladies' Fishing Society, friends like she'd not had after moving to the valley. For fifty miles, she studied the backs of Bernie and Callie's heads, memorized their hair color, their haircuts, the lines on their necks. Should she let herself get close to these women? What if one of them got cancer?

She almost laughed aloud. One of them already had it. Still, a low-grade tightness clamped her chest all the way over to Missoula.

Maggie herself dissipated the clenched feeling around Andi's heart. When the three friends walked into her room, although she looked gaunt and tired, she was laughing at something on the TV hanging on the wall. Her eyes lit up when she saw them. "Well, look who's come over! You girls on a shopping spree?"

Bernie shushed her. "Shopping, schlopping, Mrs. Ungrateful. We're a delegation from the valley telling you to get the hell better and quit giving us a fright!"

Callie added, "Lane sends a message, and I quote: 'I'm quaking in my boots for you.'"

"Of course," Bernie put in, "let it be passed over in silence that Lane won't wear boots. Thinks it's too cowboy for his delicate feet."

Maggie smiled. "I'm already better." She lay back against her pillow. "A little better, anyway. Anybody seen Victor?"

Bernie snorted. "Uh-uh. The man's up to his neck in cow shit, weaning calves from their mothers at night, then up to his eyeballs in hay-mowing dust during the day. Snow's all melted, so they're out. Doubt he has a minute to worry about you, dear."

Maggie shook her head. "Nope. Calls me every evening before he goes weaning, and every morning before haying. This morning he told me he doesn't think he could live without me. Never said that before." She patted her chest. "Be still my heart."

They laughed.

Callie said, "And since the surgery, he's been calling me every lunch break, jabbering about how you're doing."

Bernie snorted. "That man knows who he owes."

Maggie frowned. "Meaning what?"

"Girl, we all know the story—if you hadn't got him to cooperate with the sheriffs and turn that reverend in, he'd be spending fifteen years in Hardin State Prison. You saved his little butt, darlin', and he knows it."

Andi felt the shock of a sudden crystalline thought. *That man knows who he owes.* Delbo's wife had rescued him, then her relatives had called on him and he'd answered, offered what help he could, a ticket to a safer life—to the *women* in his family. It was all he had to give, but he'd given it.

He'd said it when they'd last talked. She quieted her mind, letting his words come back. *Didn't wait, Lydia.* His wife had not waited, had acted to save him. And in turn, he'd acted to save her relatives. She understood: *Like Vic, he knows who he owes.*

Andi decided it was time to call Delbo. Call in his debt yet again.

104

Andi, working to craft what to say to Delbo when she called him—if he'd answer—half-listened to Callie and Bernie's chatter in the front seat. What words could link his debt to his wife to the dead Mexican girl?

Nothing much came, and when Bernie brought up Lane Martin's latest appetizers at the Angler, Andi tuned in. She realized she was hungry. And relieved—Maggie's nurse had told them that the infection would probably require additional surgery—which was why she'd been brought over to Missoula—but would not be life-threatening. Bad news and good news.

Bernie was sighing. "I doubt there's a man on earth who could give me an orgasm as good as Lane's *hors d'oeuvres*. To die for."

Callie snorted. "Darned if I can imagine a single bite of food you *wouldn't* die for."

Bernie shrugged. "Life is short. *Hors d'oeuvres* are forever."

Andi thought of Delbo. *So is guilt.*

At her cubicle, she dialed Delbo's number and was surprised when the old man answered.

"Saw your name on the phone," he said, his voice reedy as always. "What?"

Good sign. The fear's doing its work. "I was talking with some friends this afternoon. Something I heard made me think of you."

A silence. "Waste of time, thinking of me."

"No, sir, it's not. I heard about a man who realized his debt to his wife. It nearly cost him his life, like yours."

She listened to the sound of his breathing, which had grown heavier.

"Debt?"

"Yes, sir. A woman saved you, and you've spent you life repaying that debt. Am I wrong?"

Silence.

"Sir? You there?"

"Not wrong. Saved my life in Bataan. I owe her."

"But you've been repaying that debt to many women, not just Lydia."

"Asked, she did. Asked."

Andi saw the opening. Although she wanted to push him for

more information on the cult, she elected to wait. No. He'd answered, he'd agreed with her, the fear was working on him. And perhaps his guilt. She'd wait—for the moment.

Then she changed her mind. She said, "What would Lydia ask of you—"

Too late. Delbo hung up.

She dialed right back, but this time, he didn't answer.

105

Late that evening, Andi's cell phone buzzed. She was tired and didn't want to answer. Losing her chance with Delbo weighed on her and she'd been trying to relax with Ed in front of the fire. *Damn it, just answer the thing.*

"Been thinking." It was Cassius Delbo.

Her heart skipped. "Hey, Mr. Delbo. What've you been thinking?"

"Lydia asked, I said. She asked, take care of women. Women."

"Yes, sir, I remember." She noticed the two pronouns.

"Ought to, just said it this afternoon."

She chuckled. "It's been a long day. I could forget my own name."

"Well. If I owe women, what about the girl burned in the fire? The other girls they bring through?"

"You're asking me?"

"I ask you."

She paused, seeing her chance; then, suddenly conscience-stricken, she abandoned it. "No, Mr. Delbo. You've been paying your debt all your life since the war. I don't think you owe anything more."

He was silent. Then, "Didn't expect that."

She said, "I was thinking of using your gratitude to women to force you to tell me who the bishop is. But you've been a good man...I won't manipulate you that way." She saw Ed watching her, curiosity in his eyes.

Again, Delbo took a long pause before speaking. "Women. All gone now, my Filipino family. Wife's family. No more to help, now that granddaughter's safe." He gave a long sigh. "I can help you, maybe, save some other women." He paused, cleared his throat. Andi could feel his tension as if it were flowing over the phone line. "Look at Scopus. At the funeral home."

In his voice, Andi heard a man who believes he has agreed to sacrifice his life. She braced herself. "I've talked to him. There's nothing there."

Delbo waited a very long moment before saying, "Foolish, that. Talk harder to him, girl. He's their bishop."

PART FOUR

SUNDAY

106

Six a.m. Xavier Contrerez, Lannie McAlister, and Chipper Coleman were already yawning and talking quietly in the conference room when Andi got there. Immediately after Delbo's call, she'd called Pete and Ben with his tip, and they'd set a meeting for this morning to plan their move. Ben told Pete not to bring Ordrew in, since he was the prime suspect in the theft of the evidence. She poured a cup of coffee and slid into her chair.

Chip mock-frowned. "Hey, Andi. This tip's big enough we gotta miss our beauty sleep on Sunday morning?"

"Exactly." She fought off a yawn. "Our informant's given us the identity of the leader of the group that we think killed that young girl. He's—"

The door opened and Ben came in, followed by Pete. Both held hot cups of coffee, and Ben's grin was wide.

She paused. "Take over, Ben?"

Ben shook his head. "Talked to Doc last night. He's signin' my ticket. I'm back on the job. But you're lead on this."

If he could have grinned wider, he would have.

Lannie said. "Hell, boss, you've been on the job all along." Everyone laughed and stood up to shake Ben's hand.

"Sure you don't want to run this meeting?" Andi repeated.

Ben kept his grin, but shook his head. "Ain't my show, Andi."

She nodded and resumed her briefing. "Our informant says Richard Scopus, the Carlton funeral director, is the local leader of the Warriors of Yahweh. He's called 'Bishop.' He's a very dangerous man." She paused. "I've thought all along that a man named Guy Flandreau was the leader, and I still want to find him. But we're going after Scopus."

Chip raised his hand. "Flandreau's the boyfriend of your witness, the one who said the bishop burned the woman?"

"That's him. So finding him might help us locate her." She glanced at some notes she'd made last evening. "So let me outline what I think we should do, and you guys add anything you think will work better. Okay?"

Nods.

"First, Pete was going to get a search warrant for the Carlton Mortuary and Crematory." She looked his way.

Pete held up the warrant, handed it to Andi. She put it in her pocket. He said, "Woke up Judge Flure at 5:30 to get it signed."

Ben chuckled. "Bet a buck Dickie Flure said our probable cause was 'thin.'"

Pete smiled, said, "You'd win. But he signed anyway. I told him if he didn't sign, we'd go in under exigent circumstances. Thought he'd toss it back on us, but he just grunted and signed. I don't think he was all awake."

Andi smiled. "Thanks, Pete." She looked around the room. "Xav, you, Lannie, and Chip are backup." She handed them a copy of a map. "This is Carlton's street grid." As they leaned over it, she said, "I want you stationed a block away from the funeral home. Here." She put her finger on a red star she'd printed on the map. "You'll be right around the corner from the funeral home, which I've marked with the blue star." She tapped the blue star. "Pete and I will be in the second vehicle. We'll wait a couple blocks away till you're in place. When you're ready, call me on my cell."

Lannie raised his hand. "Why not the radio?"

Pete answered that. "Scanners. Some funeral homes leave scanners on to listen for accidents."

Chip was frowning. "That legal?"

"A hundred percent," Ben said. "Ain't my idea of a good thing, but anybody can own a scanner."

Xavier raised his hand.

"Question, Xav?"

"Yeah. Shouldn't we let Carlton do this? Or at least have one of their people there. If we find anything, it could all go up in smoke if there's a jurisdiction foul."

Ben cleared his throat. "Won't be. Under the circumstances, we got us a reason to follow the lead outside our county. I'll handle Sheriff Vogel. He's already tuned in on this and he's been cooperative. Even assigned one of his guys to help Andi." He paused, thinking. "But Xavier, you ain't wrong, from the courtesy angle." He turned to Andi. "Why don't you call your guy; he's been in on this from the start."

"I'll call him after this meeting." It occurred to her that she hadn't talked with Mike since he'd been upset with her for pressing Delbo.

Lannie asked, "Andi, do you think you and Pete going in is enough? If they're as dangerous as you say, who knows what you'll run into?"

"Good point. How about we do it this way: Xav, you join Pete and me going in. Mike'll be there too. Lannie, you and Chip ride backup, but come in fast if we call. No sirens and lights. Quiet. I don't want to give any of these Warriors a reason to run and hide."

Ben shook his head. "Uh-uh. Siren-and-lights is procedure in an emergency. Rather save a life, even if you lose some bad guys."

She grimaced. "Good point. And this mission isn't about the troops, it's about the bishop," she said. "Okay, good. You guys come in hard and loud if one of us calls. Lannie, you'll get the call, so make sure your phone's on and charged. What's your number?"

He dictated it, and they all checked that they had it in their phones.

"What's the suspect's name again?" asked Chip Coleman.

"Richard Epi Scopus."

"Funny name."

"If he's the bishop, he's not funny."

107

While Lannie and Chip drove ahead to set up near the Carlton funeral home, Pete parked at the edge of town. In a minute, Andi's phone buzzed.

"Lannie here. We're in place and good to go."

"Okay, good. I'll call Mike Payne now, then we'll roll." She dialed him. "Mike, we're here. You ready?" She'd called him before leaving Jefferson, so he knew what was going down. He hadn't sounded convinced that Delbo's tip about Scopus was real.

But this time, his voice was friendlier. "Who is *we*, exactly? You're not alone?"

"No, I'm not alone. I'm with Deputies Peterson and Contrerez, and two more are backup, a block away." She waited a moment. "You'll meet us there? We'll be there in under five minutes."

"I'll be there."

She nodded to Pete as she ended the call. "Let's roll."

Two minutes later, they passed Lannie and Chip in their unmarked. No one waved. Pete approached the Carlton Mortuary and Crematory, driving slowly. It took another minute. He parked in front. Andi pressed Lannie's number. "We're here. The Carlton deputy should be here in a couple of minutes." She listened. "Yep, careful it is. We're going in."

She turned to Pete and Xavier and took a deep breath. "I don't want to wait. Go."

When they walked in the front door, Andi said, "Hello?" and Rick Scopus called, "Right with you." His face, when he joined them, quickly closed down into bland neutrality. "Well, *three* deputies. Welcome back, Andi. What can I do for you this time?"

Andi introduced her partners, then said, "We're following up on Beatrice John and Guy Flandreau, sir. Last time we were here, you said Guy had left town. Have you had any contact with him since?"

"Well, frankly, no. He never even came around to pick up the things he left."

"May we take a look at Guy's things, please?" If he'd give consent, they might not need the warrant.

"When it comes to that, I think not. The funeral business is sensitive, deputy, and if the public became aware of police activity here..." His voice, trailing off, left his implication unspoken—and unclear.

"Sir? People will be aware. Our vehicle's out front."

As Andi waited for an answer, a young man walked past the open parlor, glanced in at them, and went out the door. Scopus's eyes widened—Andi registered his look of alarm. She swung around, saw the man's back and a light orange ball cap—the color Ed had described. She called out loudly, "Guy Flandreau?"

The man whirled and looked at her, then glanced wildly at the Adams County vehicle parked in front, and bolted down the street toward where Lannie and Chip waited. Andi dashed out the door, calling back to Pete and Xav, "Sit on him!" and ran after Flandreau. She was forty-nine, in good shape, but Flandreau was young and faster. She kept him in sight. Before the corner where her backups waited, he cut into an alley, stumbled, dropped something. He stopped, looked back at her, measuring her speed. Her legs burned; she was slowing, but she'd catch him if he came back for what he'd dropped. She unhitched her holster.

He didn't come back, but whirled, dashed into the alley. She lost sight of him. When she reached the alley, she saw him, a long half-block away. She started to draw her weapon, but the houses were too close together. She bent and scooped what he'd dropped. A wallet. She stuffed it in her pocket and grabbed her cell phone, hit Lannie's number, running again. "A guy'll run out of an alley...coming your way...I'm chasing him. Get him!"

Flandreau, a full block away now, burst from the alley and pivoted left. *Shit*. Lannie was to the right. She ran to the end of the alley. At its exit, she knew she'd lost him. She ran left to the corner, dialed Lannie. "See him?" She knew he hadn't.

"Nope. Nothing."

"Damn. I'm betting it was Flandreau. Orange ball cap. If you see him..."

"We'll grab him."

"Good. I'm going back to the funeral home. I'll call if we need you."

As she retraced her steps, she fished the wallet out of her pocket, opened it, and pulled out an ID card. *Beatrice John.*

108

When Andi ran out, Rick Scopus had shaken his head. "That's not Flandreau," he said to Pete. "Your partner is wasting her time."

"Then why did he run when she called his name?"

"I have no idea. Perhaps the fellow stole something from my business. I just hired him."

Behind Scopus's half-smile and suave words, Pete detected tension. He pulled out his notebook. "What's his name?"

"Uh, John. John Walter."

Pete noted the slight hesitation. He wrote the name down. Scopus cleared his throat. Just then, Mike Payne knocked on the front door and walked in.

Pete introduced himself and Xavier, and the deputies shook hands.

Mike turned to Scopus. "Sir, I'm here representing Carlton County."

Pete said, "Mr. Scopus, we have a warrant to search your building. Deputy Pelton has it. When she gets back, we'd prefer your cooperation, but in either case, we're going to search the premises."

Scopus's reply was mild. "I'm afraid I have an appointment out of the office, Deputy. You and your friends are welcome to wait here in the parlor." His gray eyes were calm, his face sad, as if the deputies were grief-stricken customers he was consoling.

Pete shook his head. "No, sir. We'd like your permission to begin our search."

His eyes flashed. "You realize that your being here will damage my business."

"No doubt you know your business better than I do, sir. But

whether you okay the search now or we wait till Deputy Pelton returns with the warrant, we *will* search your premises." He glanced at Xav, who nodded. Pete added, "And if you try to leave, I'll arrest you."

"Don't be foolish. You have neither a justification nor the jurisdiction to arrest me." His voice had turned cold, its soothing tone abandoned.

Pete shook his head. "We're investigating a murder, sir, in our county, which we have reason to think may be connected with this business." He didn't want to alert Scopus to his status as the prime suspect yet. "So, with all due respect, if you do not sit down, I will arrest you on suspicion of hiding a fugitive, Guy Flandreau, and of interfering with a police investigation."

Apparently deciding not to test him, Scopus sat down and lifted the telephone receiver on the table beside him. "Then, you'll at least allow me to call my appointment?"

Pete nodded.

Scopus dialed, and after a moment, spoke softly, "I'm afraid I must cancel our, ah, meeting. Yes, there are Adams County deputies here with me and I want to cooperate with them....Something about a former employee....Yes, if you don't mind." He hung up and folded his hands calmly on his lap.

Pete and Xavier sat on chairs opposite him. Mike leaned against the doorframe, looking uncomfortable. Andi hadn't returned. After five minutes, there was a rustling at the door and in walked a white-haired man whose enormous belly strained the buttons of his uniform shirt. Mike stood up straight. Pete and Xavier stood, and Pete reached out his hand. "Nice to see you, Sheriff Vogel."

Harley Vogel nodded. "Pete, Xavier. Been a long time." He shook their hands. "I just got off the phone with Ben Stewart," he said. "Told me what's going on, asked me to have a look-see." He looked around. "Where's Andi?"

"She's chasing a man we think is involved with our murder. She has a search warrant, but Mr. Scopus is refusing to permit us to start the search."

Scopus stood up, visibly angry. "Sheriff, tell these people they have no business disturbing me and my business."

Vogel smiled. "You got a reason to hide something, Rick?"

"Of course not, Sheriff. But I object to these officers from another county doing it. I demand that they wait here and let Deputy Payne search the building for whatever it is they think is here."

Vogel shook his head. "They got themselves a murder case that points here, it's their legal right to follow the lead."

"It's absurd, Sheriff. We deal in death here, we don't cause it."

The door opened and Andi came in. She stopped when she saw Harley Vogel. "Hi, Sheriff. We've got a situation here."

Vogel nodded. "You're right about that. You have that warrant?"

"I do. And I have something else." She pulled out the wallet. "The man I was chasing dropped this." She looked hard at Scopus, who glared back. "It's Beatrice John's wallet and ID." She took out the search warrant. "We have a search warrant, Mr. Scopus, and we're going to search your premises for anything pertaining to the possible disappearance of Ms. Beatrice John, as well as the murder of an unknown woman on September first. And possibly to the gang known as the Warriors of Yahweh."

Scopus's face tightened, the irises of his eyes like steel balls. He ignored Andi and said to Vogel, "Sheriff, I object to this on any grounds that pertain. It's outrageous that I and my business are being subjected to—"

Vogel waved him silent. "Not my call, Rick. She's doing this by the book and you've got no choice, 'specially with that ID card she's got there. You can sit up here or you can go along with the searchers, but you can't stop them."

Mike said to the sheriff, "Sir, Mr. Scopus seems to be objecting on jurisdictional grounds. Would it help if I did the search?"

Vogel looked at Scopus, who nodded.

Andi put up her hand. "Not going to happen. It's our warrant and our investigation, not Carlton's. All due respect, Sheriff, to your department."

Vogel shrugged. "'Fraid she's right. Rick."

Andi turned to Pete and Xav. "We'll start with the basement and move up."

109

Scopus led the way down the stairs with Andi close behind. At the foot of the stairs, on the right, a door stood open. As Scopus reached to close it, Andi caught a glimpse of a woman's body lying naked on a metal table. Scopus quickly shut the door.

On the door, a sign: *Crematory*.

Andi asked, "What's that room, sir?"

"I'll ask you to respect the dignity of the dead, Deputy. That is a person who is awaiting cremation, and I will not allow you to desecrate her final hours."

"I have no intention of desecrating them or her, sir, but I *will* search that room. Now."

Scopus looked at Vogel, who shook his head. "Her warrant's good."

Scopus paused. "Allow me a moment to dignify the body." He opened the door narrowly, stepped inside, and slammed it shut.

Andi moved nearly as fast, but as she grabbed the handle, the lock clicked. "Scopus! Open this door!"

No answer. Quickly, Andi stepped aside. "Kick it, Pete."

He reared back and slammed his boot against the door, but it held. "One more," he grunted, gathered himself, and kicked the door hard. It slammed open.

Andi stepped in, took in the room, fast. Tight, nine-by-nine, a metal table attached with hinges to a steel chamber, a heavy glass fire door—the cremation firebox. The dead woman lay naked on the table, her head against the fire door. Three feet of space on either side of the table, four feet at the table's foot. On the table's right, a gurney filled the narrow space. On the far side, Scopus hovered over the body, reaching toward the firebox's red switch.

Andi moved fast around the foot of the table into the narrow space with Scopus, five feet from him, drawing her weapon. She stood beside the body's feet, aimed her gun at him. He pressed the switch. The glass door began to rise. Intense heat blasted the room. At the same moment, the foot of the table began to rise; in a moment, the body would slide into the fire. Andi stepped a foot closer. Her gun was only a couple feet from Scopus's chest. "Turn it off, Scopus."

He sneered. "You have thirty seconds, bitch. Then she slides into the fire."

Shoot the switch? *No, ricochet.* And would it even stop the mechanism?

Pete had crowded in behind her at the foot of the table, his weapon leveled at Scopus as well.

Scopus laughed. "Kill me, you lose everything I know. Go ahead, fools."

Does he want me to shoot? Andi thought. Suicide by cop? *No way.*

Shoot low? No! Ricochet could hit anyone: her, Pete, Harley Vogel now behind Pete. She rushed Scopus, swinging her gun toward the side of his head. His left hand stopped her blow, and he struck like a viper, grabbing her shoulder, spinning her around, pulling her back against him, and from nowhere pressing a knife against her throat. She crooked her arm up. Jammed her gun against his cheek, hard. Should she shoot? His death jerk could sever her throat. *No time!* Wildly, desperately, she flared her other hand out and back. She couldn't see, but felt it hit the switch. The machine stopped. She felt the heat diminish as the fire door closed.

Scopus snarled. "That was a bad move, bitch," and he pressed the knife harder.

Her mind flashed to Ed's porch, the swing, Grace driving up in her PV, waving gaily. The twinkle of evening lights below, the red lining of the evening clouds above. A pang of regret tore through her. No family, no seeing her step-girlfriend grow up.

Pete, his weapon trained on Scopus's forehead, moved carefully closer. "If that knife moves a hair, you're dead."

But Scopus was shielded with Andi held tight against his body.

Behind Pete, his own weapon drawn, Vogel said, "Drop the knife and let her go, Rick. Don't make this any worse for yourself than it is."

Scopus raised his voice. "Payne! Take control."

Vogel looked puzzled, and backed to the door. Without taking his weapon off Scopus—and Andi—he said, "What's he mean, Mike?"

Mike glanced at Xavier standing behind him, weapon drawn, pointed at the floor, ready. He shrugged. "No idea, boss."

Vogel moved back in close. "Rick, you can't get out of this alive unless you drop the damn knife."

The blade pressed harder against Andi's neck. Scopus whispered in her ear, "Send them out. I deal with you only."

She whispered, "Okay," and let her body relax. As Scopus's arm loosened, she whirled, still in his embrace—a lethal intimacy—her gun hand striking his face, hard. The knife sliced across her neck, and the pain spurred her. She kneed him, slightly off center. He went white, but stayed up. He jabbed the knife into her shoulder. She drove one hand into his throat and tried to pull away from the knife. He gagged, but jabbed the knife deeper into her shoulder while his other hand groped for the fire switch behind him.

Suddenly, his hand dropped toward the corpse's face.

The woman's arm had lifted, seized Scopus's wrist, and pulled it to her lips. Scopus shrieked. The woman crushed his fingers firmly in her teeth.

Again, Andi swung her gun hard against Scopus's head, and he fell, his fingers still grasped in the woman's mouth. The knife clattered on the floor.

Suddenly, Andi felt herself pulled roughly back and down, away from Scopus, felt Pete vault above her, saw him drive Scopus to the floor beside the fire chamber.

As they went down, the woman on the table sat up gracefully, agile as an athlete.

110

Woozy, Andi supported herself by leaning on the table, her hands inches from the woman's bare leg. Blood from her neck and shoulder ran down her chest. Harley Vogel stood where Pete had been, gun still on Scopus as Pete roughly cuffed him. When Pete straightened up, he looked at Andi, his face flushed. "You're bleeding—a lot."

She nodded, feeling lightheaded, her head bowed. Her face was only inches from the woman. The ooze of blood on her skin and smell of the woman's scorched hair sickened her.

On the floor, Scopus cringed against the wall, his bleeding fingers cradled in his other hand.

"Let's get you out of here," Pete said, putting his arm around Andi, helping her stand upright.

She grimaced. "Feel faint. Did he get an artery?"

Pete searched. "Lots of blood dripping, but no pumping. I think he missed." To Vogel, still holding his weapon on Scopus, Pete said, "Watch the bastard, Sheriff. Xav, grab us a chair and bring it into the hall." Pete supported Andi as she struggled out of the room, squeezing past the beefy sheriff. At the door, Pete said, "I'm calling you an ambulance."

Andi shook her head, which sent a shock of pain from her neck wound. "No ambulance. Just let me sit for a minute. I'll be fine..."

Pete helped her into the chair. Xavier brought wet paper towels from the restroom, and Pete gently held them against the neck wound. "Doesn't look life-threatening."

Blood still oozed; she felt it warm on her neck.

"You might need stitches. How about the shoulder?"

She touched it, felt the blood soaking through her shirt. "Bleeding. Sore...but I think it's okay for now. I'll check it later. Help her out of there," she said, lifting her hand toward the woman on the table. "Xav, we'll need another chair." Her voice felt shivery.

Pete went in and found a blanket on the shelf beneath the gurney. He unfolded it and covered the woman. He gently touched her arm. "Ma'am, can you get off the table? It's very hot in here."

"Got that right," Vogel said. "Rick, stand your ass up."

Scopus whimpered, "She broke my fingers. I need a tetanus shot."

Vogel kicked his foot hard. "Get up, you son of a bitch or I'll give you a real shot."

Pete said, "Harley, let me help this lady out of here before you stand him up. He might have another knife somewhere and then we'd have a hostage situation on top of everything."

"He's cuffed, but good point anyway," Vogel said. "You heard, Rick. Stay where you are till we clear the room."

Scopus snarled, "You people will pay for this with blood."

Seeing that Vogel had control, Pete turned away and helped the woman off the table. She flinched at his touch, so he let her move out of the room on her own. She walked fluidly, as if floating, beside Andi, and lowered herself onto the second chair Xav had just dragged across the hall. As she did, Vogel called out from inside the crematory. "Mike, give me a hand in here!"

There was no answer; the sheriff's voice came through the door. "Where's Mike?"

Xav answered, "Upstairs. Somebody came in—we heard the bell ring and he went up to intercept them."

"Okay, Xav, you give me a hand then." Together, they dragged Scopus into the room where Xav had found the chairs. In a moment, Vogel emerged, saying, "Keep him there till Mike gets back."

Just then he came down the stairs. "No problem—just a neighbor, wanted to know why we've got three squad cars out front."

111

Waves of vertigo washed over Andi. To steady herself, she pressed her hand flat against the wall behind her chair. With each surge, she breathed as calmly as she could till the dizziness passed.

The woman beside her looked at no one.

During a moment of calm, Andi said to Pete, who'd closed the crematory door, "Pete, did you hear Scopus yell for Mike to take control?"

He looked puzzled. "Don't think so. It was pretty intense for a couple minutes."

"Damn. I thought I heard it." She tried to stand. Another rush of vertigo struck; she would have fallen against the woman, but Pete steadied her.

"I want to take you to the ER, Andi."

"No, Pete, I'll be okay," Andi said. "I'll just sit a couple more minutes." She turned to the woman, who remained immobile. "I have to thank you, ma'am. I believe you saved my life." She drew in a long breath, not against lightheadedness, but to work through the ugliness of feeling Scopus's arm around her chest, the knife at her throat, and the momentary vision of her life with Ed and Grace being cut short. After a moment, she turned to the woman. "I thought you were dead."

The woman turned slowly to look at her, then faintly shook her head. "No, but not alive either. He kept us in hell. But I watched."

The answer was odd, but fit what Ed had told her about multiple personalities. "Speaking of hell, your hair is badly burned. You must be in pain."

"I do not feel pain. That is the work of others."

Andi felt herself steadying. Her own pain seemed less. Moving slowly to prevent another wave of dizziness, she took the wallet out of her pocket and showed it to the woman. "Does this look like yours?"

The flat dark eyes narrowed.

"Ma'am, are you Beatrice John?"

The woman stared at her, as if from far away. "That is the name of this body. I am the Protector."

Andi felt a chill. "Thank you. We'll talk about that later." She pointed toward the second room. "Scopus will be going away for a very long time. It's over now."

The woman shook her head so faintly that Andi barely noticed. "No. It will never be over."

112

Xavier and Sheriff Vogel came into the hall. Vogel said, "Mike's on it, Andi. Scopus is cuffed to the table leg." He turned to Xav. "You hang by the door till we figure out what's next."

Andi got carefully to her feet, a hand on the back of the Protector's chair. The woman put her own hand on Andi's elbow, helped her up. "Thanks. There's what I need," Andi said, pointing at the restroom.

Inside, she removed her shirt; slipping her arm out of the sleeve gave a jolt of pain in her shoulder. She gingerly removed the wet paper towels and examined the wounds. Her shoulder still bled, and hurt fiercely. The pain stunned her as she held fresh towels tightly against the wound. She leaned her back against the wall. In a few minutes, the shoulder bled less and the slice on her neck was a slow ooze. Pete was right, she'd need stitches.

When she felt ready, she gently dabbed both areas with soapy paper towels. The soap burned, but she wanted it clean till she got to an ER.

Done, the bleeding managed, she buttoned her shirt, its collar and shoulder area warm with blood, and went back out to the hall.

Vogel said, "Andi, can you go up the stairs?" He was holding Scopus's knife in an evidence bag. "We need to talk privately, and it's too damn hot in there." He pointed at the crematory. "Xav, can I trouble you to help this young lady to the hospital?" He nodded toward Beatrice John. He lowered his voice, "Under custody till one of my guys relieves you."

"Sure thing, Sheriff." Xav extended his hand. "Ma'am?"

She did not take it, but rose smoothly from the chair, pulling the blanket tightly around her. Everyone flinched at the sight of her charred hair.

After Xav and Beatrice left. Andi said, "Let's go up."

It was slow going, Pete at her side in the narrow stairwell, but she only felt a slight lightheadedness. The bloodstain from her shoulder spread, but slowly. They went into Scopus's office and closed the door.

Vogel rubbed his hands. "I'm going to arrest Scopus, two counts of attempted murder."

Andi asked, "Two counts?"

"The lady on the table, who wasn't dead after all—wasn't that the damnedest thing?"

"Ed Northrup can probably explain that. Who's the second count?"

He looked surprised. Pete chuckled. "You, Andi. He had a knife to your throat, and he cut you twice. If you hadn't reacted like you did, you were dead."

She felt a shiver run down her back. "Ah." She took a long breath. "Sheriff, all due respect, this is my arrest. I want to take Scopus over to Adams County, suspicion of arson and murder, and probably a long history of sex trafficking."

Vogel scratched his head. "I'm thinking different, Andi. What went down here's attempted murder. At the moment, I don't believe we've got any direct tie to your murder, do we?"

"We have Ms. John's statement to Ed Northrup that suggests she's a witness."

"What'd she say?"

"She said, 'Bishop burned the lady in the fire.'"

Vogel contemplated that. "Don't see how that clears anything up. 'Bishop' could be anybody."

"I also have an informant who says Scopus is the bishop of a group called the Warriors of Yahweh, and they're very likely the ones behind the murder. Unless he wanted to get rid of evidence, why did Scopus try to burn Ms. John before we got a chance to identify her?"

"There's that."

"I want to take him back to Jefferson, Harley. I believe he's my guy. And I have an informant I trust."

Vogel shook his head. "Sorry, but I can't see my way to that. The attempted murders happened in my county. Look, I'll arrest him, like I say, and we'll try him on the attempted murder charge. The day you link him to your murder, you can charge him with that in Adams County, and I'll surrender him to you for trial. That fair?"

Yes and no. But she saw his reasoning. "Okay. I take your point. But the minute I find my link, I'll be on my way to pick him up." She didn't like it, but Vogel was probably right.

She frowned, partly because she couldn't think clearly enough to argue any further, and partly because the throb in her shoulder was distracting her.

"There's one more thing," she said, trying to put her thoughts in order. "The guy I chased, I'm pretty sure is the link I need, Guy Flandreau, Beatrice's boyfriend—or whatever the hell he actually was.

We've got an APB out on him, but unless he's already in the wind, he's probably somewhere in Carlton, or at least close. Appreciate any help..." It felt garbled in her head.

"You got it, Andi. Pete, you go down and help Mike bring Scopus up. We'll Mirandize him right here."

Andi sank into a chair, breathing heavily. After a couple of minutes, Pete and Mike came in, Scopus between them.

Mike flinched. "Good God, Andi, you look like you need the ER bad."

Vogel said, "Mike, read Mr. Scopus his rights and book him."

"What's the charge?"

"Attempted murder, two counts."

"You got it, boss." Pulling out the Miranda card from his pocket, he briefly shot Andi a look of sympathy. She smiled. He read the card aloud.

When Mike finished, Scopus said softly, "Fuck you all."

Andi said, "Mr. Scopus, Adams County'll be charging you with suspicion of first degree murder, felonious arson, and sex trafficking. For starters."

"Charge anything you want, bitch."

Vogel stepped forward and slapped his face. "Shut your mouth, Rick! Never saw you as anything but forgettable, but today..." He didn't finish, only shook his head angrily.

Andi sighed. She hoped the slap wouldn't gum up the case.

Pete said, "Andi? Lannie and Chip? They're still on backup."

"Ah." She pulled out her cell phone. "Come on in, it's all over," she told Lannie, and ended the call.

Pete asked, "Okay, *now* we go to the ER?"

She grimaced. "No. Now we're going to tear this goddamn place apart."

113

While her partners started the search, Andi walked with Mike as he escorted Scopus to the waiting squad car, Scopus's handcuffed right arm in his grasp. When they left the mortuary, she moved around to

Scopus's left side and grabbed his elbow. Hard.

"Fuck you, bitch!"

She ignored him. She was thinking how to say what she wanted to say. "Mike," she started, talking around Scopus. "You need extra security on him."

Mike looked surprised. "Because?"

"He's the head of the traffickers."

Scopus snorted. "Deputy, like all cunts, you're stupid. Traffickers? I'm a mortician, for God's sake."

Mike jerked Scopus's elbow hard, pulling him sharply. "Knock off the language, asshole."

She ignored Scopus's obscenity, considered Mike's defending her. *Guess I didn't hear Scopus call to Mike.* "His gang operates from maximum security prisons, and its members are hardened. I don't think they'd hesitate to do whatever's necessary to break him out."

Mike nodded, "Sounds like a vicious bunch." He pushed Scopus toward the squad car. "I'll bring it up with Harley. We'll sit on him."

"Thanks, Mike."

He gave her a quick smile as he pushed Scopus into the squad car, a hand on his head to prevent it bumping the doorframe.

Her cell phone buzzed. "Pete, talk to me."

"Andi, we found the ledgers."

"Jesus. I'm on my way."

114

Four hours later, their search of the funeral home complete, Pete pulled the squad up to the Jefferson hospital ER entrance. Andi climbed out.

Ben was waiting, agitated. He saw her bloody shirt and fresh blood on her neck, and his face went white. "Jesus in a sidecar, Andi! What the hell?"

On the drive back to Jefferson, Pete had called him to report the outcome, and at her insistence had downplayed her injuries. But the blood staining the whole side and neck of her shirt looked like a butcher's apron.

"Really, Ben. I'm fine." It wasn't true; the wounds hurt badly and still bled if she turned her head too far. The dizziness seemed to have passed. Thank God for that.

Grabbing a wheelchair by the door, he swung it toward her. "My God, you look as bad as when you got shot! Christ!" After she lowered herself into it, he pushed her—fast—through the emergency entrance.

An hour later, a white bandage wrapped around her stinging neck, another clamped around her shoulder, which ached more than stung, Ben drove her back to the department. Coming in, he barked to Callie, "Get Ed over here soon's he's got a minute. Andi needs to get home."

"No I don't, Ben." At first, Ben's concern had warmed her, but after an hour of his mother-henning, she was done. "Only needed two stitches in the neck and three in the shoulder, and Doc said I don't need time off unless I want it. I don't want it." She wanted to find the link that Harley Vogel needed to transfer Scopus to Adams County.

"Well, I ain't havin' a deputy hangin' around the office lookin' like the war of the zombies. Ain't good for our image. At least go home and clean up."

"Ben, stop it. I'm not shot, I'm not dying, I'm fine. There's still a lot we need to sort out about Scopus and his operation—and Guy Flandreau is still in the wind and Beatrice John's status has to be decided. I'm not going home till you, Pete, and I talk."

Callie chuckled. "You got told, Ben."

Ben scowled. "Guess bein' sheriff around here's nothin' more'n an honorary post." For a moment he frowned, then gave a little smile. "You bagged a big one today."

"Let's go talk about it."

They settled in Ben's office. Before they dug into the case, she said, "I have to say, I didn't like Harley Vogel taking custody of Scopus."

Ben shrugged. "Guess I'd handle it the same way if it happened here. And when you find a solid connection between Scopus and your murder, sounds like Harley'll hustle him over for court."

"Can we trust him?"

"Harley? He ain't let me down in more'n thirty years. You can trust him."

A sudden burst of heat overtook her, flushing her face. She felt sweat bead on her breasts and back. After moment, some sweat dripped into the wound. Stung. She blew a long breath.

"You all right?" Ben asked.

"Hot flash. Least of my worries."

Pete joined them, and Ben asked him, "Tell me what we got outa the search."

"The ledgers, the rest of the missing evidence, Scopus's computer, some thumb drives, and a scanner. I'm guessing either the computer or the drives'll contain records since 1946."

"Ain't no computers around in 1946."

Andi said, "Even if the Warriors don't care, we know the locals were compulsive record-keepers, so I'm guessing they kept paper records from 1946 until computer and scanning technology came along. That'd mean they could destroy the physical evidence for security, and I'll bet Scopus was going to do the same with the seven old books we had. Anyway, I want DCI to fingerprint the ledgers."

"We can do it here," Pete said.

She shook her head; her neck pulled against the stitches. She took a moment for the sting to fade. "The ledgers are fragile and our fingerprinting skills are no match for DCI's. I don't want to mess this up."

Ben said, "Call 'em. Tell 'em I want a rush job. You clear on what the ledgers really are?"

"I think they track every group of women trafficked through Carlton since 1907."

"Jesus H. And we ain't never had a clue."

"Now, about Beatrice John."

Pete said, "Weirdest thing I've ever seen, Ben. I'd have sworn she was dead on that table. Even when the heat was burning her hair, not a twitch. Then, after Andi shuts the firebox down and Scopus reaches across Beatrice's face to hit the switch again, wham, she damn near bites his fingers off!"

Andi said, "When I asked her if she was Beatrice John she said, 'That's the name of this body. I am the Protector.'"

Ben shook his head. "'. . . the name of this body?' Lord, sounds like she's playin' in your boyfriend's sandbox."

"Yeah," Andi said. "Look, I'll call the Carlton hospital tomorrow morning, see when we can bring her over here."

Ben's eyebrows went up. "You got enough to be thinkin' of arrestin' her?"

"No, protecting her. She's a witness, if we can get her to talk." Suddenly, the intensity of the standoff in the crematory and her brush with death stunned her. She felt herself begin to tremble. "Maybe you're right about going home. I could use a little down time right about now."

Pete stood. "I'll drive you home."

She stood too, suddenly weak. "I'll go across to Ed's office."

Ben shook his head and pointed at her bloody uniform. "Ain't the best idea. You'd scare the liver outa the civilians." He punched a number on his desk phone, said, "Callie, call Ed and tell him to get his butt over here on the double. Emergency." He listened a moment. "Yeah, she needs a ride home." Hanging up, he looked at Andi, his eyes sad. "You ain't thinkin' so clear."

She leaned one arm on Ben's desk. Pete stood and rested his hand under her other elbow. "You all right?"

She smiled through the weakness. "Could have been a lot worse." She turned to go.

Ben said, "Andi."

She stopped and looked back.

Ben's eyes were damp. "Nice work, kid." His voice was rough.

MONDAY

115

Andi slept all night and well into the morning. She woke stiff and sore, the neck and shoulder wounds pulsing. Blood had seeped through the bandage onto the pillow. Though she felt like a truck had run over her throat, she pulled the pillowcase off and took it with her to the bathroom, dropping it into the washing machine on the way so it wouldn't stain the other clothes in the laundry hamper. After using the bathroom, she half-stumbled into the kitchen. Ed sat at the table, his hands wrapped around a mug of coffee. He looked up.

"You're not at work?" Her voice came out a croak.

"No patients today." His eyes looked haunted. "How're you doing?"

"I could use a dozen pain killers and a cup of coffee."

Ed jumped up and went into the bathroom.

She called after him, "What're you doing?"

He called back, "How many pills are you supposed to take?"

"I already took the first dose."

He came back to the kitchen and poured her a cup of coffee. "Can you talk?"

Last night when Ed drove her out to his cabin, she hadn't wanted to talk about what happened. The shock on Ed's face when he saw her bloodied shirt dismayed her: It was his nightmare come true. Telling him would only hurt him more, and she couldn't bear it. "It's not as bad as it looks, Ed. We'll talk in the morning. I'll feel better."

Wrong. But she owed him the story. "I need to eat something to go with the pills. How about some breakfast and then I'll tell you."

But after a quiet meal of poached eggs on toast, and a couple of coffees, during which they stayed carefully away from the story, she said, "It's too ugly to tell it here, Ed. I feel like it'll poison the cabin."

"Outside? Or maybe at the grotto?"

The grotto was a narrow spot on the river where huge erratic boulders created a dark, cool cathedral through which shadowed water flowed slowly, eddying, quiet.

"Perfect. I always feel safe there," she said.

Ed drove them into town, then onto the highway and south to the grotto. After the snow two weeks ago had melted, the temperature had warmed into the fifties. The morning was crisp, blue, tinged with a golden glow from the turning leaves. Flocks of geese gathered, moving south already.

As they drove, Andi watched the birds' wavering V moving across the azure sky. "Moments like this, I wouldn't mind migrating somewhere quiet."

Ed looked at her, then back at the road. "Someplace free of the danger."

"Got that right."

He pulled off the highway onto the dirt road that led down the sloping field to the river and the trail to the grotto. Andi moved slowly through the boulders, as much from a grief gathering in her heart as from blood loss and pain.

Inside the grotto, it was ten degrees cooler. Somewhere high behind them, perhaps in a stand of Ponderosa on the foothills, an osprey called, a loud series of whistles. Andi moved to her good side and took Ed's arm and leaned against him. "I must've looked like, uh..."

". . . like death." His eyes filled.

"Let's sit down," she said, pointing at a flat boulder at the edge of the water. Her energy was fading even though they'd walked slowly. She watched the flowage for a few moments, aware of the ache of grief, not sure how to find words for it.

She told Ed what had happened in the crematory basement. She felt his breathing speed up as she talked, and glanced at him. His eyes were still wet. "You all right?" she asked him.

He nodded, but for a moment he didn't speak. "That's my nightmare." He wiped his eyes. "Andi, if—"

She touched his lips. "I know. And I feel that way about you. But we caught a murderer—or at least an attempted murderer—and if I'm right, we found the bishop who burned the woman in the fire."

He put his arm around her shoulders and she flinched when he touched the wounded spot.

"My God," he said. "I'm sorry."

Saying nothing, she snuggled against him. "Incidents like yesterday, they wear down a little more of me each time." *That* was her grief, finally in words: This job she loved was abrading her.

Ed nodded beside her. "Things like yesterday, they're what we live with."

"Yeah, we live with them. I love my job, but I don't want it to kill me."

Ed swallowed hard, and she wondered which of them was closer to tears.

From high above and to the west came fast, staccato chirps: *tewp, tewp, teelee, teelee, tewp.* Ed said, his soft voice quavering, "Osprey," and they searched the sky, finding the bird soaring toward the mountains.

Ed said, "Well, you caught the bishop, that's the silver lining, eh?"

She watched the osprey soaring, and started to feel better. "Oh, there's other good news. We found the ledger books and the other evidence stolen from our evidence room. It was all in the funeral home."

Ed raised his eyebrows. "Stolen? You never told me it was stolen."

Damn. Shouldn't have mentioned it. "Couldn't. If word got out that we don't properly manage our evidence room, anybody convicted on evidence we'd presented would demand a retrial. Chaos." She looked at him. "Please don't tell anybody about this."

"Of course not. So it was your bishop stole it?"

She nodded, which hurt her neck. "Yeah, or somebody working for him. I suspected Ordrew all along, but I can't believe he's involved with the Warriors of Yahweh."

"You have any suspicions?"

She sighed. "Well, we know Guy Flandreau is loose, and so's Virgil Stark. It could've been either one of them. Though I can't figure out how they got my ID. And something happened during the, ah, incident that made me wonder about Mike."

"What about him?"

She told him about Scopus's call-out to Mike. "But Pete didn't hear it, so I have to think having a knife to my throat makes me less than a good witness."

He shook his head. "How the hell could you be?"

"Yeah. How the hell could I be?" She sighed, then leaned over and picked up a pebble, tossed it into the water. "Too damn many questions."

Ed started to say something, but Andi put her hand on his arm. "Do you think we could go home? Those pills knock the pain down, but I could use some more sleep."

They made their way back to Ed's truck, threading the narrow trail among the boulders. She held onto his arm, glad for his steadiness. They reached the truck parked at the edge of the river. The high sun—it was nearly noon—glinted off the windshield. Ed helped her into the truck—she didn't really need help, but his touch comforted her.

They sat in the truck, quietly, looking toward the mountains. High above the grotto, streaks of autumn yellow were painted across the forested mountainsides, and the air seemed hazed, infused with a soft and golden light.

Andi said, "Just a minute," and got out and walked to the water's edge. She tossed a few stones in, watching the circles ripple out and drift downstream. Ed came up beside her, and she turned easily into his arms and they kissed.

Ed said, "Will you..." he stopped.

"Will I what?"

"Never mind, pal."

She looked at him, then said, "Let's go, big guy."

They went to his truck, and again he helped her in. Again, she liked it. As he started the truck, she took a deep breath. "When Scopus had me, I pictured you and Grace. And your cabin, actually."

"A knife at your throat and you think of my cabin? Wow, ice-water veins."

She smiled. "Not that way. I think my unconscious was telling me what I want."

"Yeah?"

She nodded, which hurt a little. "I don't want to change what we have now. Two lives intersecting, making this weird, good family with Grace. Our love seems big enough for that."

Ed didn't say anything, and Andi hoped she hadn't hurt him.

After a moment, he spoke. "So you're saying no."

"No. I'm just saying what I said: I like—no—I *love* our life. You and Grace and me: two houses, one family. I don't want anything to change that."

"How about living together? Would that be changing things?" He looked at her.

Andi felt a moment's hesitation, then answered him. "Yeah, I think it would."

He nodded, shifted into reverse, backed the truck around. But not angrily, she noticed. When he spoke, his voice was soft, then trailed off. "I feel the same..."

Andi glanced over at him, but his face looked calm.

Her cell phone buzzed. She sighed. "Damn."

116

It was Charlie Begay from DCI. "Hey, Andi. I have something for you, but it probably will not help."

She grabbed a notebook from Ed's glove compartment. "Hold on, Charlie. Let me find a pencil." Ed heard, handed her a pen from his pocket. "Okay, shoot."

"The first thing is, the latents guy only got one print off those ledgers you sent us. Looks like they wiped the books or handled them with gloves, but there was one print on the last ledger. Turns out it belongs to Deputy Michael Payne. He is the guy we met up at the murder scene, correct?"

Andi's heart started pounding, and her throat tightened. "Yeah, that's him."

Charlie went on, "Since he is working the case with you, we figured he had a reason to handle the ledgers, so I believe we came up empty."

Her breath caught. *Mike. Damn.* "No, Charlie, he never handled the ledgers when we had them." It fell into place: Scopus's call-out "*Payne! Take control.*" She felt a cloud of clashing emotions—excitement, dark disappointment, anger, embarrassment. Mostly a mix of anger and mortification that Mike had played her so well. She focused on Charlie. "I'll call Sheriff Vogel about Payne."

At the mention of Mike's name, Ed's head jerked around toward her. She held up a finger. *One minute.*

"Anything else, Charlie?"

"Not at this time. We will get those ledgers back to you a.s.a.p. The techies are working on the computers and storage devices as I speak. They tell me there are some suspicious-looking spreadsheets, set up similarly to the ledgers. Dates start in November 1947. Soon as we know more, I'll get back to you."

"Thanks, Charlie. Your people have any ideas what the records might represent?"

He was quiet a moment. "It's speculative, but our forensic accountant thinks they might be records of women the group processed over the years."

Yes! She ended the call, her heart beating fast. She wanted to shout and wanted to hide. How had she missed it? Mike's kindness, his helpfulness, his subtle flirtation...And she'd fallen for it.

Ed looked over at her and asked, "News?"

She explained about Mike Payne.

"You thinking he's one of the gang?"

She was grateful he wasn't rubbing it in. "Maybe. But there's no sure way to know if he broke into the evidence room or somebody else did it. He could have touched the ledger at the mortuary, but he wasn't in on the search. So if he touched it there, he's one of them."

Ed drove slowly out to the highway, turned north toward Jefferson. "Assume it was Payne stole the evidence. How'd he get in, and why didn't anybody see him?"

She sighed. "The night of the burglary, the station was empty for about forty-five minutes around the time of the theft. If he'd been watching, he could've gotten in unnoticed. The problem is, how'd he get my ID?"

Ed drove, but didn't say anything.

Suddenly, she knew how. "I went to the restroom and left my bag on the chair in the Angler, that day you met him. Didn't need it, I only had to pee. I was gone maybe eight, ten minutes—there was a line in the restroom. He had time and opportunity to get my ID." She reached under the seat for her purse, ignoring the stab of pain in her shoulder, and opened her wallet. "Probably copied the number and just put it back."

"Is it possible to fingerprint your ID card?"

"As soon as I get to the department."

"So we're not going home?"

"You kidding? I want that print."

117

Andi left Ed visiting with Callie, got the fingerprint kit, and dusted her ID card. The card yielded her own prints, of course, but there was a good partial of a different one; she took a picture with her cell phone and emailed it to DCI. Then she called Charlie Begay and asked him to check it against their database. "I think it's Mike Payne's. If not, see if it matches anything in your databases."

He called her back in ten minutes. "That partial? It looks like

Payne's all right."

"You a hundred percent sure?"

"I am never one-hundred percent sure. Let me say ninety-five percent."

"That's good enough for me." She ended that call and dialed Carlton County. "I need to speak with Sheriff Vogel, please. It's Deputy Pelton from Adams County."

"I'm sorry, Deputy. The sheriff's pretty busy right now. We've got a problem here at the jail. Can I have him call you back?"

A problem at the jail? Scopus? "I've got some urgent information that he needs. Please, have him call back a.s.a.p."

"You got it, Deputy."

She waited impatiently. Ed had gone to his office to do paperwork, and she thought about going over there, but if Harley Vogel called...

But it only took ten minutes. Callie buzzed in to the squad room. "Harley Vogel on line 1, Andi."

"Andi, it's Vogel. I got lousy news. Our prisoner escaped last night. We have no idea how he got out, but there was a strange piece of colored paper on his bunk this morning when his breakfast was delivered. His cell door was still locked."

"Crap! It was the Warriors of Yahweh, I'm sure of it. They must've had a key."

Vogel said, "Looks that way. Which makes it an inside job, only way I can figure it."

Her anger blazed. "Sheriff, I can help you with that." She told him about Payne's fingerprint on the stolen ledgers and on her ID card.

Vogel was silent for a moment, then he simply said, "Fuck me." Another silence. Andi waited. "Okay, I'm on it, Andi. Call you back when I find the asshole."

"Wait, Sheriff. Did the paper have anything on it?"

"Five god-damned words: '*You will pay with blood.*'"

118

Ed came into the squad room twenty minutes after Vogel's call. "First time I've caught up on paperwork since last winter." He sounded pleased.

She sighed and typed the last words of her report. "Scopus escaped."

Ed's face paled. "My God. Do you think he's—"

"I don't know. I can't see him staying around here—too much risk of being caught again. So I'm thinking he's in the wind. With whoever broke him out, which I'll bet is Mike Payne." She tapped a key to save the report and looked up at Ed. "Look, I'm sorry to keep you hanging around."

"I feel better staying close to you."

"I'll be ready to leave in a minute. I have to get the bloodstains out of my uniform. Can you drop me at my place?"

"Your uniform's out at my cabin. Clean it there."

"Oh, right." Andi looked into his eyes. "Did I hurt you with what I said? At the grotto?"

He took a long breath. "When I walked in here last night and saw you all bloody, my insides turned to ice. I just went on autopilot. But later, when you were sleeping, I realized you were all right, more or less, and I also knew I couldn't bear to lose you, married or not. So yeah, it hurt, but nothing like losing you would. Or driving you away."

Her chest filled. "Okay. Your place."

Andi sprayed her uniform shirt with stain remover, but she knew she couldn't save it. Her mind raced over details of her times with Mike, trying to see what she'd obviously missed. He'd helped Scopus escape, she had no doubt. Couple that with the fingerprints and Scopus's cry, "Payne! Take control," she had to make him as a likely member of the Warriors of Yahweh. And she'd bet the price of a new uniform she knew the color of the scrap of paper left on the bunk in Harley Vogel's jail.

As she pushed the hopeless shirt into the washer, her cell phone buzzed again.

Harley Vogel sputtered, "Payne's gone. Vehicle's gone, nobody can find him. I added Payne to Scopus and Flandreau's APBs just now." He paused. "We'll get them, Andi. And when we do, they're all yours."

Andi stood silently, staring at the dials on the washing machine, seeing nothing, feeling as hopeless as her shirt. "They're in the Warriors of Yahweh, Sheriff. We'll never get them."

WEDNESDAY

119

Ed parked outside the Carlton Community Hospital and found his way to Beatrice John's room. The deputy outside her room was reading a newspaper. "Nice to see you, Doc. Good timing, too—just finished reading this damn paper the third time. I'll head out for a smoke. Your patient's inside."

"She's not my patient, at the moment. I'm here to interview her for Adams County."

"Ah. Well, good luck. She doesn't talk."

Ed nodded. "So I hear."

He knocked quietly on the door. No response. He opened it slightly and said, "Ms. John, may I come in? I'm the psychologist, Ed Northrup. We met about six weeks ago in Jefferson. You wanted help with headaches."

Still no response.

He stuck his head a little further in. "I'm sorry to intrude, Ms. John, but Deputy Pelton wants me to talk with you." He heard a rustling sound, sheets moving.

"I have no answers."

"May I come in, ma'm?"

"Come in, but I have no answers."

As he pulled a chair closer to her bed, he winced at the sight of her singed hair and the burned skin on her forehead. "I'm sorry about your burns. Are they very painful?"

She gave a long sigh, then closed her eyes. Her body sagged, and after a moment, it stiffened again and her eyes opened. "I am the

Protector. I do not feel pain."

"That's fortunate." He felt a momentary debt of gratitude to this woman. "Deputy Pelton told me how you saved her life."

Protector nodded. "That is why I let you come in. *She* saved *our* lives."

Our lives. Not my life. Ed explained that he was there officially, as a consultant to Adams County, which was preparing a murder case against Scopus.

Protector interrupted. "You will never find him."

"Deputy Pelton said there is a large search for him, and a warrant for his arrest."

"For what?"

"For attempting to kill you and Deputy Pelton, and for the murder of a young Mexican woman."

Protector nodded. "I was there. It was not good. One of our Others had to be cruel." She looked down.

She's ashamed. "What happened?"

"She slapped the girls."

He wondered, *Who is "she"*? "That upsets you?"

"I am the Protector, but I do not like cruelty. And I was not able to protect her from Bishop."

"Her?"

Her eyes narrowed, and she hesitated. "I am not to say."

"Can you say whom you protect her *from*?"

Protector grimaced. She said nothing, and her eyes closed. Ed thought, *Struggle.* A long pause, then her eyes opened. "Because of Deputy Pelton's sacrifice for us, I am permitted to speak. I protect her from outside people who hurt us. It is why I do not feel pain." She looked hesitant. "And from One who is inside...with us."

"Are you in danger, then? From inside?"

"I? No. But the one I protect is."

"May I ask—?"

"No. She is young and weak."

Ed remembered the childish voice: *Bishop burned the lady in the fire.* As gently as he could, he murmured, "Yes. I believe she spoke to me."

Protector looked away, shame coloring her face. "I failed to keep her inside. That is why Bishop punished us."

Ed hesitated. Andi had warned him not to go into details about the murder, just to learn something of Beatrice John's mental state and her willingness to testify. He pondered the next question. "So, there are others inside, beside the young one and the one who you protect against?"

"Yes.

"I heard about your imprisonment in the crematory. Can you tell me how...how that happened?"

"Bishop controls us."

"How does he control you?"

"With his words. They confuse us, and then we sleep. He makes us dream a deep place and to go there, with his words."

Hypnosis. He decided to play a hunch. "Does he count numbers to help you go deeper?"

Protector looked alarmed. "You know this? Will you—?"

"No, not at all. It sounds to me like Bishop is trained in hypnosis."

She looked thoughtful, the distress leaving her face. "As we are trained in obedience." She searched his face with her eyes. "Why did Deputy Pelton send you?"

"She wants me to ask your help against Bishop."

"We can do nothing against him. He will kill us."

"Absolutely not. You will be protected."

She simply stared at him "No one protects us." Her eyes began blinking rapidly, and to Ed it seemed she had dimmed somehow, faded. The light went from her eyes. But after a moment, it returned and she said, "I am permitted to ask what Deputy Pelton wants us to do."

"She wants your permission to ask you what happened...ah, when the Bishop burned the lady, and later to testify in court."

"For that, we will be killed."

"Your testimony will put him in prison a long time." *If they catch him.*

Protector shook her head. "He is one of many. Others will kill us."

"You're right, no one can foretell the future, but I can promise you that Deputy Pelton and I will do everything in our power to keep you safe."

"In return for our testimony."

He considered that, took a plunge. "No, not just that. Even if you don't testify, I will help you. Come to Jefferson. We'll find an apartment for you, and I will offer you my help. And Deputy Pelton's."

"Why?"

It was his turn to tell the truth. "You saved Deputy Pelton's life." He cleared his thickening throat. "I love her very much."

Protector looked at him for a long moment, her head slightly tilted. Finally, she said, "I cannot decide this alone. I will confer with the others within. You must return for our decision."

Ed began to speak, but the body, named Beatrice John, appeared suddenly asleep. Protector had left it.

120

Andi had taken both Monday and Tuesday off. She'd begun feeling better as Tuesday wore on, so this morning, she drove into the department. The ridgelines of the Monasteries glowed pink in the early light. The early snow had melted. Her neck and shoulder hurt, but not as much as they had the last couple of days. She wanted to talk to Harley Vogel about the Warriors and find out more about Payne, details that might help her catch the bastard.

Brad Ordrew was already in the squad room when she came in. "You got your guy. Good work." Genuine?

"Got him, and then lost him. The cult broke him out of Carlton's jail Sunday night."

"Hell, Andi. It must be painful to lose so much." The gibe almost sounded sympathetic.

Before she could answer, her cell phone buzzed. The screen read *Begay, C.*

She answered.

"Morning, Andi. Did you hear Sheriff Vogel passed the investigation into Scopus's escape to us?"

"No, I've been off a couple days."

"Well, I have some news that will make your day."

"Oh, man, hit me. I can use some good news." From the corner of her eye, she saw Ordrew look over toward her.

"Border Patrol in San Diego got in touch. They were looking at another trafficking gang and they came across the APBs on your guys, Scopus, Flandreau, and Payne. They caught Scopus and Payne crossing into Mexico."

"God, that's fabulous! Where are they?" She felt the grin spread across her face.

"San Diego. But that is not all. Payne started bargaining right away, though Scopus is shut up tight as a clam. Payne is offering to trade Guy Flandreau and the name of the guy who actually started the fire that killed the girl, and says he would testify about Scopus's sex trafficking operation, if we drop any charges."

"What a weasel. So we might find out more about the Warriors of Yahweh?"

"Presumably."

"What's Payne being charged with?"

"That will be something we will work out based on our evidence here and yours there. The only charges we are sure of at this moment are aiding and abetting Scopus's escape, and evidence tampering. The San Diego people asked me if we can put him at the arson scene, or if we have any evidence that he actually participated in the murder or the trafficking. Ox and I do not think so, but maybe you have come up with something we are unaware of."

"We have a witness, I think, who might be willing to tell us if he was at the murder scene. But it's not clear yet she'll help us." She wondered how Ed's interview with Beatrice John was going.

"That is thin. I hate to think Payne is going to walk, but if we drop the two charges he will."

She shook her head. "What about charging him with human trafficking anyway, then offer immunity on the trafficking in return for his testimony?"

"Hmm. That might work, and he'll still do some time for the

stolen evidence and aiding and abetting." He paused. "Actually, I have been working on another idea I think the San Diego people will go for. I already ran it by our boss in Great Falls. How about dropping the evidence tampering charge as well?"

"God, that'd be an answer to a prayer. We've been worried if word leaks..." she glanced at Brad Ordrew at his desk, lowered her voice. "There'd be a flood of..." She almost whispered the last word. "Retrials. What'd your boss say?"

"He thinks evidence tampering complicates things too much. He has the same worry you do, that it would open a can of worms for convictions based on your evidence chain. So, I take it you are comfortable dropping that charge?"

Andi drew in a long, relieved breath. "God, yes. You're thinking San Diego will go for that?" She shouldn't be talking for Pete—or Ben—but knew they'd approve.

"I am."

She took another deep breath, hesitated to let her excitement grow. "Good then. Call me when you know for sure, okay?" She gave up and let her excitement bloom. Dropping both the tampering and the trafficking charges might persuade Payne to cooperate, and he'd still do some short time for the abetting charge. And for the department, leaving the evidence theft quiet would be the best outcome she could have hoped for. Payne's testimony, and Beatrice John's if she'd give it, would make a strong case against Scopus.

She glanced at Ordrew, who now was studying her, obviously curious. Before he could ask, she told him, "Got an update on the case. The Carlton deputy and Scopus got caught and the deputy's probably going to testify." She didn't add the "maybe." "Looks like we'll break the case."

He lifted his eyebrows. "That your DCI guy?"

"Yup."

He turned back to his computer. "So *they* broke it, right?"

The put-down was so predictable, she laughed. "So true, Bradley, so true."

121

Around three that afternoon, Andi had received a text from Maggie Sobstak:

Emergency meeting of the Ladies' Fishing Society, 6 p.m. tonight, back room at the Angler. Be there or be square.

Now, a few minutes before six, Ted Coldry waved when Andi came in. "They're back in the River Room, Andrea. I believe congratulations are in order."

"Congratulations?"

"Rumor has it you solved your murder case."

Ah. The gossip lines. "We hope so. Lots of loose ends to tie up." Gossip in the valley could spread as fast as a virus in a schoolroom. Maybe she should get ahead of the rumors on the jail escape, and Ted was the perfect person to spread the news. "Our suspect escaped from the Carlton jail, with help. But they were caught in San Diego, so all's well after all."

"That story could give a person whiplash, Andrea. So those animals will be punished?"

"That's where those loose ends come in. We've got more work before the case is ready for trial."

"Ah. Well, excellent work so far, then. A Pinot Noir?"

"Perfect."

"Go on back to the River Room. I'll bring the wine."

She saw Maggie first, and went to her, holding out her arms. They hugged, gingerly—Andi was too aware that Maggie's breast might be sore after the surgeries. But the hug ended when Andi flinched at the pain in her shoulder.

Maggie said, "Oh!"

"No problem, just a little sore." Andi saw that Maggie had lost weight, had dark circles under her eyes. "You're better?"

"Fairly miserable for a while there, but I'm back home." She smiled and took Andi's hand.

Bernie squealed. "Darling! The valley's safe again. But give me a look at the wounds!" She rushed close and pulled down Andi's collar to see the bandage. "Nearly cut your throat, I hear."

Andi laughed. "He *did* cut my throat. No lasting damage, though."

Lane had come into the River Room just as Andi spoke, carrying a silver tray. "That's a good thing. We've never had a funeral in the Society. I wouldn't know the appropriate *hors d'oeuvres*."

Andi chuckled. "I'd come back from the dead for your *hors d'oeuvres*."

He put the tray down and gave Andi a gentle one-side-only hug. "I'm delighted about your success," he said. "Ted and I were entirely confident you'd solve it."

She wondered how much of their evidence analysis Ted had shared with Lane. "More confident than I was." Everyone laughed.

"So, girl, tell us the entire gruesome story," Bernie said. "Include the knife part." She rubbed her hands.

Andi hesitated. "Probably shouldn't." The truth was, she didn't want to talk about it. "You know, it's still pretty raw..."

"Sweetheart," Bernie said, "the valley's buzzing. Nobody cares about facts. I heard that after he cut you, you turned around, looked him in the eye, and kicked him in the balls. The bastard dropped like a rag."

Andi smiled, but stiffened a bit. "Didn't happen quite that way, but I guess I'm really not comfortable talking about it. Is that okay?"

Callie nodded. "End of discussion, then." She looked sternly at Bernie.

Who ignored her. "Word is," Bernie said, "a deputy in Carlton's involved. I hear he broke the ringleader out of jail and they're both gone missing."

Andi waited, irked, but also amazed. How did such information leak out into the valley? She looked at Callie, who shrugged. "Nobody heard it from me," she said. Probably somebody in Carlton's sheriff's office told a cousin in Phillipsburg, who called another cousin in Dillon, who called another cousin in Jackson, who called a fifth cousin here in Jeff.

Why not enlist the Ladies' Fishing Society to help Ted spread the truth? She nodded. "Yeah, but they've been caught in San Diego." After a moment's thought, she added, "The deputy's offering to testify against the ringleader, in return for dropping the major charges."

Bernie shook her head. "I wouldn't trust a guy like that as far as I could stretch his dick."

They all laughed, then Callie turned to Maggie. "So what's this emergency?"

Maggie looked uncomfortable. "I...I have some news. I wanted to tell you face to face, before you heard it from somebody else."

Andi felt her good mood drain away, invaded by an emptiness. Her mother had used the same words, *I have some news,* to announce that she'd stopped her chemotherapy and decided to *live* the last few months, rather than vomiting and lying sick and tormented in bed.

Maggie said, "Vic and I talked. I get the radiation for six weeks, then the treatment's over. But he said to me, 'Maggie girl, the cancer got me thinking. We work all the time, twelve months of the year. Ain't taken a vacation since we got married.'"

Bernie clapped her hands. "You're going to Mexico for a vacation!"

Maggie shook her head. "We're selling the ranch. Victor wants to move us to San José, where his brother lives. Says he wants to really live the life we got left, not just work it." Maggie had tears in her eyes.

Andi looked hard at her, and waited a moment. "You don't want to go, do you?"

Maggie shook her head. "Naw. Lived my whole life in the valley. But I guess the cancer took the gumption outa me. I don't know how to tell him. So I need your help. You know Vic." She chuckled. "An idea gets lodged in his brain, you need a crowbar to pry it loose."

Bernie grunted. "So *use* a crowbar—to the side of his head. We'll testify for you."

Andi felt the hollowness again. To lose Maggie now, when their brief friendship was in its springtime, was wrong. She felt a stab of anger at Vic, making such a selfish decision.

Callie said to Maggie, "Say no, girl. Then take that man to see Ed Northrup. He'll talk sense into him."

Andi thought about Ed. How he was listening to her, respecting her ambivalence. Despite their tension over whether to marry, she felt safe with him in a way she hadn't before. Ed, sitting quietly beside her in the grotto, listening without objection to her saying she wanted to keep their lives the same. Warmth spread through her chest.

Maggie was asking Callie, "What kind of sense does Vic need talking into? There's sense and there's sense. This cancer's no fun, but Vic's being so good—it's nice. Maybe a few more years of that, even in California, might not be a tragedy." She laughed a little. "I'm of two minds."

Andi said, "Go see Ed. He's real good when people have two minds." As everyone laughed, she thought, *Two minds—that's me, too.*

Lane pointed to the silver tray. "So when Maggie called and asked to use this room, Ted and I made some special appetizers." He delicately picked one up. "This is the first one. They're called mushroom-polenta diamonds. The recipe comes courtesy of Martha Stewart."

Bernie scrunched up her face. "You know Martha Stewart? Hon, you queer boys have ins I'd never guess!"

Lane smiled. "My 'in,' as you call it, is Martha Stewart's website."

Andi savored the mushroom-polenta diamonds. "These are delicious, Lane." As she spoke, a flash of heat swept over her. She closed her eyes, waiting for it to pass. Callie looked at her. "You all right, girl?"

For a moment, she held back. But seeing them all looking at her, eyes warm, concerned, she stopped hiding. *You wanted friends,* she thought. *So let them be friends.* "Hot flash."

Bernie laughed. "Darlin', my advice is you should use 'em. Get your Ed to feel sorry for you."

"No need for that," Andi grinned, suddenly amused. "Getting sliced up by a bad guy is all I need." She remembered what Ben had said. "My boss says he's been walking with a bunch of you neighbors."

"Hon, he tries to keep up, but he's a guy. He hangs back and watches my butt, which at my age is all I can expect."

Callie tsked, "Don't count yourself out, Bernie. You've still got your girlish figure."

"Sweetness, I got me enough figure for two or three girls."

THURSDAY

122

When Ed got up, Andi was sitting on the porch in the morning twilight, a few minutes before sunrise. He poured a cup of coffee and joined her. "You're out early."

She nodded. "Too much drama lately. I felt like watching the first light touch the mountains. Start my day off peaceful." She patted the seat beside her. "Snuggle up. Keep me warm."

He did, feeling her warmth beside him. Over the Monasteries, the dawn brightened the sky, then, with the slightest touch, tinged the ridges, pinking last night's new snow high on their crests. Below, the tree line stretched gray-green across the mountains' flanks. The morning star glistened, sharp white against the still-dusky sky over Hunter's Peak. Gradually the pink light shifted toward gold and red, and drifted down the granite peaks toward the treeline.

For the entire time, neither spoke. The silence—theirs, matched by the morning world's—pleased him.

Then, "This is the first morning in forever I've felt easy," Andi murmured. "I love this place."

Ed nodded. Steam from his cup rose in wisps as he sipped. "You're right. We haven't sat out here at dawn in ages."

Andi looked at her watch, sighed. "Well, gotta get in to work. This'll count as the start of a good day."

"You hope." He felt the familiar tug, wanting her not to return to the dangers she faced, but unwilling to keep her from the job she loved.

"I sure do. I'm going up to Wallace's Corner to thank Delbo for his help." She went inside and got her gear.

As she was getting into her SUV, she paused and yelled over the top of the vehicle. "Expect a call from Maggie."

"Why? What's wrong?"

"Nothing. She and Vic need to talk about their future."

"Ah." He looked at her. "Damn good topic for a couple."

She came around to the front of her SUV, facing him. Ed saw the thin first light touch her face. "Don't start, bucko. You know how I feel."

"Sure do. Independent but intertwining lives." He felt no anger or hurt, just a tender gratitude. She was here. That was enough.

"A lot to be said for it." She climbed into her SUV, then got out again and called to him, "And I know there's something to be said for marriage, too." She looked up toward the lightening sky. "Feels like nice weather coming. You free some afternoon this week?"

He nodded. "I'm free as a bird Saturday. What've you got in mind?"

"Let's climb the Coliseum. Celebrate breaking the case."

Perfect, he thought. "You feel up to it?"

She just looked at him.

"Okay, yeah. You wouldn't suggest it if you didn't feel up to it. You're on."

She laughed, waved, and climbed into the SUV. He loved her smile, but couldn't hear her whisper something to herself.

123

Despite the peaceful start to the morning, as Andi drove up Highway 36 toward Wallace's Corner, a wash of anger, fear, and repulsion from her confrontation with Scopus flared up. The stench of Beatrice John's burned hair, the sting of the knife against her throat, Scopus's arm pressing against her breasts, the disgusting intimacy of being held tight against his body. She touched the bandage on her neck. She'd thought the drive into the mountains would prolong the dawn's peace, but instead, the highway triggered images of the crematory. *Guess I don't bounce back like I used to.* She ignored the thought that followed: *Too old*.

She slowed as she approached Wallace's Corner, collecting herself. A few yards from the highway shoulder, beside the driveway, a For Sale sign swayed in the breeze.

"What the—?" she muttered. She pulled into the yard and got out. The place felt deserted. She pounded on the door of the house, and then the door of the workshop. She peered into Guy Flandreau and Beatrice John's empty cabin. The battered old pickup was gone. Her disappointment welled. She owed the old man a lot. Back on the highway, she read the For Sale sign and dialed the listing agent's number.

"Mr. Delbo has left Montana," the agent told her. "He was rather urgent about it." She paused. "Are you interested in the property?"

"No, I'm Deputy Andrea Pelton of the Adams County Sheriff's. I'm urgent too—I need to reach him. Has he left you a forwarding address?"

"I'm afraid not, Deputy. But I do have a cell phone number. Would that help?"

"Yes, thank you. The cell phone number will be fine."

She wrote it down, then sat for a long while behind the wheel, gazing at Wallace's Corner. Questions nagged her. Would Payne give them Guy Flandreau? Would Payne testify against Scopus? For that matter, would Flandreau? Would they be able to convict Scopus? Or would the Warriors of Yahweh simply move on to another quiet, lonely mountainside, soldiering on in their evil? Would "bishops" keep burning women?

She dialed Delbo's phone number. After many rings, it rolled over to voice mail. She listened to the guttural, old-man voice, no subjects for his verbs. "Not answering. Leave message."

She took a deep breath. "Mr. Delbo, this is Andrea Pelton. I want to thank you, sir, for your service...to our country in the Philippines and to our county in Montana. We got Scopus and his helper. If you want to return to your home, you're safe." She paused, thinking of how to say it. "Thanks to you, we have the bishop."

Hanging up, she made a decision, and dialled another call.

124

Midday, Ed's phone rang at the office.

"Ed? Lynn here. I was writing you an email, but it's better we talk personally."

He caught his breath. "Does your email start, 'Dear John'?"

She laughed. "No. I'm sending you my ideas for a contract—to join your practice."

Ed grinned, and silently pumped his fist in the air. "So you and Rachel are going to do it?"

A silence. "No, Rachel's not ready for this. We're staying together, but I'm going to accept your offer. She and I will have a part-time long-distance thing for a year, and evaluate things then."

Ed considered that, his grin evaporating. He closed his eyes. He could foresee a tough meeting in a year, could imagine Lynn telling him the long-distance thing wasn't working. He took a long breath. "That's tenuous, Lynn. I'm not getting any younger, and I need to be thinking about the future of my practice." He had a fleeting image of Andi shaking her head at him playing the age card.

"I know that, Ed. And I hate to be tentative. But I'd like to give this a whirl, and I'm sure Rachel will end up on board."

Lots of women tentative about committing to me, he thought, then shook off that twinge of self-pity. After all, Andi *was* committed to him, just not to being *married* to him. After a moment, he said, "If you think she'll come around, let's go for it. When would you like to start?"

"How does the first of May sound?"

Six and a half months? "Your commitments will take that long to straighten out?"

"Pretty much. My boss at both of my jobs asked me to stay six months, because he's worried there aren't many therapists around willing to work just a day and a half each week."

Ed rubbed his eyes. It was happening, but six and a half months? A lot could go wrong in that time. Still, she could work the other half-day she was in Jeff, after her high school job in the mornings. It'd give her time to build a practice. "Okay, then. Shoot me the email, and I'll look it over. When you're down here next, we can meet over lunch and work out the details."

"Perfect. And, Ed? Like I've said, for me this is a dream come true. I've wanted private practice since I was in grad school."

Ed relaxed, let himself imagine things working out. "My dream too, Lynn, only I didn't know I was dreaming it till six weeks ago."

125

"Northrup?"

They had been reading on the couch—Ed a journal article on multiple personalities, Grace her homework. After his morning patients, he'd driven over to Carlton to hear Beatrice John's—that is, Protector's—decision. She answered his knock this time. She'd agreed, on behalf of "the Others," to come to Jefferson and talk to Andi. He'd asked if she still wanted to consider entering therapy with him, and she'd nodded, but added nothing. Tonight, Andi was staying in town at her place, doing laundry. *Intertwining independence.* Quiet music played on the radio. He looked at Grace. "What's up?"

"I've got two things to talk about."

"Okay, shoot."

"First thing, Jared's mom told me today that he's not coming home from Missoula after all. She said he'll be over there for at least six months. I want to start visiting him every two weeks. Last time we went he was so lonely, he couldn't talk. I can't let him stay over there all alone. You okay with that?"

Ed put down his journal. He felt a tug of emotions: pride in his daughter, and a flood of sadness about how poorly Jared's surgery had turned out. And there was practicality: Three hours on winter roads wasn't a recipe for safety.

"Going every two weeks may be tough, with senior year getting busy. And the roads, come winter."

"I know, Northrup. But Jared's so sick and he's all alone."

He looked at her. "That's really generous of you, Grace."

"Yeah, well. If you or Andi can't go with me, would it be okay if I drive over myself or with my girls?"

Ed swallowed. His girl was growing up. "Okay, you're on, unless there's bad weather. But I'll do my best to ride with you as often as I can."

For a while, she was quiet.

He nudged. "So: the second thing?"

"I've decided where I'm going to college." Her sudden smile lit the room like a small sun.

"Wow. I didn't know you were that far along in the process." He took a breath. "We were going on that college trip next week, right?"

"Yeah, we can still go. It'll be fun, like a road trip. But I've decided, so there's no reason to wait."

"Okay, so who's the big winner?"

She smiled again. "You mean, who gets to put up with me if my SATs are high enough and they accept my application?"

"Yeah, something like that."

"Montana." She raised a fist. "Go Griz!"

"Missoula!" He wasn't surprised, but he put surprise into his voice.

"Northrup, don't fake it. You knew I was going to pick Missoula."

"Because Zach's going there."

She shifted on the couch, clearing her throat. "Okay, that's reason number three."

He lifted his eyebrows. "So what're reasons number one and two?"

"Reason number two is, Jared's over there in rehab. I want to be near him, so he knows somebody from school still cares about him."

Ed didn't brush away the blur in his eyes. Physically, Jared was losing ground every week. But the real damage was psychological. Since the surgery, he lived on autopilot, could no longer make decisions or plan anything, felt very little detectable emotion; and whatever feeling he experienced faded quickly. Ed knew Jared wouldn't recover enough to come home now, and probably not in six months. Probably not ever. Ed hadn't told Grace what he thought. She maintained a sturdy hope for his eventual recovery, and it would break her heart. "What if he doesn't need to stay in Missoula next year?"

Grace's eyes filled too. She rubbed them. She looked at him. "Northrup, *you* know." Her voice caught. "Jared's never coming home."

They sat quietly, each seeing through filmed eyes. Ed reached his hand to her cheek, touching it gently. Grace didn't move away.

After a while, Ed asked, "Okay, reason number one?"

Grace looked at him. Her eyes had cleared. "You know your friend Merwin? That beach-ball-shaped guy with the pink face?"

Ed grinned. "Sure. My best buddy in grad school."

"I called him."

He turned on the couch and faced her fully. "You did? Why?"

"We talked about schools I should think about. He called the department I want and talked to their chair. He said she's very good and the department's really solid. So I picked Montana."

"Huh." *Definitely growing up*, he thought. "Good for you, honey. Merwin's tuned in to most good schools in the country." He framed the big question. "So, what's the department?"

She blushed. "Psychology." She turned away, looking shy. Then turned back, smiling. "And my name's Grace, not honey."

For a moment, he couldn't speak. Her choice filled him with a delight he could never have imagined. He chuckled. "You're right. Grace *is* better than honey."

SATURDAY

126

October's bluest day glowed as Ed and Andi drove up Mount Adams to the trailhead below the high rim of the Coliseum. Beside the narrow, curving mountain roadway, the Monastery River poured down fast, no wider here than a creek, but filled to its banks with snowmelt. Aspen, birch, and larch shone like towering torches, draping the higher slopes in yellow. They'd spoken very little down the valley and up the mountain, and they pulled into the trailhead parking lot on the shore of St. Mary's Lake in a contented quiet.

During the ride, Andi had glanced over at Ed many times, gauging his mood. His face showed no tension. She hoped her anticipation wasn't too evident.

Ed pulled his truck into a slot beside the single other vehicle in the lot. "Somebody else climbing the Coliseum. Perfect day for it."

"You got that right. Perfect day for lots of things." She hid her excitement.

They left the truck and put on their packs. The trail climbed from the parking area, up the gentle first half-mile for fifteen minutes, then twisted back and forth up a set of switchbacks that, after twenty-five more minutes, left them breathing heavily, standing on a ledge overlooking the lake below.

"Happy?" Andi asked him.

"I love this mountain," he answered. Ed unshouldered his pack and took out a water bottle. "Drink?"

"Got my own." They rested a few minutes. She loved the silence.

Around them, mice skittered in the undergrowth beneath the dense cedars, and above them, birds spoke softly. Ed stood. "Ready to go?"

"Got a question first." Andi smiled. "You still want to be married?"

"Hmm. I was just thinking about that as we climbed. About what you said. You're right, what we've got together is good..." His voice faltered. "I told you, when I saw you all covered in blood, I knew that having you with me is all I actually want." He took a long breath. "All I need."

"So you're okay if we don't get married."

"However it works out, if we're together, I win."

Andi smiled. "Okay then. Let's go up." She stayed behind him, so he wouldn't see her grin.

The trail emerged from the cedars and led across a meadow to the second set of switchbacks. After twenty minutes of steady climbing, they emerged onto the meadow at the top of the Coliseum, breathing heavily. On the far side, where the forest touched the brink of the cirque, a man stood alone, gazing over the long valley. Andi and Ed approached the edge, looked down 1,300 feet to St. Mary's Lake, now a tiny oval, and the red tile roofs of St. Brendan's Monastery on its western shore.

From the lake, the river flowed down into the valley, where it made a long westerly arc, then turned north. Sunlight glinted gold on its northern stretch.

Andi turned toward him. "Let's go talk to that guy." She nodded toward the man who now stood quietly, turned toward them.

"Do you know him?"

She leaned against him. "Yeah. And you do too."

"I do?" And no sooner than he'd said it, he recognized his dear friend, Jim Hamilton, once the priest at St. Bernard's parish in Jefferson. He looked at Andi. "Why...?"

She smiled. "Go ask him."

Ed walked across the meadow. "What the hell are you—"

"Doing here?" Jim laughed. "I'm performing a marriage."

"A...what?" Ed looked at Andi, who had joined them.

She was beaming. "Looks like you win all around, big guy." She turned to hug Jim. "You ready?"

The former priest grinned. "Don't even need a prayer book for this one," he said.

THE END

AUTHOR'S NOTE

Sex trafficking, which Andi and Ed investigate in *The Bishop Burned the Lady,* is a world-wide scourge. EqualityNow.com notes, "Trafficking women and children for sexual exploitation is the fastest growing criminal enterprise in the world." The International Labor Organization estimates that upward of 20.9 million adults and children are "bought and sold worldwide" each year, and of that number, UNICEF believes more than two million are children. The National Human Trafficking Hotline reports that in Montana alone, there were fifteen cases received by the hotline in 2016, of which ten were for sexual slavery. The annual average in Montana from 2012 to 2016, was 13.2 cases. Roughly three-quarters were for sexual exploitation. And who knows the number who never call in?

As a psychologist, I have worked with a number of women who had at one time been trafficked or otherwise exploited for sexual purposes. Now, as a writer, I am honored to tell a small sliver of what they—and the courageous folks who work against the traffickers—taught me, not just about human evil, but about human resilience and the power of hope.

During the years when I consulted for various police departments, I learned that for every troubled cop—whom we see in the news all too often—there are thousands of dogged and skillful police officers pursuing criminals like the sex traffickers in this book. Although "The Job" demands that they live with danger and uncertainty every day, these dedicated cops live normal lives, struggling with the everyday challenges we all face: raising their families, being good neighbors, and trying to grow through their experiences. I wanted Andi to represent *their* story, a rich and nuanced one, which so seldom gets told.

CPSIA information can be obtained
at www.ICGtesting.com
Printed in the USA
LVHW01s0109110918
589689LV00003B/494/P

9 781684 330140